PRAIS

THE CHAIN

A Books of the Year selection for:

Time Magazine

Guardian

Daily Telegraph

Observer

Express

Amazon

Apple

The Irish Times

'Adrian McKinty is one of the most striking and most memorable crime voices to emerge on the scene in years. His plots tempt you to read at top speed, but don't give in: this writing – sharply observant, intelligent and shot through with black humor – should be savored'
Tana French

'*The Chain* has all the hallmarks of a monster hit, including a terrifying premise that had me wondering: Is this actually happening somewhere right now? And I bet I won't be the only one. Terrific'
Mick Herron

'A masterpiece. *The Chain* is one of the finest novels ever produced in the genre – up there with *Marathon Man* and *Red Dragon*. It just doesn't get any better than this. I may not read a better thriller in my lifetime'
Steve Cavanagh

'Will very likely establish McKinty as one of the finest thriller writers of his generation'
Irish Times

'Excellent . . . irresistibly alarming. This will surely be the hit McKinty deserves'
Mail on Sunday, **Thrillers of the Month**

'An adrenaline-fuelled thriller that will leave you breathless as you race to its superb finale'
Express

'Utterly brilliant'
Elly Griffiths

'Diabolical, unnerving, and gives a whole new meaning to the word "relentless." Adrian McKinty is the real deal'
Dennis Lehane

'This relentless high-suspense thriller is the book everyone is talking about. Nerve-shredding and harrowing, this story is a brilliantly executed page-turner that builds to an epic climax'
Mirror

'High concept, brilliantly conceived, beautifully written and with a propulsive page-turning quality. An electrifying thriller – one of the very best of its kind'
Fiona Cummins

'What an absolute belter of a book! Dark as hell, brilliant writing and a killer concept – I reckon this is the thriller of the year'
SJI Holliday

'A foot-to-the-floor thriller . . . Smartly plotted and hugely readable'
The i

'Fiendishly clever, highly compelling, a brilliant thriller. I loved it'
Harriet Tyce

'A brutally compelling thriller. Like Harlan Coben in a bad mood'
Mason Cross

'Wow! What a ride! Whip fast, intelligent and thought-provoking'
Adam Hamdy

'A grade-A-first-rate-edge-of-your-seat thriller. I can't believe what went through my mind while reading it'
Attica Locke

ADRIAN McKINTY was born and grew up in Carrickfergus, Northern Ireland. He studied philosophy at Oxford University on a full scholarship before immigrating to the United States. He is the author of a dozen crime novels that have won the Edgar Award, Ned Kelly Award, Barry Award, and Anthony Award and have been translated into more than twenty languages. He is a book critic for the *Sydney Morning Herald*, the *Irish Times*, and the *Guardian*. He currently lives in New York City with his wife and two daughters.

OTHER MYSTERIES AND THRILLERS
BY ADRIAN McKINTY

THE MICHAEL FORSYTHE TRILOGY
Dead I Well May Be
The Dead Yard
The Bloomsday Dead

THE SEAN DUFFY SERIES
The Cold Cold Ground
I Hear the Sirens in the Street
In the Morning I'll Be Gone
Gun Street Girl
Rain Dogs
Police at the Station and They Don't Look Friendly

STAND-ALONES
Hidden River
Fifty Grand
Falling Glass
The Sun Is God

AS EDITOR (WITH STUART NEVILLE)
Belfast Noir

THE CHAIN

ADRIAN McKINTY

ORION

An Orion paperback

First published in Great Britain in 2019
by Orion Fiction,
This paperback edition published in 2020
by Orion Fiction,
an imprint of The Orion Publishing Group Ltd.,
Carmelite House, 50 Victoria Embankment
London EC4Y 0DZ

An Hachette UK company

1 3 5 7 9 10 8 6 4 2

A CIP catalogue record for this book
is available from the British Library.

ISBN (Paperback) 978 1 409 18960 2

Typeset by Input Data Services Ltd, Somerset

Printed and bound in Great Britain by Clays Ltd, Elcograf S.p.A.

There is some wisdom to be had in taking the gloomy view and looking upon the world as a kind of hell.

Arthur Schopenhauer,
Parerga and Paralipomena, 1851

We must never break the chain.

Stevie Nicks,
"The Chain" (original demo), 1976

PART ONE

ALL THE LOST GIRLS

1

She's sitting at the bus stop checking the likes on her Insta-gram feed and doesn't even notice the man with the gun until he's almost next to her.

She could have dropped her school bag and run across the marshes. She's a nimble thirteen-year-old and she knows all the swamps and quicksands of Plum Island. There's a little morning sea fog and the man is big and clumsy. He'd be nervous about pursuit and he'd certainly have to give up the chase before the school bus came at eight o'clock.

All this goes through her head in a second.

The man is now standing right in front of her. He's wearing a black ski mask and pointing the gun at her chest. She gasps and drops her phone. This clearly isn't a joke or a prank. It's November now. Halloween was a week ago.

"Do you know what this is?" the man asks.

"It's a gun," Kylie says.

"It's a gun pointed at your heart. If you scream or struggle or try to run, I'm going to shoot you. Do you understand?"

She nods.

"All right. Good. Keep calm. Put this blindfold on. What your mother does in the next twenty-four hours will determine whether you live or die. And when . . . if we do let you go, we don't want you to be able to identify us."

Trembling, Kylie puts on the padded, elasticized blindfold.

A car pulls in next to her. The door opens.

"Get in. Watch your head," the man says.

She fumbles her way into the car. The door shuts behind her. Her mind races. She knows she shouldn't have gotten into the vehicle. That's how girls vanish. That's how girls vanish every day. If you get in the car it's over. If you get in the car, you're lost forever. You don't get in the vehicle, you turn around and you run, run, run.

Too late.

"Put her seat belt on," a woman says from the front seat.

Kylie starts to cry under the blindfold.

The man climbs into the back seat next to her and puts her seat belt on. "Please, just try to keep calm, Kylie. We really don't want to hurt you," he says.

"This has got to be a mistake," she says. "My mom doesn't have any money. She doesn't start her new job until—"

"Tell her not to talk!" the woman snaps from the front seat.

"It's not about the money, Kylie," the man says. "Look, just don't talk, OK?"

The car drives off hastily in a slew of sand and gravel. It accelerates hard and moves up through the gears.

Kylie listens as the car drives over the Plum Island bridge and with a wince she hears the tubercular grumble of the school bus go by them.

"Keep it slow," the man says.

The doors power lock and Kylie curses herself for missing a chance. She could have unclicked the seat belt, opened the door, rolled out. Blind panic is beginning to overwhelm her. "Why are you doing this?" she wails.

4

"What should I tell her?" the man asks.

"Don't tell her anything. Tell her to shut the hell up," the woman replies.

"You need to be quiet, Kylie," the man says.

The car is driving fast on what is probably Water Street near Newburyport. Kylie forces herself to breathe deep. In and out, in and out, the way the school counselors showed her in the mindfulness class. She knows that to stay alive she has to be observant and patient. She's in the eighth-grade accelerated program. Everybody says she's smart. She has to be calm and notice things and take her chances when they come.

That girl in Austria had survived and so had those girls in Cleveland. And she'd seen that Mormon girl who'd been kidnapped when she was fourteen being interviewed on *Good Morning America*. They'd all survived. They'd been lucky, but maybe it was more than luck too.

She swallows another wave of terror that almost chokes her.

Kylie hears the car drive up onto the Route 1 bridge at Newburyport. They're going over the Merrimack River toward New Hampshire.

"Not so fast," the man mutters, and the car slows for a few minutes but then gradually begins to speed up again.

Kylie thinks about her mom. She's driving to Boston this morning to see the oncologist. Her poor mom, this is going to—

"Oh my God," the woman who's driving says, suddenly horrified.

"What is it?" the man asks.

"We just passed a cop car waiting over the state line."

"It's OK, I think you're in the . . . no, oh Christ, his lights are coming on," the man says. "He's pulling you over.

You were going too fast! You have to stop."

"I know," the woman replies.

"It'll be OK. No one will have reported this car stolen yet. It's been on that side street in Boston for weeks."

"The car's not the problem, *she's* the problem. Pass me the gun."

"What are you going to do?"

"What can we do?"

"We can talk our way out of it," the man insists.

"With a blindfolded kidnapped girl in the back seat?"

"She won't say anything. Will you, Kylie?"

"No. I promise," Kylie whimpers.

"Tell her to be quiet. Take that thing off her face and tell her to lower her head and look down," the woman says.

"Keep your eyes shut tight. Don't make a sound," the man says, taking the blindfold off and pushing Kylie's head down.

The woman pulls the car over and the police vehicle presumably pulls in behind her. The woman is evidently watching the policeman in the rearview mirror. "He's writing the license plate down in his logbook. Probably called it in on the radio too," she says.

"It's OK. You'll talk to him. It'll be fine."

"All these state police prowlers have dashcams, don't they?"

"I don't know."

"They'll be looking for this car. For three people. We'll have to hide the car in the barn. Maybe for years."

"Don't overreact. He's only going to write you a speeding ticket."

Kylie hears the crunch of the state trooper's boots as he steps out of his vehicle and walks toward them.

She hears the woman roll down the driver's-side window.

"Oh God," the woman whispers as he approaches.

The state trooper's boots stop crunching by the open window.

"Is there a problem, Officer?" the woman asks.

"Ma'am, do you know how fast you were going?" the state trooper asks.

"No," the woman says.

"I clocked you at fifty-two. This is a restricted twenty-five school zone. I guess you didn't see the signs."

"No. I didn't know there was a school around here."

"It's heavily signposted, ma'am."

"I'm sorry, I just didn't see them."

"I'll have to see your . . ." the trooper begins and pauses. Kylie knows he's looking at her. She's shivering all over.

"Sir, is that your daughter in the seat next to you?" the trooper asks.

"Yes," the man says.

"Miss, can you show me your face, please?"

Kylie lifts her head but keeps her eyes tightly shut. She's still trembling. The state trooper has seen that something is amiss. A half second goes by while the cop, Kylie, the woman, and the man all decide what to do next.

The woman groans and then there is the sound of a single gunshot.

2

It's supposed to be a routine visit to the oncologist. A six-month checkup to make sure that all is OK and that her breast cancer is still in remission. Rachel has told Kylie not to worry because she feels great and everything is almost certainly fine.

Secretly, of course, she knows that things might not be fine. Her appointment had originally been scheduled for the Tuesday before Thanksgiving but she'd gotten some blood work done at the lab last week, and when Dr. Reed saw the results, she'd asked Rachel to come in this morning. First thing. Dr. Reed is a dour, even-keeled, unflustered woman originally from Nova Scotia, and she is not one for panicky overreaction.

Rachel tries not to think about it as she drives south on I-95.

What's the point of worrying? She doesn't know anything. Maybe Dr. Reed is going home for Thanksgiving and is scheduling all her appointments early.

Rachel doesn't feel sick. In fact, she hasn't felt this good in a couple of years. For a while there she had thought she was bad luck's favorite child. But all that has changed. The divorce is behind her. She's writing her philosophy lectures for the new job starting in January. Her post-chemo hair has mostly grown back, her strength has returned, and she's putting on weight. The psychic toll of the past year has been paid. She's back to the organized, in-control woman who worked two jobs to put Marty through law school and get them the house on Plum Island.

She's only thirty-five. She has her whole life ahead of her.

Knock wood, she thinks and pats a green bit of the dashboard she hopes is wood but suspects is plastic. In the arcane clutter of the Volvo 240's cargo area there's an old oak walking stick but there's no point risking life and limb reaching back for that.

The phone says it's 8:36 now. Kylie will be getting off the bus and strolling across the playground with Stuart. She texts Kylie the dumb joke she's been saving up all morning: How do you think the unthinkable?

When Kylie doesn't respond after a minute, Rachel sends her the answer: With an itheberg.

Still no response.

Do you get it? Try it with a lisp, Rachel texts.

Kylie is deliberately ignoring her. *But,* Rachel thinks with a grin, *I'll bet Stuart's laughing.* He always laughs at her dumb jokes.

It's 8:38 now and traffic is backing up.

She doesn't want to be late. She's never late. Maybe if she gets off the interstate and takes Route 1?

Canadians do Thanksgiving on a different day, she remembers. Dr. Reed must want her to come in because the test results don't look good. "No," she says out loud and shakes her head. She's not going to fall into that old spiral of negative thinking. She's moving forward. And even if she still has a passport to the Kingdom of the Sick, that won't

9

define her. That's behind her, along with the waitressing and the Uber driving and falling for Marty's lines.

She's using her full potential at last. She's a teacher now. She thinks about her opening lecture. Maybe Schopenhauer is going to be too heavy for everyone. Maybe she should begin the class with that joke about Sartre and the waitress at the Deux—

Her phone rings, startling her.

Unknown Caller, it says.

She answers with the speakerphone: "Hello?"

"Two things you must remember," a voice says through some kind of speech-distortion machine. "Number one: you are not the first and you will certainly not be the last. Number two: remember, it's not about the money—it's about The Chain."

This has to be some sort of prank, one part of her brain is saying. But other, deeper, more ancient structures in her cerebellum are beginning to react with what can only be described as pure animal terror.

"I think you must have the wrong number," she suggests.

The voice continues obliviously: "In five minutes, Rachel, you will be getting the most important phone call of your life. You are going to need to pull your car over to the shoulder. You're going to need to have your wits about you. You will be getting detailed instructions. Make sure your phone is fully charged and make sure also that you have a pen and paper to write down these instructions. I am not going to pretend that things are going to be easy for you. The coming days will be very difficult, but The Chain will get you through."

Rachel feels very cold. Her mouth tastes of old pennies. Her head is light. "I'm going to have to call the police or—"

"No police. No law enforcement of any kind. You

will do just fine, Rachel. You would not have been selected if we thought you were the sort of person who would go to pieces on us. What is being asked of you may seem impossible now but it is entirely within your capabilities."

A splinter of ice runs down her spine. A leak of the future into the present. A terrifying future that, evidently, will manifest itself in just a few minutes.

"Who are you?" she asks.

"Pray that you never find out who we are and what we are capable of."

The line goes dead.

She checks the caller ID again but the number is still not there. That voice, though. Mechanically disguised and deliberate; assured, chilly, arrogant. What can this person mean about getting the most important phone call of her life? She checks her rearview mirror and moves the Volvo out of the fast lane and into the middle lane just in case another call really is coming in.

She picks nervously at a line of thread that's coming off her red sweater just as the iPhone rings again.

Another Unknown Caller.

She stabs at the green answer key. "Hello?"

"Is this Rachel O'Neill?" a voice asks. A different voice. A woman. A woman who sounds very upset.

Rachel wants to say *No;* she wants to ward off the impending disaster by saying that actually she has started using her maiden name again—Rachel Klein—but she knows there's no point. Nothing she can say or do is going to stop this woman from telling her that the worst has happened.

"Yes," she says.

"I'm so sorry, Rachel, I've got some terrible news for

you. Have you got the pen and paper for the instructions?"

"What's happened?" she asks, really scared now.

"I've kidnapped your daughter."

3

The sky is falling. The sky is coming down. She can't breathe. She doesn't want to breathe. Her baby girl. No. It isn't true. Nobody has taken Kylie. This woman doesn't sound like a kidnapper. It's a lie. "Kylie's in school," Rachel says.

"She's not. I've got her. I've kidnapped her."

"You're not . . . it's a joke."

"I'm deadly serious. We grabbed Kylie at the bus stop. I'm sending you a picture of her."

A photo of a girl wearing a blindfold and sitting in the back seat of a car comes through as an attachment. She is wearing the same black sweater and tan wool coat that Kylie put on when she left today. She has Kylie's freckly pixie nose and brown hair with red highlights. It's her, all right.

Rachel feels sick. Her vision swims. She lets go of the steering wheel. Cars begin honking as the Volvo drifts out of its lane.

The woman is still talking. "You have to remain calm and you have to listen carefully to everything I say. You have to do it exactly the way I've done it. You must write down all the rules and you cannot deviate from them. If you break

13

the rules or call the police, you will be blamed and I will be blamed. Your daughter will be killed and my son will be killed. So write down everything that I am about to tell you."

Rachel rubs her eyes. There's a roaring in her head that sounds like a giant wave about to break on top of her. About to smash her to smithereens. The worst thing in the world is really, actually happening. *Has* really happened.

"I want to speak to Kylie, you bitch!" she screams and then grabs the steering wheel and rights the Volvo, avoiding an eighteen-wheeler by inches. She pulls the Volvo across the final lane of traffic onto the shoulder. She skids to a halt and kills the engine as scores of drivers honk and yell obscenities.

"Kylie's OK for now."

"I'm calling the cops!" Rachel cries.

"No, you're not. I need you to calm down, Rachel. I wouldn't have picked you if I thought you were the type who would lose your cool. I've researched you. I know about Harvard and your recovery from cancer. I know about your new job. You're an organized person and I know you're not going to screw this up. Because if you do, it's real simple: Kylie is going to die and my boy is going to die. Now, get a piece of paper and write this down."

Rachel takes a deep breath and grabs a datebook from her purse. "OK," she says.

"You're in The Chain now, Rachel. We both are. And The Chain is going to protect itself. So, first thing is no cops. If you ever talk to a cop, the people who run The Chain will know and they'll tell me to kill Kylie and pick a different target, and I will. They don't care about you or your family; all they care about is the security of The Chain. Got that?"

"No police," Rachel says in a daze.

14

"Second thing is burner phones. You need to buy anonymous burner phones that you use just once to make all your calls, like I'm doing now. Got it?"

"Yes."

"Third, you are going to need to download the Tor search engine, which will take you into the dark web. It's tricky but you can do it. Use Tor to look for InfinityProjects. Are you writing this down?"

"Yes."

"InfinityProjects is just a placeholder name. It doesn't mean anything, but on the site, you'll find a Bitcoin account. You can buy Bitcoin on Tor in half a dozen places by credit card or wire transfer. The transfer number for InfinityProjects is two-two-eight-nine-seven-four-four. Write that down. Once money has been wired through, it's untraceable. What The Chain wants from you is twenty-five thousand dollars."

"Twenty-five thousand dollars? How will I—"

"I don't care, Rachel. Loan shark, second mortgage, do a goddamn murder for hire. It doesn't matter. Just get it. You pay the money and that's part one. Part two is harder."

"What's part two?" Rachel asks, alarmed.

"I'm supposed to tell you that you are not the first and you are not the last. You are in The Chain and this is a process that goes back a long time. I kidnapped your daughter so that my boy will be released. He's been kidnapped and is being held by a man and woman I don't know. You must select a target and kidnap one of that person's loved ones so The Chain will go on."

"What! Are you cra—"

"You have to listen. This is important. You are going to kidnap someone to replace your daughter on The Chain."

"What are you talking about?"

"You have to select a target and hold one of that person's loved ones until the target pays the ransom and kidnaps someone in turn. You are going to have to make this exact phone call to whoever you select. What I'm doing to you is what you are going to do to your target. As soon as you carry out your kidnapping and pay the money, my son will be released. As soon as your target kidnaps someone and pays the ransom, your daughter will be released. It's that simple. That's how The Chain works and goes on forever."

"What? Who do I pick?" Rachel asks, utterly horrified.

"Someone who will not break the rules. No cops, politicians, or journalists—those are deal-breakers. Someone who will commit a kidnapping and pay the money and keep their mouth shut and keep The Chain going."

"How do you know I'll do all that?"

"If you don't, I'll kill Kylie and start again with someone else. If I screw up they will kill my son and then me. Everything's off the cliff already for us. Let me be very clear, Rachel: I will murder Kylie. I know now that I am capable of doing it."

"Please don't do this. Let her go, please, I'm begging you. As one mother to another, please. She's a wonderful child. She's all I've got in this world. I love her so much."

"I'm counting on that. Do you understand what I've told you so far?"

"Yes."

"Goodbye, Rachel."

"No! Wait!" Rachel cries but the woman has already hung up.

4

Thursday, 8:56 a.m.

Rachel begins to shake. She feels sick, nauseated, untethered. Like on the treatment days when she allowed them to poison her and burn her in the hope that it would make her better.

The traffic drums ceaselessly to her left and she sits there frozen like some long-dead explorer crashed on an alien world. Forty-five seconds have gone by since the woman hung up. It feels like forty-five years.

The phone rings, startling her. "Hello?"

"Rachel?"

"Yes."

"This is Dr. Reed. We were expecting you at nine, but you haven't signed in yet downstairs."

"I'm running late. Traffic," she says.

"That's OK. It's always a horror show at this time. When can we expect you?"

"What? Oh . . . I'm not coming in today. I can't."

"Really? Oh, dear, well—would tomorrow suit you better?"

"No. Not this week."

17

"Rachel, I need you to come in to discuss your blood work."

"I have to go," Rachel says.

"Look, I don't like to talk about these things over the phone but what we're seeing with your most recent test is very high levels of CA 15-3. We really need to talk—"

"I can't come in. Goodbye, Dr. Reed," Rachel says and hangs up the phone as flashing lights appear in the rearview mirror. A big, dark-haired Massachusetts state trooper gets out of his vehicle and approaches the Volvo 240.

She sits there, utterly adrift, tears drying on her face.

The trooper taps her window and after a moment's hesitation, she rolls it down. "Ma'am," he begins and then sees that she has been crying. "Um, ma'am, is there a problem with your vehicle?"

"No. I'm sorry."

"Well, ma'am, this shoulder is for emergency vehicles only."

Tell him, she thinks. *Tell him everything. No, I can't, they'll kill her, they will. That woman will do it.* "I know I shouldn't be parked here. I was on the phone to my oncologist. It—it looks like my cancer has come back."

The trooper gets it. He nods slowly. "Ma'am, do you think you're capable of continuing your journey at this juncture?"

"Yes."

"I'm not going to write you a moving violation, but I would ask you to proceed with your journey, please, ma'am. I'll halt traffic until you get into the lane."

"Thank you, Officer."

She turns the key in the ignition and the old Volvo grumbles back to life. The trooper stops the vehicles in the slow lane and she pulls out without any difficulty. She drives for one mile until she hits the next exit and then gets off at the slip road. South is the hospital where they can maybe fix her but she doesn't care about that now. That's utterly irrelevant. Getting Kylie back is the sun and the stars and the entire universe.

She takes I-95 northbound, pushing the Volvo harder than it has ever been pushed in its life.

Into the slow lane, into the medium lane, into the fast lane.

Sixty miles an hour, sixty-five miles an hour, seventy, seventy-five, seventy-eight, eighty.

The engine is screaming but all Rachel can think is *Go, go, go.*

Her business now is north. Get a bank loan. Get the burner phones. Get a gun and everything else she needs to get Kylie back.

5

It had all happened so fast. A gunshot and then they had driven off. Driven for how long? Kylie had lost track. Maybe seven or eight minutes before they had turned onto a smaller road, gone down a long driveway, and stopped. The woman had taken a picture of her and gotten out to make a phone call. Probably to her mom or dad.

Kylie's in the back seat of the car with the man. He is breathing hard, swearing under his breath, and making strange animal-like whimpering noises.

Shooting the policeman was clearly not part of the plan and he isn't handling it well.

Kylie hears the woman come back to the car.

"OK, it's done. She understands everything and knows what she has to do," the woman says. "Take this one down to the basement and I'll hide the car."

"OK," the man replies meekly. "You have to get out, Kylie. I'll open the door for you."

"Where are we going?" Kylie asks.

"We've set up a little room for you. Don't be worried," the man says. "You've done very well so far."

She feels the man reach over her and unclick her seat

20

belt. His breath is acrid and repulsive. The door opens next to her.

"Keep your blindfold on; I have a gun pointed at you," the woman says.

Kylie nods.

"Well, what are you waiting for? Move!" the woman says in a shrill, hysterical voice.

Kylie swings her legs out of the car and starts to get up.

"Watch your head, please," the man mutters.

She stands slowly, carefully. She listens for highway traffic or any other noise, but she doesn't hear anything. No cars, no birds, no familiar Atlantic breakers. They are somewhere well inland.

"This way," the man says. "I'm going to take your arm and lead you downstairs. Don't try anything. There's nowhere you can go and we're both prepared to shoot you, OK?"

She nods.

"Answer him," the woman insists.

"I won't try anything," she says.

She hears a bolt being dragged back and a door being opened.

"Careful, these stairs are old and sort of steep," the man says.

Kylie walks slowly down the wooden stairs while the man holds her by the elbow. When she gets to the bottom of the steps, she can feel that she's standing on concrete. Her heart sinks. If it had been a crawl space like the one beneath her house, she would have had just dirt and sand underfoot. You could dig your way through dirt and sand. You couldn't dig your way through concrete.

"Here," the man says and leads her across the room. It's a

basement, obviously. The basement of a house deep in the country, far from anyone.

Kylie thinks about her mother and feels another sob welling up in her throat. Her poor mom! She's supposed to be starting a new job soon. She's just beginning to turn her life around after the cancer and the divorce. It isn't fair.

"Sit here," the man says. "Sit all the way down. It's a mattress on the floor."

Kylie sits on the mattress, which feels like it's covered with a sheet and a sleeping bag.

She hears the click of the woman taking a photo. "OK, I'm going to the house to send her this and check Wickr. I hope to God they're not angry with us," the woman says.

"Don't tell them anything went wrong. Tell them everything went according to plan," the man says.

"I know!" she snaps.

"It's going to be OK," the man says unconvincingly.

Kylie hears the woman run up the wooden steps and close the basement door. She's alone with the man now and this scares her. He could do anything.

"It's OK," he says. "You can take your blindfold off now."

"I don't want to see your face," Kylie replies.

"It's fine, I've got the ski mask on again."

She removes the blindfold. He's standing near her, still holding the gun. He has taken his coat off. He's wearing jeans, a black sweater, and loafers caked with clay and mud. A heavy man in his forties or fifties.

The basement is rectangular, roughly twenty feet by thirty feet. There are two small square windows choked with leaves on one side. A concrete floor, a mattress, and an electric lamp next to the mattress. They've given her a

22

sleeping bag, a bucket, toilet paper, a cardboard box, and two large bottles of water. The rest of the basement is empty but for an antique cast-iron stove against one of the walls and a boiler in the far corner.

"You're going to be staying here for the next few days. Until your mother pays the ransom and does the other stuff. We're going to try to make you as comfortable as possible. You must be terrified. I can't imagine . . ." he says and begins to choke up. "We're not used to this, Kylie. We're not people like this. All of this has been forced on us. You have to understand that."

"Why have you taken me?"

"Your mother will explain everything when you get back to her. My wife doesn't want me to talk to you about it."

"You seem nicer than her. Is there any way you could possibly let—"

"No. We'll—wow—kill you if you try to escape. I mean that. You know what we're c—capable of. You were there. You heard. That poor man . . . oh my God. Put this on your left wrist," he says, handing her a handcuff. "Tight enough so you can't escape, not so tight so that it chafes you . . . that's it. A little bit tighter. Let me see."

He takes her wrist and examines it and ratchets the handcuff tighter. Then he takes the other cuff, attaches it to a heavy metal chain, and attaches that to the iron stove with a padlock.

"You've got about nine feet of chain, so you can move around a bit. Do you see that, over there by the stairs? That's a camera. We'll be keeping an eye on you even when we're not down here. The fluorescent light will always be on so we can see what you're doing. So don't try anything, OK?"

"OK."

"You've got a sleeping bag and a pillow. In that box there

23

are toiletries and more toilet paper and graham crackers and books. Do you like the Harry Potter books?"

"Yes."

"The whole series is in there. And some old stuff. Good stuff for girls your age. I know what I'm talking about. I'm an en . . . good stuff," he says.

"I'm an English teacher"? Was that what he was going to say? Kylie wonders. "Thank you," she says. *Be polite, Kylie,* she tells herself. *Be the good, scared, frightened girl who won't cause them any trouble.*

The man squats down next to her, still keeping the gun pointed at her.

"We're in the woods here. At the end of our own dirt road. If you start screaming, no one will hear you. We're on a big lot and the woods are all around. But if you do start yelling, I'll see and hear you on the camera and I won't be able to take any chances. I'll have to come down and gag you. And so you can't remove the gag, we'll have to cuff your hands behind your back. Do you understand?"

Kylie nods.

"Now, turn out your pockets and give me your shoes."

She turns out her pockets. She only has money in them anyway. No penknife or phone. The phone's back there on the dirt road on Plum Island.

The man stands and sways a little. "Sweet Jesus," he says to himself and swallows hard. He goes up the stairs shaking his head, apparently in disbelief and amazement at what he has wrought.

When the basement door closes, Kylie leans back on the mattress and exhales.

She starts to cry again. She cries herself dry and then sits up and looks at the two bottles of water. Would they poison her? The seals on the water are intact and it's Poland Spring.

24

She drinks greedily and then stops herself.

What if he doesn't come back? What if she has to make this water last for several days or weeks?

She looks in the big cardboard box. Two boxes of graham crackers, a Snickers bar, and a can of Pringles. Toothbrush, toothpaste, toilet paper, wipes, and about fifteen books. There's also a drawing pad, two pencils, and playing cards. With her back to the camera she tries to use the pencil to pick the lock on the handcuff, but after ten seconds she gives up. You'd need a paper clip or something. She looks through the books. Harry Potter, J. D. Salinger, Harper Lee, Herman Melville, Jane Austen. Yeah, probably an English teacher.

She takes another sip of water and unspools some of the toilet paper and dries the tears from her face.

She lies down on the mattress. It's cold. She gets into the sleeping bag and hunkers down under it where the camera can't see her.

She feels safer here.

If they can't see her, that's something. That's a Daffy Duck trick. If I can't see you, you don't exist.

Were they telling the truth about not wanting to harm her? You believed people until they showed you how bad they really were.

But they'd already done that, hadn't they?

That policeman. He was probably dead or dying. Oh God.

Remembering that gunshot, she wants to scream now. To scream and get someone to come and help her.

Help me, help me, help me! She mouths but doesn't say the words.

Oh my God, Kylie, how could this have happened? The thing that you were warned about: Don't get into a stranger's car. Never get into a stranger's car. Girls go missing all the time and when they go missing, they almost never come back.

But sometimes they *did* come back. There were many who disappeared forever but not all the lost girls stayed lost. Sometimes they came home again.

Elizabeth Smart—that was the Mormon girl's name. In that interview, she had been dignified and calm. She had said that there was always hope in these situations. Her faith had always given her hope.

But Kylie doesn't have any faith, which is obviously her stupid parents' fault.

So claustrophobic in here.

She pulls the sleeping bag down and takes a few panicky breaths and looks around the room again.

Are they really watching her?

Certainly at first they will be. But at three in the morning? Maybe she can move that stove. Maybe there's an old nail she can use to pick the lock. She'll wait. She'll keep cool and wait. She looks in the box and pulls out the pad and paper.

Help me, I'm a prisoner in this basement, she writes, but there's no one to give the note to.

She rips out the page and crumples it up.

She starts drawing instead. She draws the ceiling of the tomb of Senenmut from her Egypt book. This begins to calm her. She draws the moon and stars. The Egyptians thought the afterlife was located in the stars. But there is no afterlife, is there? Grandma believes in the afterlife but nobody else does. It doesn't make any sense, does it? If they kill you, you're just dead and that's that. And maybe a hundred years from now, they find your body in the woods and nobody even remembers who you were or that you'd gone missing.

You're erased from history like a shaken Etch A Sketch.

"Mommy," she whispers. "Help me. Please help me. Mommy!"

But she knows that there's no help coming.

6

When Rachel gets back to her house on Plum Island she walks into the kitchen and falls to the floor. It isn't a swoon. She's not fainting. She just can no longer remain vertical. She lies there on the linoleum like a disheveled question mark. Her pulse is racing, her throat constricting. She feels like she's having a heart attack.

But she can't have a heart attack. She has to save her daughter.

She sits up and tries to breathe and think.

They'd said don't call the police. They are probably afraid of the police.

The police will know what to do. Won't they?

She reaches for the phone but stops herself. No. She dare not risk it.

Don't call the cops. Never call the cops. If they find out she has called the cops, they'll kill Kylie immediately. There was something about that woman's voice. The desperation in it. The determination. She'll do it and she'll move on to another victim. The whole thing about The Chain is incredible and crazy and yet . . . that woman's voice . . . it had the ring of truth. The woman had clearly been terrified of The

28

Chain and its power and she believed in it.

And I believe too, Rachel thinks.

But she doesn't have to be alone. She needs help.

Marty. He'll know what to do.

She speed-dials Marty's number but it goes straight to voice mail. She tries again but again gets voice mail. She looks down her list of contacts and calls his new house in Brookline.

"Hellooo," Tammy answers in that singsongy voice of hers.

"Tammy?" Rachel asks.

"Yeah, who's this?"

"This is Rachel. I've been trying to contact Marty."

"He's out of town."

"Oh? Where is he?"

"He's in, um, oh, what's that place . . ."

"Work?"

"No. You know . . . the place where they play golf."

"Scotland?"

"No! Where everybody goes. He was so excited."

"Golfing, when did he start . . . never mind. Look, Tammy, I'm trying to reach him and it's an emergency and I can't get through on his phone."

"He's down there with the firm. They're on a retreat so they had to hand in their phones."

"But where is it, Tammy? Please, think."

"Augusta! He's in Augusta. I think I have a contact number somewhere if you need it."

"I need it."

"Yeah, hold on, lemme see, here it is, OK." She reads out a number.

"Thanks, Tammy. I better call him."

"Wait, what's the emergency?"

"Oh, it's nothing, a problem with the roof, it's leaking, that's all. No big deal. Thank you," she says and hangs up.

She dials the number Tammy gave her.

"Gleneagle Augusta Hotel," the receptionist says.

"I'd like to speak to Marty O'Neill, please. I'm his, er, wife, and I've forgotten what room he's in."

"Um, let me see . . . seventy-four. I'll put you through."

She puts Rachel through to the room, but he isn't there. She calls the front desk again and asks the receptionist to tell Marty to call her as soon as he gets back in.

She hangs up and sits down on the floor again.

She's dazed, speechless, horrified.

Given all the evil people in the world with unbalanced karmic checkbooks, why has this happened to her, especially after everything she's been through the past couple of years? It isn't fair. And poor Kylie's just a little girl, she—

The phone rings next to her. She picks it up and looks at the ID: Unknown Caller again.

Oh no.

"Calling your ex-husband?" the scary, distorted voice says. "Is that really what you want to do now? Can you trust him? Can you trust him with your life and the life of your child? You're going to need to because if he says anything to anybody, Kylie's dead, and I think we'll have to kill you too. The Chain always protects itself. Maybe have a think about that before your next phone call."

"I'm sorry. I . . . I didn't get through to him. I left a message. It's just . . . I don't know if I can do this by myself, I—"

"We might allow you to get help later. We will send you a way to contact us and you can ask us for permission. But for now, if you know what's good for you, don't talk to anyone. Just get the money and start thinking about a target.

You can do this, Rachel. You did well getting rid of that cop back there on the highway. Yes, that's right, we saw. And we'll be watching you closely until this is all over. Now get on with it," the voice says.

"I can't," Rachel protests meekly.

The voice sighs. "We don't select people who require continuous coaching. That's way too exhausting for us. We pick self-starters. Bootstrappers. That's you, Rachel. Now, get up off the goddamn floor and get moving!"

The line goes dead.

Rachel looks at the phone in horror. They *are* watching her. They know who she's calling and everything she's doing.

She pushes the phone away, gets to her feet, and staggers to the bathroom like she's walking from a car accident.

She runs the faucet and splashes water on her face. There's no mirror in here or anywhere in the house except for Kylie's room. She'd gotten rid of all the mirrors because of the visual horror of the whole hair-falling-out routine. Of course no one in her family had ever allowed her to think that she might die. Her mother, the nurse, had explained right from the get-go that it was a treatable stage 2A breast cancer that would respond well to an aggressive precision surgical intervention followed by radiation and chemotherapy. But in those first few weeks, looking in the bathroom mirror, she saw herself diminishing, hollowing out, wasting away.

Getting rid of all the mirrors had been an important step in her recovery. She didn't have to see herself become the terrible, pale skeletal spider of the dark days of the chemo. Her recovery wasn't exactly a miracle—the stage 2A five-year survival rate was 90 percent—but still, you could always be one of the 10 percent, couldn't you?

She turns the faucet off.

Good thing there's no goddamn mirror, because Mirror Rachel would be looking back at her with dead, accusing eyes. Letting a thirteen-year-old girl wait by herself at a bus stop? You think this would have happened if Kylie were with Marty?

No. It wouldn't have. Not on his watch. On yours, Rachel. Because, let's face it, you're a loser. They're completely wrong about you. Tragically mistaken. Thirty-five and you're starting your first real job? What have you been doing all this time? All that potential wasted. The Peace Corps? Nobody joins the Peace Corps. Those years drifting with Marty after Guatemala. You working after he finally decided he wanted to go to law school?

You've been faking it. But you're just a loser and now your poor daughter has gotten sucked into your loser web.

Rachel points a finger at the place where the mirror used to be. *You dumb bitch. I wish you had died. I wish you had been one of the 10 percent who'd died!*

She closes her eyes, breathes, counts down from ten, opens them again. She runs to the bedroom and changes into the black skirt and white blouse she bought for teaching. She puts on her expensive-looking leather jacket, finds a respectable pair of heels, runs a hand through her hair, and grabs her shoulder bag. She gathers her financial documents, her laptop, and the employment contract from Newburyport Community College. She gets Marty's stash of bar-exam cigarettes and the sealed bag of flood money. She runs to the kitchen, slips in the heels, almost smashes her face into the range hood, rights herself, grabs her phone, and tears out to the car.

7

The First National Bank on State Street in downtown Newburyport opens at 9:30 a.m. Rachel paces the sidewalk near the bank entrance and puffs on her Marlboro.

State Street is deserted except for a very pale, nervous, older man wearing a heavy coat and a Red Sox cap who is walking toward her.

Their eyes meet as he stops in front of her.

"Are you Rachel O'Neill?" he asks.

"Yes," she replies.

The man swallows hard and pulls his cap lower. "I'm supposed to tell you that I've been off The Chain for a year now. I'm supposed to tell you that because I did as I was told, my family is safe. I'm supposed to tell you that there are hundreds of people like me who can be recruited to bring you a message if The Chain thinks you or anyone in your family needs a message."

"I get it."

"You're—you're not pregnant, are you?" the man asks hesitantly, seemingly going off script for a moment.

"No," Rachel replies.

33

"Then this is your message," he says and, without warning, punches her in the stomach.

The air is knocked out of her and Rachel crumples to the ground. He is surprisingly strong, and the pain is terrible. It takes her ten seconds to get her breath back. She looks up at the man in incomprehension and fear.

"I'm supposed to tell you that if you need further proof of our reach, you should Google the Williams family of Dover, New Hampshire. You won't see me again but there are many others out there like me. Do not attempt to follow me," the man says and with tears of shame running down his cheeks, he turns and walks quickly back down the street.

Just then the bank door opens and the security guard sees her sprawled on the ground. He looks at the man hurrying away from her; his fists clench and it's clear that he senses something has just happened.

"Can I help you, ma'am?" he asks.

Rachel coughs and pulls herself together. "I'm fine, I guess. I, uh, took a spill."

The security guard offers her his hand and helps her to her feet.

"Thank you," she says and winces in pain.

"Are you sure you're OK, ma'am?" he asks.

"Yes, fine!"

The security guard looks at her oddly for a moment and again at the man hurrying away. She can tell that he's wondering if she's some kind of shill in a bank-robbery attempt. His hand drifts toward his gun.

"Thank you so much," she says. She lowers her voice to a whisper. "I'm not used to heels. So much for making a good impression at the bank!"

The guard relaxes. "No one saw you but me," he says. "I don't know how you walk in those things."

"This is a joke I tell my daughter: 'What do you call a dinosaur in high heels?'"

"What?"

"'My-feet-are-saurus.' She never laughs. She never laughs at my dumb jokes."

The guard smiles. "Well, I think it's funny."

"Thank you again," Rachel says. She fixes her hair, goes inside the bank, and asks to see Colin Temple, the manager.

Temple's an older guy who used to live out on the island before moving into town. He and Rachel had attended each other's barbecues, and Marty had gone fishing with him on his boat. Colin hadn't screwed her over the couple of times she had missed mortgage payments since the divorce.

"Rachel O'Neill, as I live and breathe," he says with a grin. "Oh, Rachel, why do birds suddenly appear every time that you're near?"

Because they're actually carrion crows and I'm one of the goddamn undead, she thinks but doesn't say. "Good morning, Colin, how are you?"

"I'm fine. What can I do for you, Rachel?"

She swallows the pain of the gut punch and forces a half smile onto her lips. "I'm in a bit of trouble, and I wonder if we can have a talk."

They repair to the manager's office, which is decorated with yacht pictures and tiny intricate model boats that Colin has made himself. There are several photos of a snot-nosed King Charles spaniel that she can't for the life of her remember the name of. Colin leaves the door a little bit ajar and sits behind his desk. Rachel sits opposite and tries to put a pleasant expression on her face.

"What can I do to help?" Colin asks, still pretty cheery but with suspicion creeping into his eyes.

"Well, it's the house, Colin. That roof above the kitchen

is leaking and I had a contractor in yesterday and he said the whole thing will have to be replaced before it snows or it all might come down."

"Really? It looked OK last time I was out there."

"I know. But it's the original roof. From the 1930s. And it leaks every winter. And now it's just a danger. To us, I mean. To me and Kylie. And also, you know, to the house. You guys have the mortgage and if the house was destroyed, your asset wouldn't be worth anything," she says and even manages a little fake laugh.

"How much does your contractor say he'll need?"

Rachel had thought about asking for the full twenty-five thousand but that seems ridiculous for a roof job. She has nothing in her savings account, but she can charge ten grand on her Visa. She'll worry about paying off the bill when Kylie is home safe.

"Fifteen thousand. But it's fine, Colin, I'm good for it. I'm starting a new job in January," she says.

"Oh?"

"I've been hired to teach some classes at Newburyport Community College. Introduction to Modern Philosophy. Existentialism, Schopenhauer, Wittgenstein, all that good stuff."

"Finally using that degree, eh?"

"Yeah. Look, I've brought the employment contract and the full salary details. It's not much but it's a steady paycheck and it's more than I was getting as an Uber driver. Things are really going great for us now, Colin—just, you know, apart from the roof," she says as she hands over the documents.

Colin examines the paperwork and then looks up and examines her. He knows something is wrong. She probably looks awful. Wizened, thin, worried. Like someone whose breast cancer has returned or who is in the final stages of a methamphetamine death spiral.

His eyes narrow. His mood changes. He shakes his head. "I'm afraid we can't defer any more payments and we can't add anything to the original loan. I wouldn't be allowed to do that. I have very little discretion in these matters."

"A second mortgage, then," she says.

He shakes his head again. "I'm sorry, Rachel, but your house isn't a safe enough asset for that. To be brutally honest, it's just a glorified beach shack, isn't it? And you're not even really on the beach."

"We're on the tidal basin. It's waterfront property, Colin."

"I'm very sorry. I know you and Marty talked for years about remodeling it, but you never did, did you? It's not properly winterized, there's no central air."

"The land itself, then. Property prices have been going up around here."

"You're on the unfashionable western side of Plum Island, not the Atlantic side. You face the marshes and you're in the flood zone. I'm sorry, Rachel, there's nothing I can do for you."

"But, but . . . I have this new job."

"This employment contract at the community college is only for one semester. You're a bad risk for the bank—you can see that, can't you?"

"You know I'm good for it," she insists. "You know me, Colin. I'm almost always on time. I pay my debts. I work hard."

"Yes. But that's not the issue."

"And what about Marty? He's a junior partner now. I've been letting him slide on the child-support payments because of Tammy's bankruptcy, but—"

"Tammy?"

"His new girlfriend."

"She went bankrupt?"

Crap, Rachel thinks. She knows this information will not help her case, so she tries to rush through it.

"Oh, it's nothing. She had a chocolate store in Harvard Square, and it went under. She's not a businesswoman. I think she's only about twenty-five or—"

"How do you lose money selling chocolate in the munchies capital of New England?"

"I don't know. Look, Colin. We're old friends. And I . . . I need this. I need it as soon as possible. It's an emergency."

Colin leans back in his chair.

Rachel sees him turning all this over. He's probably learned how to spot a liar . . .

"I'm sorry, Rachel, I really am. If you're looking for a contractor, I can recommend Abe Foley. He's honest and he does a good job fast. That's all I can do."

Rachel nods. "Thank you," she says meekly and, thoroughly defeated, exits his office.

8

Hmmm, this one feels different.

There's no evidence, of course, that it *is* any different. It shouldn't be any different. They *always* say the same things, act the same way, and then fall right into line. Human beings are boringly predictable. That's why the actuarial tables work so well.

And it's just a feeling—that's all. And she can shake this feeling and replace it with another. But she doesn't want to do that today. She wants to sit with the bad feeling and experience it and have it explain to her why it's here. If the feeling means anything at all, it's almost certainly about the current person on The Chain.

Perhaps it would be wise to take a look at the present state of play. She opens up the encrypted file on her computer and examines the current protagonists. Everything looks fine. Link negative two is Hank Callaghan, a dentist and Sunday-school teacher from Nashua who has done everything requested of him. Link negative one is Heather Porter, a college administrator also from New Hampshire who has done all she has been asked to do. Link zero is Rachel O'Neill or, as she calls herself now, Rachel Klein. A former waitress and Uber driver who will soon be teaching at a community college.

Is Rachel the bad apple?

It doesn't really matter if she is. As Olly is always saying, The Chain is largely a self-regulating mechanism that repairs its own broken DNA with only a little nudging from the outside.

"Don't worry. It will all sort itself out," her stepmother used to say. And she was right. It generally did all sort itself out. She was sorted out too in the end, of course.

No, Rachel won't be any trouble. None of them will be or could be. Rachel will fall into line like all the others; either that, or she and her daughter will die. And die horribly, as an example for the others.

9

On the street outside the bank, Rachel fights back tears and waves of panic. What is she going to do? She can't do anything. She has failed at the very start. *Oh my God, my poor little Kylie.*

She looks at the clock on her phone: 9:43.

She sniffs, wipes her face, takes a breath, and goes back inside.

"Miss, you can't—" someone says as she marches back into Colin's office.

He glances up from his computer looking startled and guilty, as if he'd been Googling some particularly arcane pornography. "Rachel, I told—"

She sits and resists the urge to jump over the desk, put a knife to his throat, and scream for the tellers to give her the goddamn money in nonsequential bills.

"I'll take any loan this bank offers at any rate of interest, no matter how predatory. I need the money, Colin, and I'm not going to leave this frigging office until I get it."

Her eyes, she knows, have a piratical, dangerous, bank-robber glint to them. *Look at me,* they seem to say, *I am capable of anything right now. Do you really want to begin your day with the guards dragging me out of here kicking and screaming?*

Colin takes a deep breath. "Well, um, we do offer a ninety-day emergency home finan—"

"How much can I get?" Rachel interrupts.

"Would fifteen thousand dollars cover your, er, roof?"

"Yeah."

"The rate of interest would be well above our . . ."

She tunes him out and lets him spin her the blah-blah-blah. She doesn't care about the rate of interest or the service fee. She just wants the money. When he's done talking, she smiles and says that all sounds fine.

"I'll need to do some paperwork," Colin says.

"Can I have the money transferred directly into my account?"

"You'd prefer that over a check?"

"Yes."

"We can do that."

"I'll be back to sign the paperwork in an hour," she says, then she thanks him and goes outside.

She looks at her hastily scrawled, extremely incriminating checklist.

1. Ransom
2. Burner phones
3. Research target/victim
4. Get gun, rope, duct tape, etc.
5. Research place to hide victim

She's near the Newburyport library. Maybe she can do some research on a target/victim in that hour? *Sure, yeah, move, Rachel, move.*

She runs down State Street to the library, sprints up the library steps, and finds an empty study cubicle in the

Lovecraft Wing. First thing she does is Google the Williams family of Dover, New Hampshire. A grisly robbery/home invasion gone wrong, the police thought. A mother and her two children and her new boyfriend were tied up, and all of them were shot in the head. The children had been killed hours before the mother, so she'd had plenty of time to suffer and think about it.

Utterly chilled, Rachel begins researching potential targets.

How had they found her? A pin in a map? PTA records? Uber profile?

Facebook. Goddamn Facebook.

She fires up her MacBook Air, logs on to Facebook, and spends the next forty-five minutes scrolling through names and faces of friends of friends.

There are a breathtaking number of people whose profiles and posts are public and can be viewed by anyone. *George Orwell was wrong,* she thinks. *In the future, it won't be the state that keeps tabs on everyone by extensive use of surveillance; it will be the people. They'll do the state's work for it by constantly uploading their locations, interests, food preferences, restaurant choices, political ideas, and hobbies to Facebook, Twitter, Instagram, and other social media sites. We are our own secret police.*

Some people, she discovers, helpfully update their Facebook and Instagram feeds every few minutes, giving potential kidnappers or burglars intimate temporal and geographic information on their whereabouts.

It's all good stuff and Rachel decides to hunt for targets in the Greater Boston and North Shore areas. Successful, together men and women who are unconnected to law enforcement, who have big houses but small families, and who look as if they can pay a ransom and continue The Chain.

She takes out her notebook and makes a preliminary list of candidates.

Then she closes the computer, picks up her leather jacket, puts the list in her zip pocket, and goes back to the bank.

Colin is waiting for her. She signs the forms and when all that is done, she says she'll wait while he transfers the money into her account. It's the work of a moment.

She thanks him and goes to the Panera Bread on Storey Avenue. She orders a coffee and takes a booth in the corner, then logs on to the free wireless, fires up the Mac, and downloads the Tor search engine, which looks seriously untrustworthy. Nevertheless, she clicks the icon, and just like that, she's on the dark web. She's heard of the dark web and knows it as a place where you can buy guns, restricted prescription drugs, and narcotics.

She finds a place to buy Bitcoin, reads through the procedures, sets up an account for herself, and buys ten thousand dollars' worth of Bitcoin with her Visa. Then she buys another fifteen thousand dollars' worth of Bitcoin using the recently deposited money in her First National account.

She finds the InfinityProjects Bitcoin account and transfers the money. The transaction takes less than a second.

And just like that, the ransom is paid. Jesus.

So what happens next? Would they call her? She looks at the phone and waits. She sips her coffee and stares at the other people in Panera. They have no idea they are living the dream. They have no idea how bad it can get on the other side of the looking glass.

She tugs at a loose thread on her blouse.

Her phone dings with another photo of Kylie—here she's sitting on a mattress in a basement—and a message from Unknown Caller: Further instructions coming. Remember: it's not about the money, it's about The Chain. Move on to part 2.

Move on to part 2? Did that mean they received the money? She hopes she hasn't screwed it up.

But of course, that was the easy part.

She closes the Mac and goes outside to the car.

What now? Back to the house? No, not back to the house. Now she has to get the burner phones and a gun, and the best place to do that is far from neighbors and prying eyes and the Massachusetts gun laws, over the state line in New Hampshire.

She runs to her Volvo, gets in, turns the ignition, and, with a growl of clutch and a squeal of brakes, heads north again.

10

Thursday, 10:57 a.m.

Everyone on the radio is talking about the shooting of a state trooper near Plaistow. There are only about four or five murders a year in New Hampshire, so this is big news and it's on every station.

The reports unnerve her, so she turns the radio off.

Just over the state line in Hampton, New Hampshire, she finds the place she's been looking for: Fred's Firearms and Indoor Tactical Range. She'd driven by Fred's a thousand times and never dreamed about stopping.

Until today. She parks the Volvo and goes inside. Her stomach still hurts from the punch in the gut and she winces a little as she walks.

Fred is a tall, heavy, amiable-looking sixty-year-old wearing a John Deere cap, a denim shirt, and jeans. His face is badly pockmarked but he's still a handsome old geezer. The most distinctive thing about him, perhaps, is the gun belt he wears low on his waist. There are two semiautomatics in open holsters, which, Rachel assumes, are there to deter potential thieves. "Morning, ma'am," he says. "What can I do for you?"

"I'm here for a gun. Something I could keep in my room

for, you know, personal protection. We've had reports of burglars in our neighborhood."

"You from Boston?" he asks with a look that seems to add *That city of Noam Chomsky, the Harvard debating society, and Ted Kennedy?*

"Newburyport," she says and then wonders if perhaps she should have given a fake hometown.

"You're looking for a pistol? A thirty-eight, something like that? Something simple?"

"Yes, exactly. I've brought my driver's license."

"I'll put your name in the system. There's a two-day waiting period while we check you out."

"What? No, I'll need something sooner than that," she says, trying not to sound suspicious.

"Well, ma'am, today I can sell you a rifle or a shotgun, any of these," Fred says, pointing at a row of guns. Rachel is five foot nine but they all look too big for her and too ungainly to hide under a coat while she's sidling up to some poor kid.

"Do you have anything more compact?"

Fred rubs his chin and gives her an odd, penetrating look. She wishes then that she looked prettier. Attractive women didn't get that sort of look . . . or not as much, anyway. In her twenties, Rachel had looked like Jennifer Connelly in Ang Lee's *Hulk,* according to Marty, but all that was gone now, of course. Her eyes were hollow and ringed, and the bloom was permanently missing from her cheeks.

"The law puts a lower limit on barrel length, but what about one of these?" Fred says, and from under the counter he pulls out what he says is a Remington Model 870 Express Synthetic Tactical pump-action shotgun.

"This might do," she replies.

47

"It's a 2015, used. I could let you have it for three hundred fifty."

"I'll take it."

Fred winces. Clearly he was expecting her to haggle him down but Rachel is so desperate she's willing to pay the asking price. She sees him look out into the parking lot and note that her car is a beat-up orange Volvo 240. "Tell you what," he says. "I'll throw in a box of shells and a little lesson. Do you want me to show you how to use it?"

"Yes, please."

Fred walks her to the indoor range.

"You ever fire a gun before?" he asks.

"No. I've held one. A rifle, in Guatemala. But I never fired it."

"Guatemala?"

"Peace Corps. We were making wells. Me and Marty—my ex—were liberal arts majors, so of course they sent us to the jungle to work on an irrigation project. We had no clue. We had our baby girl with us. Kylie. Crazy, really, when you think about it. Marty said he saw a jaguar stalking the camp. No one really believed him. He hurt his arm when he fired the rifle."

"Well, I'm going to teach you how to do it right," Fred says and he gives her ear protectors and shows her how to load the weapon. "Tight against your shoulder. There will be a kick, it's a twenty-gauge. No, no, much tighter. Brace it with your body. If there's a gap, the weapon will drive itself into your collarbone. Remember Newton's third law. Every force results in an equal and opposite force."

Fred pushes a button and a paper target comes up on a roof runner and stops twenty-five feet away from them. There's a claustrophobic smell in here of grease and gunpowder. The target is a scary-looking man also carrying a weapon; it's not a terrified little kid.

"Pull the trigger, that's it, go on, easy does it."

She squeezes the trigger, there's an enormous bang, and Fred is right about Newton's third law. The barrel pounds into her shoulder. When she opens her eyes and looks at the paper target, she finds that it has been obliterated. "Twenty-five feet or closer and you should be OK. If they're farther away and they're running, let them run. You get my drift?"

"Let them run toward you so you can kill them or let them run away and call the police."

He winks at her. "You catch on quick."

She takes the shells and pays with her flood money. She thanks Fred and goes out to the car and puts the shotgun on the passenger seat next to her. If they're monitoring her through her phone somehow, hopefully they will see that she's serious and that she's getting things done.

11

The Hampton Mall is the perfect place to buy burner phones. She slides the car into a spot in the parking lot, opens up the trunk, and rummages around looking for Kylie's Red Sox cap. Her own Yankees hat sometimes attracts attention; a Sox or a Pats cap never gets a second look. She finds the cap, puts it on, and pulls it low over her face.

Her phone rings and her stomach lurches. "Hello?" she says automatically without waiting to see who it is.

"Hi, Rachel, this is Jenny Montcrief, Kylie's homeroom teacher."

"Oh, Jenny, um, hi."

"We were wondering where Kylie was today?"

"Yes, she's sick. I meant to call the office."

"You have to call before nine."

"I will next time, I promise. I'm sorry. She won't be in today, she's not feeling well."

"What's the matter? Anything serious?"

"Just a cold. I hope. Oh and, um, vomiting."

"Oh, dear. I'm sorry to hear that. Hopefully we'll see her tomorrow. Rumor has it she's cooking up a great presentation on King Tut."

"Tomorrow, um, I don't know. We'll see. These things are unpredictable. Listen, I better go, I'm getting some medicine for her right now."

"How long is she going to be out?"

"I don't know. I have to go." Another call is coming in, from an Unknown Caller. "'Bye, Jenny, sick daughter, have to run," Rachel says and answers the incoming call.

"I hope you're working hard, Rachel. I'm relying on you. My boy won't get released until you get someone to take his place," the woman holding Kylie says.

"I'm doing my best," Rachel tells her.

"They said they sent you a message and told you about the Williams family?"

"They did."

"If you get out of this, you have to keep quiet or the blowback will get you like it got them."

"I'll keep quiet. I'm cooperating. I'm doing the best I can."

"Keep going, Rachel. Remember, if they tell me you're trouble, I won't hesitate to kill Kylie!"

"Please don't say that. I'm—"

But the woman has hung up.

Rachel looks at the phone. Her hands are shaking. The woman is clearly on edge. Kylie is in the hands of someone who sounds like she's on the verge of a nervous breakdown.

A young man gets out of a car in the row opposite. He looks at her strangely for a moment and then nods grimly at her.

Is he another one of The Chain's agents?

Are they everywhere?

Suppressing a whimper, she puts the phone in her bag and hurries through the double doors of the mall.

The Safeway is open and already filled with people.

She grabs a shopping basket, speeds past the displays of Thanksgiving merchandise, and finds the rack selling those inexpensive cell phones. She picks up one that looks good, an AT&T cheapo that can still do photos and video. It's $14.95. She puts a dozen of them in the basket and then throws in two more. Fourteen. Will that be enough? There are only six phones left on the rack. Hell with it. She takes those too.

She turns to see Veronica Hart, her eccentric neighbor who lives five houses down from her on Plum Island. Oh God. The very reason she'd come up here was to get away from anybody who might possibly know her. If Veronica sees the phones, she'll ask her if she's prepping for the end of the world and then she'll point out that come the apocalypse, zombies will tear down the cell-phone towers. It'll be a whole thing. Rachel lurks behind the unsold Halloween merchandise until Veronica pays and leaves.

She scans the phones at the self-serve checkout counter. After that, she goes down to the Ace Hardware and buys rope, chains, a padlock, and two rolls of duct tape.

The cashier is a hipster with long Elvis sideburns and sunglasses. "Thirty-seven fifty," he says.

She hands over two twenties.

"You're supposed to say 'It's not what you think,'" the cashier says.

Rachel has no idea what he's talking about. "What?"

"All this," he says, loading the gear into two plastic bags. "It looks like a *Fifty Shades of Grey* starter kit, but I'm sure there's a more innocent explanation."

The real explanation is much more terrifying. "Nope, that's exactly what it is," Rachel says and hurries out of the store.

12

Kylie has no phone, so she has no idea what time it is, but she thinks it might still be morning. She can't hear anything, but she can see light through the basement window.

She sits up in the sleeping bag. It's so cold down there that frost has formed on the sides of the windows. Maybe running in place will help?

Kylie worms her way out of the sleeping bag and stands in her socks on the freezing concrete floor. She walks as far as the chain will let her, which isn't very far. A small circle around the bed and back to the big old cast-iron stove. Is that thing as heavy as it looks? She goes to it and, with her back to the camera, gives it a shove. It doesn't move. Not an inch. She scurries back to the sleeping bag and waits under the covers, straining to hear if the basement door is being opened, but no one comes.

They're busy. They aren't watching her through the camera. Or at least not continually. They've probably connected it to a laptop and occasionally check in on her. If she could move the stove, then what? She'd still be chained to the stupid thing and standing there at the bottom of the stairs with no way out.

Under the sleeping bag, she examines the handcuff on her wrist. Almost no space at all between metal and skin. Maybe a couple of millimeters. Could she slide the handcuff off her wrist with that tiny amount of space? It seems unlikely. How had Houdini done it? Her friend Stuart had been into that Houdini miniseries and encouraged her to watch it. She certainly doesn't remember Houdini ever sliding a handcuff off his wrist in any of his escapes. He had always picked the locks with a hidden key. If she ever gets out of this, she'll have to learn some survival skills like that. Self-defense, handcuff-lock picking. She examines the handcuff closely. The words peerless handcuff company are stamped into the metal just below a little keyhole. What you do is put your key in the lock and turn it either clockwise or counterclockwise and the handcuff opens. What she needs is something that will do the job of the key and spring the mechanism. The sleeping-bag zip is no good. The pencil they'd given her for drawing is no good. Nothing in the cardboard box is any good, except maybe the . . .

She looks at the tube of toothpaste. What's it made of? Metal? Plastic? She knows that oil paints are kept in metal tubes, but toothpaste? She examines it carefully but can't figure it out. It's Colgate Cavity Protection. It looks like an old tube they've kept in their spare bathroom for years. Could you possibly use the pointy bit at the bottom to pick the handcuff lock?

She pokes it into the keyhole and it doesn't seem impossible. She'll have to carefully rip the bottom off the tube and attempt to fashion it into a key. The woman will kill her if she finds her trying to escape. Trying to escape is a dangerous long shot, but it's better than no shot at all.

13

There's a short man standing in front of her house. The shotgun is in the passenger seat. As Rachel pulls into the parking spot, she reaches for it. She rolls the window down and puts the shotgun across her lap. "Hello?" she says inquiringly.

The man turns. It's old Dr. Havercamp from two houses down on the tidal basin.

"Hello, Rachel," he replies cheerfully in his rural Maine accent.

Rachel puts the shotgun back in the passenger seat and gets out of the car. Dr. Havercamp is holding something.

"I think this is Kylie's," he says. "Her name is on the case."

Rachel's heart leaps. Yes, it's Kylie's iPhone—maybe that will give her some clue as to where Kylie is. She snatches the phone out of his hands and turns it on but the only thing that appears is the lock screen: a picture of Ed Sheeran playing guitar and the space to enter the four-digit code. Rachel doesn't know the code and she's sure she won't be able to guess it. If you guess wrong three times, the phone locks itself for twenty-four hours.

"It is Kylie's phone. Where did you find it?" Rachel asks, trying to sound casual.

"It was at the bus stop. I was walking Chester and I thought, *That's a phone,* and I picked it up and saw Kylie's name on the back. She must have dropped it when she was waiting for the school bus."

"She'll be so relieved. Thank you."

Rachel does not invite him in or offer him coffee. In this part of Massachusetts that's almost a capital offense, but she has no time.

"Um, I guess I better go. I have bilge to pump. Take care," he says. She watches him go down through the reeds to his boat.

When he's gone, she brings the shotgun and other supplies into the house, gets a drink of water, and turns on her Mac. The computer flares to life and she looks at it with a jaundiced eye for a moment. Are they watching her through the Mac's camera and her iPhone camera? She read somewhere that Mark Zuckerberg put a piece of masking tape over the camera on all his electronic devices as a security precaution. She gets tape from the kitchen drawer and does exactly that, covering the camera on her phone, her Mac, and her iPad.

She sits at the living-room table.

Now to the task at hand.

She has to kidnap a child? She laughs bitterly. How on earth is anything like that possible? It's madness. Complete and utter madness.

How can she do a thing like that?

Again she wonders why they picked her. What did they see in her that made them think she would be able to do something as utterly evil as kidnapping a child? She has always been the good girl. Straight-A student at Hunter College High School. She aced her SATs and nailed the Harvard interview. She never speeds; she pays her taxes; she's never late for anything; she agonizes when she gets a parking ticket. And now she's supposed to do one of the worst things anyone could ever do to a family?

She looks through the window. A beautiful, clear fall day. The tidal basin filled with birds and a few fishermen digging for bait on the mudflats. This part of Plum Island is a microcosm of this part of Massachusetts. On this side of the tidal basin, you have the smaller houses on the marsh; on the east side, you find the big empty summer houses that face the breakers of the Atlantic Ocean. The west side of the basin is all blue-collar firefighters, teachers, and crab men who live here year-round. The east side begins to fill up with the wealthy summer folk in May or June. Marty and she had thought they'd be safe out here. Safer than Boston. Safe—what a joke. Nobody's safe. Why were they naive enough to think that you could live anywhere in America and be safe?

Marty. Why doesn't he call her back? What the hell is he doing in Augusta?

She gets the list of names that she culled from Facebook and begins scrolling through them again.

All those happy, smiling faces.

A grinning little boy or little girl that she is going to point a gun at and drag into her car. And where in the name of God is she going to hold this poor soul? Her house is out of the question. The walls are made of wood, and there's no soundproofing. If someone starts screaming, half a dozen neighbors will hear. And she doesn't have a proper basement or an attic. As Colin Temple had said, this house really is little more than a glorified beach shack. Perhaps she could check into a motel? No. That's nuts. Too many questions.

She looks through the window at the big houses on the far side of the basin and suddenly a much better plan occurs to her.

14

She runs to her bedroom, pulls off her skirt, and slips on a pair of jeans and sneakers. She puts on her red sweater, Kylie's Red Sox cap, and a zip-up hoodie; she opens the French doors and goes out onto the deck.

She walks to the little sandy path that runs along the side of the basin between the reeds.

Cold wind, rotting kelp. TV and radio noise drifting down from waterfront homes.

She keeps close to the shore until she's halfway up the basin on the ocean side. Then she slips over onto Northern Boulevard and, trying to look as inconspicuous as possible, begins exploring the big beachfront houses that face the Atlantic.

All the summer people are gone, but which of these homes belong to summer folk and which belong to year-round residents? There are more year-rounders now that PI has its own water and sewage but the old-money types are creatures of habit, arriving on Memorial Day and flying off again on Labor Day like plovers.

Determining that a house is occupied is the work of a moment: lights on, a car in the driveway, voices. Determining that a house is empty but only temporarily is also fairly easy: no lights on, no car in the driveway, but mail piling up in the mailbox, and the gas is still on.

Determining that a house is empty and likely to stay empty for a while is a little trickier, but not as tricky as you might think. Lights off, electricity off, wireless off, no mail in the mailbox, gas lines turned off. But those could still be the homes of weekenders who worked in Boston or New York from Monday to Friday and showed up Saturday morning in their L. L. Bean boots and coats, somewhat surprised to find a stranger standing in the kitchen next to a kid tied to a chair.

What she's looking for is a house that's weatherproofed for the winter. Nor'easters this time of year are particularly severe, and although most of the homes facing the ocean are up on dunes above the sea, if there's a high tide and a bad storm, waves could come lashing over their decks and smash their expensive plate-glass windows. So if a house's owners weren't going to be back until Christmas or spring, they'd hammer boards over all the east-facing windows.

This had been done in several of the bigger houses, and there is one up near the point that she particularly likes. It's made of brick, which is rare around here; almost all the other houses on the island are timber-construction jobs. Even better than the brick walls is the fact that it has an actual basement belowground. This tells her that it was built before 1990, which was when bylaws had been introduced requiring all new houses on Plum Island to be floodproofed—meaning that they had to be on stilts above the ground.

Rachel walks around this promising house, investigating. The sea-facing windows are boarded up and the side ones are too. She hops over the fence and checks the fuse boxes and the lines. The gas and electricity are off and there's nothing in the mailbox at all; clearly, all the mail is being forwarded or held at the post office. A sign on the mailbox says that the house belongs to the Appenzellers. She knows these people a little bit. An older couple. He's in his late sixties, originally from Boston, a retired chemistry professor at Emory. The wife, Elaine, is a little younger, late fifties. Second marriage for both of them. If Rachel is remembering correctly, they go to Tampa in the winter.

Rachel goes up onto the east-facing rear deck. The deck has privacy walls, which means that you can sit there without being seen except by the people walking past directly ahead of you on the beach. At this time of year, there aren't many of those people.

The back entrance leads straight into the kitchen. There's a locked screen door that opens when she gives it a good tug. The kitchen door has an ordinary doorknob.

She examines it closely and takes a picture of it with her phone. She spends ten minutes Googling the image and discovers that it is a Schlage faux-Georgian F40 doorknob that, according to several locksmith sites, can be disabled with a hammer and a chisel straight down the mechanism.

What's worrying, though, is the sign on the kitchen window that says that the house is protected by Atomic Alarms. If she does open the back door, she might have thirty seconds to find the alarm's code box, and if she doesn't put the code in fast enough, all hell will break loose, won't it? The Atomic Alarms sign, however, looks very old. It was once a bright blue and it has now faded to a light gray. Will the alarm still work with the electricity turned off?

There's one other huge problem with the house. The Appenzellers are right next to one of the many paths cutting through the dunes that lead to the Plum Island beach. At this time of day no one is using the path, but in the mornings she imagines that it's busy with dog-walkers and residents taking their daily constitutionals. If a kid is screaming his head off, he will be heard unless she can soundproof the basement. A big board over the basement window might do the trick, but it won't be foolproof. Hmmm. She remembers Voltaire's warning about the perfect being the enemy of the good. She could spend a week looking for the best available empty house, a week in which Kylie will be suffering in a homemade dungeon. Apart from the alarm sticker and the dune path, the Appenzeller house is pretty close to ideal. It's a little removed from the other dwellings on this strip and partially isolated by dunes. It's off the road by about fifteen yards and the Appenzellers have planted cypress trees as further shielding from the setting western sun.

She sits in one of the Adirondack chairs on the Appenzellers' back porch and dials the number for Newbury Home Security.

"NHS, this is Jackson, how can I help you?" a man answers in a Revere accent so strong it could strip paint.

"Oh, hi. Can you help me with an alarm question?"

"I'll try."

"My name's Peggy Monroe. I live out on the island. My daughter's supposed to walk Elsie Tanner's Neapolitan mastiff while she's away, and Elsie gave her the key but there's an old Atomic Alarms sticker in the window and my daughter's worried that if she opens the door, the alarm will go off. Any suggestions?"

Rachel's new to the lying game. She isn't sure if it's better to say as little as possible or to be chatty and give names and details in order to assuage suspicion. She went with the latter plan, and now she worries that she's messed up.

Jackson yawns. "Well, ma'am, I guess I could come out

there and take a look if you want, but it's a fifty-dollar minimum."

"Fifty dollars? That's more than she's getting paid to walk the dog."

"Yeah, I figured. Look, I think your daughter should be OK. Atomic Alarms went out of business in the nineties. Breeze Security took over most of their operation, but the Breeze guys made sure they took all the old Atomic signs off the windowpanes, so chances are if there's an old Atomic Alarms sign up there, the alarm isn't connected to anything. Did she see any newer alarm signs?"

"No."

"I'd say she's going to be OK. If she does get in trouble, call me back and I'll come out there and see if there's anything I can do."

"Thank you very much."

She walks back to her house on the other side of Plum Island and finds a chisel and hammer in Marty's old toolbox. A toolbox he had never really used for anything. His brother, Pete, was the engineer, car expert, and fixer, not Marty. When they'd first moved up here, it had been Pete who had made the house livable when he was home from one of his tours.

Her heart drops. If anything happens to Kylie, it will kill Pete. Uncle and niece dote on each other. Rachel feels the tears welling up again and forces them back down. Sobbing won't get Kylie back.

She puts the hammer and chisel in a gym bag and grabs a flashlight. In case of trouble, she gets the shotgun too. It just about fits in the bag.

It begins to drizzle as she walks along the basin trail. The sky is gray now and there are ominous black clouds to the west. Rain would be good. It'd deter dog-walkers and busybodies.

She wonders if the kidnappers have Kylie somewhere warm and safe. She's a sensitive girl. She needs looking after. Rachel makes a fist and slams it into her thigh. *I'm coming, Kylie, I'm coming, I'm coming.* She puts her hood up and walks along Northern Boulevard to the Appenzellers'. Yeah, those cypress trees out front will do a pretty decent job at hiding nefarious goings-on inside. She cuts down the sandy path and hops the fence again. She examines the rectangular basement window that's six inches above the ground. It's three feet long and a foot tall. She taps the glass—it doesn't look too thick but if you covered the glass with an acrylic sheet or a thick wooden board, you could, perhaps, effectively muffle sounds.

She walks to the back porch and opens the screen door. Her heart is beating fast. It seems nuts to be doing this in broad daylight, but she has to get a move on.

She takes the chisel out of the bag and positions it in the center of the lock at the keyhole. Then she raises the hammer and hits the chisel hard. There's a metallic thud but when she tries the handle, it doesn't turn. She positions the chisel again and hits much harder. This time it's a swing and a miss, and the hammer plows into the wooden door.

Jesus, Rachel.

She lifts the hammer back and strikes a third time. The entire center mechanism collapses and bits come flying out. Rachel puts down the chisel and hammer and gingerly tries the door.

The handle turns, and when she pushes, the door creaks open.

She takes out the shotgun and the flashlight and, shaking all over, goes inside.

15

Thursday, 1:24 p.m.

She stands in the house she's just broken into. Thirty seconds of fear.

No dogs come at her. No alarm sounds. No one yells.

It isn't just luck. She has scouted it well.

The house is musty and empty. A thin layer of dust coats the kitchen surfaces. No one has been in here since early September. She closes the kitchen door behind her and explores the home.

Three uninteresting levels and a very interesting basement with brick walls and a concrete floor and nothing in it but a washing machine, a dryer, and a boiler. The house is held up by a series of concrete pillars and she could, she thinks in disgust, chain someone to one of those pillars. She checks out the little window above the dryer. She'll cover that with a board she'll get from the hardware store in town.

Rachel shivers with a mixture of fascination and revulsion. How can she think about this sort of thing so glibly? Is that what trauma does to you?

Yes.

It reminds her again of the chemo days. The numbness.

The feeling of plunging into the abyss and falling, falling, falling forever.

She goes upstairs, leaves through the back door, closes it, shuts the screen door, and makes sure the coast is completely clear before going down the back steps onto the beach.

She walks home again through the sea spray and drizzle.

She opens her MacBook at the living-room table and begins checking the Facebook feeds on her list of potential targets.

Selecting the right target is very important. You have to choose the right kind of victim with the right kind of family, people who won't lose their shit and go to the cops and who have both the money to pay the ransom and the emotional wherewithal to carry out a kidnapping to get their child back.

Again she wonders why she was singled out. She wouldn't have picked herself. No way. She was going to pick someone much more together. A married couple, maybe, with money.

She gets out her legal pad and comes up with some criteria so she can narrow down her long list. No one who knows her and might possibly recognize her voice. No one in Newburyport or Newbury or Plum Island. But also not someone who is too far away. No one in Vermont or Maine or south of Boston. People who have dough. People who look steady. No cops, journalists, or politicians.

She scrolls through names and faces and again marvels at how willing people are to spill their intimate secrets on the web for anyone to see. Addresses, phone numbers, occupations, number of kids, where their kids go to school, all their hobbies and activities.

A kid is probably the best bet. The most pliable. The least likely to struggle or escape and the most likely to pull at the heartstrings of loved ones. But kids are well watched in this day and age. It might be tricky to grab a child without being seen.

"Except for my kid. Anybody can take my kid," Rachel says and sniffs.

She goes through Facebook and Instagram and Twitter and applies the criteria. She culls her long list down to five kids. She ranks the children in order of preference.

1. Denny Patterson of Rowley, Mass.
2. Toby Dunleavy of Beverly, Mass.
3. Belinda Watson of Cambridge, Mass.
4. Chandra Singh of Cambridge, Mass.
5. Jack Fenton of Gloucester, Mass.

"I can't believe I'm doing this," Rachel says to herself. Although, of course, she doesn't *have* to do anything. She could go to the cops or the FBI.

She takes time to consider it. To really think about it. The FBI are professionals, but the woman holding her daughter isn't afraid of the criminal justice system; she's afraid of The Chain. The person above her on The Chain has her son. And if Rachel is perceived as a defector, this woman's instructions are to murder Kylie and select a new target. The woman is sounding increasingly on edge. Rachel has no doubt she will do anything to get her son back . . .

No, no FBI. And furthermore, when she makes the phone call that the woman made to her, she'll have to sound equally determined and dangerous.

She looks at the notes she's made on her various targets. Her number-one choice looks very good indeed: Denny Patterson. Twelve. Lives with his mom, Wendy, in Rowley.

Single mom, dad out of the picture. She isn't bankrupt. In fact, she seems to be quite well-off.

Rachel considers that. What is it that the operators of The Chain want? The most important thing is that The Chain itself continues. Some of the people on it will be richer than others, but more crucial than their wealth is the fact that they have to be clever and discreet enough to add another link and keep the whole thing going. Each individual link in The Chain is precious. The targets have to have money but they also have to be competent and pliable and afraid. Like she is now. A strong link with a few hundred dollars in the bank is better than a weak link who is a millionaire.

Kierkegaard said that boredom and fear lay at the root of all evil. The evil people behind The Chain want the money they collect, and what they fear is the individual who might bring the whole thing crashing to a halt.

Rachel is not going to be that person.

Back to Denny. Denny's mom had a company that was bought by AOL back in the day. Loves her son, brags about him all the time. She seems tough and unlikely to go to pieces. Forty-five years old. Ran the Boston Marathon twice, in 2013 and again last year. Faster last year. Four hours, two minutes.

Denny likes video games, Selena Gomez, and the movies, and the best thing—from Rachel's point of view—is that he's crazy about soccer. Goes to practice three times a week after school and often walks home.

Walks home.

Curly-haired, nice, normal kid. No allergies, no health problems, is not big for his age. In fact, he looks a little bit smaller than the average. Definitely not the goalkeeper for his team.

The mom has one sister; she lives in Arizona. Dad not

around. Lives in South Carolina. Remarried.

No family cop or political connections.

Wendy has embraced the digital future, Instagramming or tweeting her location and what she is up to practically every waking minute of the day. So if Rachel spies the kid at soccer practice, Wendy will let her know where the hell she is.

Kid 1 sounds very promising. She looks now at Kid 2: Toby Dunleavy, also twelve, from Beverly. Has a little sister. Mother continually updating everything they do on Facebook.

She pulls up Helen Dunleavy's Facebook page. A smiling, pleasant-looking blonde about thirty-five. *I'm not neurotic. I am too busy to be neurotic* are the words under her photo. Helen lives in Beverly with her husband, Mike, and her son and daughter, Toby and Amelia. Mike is a management consultant in Boston with Standard Chartered. Helen is a part-time kindergarten teacher at North Salem Elementary School.

Amelia is eight years old, four years younger than Toby. Rachel scrolls through the Facebook feed. Helen teaches kindergarten two mornings a week and the rest of the time she seems to spend updating her friends on Facebook about the family's doings. Mike Dunleavy apparently works long hours in Boston and most nights doesn't come home until late. Rachel knows this because Helen posts about what train Mike is coming back on and whether she is going to have the kids wait up for him or not.

Rachel finds Mike's résumé at LinkedIn. He's thirty-nine, originally from London, and recently lived in New York. No political or police background, and he looks stable enough. He likes soccer, and he used to be an auctioneer before going into management consulting. His claim to fame is selling a can of *Merda d'Artista* by Piero Manzoni.

Helen is one of three sisters. She's the middle child. Both of her sisters are homemakers. One is married to a lawyer; one is divorced from a food scientist.

The kids get picked up from school every day without fail, but what makes Toby attractive is the fact that he has just started archery. Goes twice a week to the Salem and District Archery Club.

Archery is Toby's big new passion. There's a link on his Facebook page to an adorable YouTube video of him shooting at various archery targets to the music of Ini Kamoze's "Here Comes the Hotstepper." And the great thing is that he walks home from the archery club. All by himself. He's a good boy. *Kids should be doing more of that,* Rachel thinks and then remembers that she is exactly the reason why helicopter/overprotective parents exist.

Kid 1 and Kid 2 both look promising and she has three solid backups too.

She closes the computer, gets her coat, and drives into town to visit the hardware store. In the car her phone begins to ring. "Hello?"

"Hi, could I speak to Rachel O'Neill, please."

"This is she."

"Hi, Rachel, I'm Melanie, calling from the fraud department at Chase. I wanted to alert you to some unusual activity on your Visa card this morning."

"OK."

Melanie asks her some verification questions and then gets to the point: "Apparently someone used your card to purchase ten thousand dollars' worth of Bitcoin. Do you know anything about that?"

"You didn't stop the order from going through, did you?"

"No, we didn't. Um, but we were wondering—"

"It was me. I did it. It's all fine. It's an investment I'm making with my husband. Look, I'm really in the middle of something, I have to go."

"So there's been no unusual activity?"

"Nope. Nothing unusual. All good here. But thank you for calling. I really have to go. Goodbye," Rachel says and hangs up.

At the hardware store she gets a board made for the Appenzellers' basement window and when she's on the way back home, Marty calls. Finally!

She tries not to burst into tears at his always amiable and cheery "Hey, sweetie, what's up?"

For some reason, you can't really hate Marty no matter how much you want to. Something about those green eyes and that dark wavy hair. Rachel's mother had warned her that he was a rogue, but that kind of talk has always backfired on mothers.

"Tammy said something about a leaky roof?" Marty inquires.

"What?"

"The roof. Tammy said rain was coming in?"

"Where are you, Marty?" she asks and almost adds *I need you.*

"I'm in Augusta. We're down here for the retreat."

"When are you coming back?"

"I'll be back Friday evening to take Kylie for the weekend, don't worry."

Rachel stifles a sob. "Oh, Marty," she whispers.

"That's tomorrow, hon. Hang in there."

"I will."

"This isn't about the roof, is it? What's happening, babe? Something's wrong. Tell me."

Aside from the fact that I'm probably dying and our daughter's been kidnapped? she very nearly says but doesn't. Doesn't because Marty would go straight to the police and wouldn't understand.

"Is it about money? I haven't been good, I know that. I'll do better. I promise. Have you got a contractor?"

"No. I've got no help," Rachel says in a monotone.

"How badly is the roof leaking?"

"I don't know."

"Look, hon, I checked the weather. No roofer will come out in the rain tonight. Maybe Pete could help?"

"Pete? Where is Pete?"

"He's in Worcester. I think."

"I'll send him a text. I think I'll be allowed to do that."

"What are you talking about? Allowed by whom?"

"Nothing. No one. Yes, maybe I'll ask Pete. I'll think about that."

"All right, sweetie. I really have to go, OK?"

"OK, Marty," she says sadly.

"'Bye," he says and hangs up. Without his calming baritone, the car is chilly and silent once more.

16

Unless you are a bow hunter, a paraplegic, an ancient-firearms enthusiast, or under the age of eighteen, deer-hunting season in Massachusetts doesn't begin until November 27.

Pete, however, has never really bought into the logic of the Massachusetts hunting-season dates or, indeed, most laws, rules, and ordinances.

He knows that if the rangers or a sheriff catches him, he could get fined or worse. But the rangers won't catch him. Pete knows these woods west of Worcester the way other people know the bars outside Fenway or the rotation of the girls at Hurricane Betty's. He's been hunting these forests since he was a boy. Admittedly, his senses are dulled somewhat because of his current issues, but even so, no clumsy sheriff's deputy or high-visibility-vest-wearing ranger is going to surprise him.

He often thinks about moving to Alaska, where there would be even fewer rangers and deputies, but Kylie will keep him in the state at least until she's off to college. Kylie is his only niece and he's nuts about her. They text nearly every day and he always takes her to those movies her mom can't sit through.

Pete follows the big buck deeper into the birch forest. It has no idea it is being stalked. He's upwind of it and he moves through the trees in utter silence. Pete is very good at this. In the Marines he had been an engineering officer, but after a couple of years of building bridges under mortar fire, he had taken a sabbatical to attend the basic recon course at Camp Pendleton. He finished near the top of his class. The brass had wanted him to transfer to a recon battalion but he'd done it only to test himself.

He sights the old buck in his rifle and aims under the heart, but just as he is about to squeeze the trigger, his phone vibrates in his pocket. *Should have turned it off,* he thinks. *Didn't imagine there would be a signal out here.*

He looks at it. Two new messages, one from Rachel and one from Marty. Both asking the same question: *Where are you?*

He tries to respond to Rachel, but the message won't go through. He ignores Marty's text. He doesn't hate Marty but they have little in common. There's six years between them, and by the time Marty was up walking and talking and starting to get interesting, Pete had been itching to get out of the house. And get out he had. At the age of twelve, he had "borrowed" a neighbor's Chevy Impala and driven it all the way to East Franklin, Vermont. He'd been heading for Montreal, of all places, but he was stopped at the Canadian border and arrested.

And nothing had happened. Nothing at all. The judge gave him the old blah-blah-blah and a finger-wagging. He'd stolen more cars after that but was more careful. No attempts to cross the border, no racing. He hooked up with a bad crowd in high school, but nobody cared as long as he maintained a high-B average, which he did. School bored him but he somehow managed to get accepted to Boston

University to study civil engineering. At BU he just about maintained a C average. He spent most of his time playing with the new computer-aided design software, creating outrageous suspension bridges that could never be built and old-fashioned cantilever bridges that no one wanted. He graduated in May of 2000 with no plans for or ideas about his future.

He moved to New York and attempted to make a living as a cybersecurity expert on the burgeoning World Wide Web. Everybody said that the internet was the new gold rush, but Pete must have been panning in the wrong virtual rivers. He barely made enough to keep up with the interest on his student loans.

But then a year later: September 11.

He went to Times Square the next morning. No one who was in New York then will ever forget that day after. It was a new world. At the recruiting booth, there was a line that stretched to Thirty-Fourth Street. Pete's grandfather had been in the navy. With Pete's engineering degree and background, the recruiters recommended the navy or the Marine Corps. Pete chose the Marines. And that was all she wrote for the next thirteen years. Officer Candidate School, the combat engineers, seven overseas tours, five to operational theaters. After the Marines, he'd traveled some and finally moved back to Worcester.

Now that chapter of his life is closed. Now he's just another unemployed forty-year-old who needs to take some free venison to make it through the winter.

The stag lowers its big head to take a drink at a stream. There's a scar that runs along its left flank. They've both been in the wars.

Pete has a clear shot, but something tells him that the stag is going to have to wait. He has that feeling you get in the back of the neck: Something is up. Something is wrong.

He looks at the texts again: *Where are you?*

Is Rach in some kind of trouble? He puts the rifle over his shoulder and looks for some slightly higher ground to see if he can get a signal, but now his phone says that it's got 1 percent charge.

He climbs the little hill above the waterfall and tries texting from there but in the two minutes that that takes, of course his phone dies. The big stag turns to look at him. They stare at each other for three seconds.

Spooked, it slips between the trees. Pete watches it vanish with regret. Food stamps go only so far. He secures the rifle and heads back to his truck.

And now his skin is starting to crawl. Is it that time already? He looks at the sky. It can't be three o'clock. But evidently it is. He hikes through the autumnal wood and finds his pickup truck undisturbed in the firebreak. Unfortunately, he hasn't brought his phone charger, so he will have to wait until he gets back to his apartment in Worcester to see what Rachel wants.

17

Kylie sits in the sleeping bag. She holds the toothpaste tube in one hand, her wrists aching from the effort of trying to pick the handcuff lock. She remembers a YouTube video Stuart wanted to show her about three ways to get out of handcuffs. Stuart loves that kind of thing—Houdini, magic, escapes. She hadn't watched it; she'd been on her own phone scrolling for the video about a new secret chamber someone had found in the Great Pyramid.

Next time she would pay attention.

If there is a next time, she thinks with a rush of terror.

She breathes deep and closes her eyes.

She likes magic also.

The Egyptians lived in a god-and-demon-infested world. There are demons here too, but they are human beings.

She wonders if her mom is doing the things the kidnappers want her to do. She wonders if the kidnappers have mistaken her mom for someone else. Someone with access to a bank vault or government secrets . . .

She takes a big breath, lets it out slowly, does it again.

She's calmer now. Not calm, but calmer.

She listens to the nothing.

No, not nothing. There's always something. Crickets. A jet. A very distant river. Seconds tick past, then minutes. She wants the river to take her away from this place, these people, away from all of it. It doesn't matter where. She wants to lie back and let the current float her down through the marshes to the Atlantic.

No. That's fake. A dream. *This* is real. This basement. These cuffs. *Be in the now,* the school counselor had said in that mindfulness class they had all mocked. *Be present and see* everything *there is to see in the now.*

She opens her eyes.

She looks, *really* looks.

She sees everything there is to see.

18

Wendy Patterson picks up Denny from Rowley Elementary School, takes him to soccer practice at Rowley High School, then drives into Ipswich and gets herself a soy chai latte from the Starbucks. She Instagrams a picture of the latte and a Thanksgiving cookie that she got for Denny.

Denny has changed into his soccer clothes and is doing dribbling drills with the team. Rachel watches him from her Volvo 240 parked across the street while using her phone to monitor Wendy's tweets, Facebook updates, and Instagrams. She watches him and feels sick with doubt. How can she do this? It's the most evil thing you could ever do to a mom, to a family. But then she thinks about Kylie locked in some crazy woman's basement. It's the most evil thing you can do but it has to be done.

She watches Denny play, and when the practice is over she sees that, yup, Wendy is still in Ipswich at the Starbucks. The drizzle has stopped now and it looks like Denny is going to be walking home. Wendy doesn't indicate on her Facebook feed that she is coming to pick him up.

Could Rachel grab him now?

She had thought that this would be a scouting trip, not

a snatch-and-grab mission. She hasn't prepared the Appenzeller house yet. The board isn't over the basement window; she doesn't have a mattress down there. But if the opportunity presents itself?

She follows the little boy in her car as he walks home with a friend. Obviously, she can't grab two kids, so she'll have to wait until they part.

She knows she must look very suspicious, creeping along at five miles per hour following two little boys.

She hasn't thought this through properly. She has no idea where in Rowley Denny's house is. Is he on the main road? Down a cul-de-sac? She curses herself for not figuring out the route from the high school to his house on Google Maps.

The friend hangs with Denny for a few blocks but then waves and leaves, and Denny is by himself.

Little Denny all alone.

Rachel's pulse quickens. She looks at the front passenger seat. Gun, ski mask, handcuffs, blindfold.

She rolls the window down and checks her mirrors.

There are witnesses. An old man with a dog. A high-school girl jogging. Rowley is a sleepy little community but not quite sleepy enough today. And then, just like that, Denny walks up a driveway, takes a key out of his pocket, and goes into his house.

Rachel parks the Volvo on the other side of the street and checks Wendy's Facebook feed. Now she *is* coming home, it says.

Rachel has about eight or nine minutes with Denny in there by himself. *Is* he by himself? Is there a dog or a housekeeper or something?

Can she just put on the ski mask, march across the road, and ring the doorbell? How can she get him into the car if she has to make a quick getaway? In the movies, lone kidnappers used chloroform-soaked rags to get their victims. Could you buy chloroform at the pharmacy? What if she used too much and sent the frickin' kid into cardiac arrest?

She puts her face in her hands.

How is this happening to her? When is she going to wake up from this nightmare?

She goes through these thoughts over and over until it's too late. Wendy's white VW SUV rolls up in front of the house, and Wendy gets out.

Rachel curses herself.

She's blown it. Almost on purpose. Almost on purpose out of sheer cowardice.

But as soon as his mom appears, Denny comes outside, and he and a kid from next door start playing basketball on the other kid's hoop.

She watches them both greedily. The way a predator watches its prey.

Either would do in a pinch. If she could get one of them alone . . .

She looks at her watch. Not yet five o'clock. This morning when she woke up, she had been a completely different person. As J. G. Ballard pointed out, civilization is just a thin, fragile veneer over the law of the jungle: *Better you than me. Better your kid than my kid.*

When the one-on-one basketball game is over, Denny goes back inside. A few moments later, a Lowell Police Department patrol car pulls up in front of the Pattersons' house and a six-foot-three uniformed cop gets out.

Rachel slinks down in her seat, but the cop hasn't come for her. He is carrying a giant box of Legos. He rings the Pattersons' bell and Wendy answers. She gives him a kiss, and Rachel watches the cop go inside. She watches through the living-room window as he ruffles little Denny's hair and gives him the Legos.

I guess Wendy doesn't report everything *on Facebook and Instagram,* Rachel thinks. And there goes Kid 1. No law enforcement. The rules are clear. She takes out her notebook and her phone. Kid 2 is now Kid 1.

Toby Dunleavy.

Rachel looks at Helen Dunleavy's Facebook feed. She selected Helen because she was another one of those people who felt the need to share everything that was happening to them every half an hour or so. She seems like a nice lady, though, and a good mom. That's the kind you want: a good mom who will do anything to get her child back.

She deep-dives on Mike, Helen's husband. Standard Chartered is a safe, boring enough place to work. He's probably used to dealing with stress and he'll have money to pay a ransom. Mike is English but lived in Manhattan for many years. He has a food blog and he'd written a funny post titled "What Came First, Zabar's or the Upper West Side?" Another nice guy. Not a guy you'd want to put through hell.

But then, nobody should be put through what she's going through.

She pauses and again racks her brain for any other way out of this, but nothing comes to mind. Follow The Chain. That's all. If you follow The Chain you get your kid back. If you don't . . .

Her iPhone begins ringing as she's looking at Toby's Tumblr feed. The screen says *Unknown Caller.*

"Hello?" Rachel says hesitantly.

"How are things going, Rachel?" a voice asks. It's someone speaking through a voice distorter. The original someone who contacted her this morning when she was on I-95.

"Who are you?" Rachel demands.

"I'm your friend, Rachel. A friend who will tell you the truth no matter how bitter that truth is. You're a philosopher, aren't you?"

"I guess—"

"You know what they say. The living are only a species of the dead, aren't they? And a very rare species at that. The cradle rocks over the abyss. Your daughter's named Kylie, is that right?"

"Yes. She's a great kid. She's all I have."

"If you want her to stay in the land of the living, if you want her to come back safely, you're going to have to get your hands dirty."

"I know. I'm researching targets right now."

"Good. That's what we want. Do you have a piece of paper nearby?"

"Yes."

"Write this down: 2-3-4-8-3-8-3-h-u-d-y-k-d-y-2. Say it back to me."

Rachel repeats it.

"That's the Wickr account name for this part of The Chain. That's W-i-c-k-r. You'll need to download the app on your phone. Send the details of the targets you are considering to that account. Someone here may vet this list. We may veto some of your choices. Sometimes we veto all the candidates, and occasionally we suggest some of our own. Is that clear?"

"I think so."

"Is it clear or not?"

"It is. Look, I might need help with this part, but I don't know if I can bring in Marty, my ex-husband. He might want to go straight to the cops."

"Then you'd better not bring him in," the distorted voice says quickly.

"His brother, Pete, was in the Marines, but he's definitely not a fan of law enforcement. He had some trouble with the police when he was a kid, and I think he was arrested last year in Boston."

"That doesn't mean much. I hear the Boston PD will arrest you for anything."

Rachel sees a small opportunity here. A little seed of something that might never grow but that is nevertheless a seed.

"Yeah," Rachel says and then adds with seeming indifference, "They'll arrest you for jaywalking, arrest you for banging a uey."

The distorted voice stifles a laugh and mutters, "Very true," before immediately getting back to business. "We may allow this ex-brother-in-law of yours. Send me his details on Wickr."

"I will."

"Very good. We're making progress. This is how it's worked for many, many years. The Chain will get you through, Rachel," the voice says and then the line goes dead.

The Lowell cop exits the Patterson house and walks to his car. Wendy comes to the door and waves.

It's time to leave this street and this town.

Rachel puts the key in the Volvo's ignition. The car backfires, and the cop turns to look at her. She has no choice but to wave to him through the window. Yet another person who has seen her do something weird or suspicious today.

She drives along Route 1A onto Rolfes Lane, takes the turnpike, and goes over the bridge to Plum Island.

Half a block from her house, she sees Kylie's geeky friend Stuart approaching. Shit!

She rolls her window down, stops the car. "Hello, Stu," she says casually.

"Mrs. O'Neill, um, I mean, Ms. Klein, um, I was wondering . . . I was wondering where Kylie was today? I didn't get a text from her. Mrs. M. said she was sick."

"That's right, Kylie's not well," Rachel says.

"Oh? What's wrong?"

"Um, stomach flu, that kind of thing."

"Wow. Really? She seemed OK yesterday."

"It was very sudden."

"Must have been. She texted me this morning and didn't say anything. I thought she might have been trying to get out of that Egyptology presentation, which is crazy because, you know—"

"She's the expert, I know. Like I said, it was, uh, very sudden."

Stuart seems puzzled and not entirely convinced. "Anyway, we all texted her and she never got back to us."

Rachel tries to think of a reasonable explanation. "Um, yeah, we've lost wireless in the house, which is why she's been out of touch. She can't text or Instagram or anything."

"I thought she still had minutes left on her phone?"

"Nope."

"Hey, do you want me to come over and look at your wireless? It might be a router issue."

"No, better not. I'm coming down with the flu bug as well. It's very contagious. Don't want to get you sick too. I'll definitely tell Kylie you were asking for her."

"Um, OK, 'bye," he says, and she stares at him until, intimidated, he turns and waves and walks back down the road again.

She drives the remaining fifty yards to the house. She hasn't thought of that. Kylie's school friends text and message all the time. If Kylie goes radio silent for more than an hour, it creates a big vacuum in their lives. And soon she'll start running out of plausible excuses. Another thing to worry about on top of everything else.

19

Pete isn't home yet but he can't take it anymore. He's been in the woods all day.

His skin is crawling; his skin is on fire. It is, as old man De Quincey said, the itch that can never be scratched.

He pulls the Dodge Ram off Route 2 and into the Wachusett Mountain State Reservation. There's a pond there that nobody ever goes to.

He reaches over the seat and grabs his backpack.

He looks up and down the road but there's no one around. From the backpack he removes a small plastic bag of premium-grade Mexican heroin. The DEA crackdown on legit opiates has affected all the patients who get their meds through the VA; Pete was able to fill the gap through the dark web for a while but then the feds got active there too. Heroin is actually easier to obtain than OxyContin now, and heroin is much more effective anyway, especially golden-triangle H and the new stuff coming up from Guerrero.

He takes out a spoon and his Zippo lighter and a syringe and a rubber arm tie. He cooks the heroin, ties off a vein, sucks the drug up into the syringe, and flicks the needle to get the air bubbles out.

He injects himself and then quickly puts the paraphernalia in the glove compartment in case he passes out and a National Park Service clown gets nosy.

He looks through the windshield at the fall foliage and the azure pond water. The trees aren't at their peak but they're still beautiful. Fiery oranges and reds and crazy sunburned yellows. He relaxes and lets the heroin dissolve in his bloodstream.

He's never looked at the statistics, so he has no idea how many veterans are opiate addicts of some sort, but he imagines the number is quite high. Especially for people who have done a couple of combat tours. During the '08 surge, every single member of his company had been injured or wounded. After a while people just stopped reporting themselves to the medics. What was the point? Nothing they could do about a concussion or a broken rib or a sprained back. You were just taking up a bed when your buddies were out there clearing roads and removing explosive charges from bridges.

What these opiates do, what heroin does, is remove the pain from your body temporarily. All the accumulated pain of all those decades walking the earth. Pain from the grinding of bone on bone, pain from falls, pain from people dropping girders on you, pain from the incompetent operation of machinery, pain from falling thirty feet into a wadi, pain from an overpressure shock wave from an IED thirty feet to your rear.

And that's just the physical pain.

He tilts the car seat back and lets the heroin ease his burdens in a way that even sleep cannot. The μ-opioid receptors in his brain activate a cascade that leads to a release of dopamine and a rush of well-being.

His eyes flicker and he zoetropes the strange twiggy trees on the pond's far shore, the falling leaves, and the thin-legged wading birds walking over the pond's mercury surface. Memories and images flood his mind whenever he uses. Usually bad memories. Usually the war. Sometimes 9/11. He thinks about Cara and Blair. He's just over forty, but he has been married and divorced twice. Nearly everybody he knows is in the same boat, of course, and it's worse among the enlisted men. Sergeant McGrath, a guy on his last tour, had been divorced *four* times.

Cara was just a youthful mistake—they were married for only thirteen months—but Blair . . . oh boy, Blair was a Townes Van Zandt song. She had taken a big chunk of his heart, his life, and his money.

Money. Another worry. Seven more years in the Marines and he could have retired on half pay. But the truth was that he had just barely avoided court-martial for what had happened at Bastion in September 2012.

Women, money, the goddamn war . . . hell with it all, he thinks and closes his eyes and lets the heroin fix him.

The H fixes him.

Fixes him in spades.

He sleeps for about twenty minutes and wakes and drives to a 7-Eleven to buy a pack of Marlboros and a Gatorade. The worry about Rachel has temporarily slipped his mind.

He gets back in the cab and turns on the radio. They're playing Springsteen. It's new Springsteen and he doesn't know new Springsteen but it's all right. He lights himself a cigarette and sips the Gatorade and then drives to Holden, where he takes 122A into town.

He's been back in Worcester about two months now. He doesn't feel sentimental about the place. He has no family left here and very few friends from the old days.

The apartment is in an old mill that has been converted into condos. It's only a flop to crash in and get mail.

He parks the car and goes inside.

He grabs a Sam Adams from the fridge and plugs the iPhone into the charger. When it comes back to life, he looks at a second text from Rachel.

They said it was OK for me to bring you in. Call me, please! it says.

He dials her number and she answers immediately. "Pete?" she asks.

"Yeah, what's up?"

"Are you home?"

"Yeah. What's going on?"

"I'll call you right back," she says.

The phone rings. It says *Unknown Caller*. "Rachel?"

"I'm calling you from a burner phone. Oh, Pete, I need to talk to somebody. I tried to talk to Marty but he's in Georgia. Oh God," she begins and dissolves into sobs.

"Have you been in an accident? What's happening?" he asks.

"It's Kylie. They've taken Kylie. They've kidnapped her."

"What? Are you sure she's not just—"

"They've taken her, Pete!"

"Have you called the police?"

"I can't call the cops, Pete. I can't call anybody."

"Call the police, Rachel. Call them now!"

"I can't, Pete, it's complicated. It's so much worse than you can imagine."

20

Pete has the same recurring thought as Rachel does: If they harm one hair on Kylie's head, he will scorch their world and stamp on the smoldering ashes. He will spend the rest of his life hunting them down and killing them all.

No one is going to harm Kylie, and they are going to get her back.

Pete drives the Dodge Ram hard to the front gate of the self-storage yard on Route 9. He parks outside locker 33. It's the biggest locker you can get, the size of a couple of garages. He had graduated from the small locker to the medium one and now to their "deluxe storage facility." He opens the padlock, rolls up the metal door, finds the light switch, and pulls the door closed behind him.

When his mom sold the house and moved to that place near Scottsdale, Pete had just taken all his stuff and dumped it in here, adding to it over the years. Until he bought the apartment he's in now, he had never really had a civilian house. He'd lived in the married quarters at Camp Lejeune and a succession of billets in Iraq, Qatar, Okinawa, and Afghanistan. This anonymous self-storage place between the road and the old ruined freight railway is the closest thing he's got to a permanent home.

He can spend hours here going through his old crap but today he ignores the nostalgia boxes and goes straight to the gun cabinet on the wall at the back. Rachel was confused and unclear on the phone. Kylie had been kidnapped and at this stage Rachel didn't want to go to the police. She wanted to cooperate with the kidnappers and do what they asked. If he can't persuade her to bring in the FBI, the two of them will need to be well armed. He unlocks the gun cabinet and takes out both of his handguns—his grandfather's navy-issue .45 ACP and his own Glock 19—and finally his Winchester twelve-gauge. His rifle is in the cab already.

He takes spare ammo for all the weapons and grabs a couple of flash-bang stun grenades he'd smuggled home. If this becomes a rescue mission, what else will he need? He gets his B-and-E equipment—lock-pick kit, sledgehammer, EM-alarm jammer, latex gloves, flashlight—and the bugging and anti-bugging gear he'd acquired for his post Corps corporate work.

He loads everything into the Dodge Ram and wonders, *What else?*

He takes the zip-lock bag containing his stash of heroin out of the glove compartment.

This would be the time to go cold turkey. To end it. Leave it here and drive away without it.

He has other priorities now.

Never going to get another opportunity like this one.

Torch it. Ride the pain. Get Kylie back.

Two roads. Yellow wood. All that shit.

He stands there.

Hesitating.

Thinking.

He shakes his head, puts the plastic bag in his jacket pocket, closes the locker, exits the storage yard, and heads for the highway.

21

Thursday, 8:30 p.m.

Rachel has researched the Dunleavy family until her eyes are tearing and her head is spinning. She knows them better than they know themselves.

She's read every blog and Facebook feed and Instagram post. Every tweet and retweet. She knows that Toby took up archery because he was inspired by a Danish speed archer in a YouTube video, not his father's bow-hunting proclivities. She knows that Amelia Dunleavy has a peanut allergy and that her elementary school has banned peanuts because of it.

She's read all of Mike's newish bow-hunting blog and his food blog all the way back to his very first post, in 2012, a recipe for a chocolate Bundt cake.

She knows that Helen wanted to return to work full-time but was worried she didn't have the energy required to be a fifth-grade teacher. Tons of stuff like that. Some of it helpful to Rachel; most of it not.

She closes the files on her computer and looks at her notes. She's printed out a map of Beverly and drawn the possible routes back from the archery club to the Dunleavy house. It'll have to be researched on the ground. She has prepared a B target and a C target, but she knows little Toby

94

Dunleavy is going to be the one.

Full dark now on the basin. The boats are in for the night.

Clothes are everywhere, the cat's litter box is unemptied, the breakfast dishes are still there—the house is a goddamn Tracey Emin piece of modern art commemorating a more innocent time that is never coming back.

Rachel examines her left breast. It doesn't feel any different, but the doctor is probably right to be concerned—there could well be something malignant growing in there again. If she does nothing, the malignant entity will kill her, erase her from existence. How pleasant that would be.

She stares through the window. The clarity of the light has faded and the agitated sky has turned dark blue and black.

The drizzle has become rain.

She hears what sounds like a pickup truck coming down the lane.

She sprints outside.

Pete gets out of the cab and she runs to him and he puts his arms around her and they stand there in the downpour saying nothing for fifteen seconds. Pete helps her back inside and they sit at the living-room table.

"Tell me the whole story from the beginning," Pete says.

Rachel tells Pete everything that happened since that first phone call, including everything she has done: paid the ransom, gotten the phones, gotten a gun, broken into the Appenzellers' house, tried to figure out exactly whom to kidnap. She doesn't tell him about the renewed concerns of her oncologist—that's between her and death.

Pete listens but says nothing. He lets her talk.

He tries to take it all in.

It's incredible.

He has seen evil up close in Afghanistan and Iraq, but he wasn't expecting something this clinical and diabolical in America. Never in his wildest dreams did he imagine a malevolent force like this coming near his family. This is some serious organized-crime or cartel shit.

"What do you think?" Rachel asks when she's done.

"I think we have to go to the cops, Rachel," he says soberly.

She's been expecting this answer. She shows him the story about the Williams family on her laptop, and while he's reading it, she tells him about the man outside the bank. She takes his hand. "You didn't speak to them, Pete. I did. That woman holding Kylie is terrified for her son. If they tell her to kill Kylie, she will. I know she will. She'll kill Kylie and select another victim to stay good with them. Keeping The Chain going is our only option."

She knows she sounds like someone in a cult, but that pretty much sums it up. She's all in now, she believes them, and she wants Pete to believe them too.

"So to get Kylie back, we'll have to kidnap someone," he says, shaking his head in horror.

"We have to, Pete. If we don't, they kill her. If we go to the police, they kill her. If we ever talk about it, they kill her."

Pete's mind goes back to that class he had been forced to take on ethics at Quantico. The Israeli IDF guest lecturer had given them a presentation on why it was ethical to disobey an illegal order. Morality entered into the equation even in the military. And what Rachel is contemplating now is not only illegal but absolutely morally wrong. Morally wrong from every conceivable angle. The ethically right play would be to go to the FBI immediately. Find the nearest FBI field office and tell them the whole story.

But that will get Kylie killed. Rachel believes that, and he believes her. And Kylie's safe return is the only thing Pete cares about.

The decision's been made. If they have to kidnap someone to get her back, he'll do it. If he has to kill someone to get her back, he'll do it. If he gets her back and they stick him in a cage for fifty years, it will be easy time, easy because Kylie will be safe.

"This morning they sent me a photo of Kylie to show me that she's safe," Rachel says. Shaking, she gives Pete her phone.

Pete looks at the photo of little Kylie blindfolded and sitting on a mattress in a basement. There are few clues to her location that he can see. She's been given Poland Spring water and she's got graham crackers, but those you can get anywhere. Kylie does not seem to have been physically abused but of course she must be terrified beyond belief.

He goes to the kitchen and pours himself some coffee. He takes a moment to assess the situation. "We're ruling out the police? Definitely?" he asks.

"The Chain voice and the woman holding Kylie were both very clear. They said that if I break any of the rules, they'll have to kill Kylie and move on to another target."

"How will they know if you're breaking any of the rules?"

"I don't know."

"Have they bugged your house? Have you had a break-in recently or any unusual visitors?"

"No, nothing like that, but I think they hacked my phone earlier today. They knew a police car was behind me on the highway. And they know who I'm calling and what I'm talking about. They seem to know where I am at all times. I think they might have been looking through the phone's camera. Can they do that?"

Pete nods, turns off Rachel's iPhone, and puts it in a drawer. He closes her MacBook and places it with the phone. "Sure. You say you bought disposable phones?"

"Yes."

"Use them for all outgoing calls from now on. And don't use your computer again. I've brought mine. They've probably hijacked the camera on your phone and computer and disabled the camera light so that they can see you and you don't even know it's on. The stuff that goes on in intel black ops would blow your mind."

"I covered the camera with a piece of tape."

"That's a good idea, but just be aware that they might be listening too. I'll search the house for bugs. You say you haven't had a break-in? What about an unscheduled TV-repair guy or plumber or anything like that?"

"Nothing like that."

"Good. Could just be spyware. Now, what have you told Marty?"

"Nothing so far. He's in Augusta, playing golf."

"He's my little brother and I love him, but Marty's got a mouth, and if you're worried about security or someone going to the FBI . . ."

"Nothing that will risk Kylie," she says.

Pete takes her cold, trembling hand in his. "It's going to be OK," he says.

She nods and looks into his dark, steady eyes. "Are you sure?"

"I'm sure. We're going to get her back."

"Why me, do you think? Why my family?" she asks.

"I don't know."

"She said she researched me online. She saw that Marty and I did that Peace Corps project in Guatemala. She saw Harvard and cancer survivor and all my jobs and she thought

I seemed like someone who had her act together. I'm not. I'm a loser, Pete. I'm weak."

"You're not, you're—"

"I've screwed up my whole life. I invested everything in Marty. I can't even look after my own daughter!"

"Stop it, Rach."

"I don't own a gun. I had to buy one. Today."

"Another smart move."

"Today was the first time I've ever fired one."

Pete now takes both of her hands in his. "Trust me, Rachel. You're handling this. And now I'm here to help you."

"In the Marines, I know you were an engineer, but did you ever, have you ever had occasion to . . ."

"Yes," he says simply.

"More than once?"

"Yes."

She nods and takes a deep breath. "I drove up to New Hampshire to get the gun and the other supplies. I was nearly seen by someone on the island but I think I gave her the slip."

"That's good too."

"How can anyone carry out any kind of criminal enterprise in New England when everybody knows everybody?"

Pete smiles. "We'll figure it out, Rach. What else have you done?"

"Here are my targets," she says, handing Pete the list of vulnerable kids who fit the criteria.

"You want stable parents who look as if they won't go to the cops and who'll carry out a kidnapping?" Pete asks.

"They can't be broke, and they can't have any connection to cops, journalists, or politicians. And they have to have kids of the right age. No kids with special needs. No diabetics or anything like that."

"What about kidnapping a spouse instead of a child?" Pete asks.

"You can't be sure of how someone will feel about a spouse. Look at us. Three divorces between us. But all parents love their kids, right?"

"Right. Well, this seems OK. Toby Dunleavy, that's your number-one target?"

"Yup. I had a different number one, but the mom was dating a cop."

"Have you been over to the Dunleavy house?"

"Nope. Gonna do that later tonight. But first I need your help with the mattress and the board at the Appenzellers'."

"Where is this place?"

"Just across the basin. Come on, I'll take you."

They go outside in the rain and walk along the basin trail. "A lot of these big houses are vacant this time of year," Rachel explains.

"You broke into one of these by yourself?" Pete asks.

"Yup. I knew the Appenzellers were gone. I was a little worried about an alarm but there wasn't one."

"You did well. I've done a few B-and-Es myself and it's always scary."

"We can go in through the back," Rachel says when they reach the path next to the Appenzeller house.

"This place is a good choice, Rach. I like the brick," Pete says. "How did you pick the lock?"

"I didn't. I hit the mechanism with a chisel."

"Where did you learn how to do that?"

"Google."

They go inside and up on the first floor they grab a mattress and bedding from the spare bedroom. They manhandle it down to the basement. Rachel has already brought over the board to cover the window. "We'll put it up with Marty's old electric drill. I think that will make less noise than a hammer," Pete says.

They put up the board and try to make the basement as pleasant as possible with sheets and blankets and a few toys and games Rachel brought over earlier. It's devastating to think that if this actually works and they don't get killed or arrested, a scared little boy will be down here soon. Rachel has attached a heavy chain to a concrete pillar near the mattress, and this sends a shiver down Pete's spine.

They close the back door of the Appenzellers' and return to Rachel's house.

"Now what?" Pete wonders.

"Search my house for bugs. I hate the idea that they're watching everything I do."

Pete nods. "I can do that."

He takes the wireless detector out of his bag. In the old days of analog-bugging equipment, you needed a radio receiver and complex equipment, but now a fifty-buck wireless detector can do the job. He goes through the house and then he gets to work on the phone and the computer.

"It's largely a negative," he says at last. "I did a thorough scan of the entire house from top to bottom. I looked in the basement and I even looked in the crawl space above the kitchen."

"Did you say *largely* negative?"

"I did. You don't have any bugs in the house. However, as I suspected, your Mac has been completely compromised."

"How?"

"There's a spyware bot on your Mac that, when connected to the wireless network, slaves the camera and also shows a live screenshot of whatever is on your home screen. It was fairly easy to capture your passwords after that. The bot has a randomly generated name that doesn't mean anything. Its destination is also encrypted."

"How do you know how to do all this?" Rachel asks, impressed.

"Well, you know me, I've been tinkering with computers since the Stone Age days of the internet. Trying to get back into it more seriously. Private security is a big growth sector for former servicemen."

"Can you remove the bot thing?"

"That's a fairly easy task. But if I do, its absence will be noticed immediately."

"Whoever it is that's hacking me will know that I'm onto them?"

"Exactly. And if they know that you're onto them, they will undoubtedly deploy further countermeasures. Just don't use your Mac and phone until Kylie is back. Then I'll kill the bot and wipe your machines."

"They're going to be calling me on my iPhone. I need it."

"Just be aware, then, that they'll be listening in on you, and your phone, of course, is also a GPS transmitter."

"Could they be physically watching the house?" Rachel asks.

"They could," Pete says. "They could be watching us right now. My guess is they're not."

Rachel shudders. "I keep seeing Kylie in that basement. She must be terrified."

"She's a resilient kid. She's a tough little cookie." *Maybe too tough,* Pete thinks. *I hope she doesn't try anything stupid.*

22

Kylie waits until she thinks it's very late, but naturally she has no way of telling the time. No iPhone, no iPad, no Mac. No watch, of course, but who wears a watch these days?

As she lies on the mattress, she can hear traffic on a distant road, and she can occasionally hear planes change the thrust of their engines as they descend toward Logan. Very distant planes going to a very distant Logan Airport.

She sits on the mattress with her back to the eye of the camera and nibbles at a graham cracker. Her first plan has failed. The toothpaste tube cannot be used to open the handcuffs. She tried for hours, but it was a total bust. Her second plan, however, might work a little better.

Just after dark, the man had brought her a hot dog and a glass of milk. He set the tray on the floor next to her. The gun was in a pocket in his sweatshirt. The woman had come down to take the tray away with the gun in her right hand. They're always armed. She's a thirteen-year-old chained to a two-hundred-pound stove but they aren't taking any chances. They always come down here with a gun.

And that, Kylie realized, was what was going to help her.

She had spotted it earlier this afternoon. As the sun moved slowly across the sky, she had seen a glint in a corner of the basement. Moving as close as she could, she saw that the glint was a wrench just barely visible against the wall under the boiler. A wrench that had been dropped there and forgotten about, maybe years earlier. They had obviously prepped this basement, but to see the wrench you'd have to be lying on the floor looking directly at the boiler as the sun streamed through the window in the afternoon.

The wrench is the key.

She waits. And waits.

In what are, perhaps, the wee hours, the traffic seems to slow on the road and the planes grow less frequent.

She keeps thinking about that state trooper. Had they killed him? They must have killed him. That means she is being held by two murderers. They don't seem like murderers, but they are. She tries to fight the terror of that thought but wherever she goes in her mind, it's lurking there . . .

She thinks about her mom.

Her mom will be worried sick. She'll go to pieces. She isn't as strong as she pretends to be. It hasn't even been a year since she finished her chemo. And her dad—her dad's awesome but maybe not the most dependable guy in the world.

She looks at the camera by the stairs again. How late is it now? Will they sleep at all tonight? They have to get some sleep.

Still she waits.

It's maybe two in the morning now. *OK, here goes,* she thinks.

She stands, takes the slack out of the chain, and with all her might begins tugging at the stove. It's enormously heavy, of course, but the floor is smooth concrete without much friction. Earlier, she poured water under the stove's cast-iron feet and sloshed it around, hoping that might help too.

She pulls at the chain with everything she has, leaning back like a tug-of-war competitor. She's sweating and her muscles ache and it's seemingly impossible for a little girl to—

The oven jolts. Her feet give way and she falls to the floor, landing on her tailbone with a *thwack*.

She bites her lip and has to stop herself from yelling.

She rolls around on the ground. *Damn, damn, damn.*

The pain starts to subside and she examines herself as best she can. Nothing seems broken. She has never broken a bone before, but she imagines the pain would be a lot worse than this. When Stuart broke his wrist ice-skating on the frozen pond at Newbury Common, he had howled and howled.

But then again, that's Stuart.

She stands up and shakes the pain out of her limbs. Pain is weakness leaving the body, her crazy uncle Pete had once said. *So I'm way stronger now,* she tells herself, but she doesn't really believe it.

She grabs hold of the chain and pulls hard, and again the oven jolts, and this time it keeps moving ever so slowly as she keeps pulling. It is, she remembers from science class, all about friction and momentum. The oven is huge but the wet floor is smooth.

It's heavy, so very heavy, but it's moving. The noise is ugly, a high-pitched screeching and scraping that is, hopefully, not quite loud enough to be heard outside the basement, never mind in the house.

She sweats and pulls for two minutes and then stops,

utterly exhausted. She sits down on the edge of her mattress and breathes hard.

Self-consciously, she looks back at the camera, but that isn't going to tell her anything. There's no light above it showing when it's on. You have to assume that it's *always* on.

She crawls toward the wrench under the boiler. The chain on her left wrist tightens and when she stretches herself like Mister Fantastic, she is about three feet away. She climbs back into the sleeping bag and does some calculating. She can maybe move the oven another foot tonight. It will probably take another full night to get the wrench, but get it she will.

She's elated. She has a plan, and now she has a way to implement it. It might get her killed. But doing nothing might get her killed too.

23

Poseidon Street is a little bit outside Beverly Town Center and close to the water. It's a typical New England tree-lined suburban road, a neighborhood of small two-story colonials with tiny windows and steep roofs sitting uneasily beside newer houses with larger footprints and bigger windows. Number 14 Poseidon Street, where the Dunleavy family lives, is one of the newer homes, a three-floor faux-Georgian oak-frame job painted a retro mustardy brown. In the front yard, there's a beautiful red maple tree to which a swing has been attached. In the ambient street light, you can see children's toys, a football, and a catcher's mitt lying on the grass.

Rachel and Pete have parked on the far side of the street in the shadow of a big drooping willow tree that still has some of its leaves.

They can't help looking slightly suspicious. Fortunately, although this isn't the kind of neighborhood where people sleep in their cars, it is the kind of neighborhood where people pretend not to see someone half asleep in a car at four in the morning.

Pete is looking at the Dunleavys' social media activity on

his laptop. "Nobody's awake yet," he says.

"Mike will be up in about an hour, then Helen, then the kids. Mike sometimes catches the six o'clock train to South Station, sometimes the six thirty," Rachel tells him.

"He should drive, there's no traffic at this hour," Pete says. "Hey, you know what we have to watch out for?"

"What?"

"GPS tags in the shoes. A lot of helicopter parents put GPS tags in their kids' backpacks and shoes. That way if they go missing, the parents can find them with an app in a few seconds."

"Is that for real?" Rachel says, aghast.

"Oh yeah, grab a kid with one of those little buggers, and the FBI will be up our ass before we know what hit us."

"How do we stop that?"

"I can scan the kid to see if he's transmitting. And then toss his iPhone and GPS shoes, and we should be OK."

"Helen seems the type to brag about using that system to find her kids, but she hasn't mentioned it," Rachel says, surprising herself with the bitterness of this observation. She remembers that Tacitus line about how you always hate those you have wronged. Or those you are about to wrong in this case.

"Maybe you're right," Pete says. "But we'll check the shoes anyway."

They watch the house and sip coffee and wait.

No life at all on the street. The days of the milkman are long over. The first dog-walker doesn't appear until 5:30 a.m.

The earliest indication that anybody is up in the Dunleavy house comes at 6:01 a.m., when Mike retweets a tweet from Tom Brady. Then Helen wakes and begins Facebooking. She Likes a dozen posts from her friends and shares a video about women soldiers fighting Isis in Syria. Helen is a moderate Democrat. Her husband seems to be a moderate Republican. They care about the world, the environment, and their kids. They are harmless, and in completely different circumstances, Rachel could imagine being their friend.

The kids are lovely too. Not spoiled, not bratty, just great little kids.

"Look at this," Pete says. "Helen has just Instagrammed a picture of the Seafarer Restaurant on Webb Street in Salem."

"It's on Facebook now too," Rachel says.

"She says she's having breakfast there with her friend Debbie. How far is Salem from here?"

"Not that far. Five minutes, maybe ten if there's traffic."

"Not ideal. But a breakfast with an old friend has gotta take a minimum of forty-five minutes, right?"

Rachel shakes her head. "I don't know. If it's only coffee and muffins, it could be less. But then again, they'd go to Starbucks if they were just getting coffee and muffins. Why, what are you thinking?"

"I'm thinking that once Mike's gone and the kids are safely at school and Helen is safely at her breakfast, the house will be empty."

"And then what?"

"I go in the back door. Scout the place. Maybe upload a little spyware bug of our own onto the family desktop."

"You can do that?"

"Oh yes."

"How?"

"The B-and-E stuff is pretty easy, as you found out at the Appenzellers'. The bugging tech I learned from my buddy Stan when I worked for him after the Corps."

Rachel shakes her head. "I don't know."

"Gives us an advantage. We'll know what they're

thinking. The shit's going to get real when we take Toby."

"Is it safe?"

"Is anything we're doing safe?"

Mike Dunleavy finally leaves for work at 7:15. He drives himself to the Beverly train station and leaves his BMW in the lot. Helen gets her kids outside at 8:01. It's not really cold enough for winter coats but Helen has bundled them up anyway. Rachel thinks they look adorable in their over-size parkas and their hats and scarves.

"Do you want to follow them?" Pete asks.

Rachel shakes her head. "No point. Helen will let us know when she drops them off at school and gets to the restaurant."

They sit in the Volvo and wait, and, sure enough, at 8:15, Helen Facebooks a selfie taken inside the Seafarer.

Pete scans the street. A college-age kid is shooting hoops down the block, and across the street, a little girl comes out of her house and starts jumping up and down on an enclosed trampoline. "Look over there—front door's closed, kid's on that trampoline by herself. She'd be perfect," Pete says.

"Yes," Rachel agrees. "But that's not the plan."

"No? OK, I'm going in."

Rachel grabs his hand. "Are you sure about this, Pete?"

"We need all the information we can get about these people. In a raid, you gather all the intel you can for days, sometimes weeks, before you move. But we don't have days or weeks, so we gotta get as much info as quickly as possible."

Rachel can see the sense of that.

"Which is why I'm going in now while the house is, presumably, empty. If crazy old Uncle Kevin's in there with a shotgun, I guess I'm screwed. If I'm not back in fifteen minutes or so, you should go."

"What are you actually going to do?"

"Whatever I can in fifteen minutes."

"OK, so that would be eight thirty."

"Yeah."

"What does it mean if you're not back by eight thirty?"

"It means I'm compromised somehow. I won't talk, of course, but you should move on to target B or, better yet, make a completely new target list that I don't know anything about."

"I'll call you if there's trouble in the street."

"OK, but if things are looking hairy, just get out of here."

Pete puts his backpack over his shoulder, checks to see that no one is looking, and runs to the fence between the Dunleavy house and a little patch of wood sandwiched between the beach and the road. Rachel sees him climb over the fence into the Dunleavys' backyard.

She listens for the sound of screaming or crazy Uncle Kevin firing his shotgun, but there's nothing like that.

In the rearview, she watches the little girl across the street play on her trampoline. There doesn't seem to be anyone supervising her. The front door of her house is firmly closed. It would, in fact, be easy to walk over there and take the child.

Jesus Christ, who thinks things like this? What the hell have you become, Rachel?

She turns on her phone and looks at the time: 8:22.

She closes her eyes and thinks about Kylie. Has she been able to sleep? Knowing Kylie, she was probably thinking about her mom and dad the whole night, worrying about them.

Oh God, Kylie, I'm coming for you. I'll get you back. Never let you out of my sight. Be a better mom. Keep you safe. Kill social media. Trust nobody. Full tinfoil hat.

She looks at the phone again: 8:23.

A white van drives slowly along the street, the kind of beat-up white van that's always up to no damn good. The driver, however, pays no attention to her, and the van keeps going.

She rummages in her coat pocket for Marty's cigarettes, but she can't find them. A dog is barking like crazy somewhere.

Barking where? The Dunleavys do not have a dog. Rachel would know.

Maybe their neighbors? Maybe a dog next door saw Pete go into the house and recognized him as a stranger?

The phone reads 8:28.

She puts on the radio. It's one of those endless reruns of *Car Talk*. One of the two brothers is ranting about the VW microbus.

Now it's 8:31.

Where's Pete?

The dog is barking louder now.

The little girl gets off the trampoline, picks up what seems to be a can of soda, and gets back on the trampoline.

Not a good idea, sweetie. Not in your nice dress, Rachel thinks.

It's 8:34.

A black-and-white from the Beverly Police Department appears in her rearview mirror. "Oh no," Rachel mutters. She turns the key in the Volvo's ignition and the reliable old engine roars to life.

The police car starts driving slowly down the street. There are two officers inside. They're coming right toward her.

And now it's 8:37.

The dog's barking gets louder still.

The police car gets closer.

She slips the Volvo into first gear, her left foot on the clutch, her right ready on the gas.

The little girl on the trampoline does the inevitable and manages to upend the soda all over herself. She starts screaming. The two cops turn to look at her.

Pete appears on top of the Dunleavys' fence. He drops down to the little patch of woods, runs to the Volvo, and gets in the back seat, panting heavily. "Go!" he says.

"Everything OK?" Rachel asks, alarmed.

"Yeah. Fine. Go!"

Rachel lets the clutch out and drives away. She heads east toward Manchester and then north to Ipswich and Route 1A. The cops are not following her. Pete is in the back, fiddling with his phone.

"Is everything all right?" she asks again.

"Yes, fine."

"What happened in there?"

"Nothing. It was a breeze. The back window was open, so I was in in two seconds. I found a desktop PC in a downstairs study that was still on. I loaded a worm on that. I couldn't find the home phone, so I couldn't load a bug there, unfortunately. Lot of people don't have a landline anymore. But as soon as they fire up the desktop, I'll be able to read their e-mail, Skype, FaceTime, and iMessage passwords."

"Holy crap," Rachel says, impressed.

"Yeah," Pete replies.

"Your buddy Stan taught you all of that?"

"Most of it. I always had a bit of an outlaw mind-set."

"Yes, Marty told me about you stealing a car and driving to Canada when you were eleven."

"Nah, I didn't make it to Canada. And I was twelve," Pete says with false modesty.

"You went past the fifteen-minute time limit in there."

"I know. I found Toby's room. I did a little investigating.

Normal kid. No health issues that I can see. Likes the Red Sox, the X-Men, and a TV show called *Stranger Things*. Totally normal kid."

"So he'll do?" Rachel asks miserably.

"Yeah, he'll do."

They drive over the bridge and onto Plum Island.

Rachel yawns when they arrive at the house.

"When was the last time you slept?" Pete asks her with concern.

She brushes off the question. "I'll make some more coffee. We've got work to do."

Rachel goes upstairs to get the whiteboard from Kylie's room. She opens the door, half expecting Kylie to be hiding in there, for this to be some cruel, crazy prank.

It's empty, but the room smells of her little girl. That cheap Forever 21 perfume she loves. The seashell collection, the clothes overflowing the laundry bin, the books on astronomy and Egypt. A box that holds every birthday card she's ever gotten. The posters of Brockhampton and the Keira Knightley version of *Pride and Prejudice*. Her neatly arranged homework binders. Her photo montage of friends and family.

Rachel feels herself begin to sway. She grabs the whiteboard and steps into the hall and gently closes the door.

Downstairs they plot little Toby's life on a flow chart. He has archery tonight and Sunday night. Archery finishes at seven and he walks home. That's the window of opportunity. "The archery club meets at something called the Old Customs Hall near the water in Beverly. It's a little less than a one-klick walk from there to the Dunleavys' house," Pete says, looking at Google Maps.

"What's a klick?"

"Sorry—one kilometer. I've been over the route on

Google street view a few times now. He walks from the Old Customs Hall up Revenue Street, then he turns left on Standore Street, right on Poseidon Street, and he's at his house. It should take him no more than seven or eight minutes. Maybe ten at the most."

It's a pretty tight schedule and they know it.

"We have to hit him between seven o'clock and seven ten. In fact, if this is going to work, we have to get him when he's on Standore Street, since there will be too many people milling about on Revenue Street and we can't grab him right in front of his house on Poseidon because his mom might be waiting for him," Rachel says.

Pete rubs his chin. It's a very narrow window indeed, both temporally and geographically, but he doesn't bring that up. This is the kid they have done the planning for. Rachel stifles a yawn. "Why don't you take a nap and I'll drive down there again and check the entire route this time," Pete suggests.

"No nap necessary. Let's go."

"Now?"

"Yes."

They go outside, get in the Volvo, and reach Beverly in a mere fifteen minutes. The town is maybe a little too close to Rachel's town for comfort, but that can't be helped.

It's busier now. There are, Rachel thinks, a worrying number of assholes walking their dogs or out for a stroll. Assholes, because why should they be so unconcerned and happy when the sky is falling? *Has* fallen. The Old Customs Hall is near the water, and this too is a popular dog-walking and hangout locale.

"Updated weather forecast," Pete says, looking at his laptop. "Drizzle tonight, not rain. Hopefully that'll be enough moisture to deter casual foot traffic but not so much that his mom comes to pick him up."

"When I get Kylie back, I'm not letting her walk anywhere by herself until she's fifty," Rachel mutters, knowing this is a pitiful horse/barn-door statement.

They drive from the Old Customs Hall along Revenue Street and Standore Street and up Poseidon Street, about a three-minute run through unremarkable suburban New England. Standore Street is lined with big old-growth oak trees that still have leaves. "Excellent cover," Pete notes.

They turn and head back to the center of town.

"All right, this is the plan," Rachel announces. "One, we drive to the Old Customs Hall. Two, we wait for the kids to come out. Three, we follow Toby home along Revenue and Standore Streets. Please, God, let Toby be by himself. Four, we pull up the car next to him. Five, we grab him and throw him inside. Six, we drive off."

"Do you want me to grab him?"

She nods. "And I'll drive."

"OK, then."

She looks at him. "There are so many things that can go wrong, Pete. I'm glad you're with me."

Pete thinks back to that night at Camp Bastion in September of 2012 when everything went wrong. He bites his lip. "Yeah, it'll be fine, Rach," he says.

"But even if it all goes right," she replies wretchedly, "it'll still be absolutely terrible."

24

Kylie wakes up in a sleeping bag. Where—
   With a gasp of horror she remembers where she is and what has happened. She's in a basement somewhere north of Newburyport where two people, a husband and wife, are keeping her until her mother pays a ransom. Kylie's throat constricts. She sits up in the sleeping bag and hyperventilates. The air down here is musty and thick.

She pulls it into her lungs nevertheless and forces herself to calm the hell down. *They're going to kill me, they're going to kill me, they . . . no. They're not. They're not psychopaths. They aren't going to harm me if Mom does what they want. What happened with the state trooper was an accident.*

And she's not dead yet.

She's been working on a plan. The wrench . . . yes!

Judging from the sun, she probably slept late. Amazing that she slept at all. She needs to pee real bad now. She turns her back to the camera, grabs the pee bucket, and uses the scrunched-up sleeping bag as a shield.

A few minutes later the door opens, and she can see the man at the top of the stairs. Beyond him are a yard and a tree. He leaves the door open as he comes downstairs holding a

117

tray. He's wearing pajamas and he has his ski mask on. She can hear him breathing heavily, as if coming down the stairs has been a bit of an effort.

"Good morning," he says. "If it is still morning. It is, I think. I brought you, a, um, late breakfast. Cheerios. You like Cheerios, yeah?"

"Sure."

He walks across the basement floor and sets the tray down next to her. A bowl of Cheerios and milk, a glass of orange juice, another bottle of water. The gun handle is poking out of his pajama pants pocket.

"Apologies about the hour. We didn't get to bed until very late last night. We weren't, um, expecting things yesterday to go so . . . you must be hungry. Did you get any sleep?" he asks.

She shakes her head noncommittally.

"It's not surprising," he replies. "This is a crazy set of circumstances. Never in my wildest dreams . . ."

"Why *are* you doing it?" Kylie asks.

He takes a deep breath. "Because they've got our boy," he says softly and shakes his head. "Did you get a chance to look at the books?"

Kylie sees a little opening here. "Yes. I'd never read *Moby-Dick* before. I always thought it would be boring."

"But you liked it?" the man asks excitedly.

"Yes. What I read of it."

"Oh, that's wonderful. A classic. Boring at first, maybe, for someone of your generation. But once you let your mind get into that way of thinking, it just sort of flows along."

"Yeah, you're right. I liked the tattooed guy."

"Queequeg? Isn't he wonderful! Melville lived with the South Pacific Islanders for nearly a year, and his portrayal of them is quite affectionate, don't you think?"

Kylie desperately tries to come up with something to say, something that would have impressed her English teacher if she was put on the spot in class about a book she hadn't read.

"Yeah, and the whole book—it's all a big metaphor, isn't it?" she says.

"Of course it is. Yes! Very good. You're—"

"Just leave the tray and come back up!" a voice says from the top of the stairs.

"I better go," the man whispers. "Eat up and relax and please don't try anything. I've never seen her like this."

"Come on!" the woman screams, and the man goes up the stairs and locks the door behind him, leaving Kylie alone again.

This time too he came down with the gun.

The gun is the key to the whole thing.

25

Her phone chimes. She set an alert to let her know when the latest batch of ransom money cleared the Bitcoin system and landed in their Swiss bank account. Sometimes Visa or MasterCard or, especially, AmEx blocks the charge, but apparently now it has been paid in full.

Her brother mocks her for this kind of micromanaging. When she lets him run The Chain, he claims he does almost nothing. He says he pretty much lets the whole thing self-police. But she's more hands-on. It's *her* baby.

She looks at her phone. Yup, twenty-five thousand untraceable dollars have come through the Bitcoin laundry.

That's good in one way, but when they came up with the money this quickly, it meant that they could have paid a lot more. This is her mistake. *She* set the ransom amount. *She* looked at Rachel's bank account and income and thought twenty-five thousand would be pushing it. *I mean, come on, she was working as an Uber driver until a few weeks ago and there's no family money.*

The philosophy isn't to soak people for all they have but to keep the sums manageable. *It's not about the money, blah-blah-blah.*

Still . . .

She mirrors Rachel's computer on her phone, but Rachel hasn't turned on the Mac since last night. She's evidently using a different computer now. This is a hint that Rachel isn't a total idiot.

She looks out the window at the rain falling pointlessly into Boston Harbor. Is Rachel trying to outsmart her? That would be a terrible mistake for her to make.

She opens the Wickr app and sends Rachel a message: Are you ready to proceed with your target, Toby Dunleavy?

There's a five-minute pause before Rachel replies: Yes. We're doing it tonight if we can and Sunday night if tonight doesn't work.

Why not tomorrow night? Or tomorrow morning? she types.

The boy takes archery lessons and walks home from there. Archery is tonight and Sunday night, Rachel replies.

She doesn't like Rachel's tone. It isn't scared enough. It isn't humble enough. Rachel doesn't realize that she's the gamma bitch talking to the alpha.

I can exterminate you, Rachel, she thinks. *Just snap my fingers and you're dead as a D Street crack whore.*

Message me on Wickr as soon as you get the boy, she texts. And I will make the first call to the family. You will call them five minutes later. The first thing you will say is "You must remember that you are not the first or the last. It is not about the money, it's about The Chain." Do you understand?

Yes, Rachel texts.

Again, it seems curt and confident. She does not like that.

She closes the message thread and thinks things over for a few minutes.

Olly is always telling her not to let things get into the realm of the personal. Like he's older and wiser. Yes, older by fifteen minutes. It is true that there is no need to do any of this hastily. It isn't about speed. All that matters is that it keeps going.

According to Olly's modeling, the more people that are added to The Chain, the more likely it is that there will be a major defection. That's why fear is so important. That's the whole mental component.

Human beings are creatures whose lives are governed by deep instincts. They are like mice, these people, mice in the hay fields, and she's the peregrine swooping over them, seeing every little thing they do.

She thinks about Noah Lippman. She'd been serious about Noah, but he had broken up with her and moved to New Mexico with a new girlfriend. The Chain, however, had somehow stretched its tentacles way out there to the high desert. In Taos, his life had taken several disastrous turns. His girlfriend had been killed in a hit-and-run, he had been fired from his hospital job, and he had been mugged and badly beaten, and now he's a poorly paid and overworked nurse in a Santa Fe hospice. Gray hairs Noah has now, and he's walked with a limp since his assault.

The Chain didn't always have to be a bad thing, she supposes. Sometimes it helped people. Helped people focus on what was really important. And in a way, she's doing these mice in the hay field a favor. *I mean,* she thinks, *now you know what your purpose is, don't you, Rachel? Now you know what you have to do if you want to see sweet little Kylie again. That blind panic that you're feeling? That adrenaline rush? That call to action? The Chain gave you that. The Chain has set you free.*

She closes the laptop.

Don't interfere, Olly says, leave it alone.

But sometimes one can have a little fun.

She clicks on the Wickr app again and messages Heather Porter: The ransom for Rachel to pay has doubled to fifty thousand dollars. The balance must be paid today. Inform her immediately. Furthermore, she must complete part 2 of the process today. If she doesn't pay the new ransom and complete her kidnapping by midnight, you must kill Kylie O'Neill and search for a new target.

Yes, that will fix things, she thinks with some measure of satisfaction.

26

Rachel stands under the shower. She scalds herself and freezes herself, but the water doesn't help—she's still inside the bad dream. *Other* people lose their kids, people who don't pay close enough attention. People who let thirteen-year-olds walk home from lonely bus stops in Mississippi or Alabama. This kind of thing doesn't take place in urbane, civilized, safe northern Massachusetts.

She steps out onto the chilly bathroom floor and shakes her head. That's the sort of complacency and snobbery that allowed them to kidnap her daughter in the first place. Her head is light. Her left breast hurts. She's utterly unmoored. She imagines her face again in the nonexistent bathroom mirror. That gaunt, hollow, ugly, un–Jennifer Connelly stupid face. Getting rid of the mirrors—what a joke that was. Just hiding the truth. All those smashed mirrors in the town dump. All that bad luck circling back to her.

Camus said, "In the depths of winter, I finally learned that within me there lay an invincible summer."

What bullshit.

All she feels is pain and fear and misery. Fear above all. And, yes, this is the depth of winter, all right. This is the middle of the Ice Age at the sunless North Pole. *My daughter has been kidnapped and to get her back I'm going to have to grab a sweet little boy off the street and threaten him and threaten his family and mean it. Mean it when I say I'm going to kill him, because if I don't I'll never see Kylie again.*

She pulls on a T-shirt, her red sweater, and jeans and walks into the living room.

Pete looks up from his computer.

He can't know about the torment within her. He can't know about the fear and the doubts. He doesn't want to do it. He's a good man. A veteran. She needs to Lady Macbeth it. "Right, so we're all set, then," she says coldly.

Pete nods. He has just come back from the Appenzellers'.

"How does the house look?" she asks.

"Perfect. Super-quiet down in the basement. A bucket to pee in. I got the kid some comic books so he won't get bored. Few stuffed animals and games as well. Some candy."

"Latest weather?"

"Still drizzle. Not heavy rain."

"What is the family doing right now?" Rachel asks.

"Mike's still at work. Rest of the family is home. Helen Dunleavy is currently writing a lengthy Facebook post about the fig tree in her backyard. Oh, and Toby definitely does not have the peanut allergy."

"Good. I was on a plane once with a woman who was allergic to peanuts, and she had a meltdown just from the smell of someone's peanut-butter sandwich. Nightmare," she says and lets out a huge sigh. "Thank you for coming, Pete. You're a rock. I couldn't get through this without you."

Pete looks at her and swallows. His mouth opens and closes. He has two things to tell her. He has to tell her about the heroin and he has to tell her about the Camp Bastion incident. He's not a rock. He's unreliable. He's a failure. He would have been court-martialed if he hadn't resigned first. "There's something you should know . . ." he begins.

Rachel's iPhone rings: *Unknown Caller.*

She answers it on speaker so Pete can hear. "Yes?" she says.

"There's been a change of plan," the woman holding Kylie says.

"What do you mean?"

"You are required to deposit an additional twenty-five thousand dollars into the InfinityProjects account."

"We already paid the ransom. It's—"

"It's been changed. Sometimes they change things. You need to pay another twenty-five thousand. Furthermore, you need to complete part two of the process today. Do you understand? If you don't do these things *today,* I'm supposed to kill Kylie."

"No, please! I've done everything you've said. I'm cooperating!"

"I know you are. They just messaged me. We have to do what they say, Rachel. Another twenty-five thousand by midnight and part two done by midnight. If you don't do it, I have to kill Kylie. And if I don't do that, they'll kill my son, so I have to do it."

"No, that's crazy. We're cooperating, we're doing—"

"Do you understand what I've told you, Rachel?"

"Yes, I—"

The line goes dead.

Another twenty-five thousand today? How?

"Car coming!" Pete says, looking through the living-room window.

"It's coming here?"

"It's coming here," Pete says. "Two occupants. A man

126

and a woman. Parking next to my truck. What does Marty drive now?"

Rachel sprints to the kitchen window. The car is a white Mercedes; the man in the driver's seat is Marty, and she's sure that the woman next to him is Tammy. Rachel's met Tammy only once, at one of the Kylie handovers, but Tammy is a leggy blonde with a cute bob haircut and Marty's passenger certainly has the haircut.

"It is Marty!"

Pete runs to the kitchen window. "Jesus, you're right. What is he doing here? I thought you said he was in Georgia."

Rachel groans. "It's Friday evening. He's come to take Kylie for the weekend."

"We're on the clock here; we need to get rid of them."

"I know!"

Marty waves to her through the window. Rachel remains standing, aghast, at the kitchen sink and watches as Marty and Tammy come up the outside steps. Marty opens the kitchen door, smiles at her, leans forward, and kisses her on the cheek. He looks good. Very handsome. Movie-star handsome. He's lost a little weight, there's color to his cheeks, and he's finally gone to a barber who knows how to cut his thick, wavy hair. His green eyes are twinkling, but his heavy eyebrows are knit together with concern when he looks at her.

She fights the weak, atavistic urge to collapse onto Marty's chest, throw her arms around his neck, and weep. She sniffs and pulls herself together and smiles.

"Well, you're looking terrific." Marty lies like a frickin' trouper. There's a little clearing of the throat from behind him and he brings Tammy forward. "Of course you remember Tam," he says.

Tammy is tall and pretty with boring blue eyes. "Rachel!"

Tammy declares and gives her a hug. "How are you doing?" she asks.

"I'm OK," Rachel says and takes a deep breath.

Now that she's over the shock of seeing them, she has only two objectives: get them out as quickly as possible and without raising any suspicions about Kylie's absence.

"Pete, what are you doing here?" Marty asks.

Pete marches across the room and gives his brother a hug. "Hey, Marty."

"Pete, Jesus, it's great to see you. Wow, you are as brown as a berry. Look at you. Tammy, this is my big brother, Pete," Marty says.

"Nice to finally meet you in the flesh," she says and kisses him on the cheek.

"I think it's obvious that I got the looks and the brains in the family," Marty quips. "What brought you up here, big brother?"

Rachel can see the cogs turning in Pete's brain as he tries to think of something. "I called Pete to help me with the roof," she says.

"Yeah, the roof," Pete agrees. "I took care of it."

"Sorry about that, honey," Marty says, chagrined. "You sounded really upset on the phone."

"It's fine now," Rachel replies, glancing at the clock.

"So where's my golden girl? Are we a little early?" Marty says, evidently relieved to have avoided a gigantic fight about the leaky roof. He looks around for Kylie.

"Are you taking Kylie somewhere?" Pete asks, trying too hard to sound casual.

"Taking Kylie for a little daddy time and a little crazy-auntie time. I'm the crazy auntie in this setup," Tammy says.

"Kylie!" Marty shouts upstairs.

"Oh, I nearly forgot, this is for you," Tammy says. She

128

reaches into a shopping bag and gives Rachel a bottle of champagne. "It's your one-year anniversary coming up soon."

"One year?" Rachel wonders out loud. "We've only been divorced since February."

"Not that. It's about a year since your last chemo. That's what Marty said. It's been a year and it hasn't come back."

"Oh, yeah, that. Is it a year? Jesus, how time flies, huh?" Rachel says, still furious at herself for forgetting that Marty was coming.

"A year of full remission. That's something," Marty says. "You should celebrate. You've got the rest of the weekend off. Treat yourself. Go to that Max Richter concert you could never drag me to!"

Rachel puts the now-riddled-with-irony champagne bottle on the countertop. The polite thing would be to offer them a drink, but that would eat up more precious minutes. Her mind is racing. How is she going to explain this? She can't say Kylie is sick. Marty would insist on seeing her.

"So, um, Augusta?" Pete asks hesitantly, not wanting to initiate a conversation but trying to buy some thinking time.

"Why did you mention that?" Tammy says and mimes hanging herself.

"Oh, man, yeah, Augusta National is just beautiful and—" Marty begins.

"Where's Kylie? Is she getting ready?" Tammy wonders. She takes Rachel's hand, gives her a big smile, and checks a ping on her phone.

Really, these kids are too much, Rachel thinks, disengaging her hand. *I mean, you can hide anything behind a smile.*

Anything at—

Something occurs to her.

Something terrible.

Something diabolical.

"That's a lovely necklace you've got there," she says to Tammy. "I've been thinking of getting a *chain*. What do you think?"

Tammy looks up from her phone. "What?"

"I've been thinking of getting a chain. Like yours. It's not about the money, is it? It's about the chain."

"You can have this if you want, sweetie. I got it at Filene's. On sale."

Not a flicker. The Chain has nothing whatsoever to do with her. It couldn't. The selection process is almost entirely random. That's the genius of it. Rachel turns to her ex-husband. "Marty, look, I'm really embarrassed about this. I screwed up. I should have called you. Kylie's gone."

"Gone?"

"It's all my fault, you two driving up here. I completely forgot you were coming today. I'm so stressed about teaching after all these years and about the roof and I was trying to write my lectures, and I just forgot," Rachel says.

"Where is Kylie?"

"She went to New York," Rachel says.

"New York?" Marty asks, puzzled.

"Yes, she's been working on this school project about King Tut and they have that mini-exhibition there at the Met and she did so well in school this term, I let her go see it."

"In New York?"

"Yup, I saw her onto the bus and her grandma picked her up at Port Authority and took her to the apartment in Brooklyn. She's staying there for a couple of days and getting all the Egypt she'll ever want," Rachel says.

Marty's brow furrows. "It's November. Isn't your mother down in Florida?"

"No, not this year. She's staying in New York a little longer because the weather's been so warm."

"When is Kylie coming back?"

"In a couple of days. They might take in a show. Um, Mom has a line on some *Hamilton* tickets."

"Oh, I gotta ask Kylie about that. What night is she actually going? I'll text her," Tammy says.

"Do you have Kylie's number?" Rachel asks, horrified.

"Of course. And we follow each other on Instagram. Don't think she's posted anything about New York, though."

"No, um—"

"This is weird," Tammy says, staring at her phone. "Kylie hasn't posted anything on Instagram since yesterday morning. Normally she posts two or three times a day."

"Are you sure she's OK?" Marty asks with concern.

"Yes, she's completely fine," Rachel insists. "Her grandmother probably confiscated her iPhone. She's always going on about looking at the real world instead of burying your head in a screen a few inches from your nose."

Marty nods. "That sounds like Judith," he says. "But I mean, hell, Rachel, why couldn't you have just called us? A simple text, you know? Save us all a lot of hassle."

Rachel's hackles rise. How dare he? He's the man who was golfing in Augusta while his daughter was kidnapped. He's the man who left his wife, who was recovering from cancer, for a younger woman. He's the man—

No.

This is not the time for a war. She has to be super-contrite and end this. "I'm really sorry, Marty. I messed up. I'm a total schmuck. I'm under a lot of pressure, you know? New job. Teaching. The roof. I'm sorry."

Marty is taken aback by Rachel's self-reproach. "Oh, right, yeah. Look, that's OK, sweetie, these things happen."

Get them out now! a voice is bellowing in Rachel's head.

"Do you want to stay for dinner?" she asks, taking a gamble. "It seems a shame for you to come all the way up here and have to go straight back. I could make"—she tries to think of Marty's least-favorite food. Mussels? Yeah. He's always hated mussels in garlic—"a big salad and they've got some amazing mussels in at the fish market."

Marty shakes his head. "No, no, we'd better go if we're going to beat the traffic back."

"Traffic?" Tammy says, puzzled. "The traffic will be going the other way."

"There will be traffic," Marty insists.

"I'm so sorry I screwed up," Rachel says.

Marty gives her a sympathetic nod. "It's OK. Shall we say next weekend?"

"Yes, and I'll bring her down to Boston so you don't have to come up again. Least I can do," Rachel says, wondering if Kylie will be back next weekend. If she is and if she's safe, nothing else will matter. Marty can take her to the damn aquarium every weekend until the end of time.

"That won't be necessary," he says, giving her a parting hug. Tammy gives her a kiss on the cheek. In five minutes they are back outside and climbing into their car.

Pete and Rachel wave goodbye from the doorstep, go inside, and close the door.

Five twenty now. So much time wasted. Archery begins at six, and Toby Dunleavy's walk home begins at seven o'clock.

"They want another twenty-five thousand by midnight or they'll kill Kylie," Rachel says, trying to ward off panic.

"I'm already on that," Pete replies, and she watches as he logs on to a Bitcoin buying site on the dark web.

"What are you going to do?" Rachel asks.

"Fifteen-thousand credit limit on one card, ten-thousand limit on the other, no problem," Pete says.

"Do you have money in the bank to cover that?"

"It doesn't matter, does it? Getting Kylie home is all that matters."

Rachel kisses him on the back of the neck and helps him set up an account and transfer the funds.

"Are you watching the clock?" she asks him.

"Nearly done," he says. "Get the Dodge warmed up. Make sure the masks and gloves are packed."

She runs outside, loads the vehicle, puts the key in the ignition, and starts the engine.

It's five minutes to six now.

"Done," Pete says when she comes back in. He looks at Helen Dunleavy's Facebook feed. "She's on her way to the archery club. We better go too. I'll get the gun."

"I don't want this boy hurt," Rachel says.

"I don't think we'll need to hurt anyone, but we might need to fire a shot in the air to scare off any Good Samaritans. I've got a loud Colt .45 that'll do that," Pete assures her.

Rachel nods. She thinks of those words, *I don't want this boy hurt*. This boy. This boy has a name: Toby. He's Toby Dunleavy. But it will be easier to think of him as *this boy*. An abstract thing. Not a human being. Not a human child. They might need to threaten *this boy*. They might, in fact, need to carry out the threat.

She shudders. Pete stares at her.

"All right. Let's go," she says.

They get in the Dodge and drive down Route 1 toward Beverly. Traffic is heavier than normal, but they aren't worried. It's only a twenty-minute run and they have an hour before archery gets out.

Pete takes her hand and gives it a little squeeze. "Maybe

you better call your mother and prep her in case Marty calls looking for Kylie."

"Good idea," she says and dials her mother in Florida.

"I'm about to play bridge, what is it?" Judith answers.

"Mom, listen, I just told Marty that Kylie is staying with you in New York."

"What? Why did you do that?"

"He came over today and it's one of his weekends but Kylie hates Marty's new girlfriend and didn't want to go stay with him, so I just sort of panicked and said that she was with you for a couple of days in New York."

"But I'm in Florida."

"Mom, I know you're in Florida, but if Marty calls, you have to tell him that you're in Brooklyn and Kylie's with you."

"What are we doing in New York?"

"Kylie wants to see all the Egypt stuff at the Met."

"She would like that."

"And you guys got tickets to see *Hamilton*."

"How did we manage to do that?"

"I don't know, maybe you know some old lady who isn't using her tickets."

There's a long silence on the line while Judith thinks about it. "This is quite the web of lies you've hooked me into, Rachel. Now I'm going to have to pretend I've seen *Hamilton* if my ex-son-in-law calls. What am I going to say?"

"Hell, Mom, can you not think on your feet? Oh, and you've confiscated Kylie's phone," Rachel snaps as they pass a sign that reads BEVERLY, NEXT EXIT.

"Why would I take my thirteen-year-old granddaughter's phone?"

"Because you're sick of her coming all the way to New

York City and then just staring at a piece of glass six inches from her face the whole time she's there."

"Yeah, I guess that makes sense," Judith says.

"OK, Mom, thanks a lot, you're a lifesaver. I better go," Rachel says as they arrive in Beverly.

"Take care of yourself, honey, I worry about you."

"I'm fine, Mom. Everything's fine."

She hangs up. It's drizzling and a chill wind is blowing in from the water. "Don't like this weather," Pete says. "Helen might change her mind and pick up Toby instead of letting him walk. I better check."

There's nothing on Facebook, but using the worm on the home PC, they find Helen writing a text to her sister to say that, per her recommendation, she is watching *Atomic Blonde* with Mike.

They have their window.

They park on Revenue Street at six thirty, but for some reason a line of kids and adults are coming out of the Old Customs Hall.

"What the hell? Who are those kids? Jesus, I think that's the archery club!" Pete cries.

"Look at all those bows and stuff. It *is* them! We've screwed it up already!" Rachel exclaims.

"Go! Run the route!" Pete says, and Rachel puts the car in gear.

"I'm going."

"I don't understand it. They're supposed to get out at seven o'clock. Why would they leave early? And half an hour early! It makes no sense," Pete says.

"Oh God, oh God," Rachel is saying over and over.

"It's all right," Pete says evenly. "They're only just getting out. We'll be OK."

Rachel drives quickly up Revenue Street. She turns on

Standore Street, and there, about a hundred yards up the road, is a kid in a parka carrying a sports bag with what looks to be a composite bow sticking out of it. The kid has his hood up and is walking in the direction of the Dunleavys' house.

"Is that him?" Rachel asks.

"No idea, but that sure looks like the end of a bow in his bag. And there's nobody on either side of the street. For the moment."

"Ski masks on," Rachel says, desperately trying to keep the blind panic out of her voice.

"Coast is clear," Pete says. In the end they hadn't needed the trees or the dark to hide them because the rain deterred any potential witnesses. Rachel puts the wipers on, kills the lights, drives the car up the street, and stops in front of the child.

"No one around," Pete says, scanning both sides of the road.

"Go, then!" Rachel says.

Pete jumps out the passenger-side door with the .45. Rachel sees him talk to the kid. He turns and shakes his head at her.

Something's wrong. Pete comes back to the car without the boy.

What the hell is happening?

"What's the problem?" she demands.

"It's a girl," Pete says.

Rachel pulls her ski mask down and gets out. And sure enough, it's a little, skinny, brown-haired girl about eight or nine years old. She's carrying a gym bag that looks far too big for her.

"Did you just come from the archery club?" Rachel asks her.

"Yes," the girl replies.

"Why did they get out early?" Pete asks.

"The heating was broken so we had to come home. Why are you wearing those things on your faces?"

"What's your name?" Rachel asks.

"Amelia Dunleavy."

"Where's your brother, Toby?"

"He went to Liam's house. He told me to take his bag home."

"What are we going to do now?" Pete asks Rachel.

"We're taking her," Rachel says grimly.

"That wasn't the plan."

"It's the plan now," Rachel tells him. She knows she'll never be able to go through this again. And if she can't go through with it, Kylie's dead.

"Come on, Amelia," Pete says. "We're giving you a ride home."

He puts her in the car, clasps her seat belt, sits beside her, and locks the door. Rachel makes a U-turn and drives toward the Route 1A exit.

"Are we really doing this? What about her health issues?" Pete asks.

"We'll deal with them. No peanuts or peanut products. We'll get an EpiPen . . . shit!" Rachel exclaims and punches the dashboard.

"You shouldn't use that word," Amelia says.

"You're right," Rachel replies. "Sorry, sweetie. How old are you, honey?"

"I'm eight," Amelia says. "I'll be nine in December."

"Who lets an eight-year-old walk home by herself at night in this day and age? In the rain? Who does that?" Rachel mutters.

"Toby was supposed to be here. It was my very first time

137

at archery tonight. I can use the junior bow now. And he was supposed to walk me home, but he went to Liam's because we got out early."

"And Toby let you go home by yourself?"

"He said I was a big girl. He let me carry his bag," Amelia says.

"Well, you have to come with us now. Your mom said it was OK. It's an adventure," Rachel tells her.

She sees Amelia shake her head in the rearview mirror. "I don't want to go with you. I want to go home," she says.

"You can't go home. You have to come with us," Rachel insists.

"I want to go home!" Amelia says and begins to wail.

Rachel gags as Amelia begins to thrash and claw at the seat belt.

"I want to go home!" Amelia yells and Pete holds the struggling little girl with his big hands.

When she's out of town, Rachel skids the Dodge to the side of the road on an isolated bit of Route 1A somewhere in the marshy woods between Beverly and Wenham. She climbs out of the cab, takes off the ski mask, and vomits.

She spits and vomits again. Her mouth is acrid and her throat burns. Tears are pouring down her cheeks.

She vomits until she's only dry-heaving.

Pete opens the car door and throws out Amelia's shoes and the gym bag. "Better sink those in the swamp," he says. "Just to be on the safe side. Might be a GPS transmitter in them."

Rachel puts the shoes in the gym bag, partially zips it, and throws it in the marsh, where it floats. She doesn't have time for a Norman Bates–style car-sinking scene, so she wades into the swamp and sinks the bastard with her foot. Then she puts the ski mask back on.

"Do you want me to drive?" Pete asks as Rachel climbs back into the pickup. She shakes her head and turns to Amelia, who has tears streaming down her little face. Her eyes are wide and she's clearly terrified.

"It's going to be OK, darling," Rachel says. "We're just taking you for a couple of days. It's a game we're playing. Your mommy and daddy know all about it."

"Are they playing the game too?" Amelia asks, surprised.

"Yes, they are. It's going to be OK. I promise," Rachel says and puts the car in gear and drives again.

"You're going to have to wear this blindfold now, honey," Pete says. "It's part of the game."

"Like blindman's buff?" Amelia asks.

"Sure," Pete says.

"I've played that one before."

She puts the blindfold on, and Pete and Rachel take their ski masks off.

They are just outside of Newbury when Rachel sees the state police car in her rearview mirror. "Cops," she says calmly.

Pete looks back. "We haven't done anything wrong. Just keep driving, don't speed, don't go slow," he says.

"I know," she snarls at him. "But give me a gun. If they stop us, there will be no talking our way out of this."

"Rachel—"

"Give it to me!"

Pete hands her the .45 and she puts it in her lap. "You know how to use it?" he asks.

"Yes. We're agreed on what we're going to do if we're stopped?"

"Yes," he says and holds his breath.

27

The cops tailgate them for thirty seconds, slowly come alongside, and then zoom by in the passing lane.

Of course they do.

Rachel has done nothing wrong.

She drives straight to the Appenzellers'.

Amelia is either dazed or terrified. It doesn't matter which—she's compliant, and that's what counts. "You get her inside and I'll make the phone calls," Rachel tells Pete.

When the street is deserted Pete takes Amelia out of the Dodge and down into the basement.

Rachel stays in the cab and pulls up the Wickr app on her phone. It's done, she types to her contact.

What's done? a message comes back.

I've kidnapped Amelia Dunleavy. I'm holding her right now.

Rachel's phone rings. "Good. Very good," the distorted voice says. "I will call her family now. You will then call and ask for a hundred thousand dollars, payable in Bitcoin to the same account as before."

"A hundred thousand! That seems—"

"That represents only half the amount they have in their

savings account. They can pay that easily. It's not about the money, Rachel."

"I know. It's about The Chain."

"That's right. I will call them and tell them to get a pen and paper. You will talk to them five minutes from now on a burner phone. They will be waiting by the telephone for your call."

The line goes dead.

Rachel calls Pete on a burner phone.

"Hello?" he says.

"Is everything OK?" she asks.

"She's freaked, obviously. Scared. I'm saying that we're friends of the family. She sort of believes it and sort of doesn't."

"Keep her safe, Pete. Keep her away from nuts. I don't know how sensitive she is, but we have to err on the side of caution. Let's not be the stupid babysitter in one of those movies."

"We won't be."

"We have to read all the labels of everything we give to her and we'll need to get an EpiPen."

"We will. I'll look into that. I think you can get them on eBay. Have you called the family yet?"

"Doing it now."

"Use a different phone than this one. Drive away from the house to make the call."

"Good idea. I will."

She drives quickly to the parking lot by the ocean. She dials the Dunleavys' number. "Hello?" a woman says anxiously.

"I've taken your daughter, Amelia. She's been kidnapped. You are not to call the police. If you call the police or any law enforcement agency, I'll kill her. Do you understand?"

Helen begins to scream.

Rachel calms her down by telling her that if she doesn't calm down, she is going to put a bullet in her daughter's brain.

The conversation takes ten minutes.

When it's over, Rachel gets out of the car and throws up again and again until there's nothing left.

She stares at the black ocean breaking on the shore.

She sits on the sand as a very cold, hard rain begins to fall.

Her head's hurting. She feels as if her skull is going to explode.

She sits for five more minutes and then stands and stamps on the burner phone and throws the pieces into the sea. She tilts her face up into the downpour and begs the water to cleanse her. It doesn't work.

She calls Pete on a new burner phone. "It's done. Everything OK there?"

"Not so great. I put the handcuff on and chained her to the pillar. She didn't mind that too much. And she's not screaming or anything, but she's crying and wants her mom and says she can't stay here without Mr. Boo. He's a bear, apparently. There's plenty of other stuffed toys but only Mr. Boo will do."

"I understand," Rachel says.

She drives home and goes upstairs into Kylie's room. She finds Marshmallow, Kylie's pink stuffed bunny. How is Kylie able to sleep without Marshmallow or her cat?

She takes Marshmallow, puts on a hoodie, and runs through the rain to the Appenzellers'.

She taps on the back door and Pete lets her in. He's on the phone. He looks worried.

"What's the matter?" she whispers.

"AmEx is verifying the charge," he says, putting his hand over the receiver.

"Visa did that with me too. If the money doesn't go through tonight, they kill Kylie."

"I know. I'll take care of it," he replies. Pete doesn't look good; he's twitchy, bug-eyed, sweating.

"Are you OK?"

"Yeah, I'm fine. I'll take care of it."

Rachel puts on her ski mask and goes down to the basement.

Amelia is exhausted. She has cried and fought and cried some more and all she probably wants to do now is sleep but she can't without Mr. Boo. She's sitting on the sleeping bag on the mattress surrounded by Legos and games and the wrong stuffed animals.

Rachel sits next to her. "I know you're scared, honey, but there's nothing to be scared of. You're safe here, I promise. I won't let anything happen to you."

"I want my mom," Amelia says.

"I know. We'll get you back to her soon. Look, I heard about Mr. Boo and although we don't have Mr. Boo, this is my little girl's special friend Marshmallow. She's had it since the day she was born. He's very, very special. He's got thirteen years of love in him."

Amelia looks at Marshmallow suspiciously. "I want Mr. Boo."

"We don't have Mr. Boo, but we have Marshmallow," Rachel says. "Marshmallow is Mr. Boo's friend."

"Is he?"

"Oh yes, they're very good friends." Rachel passes him over and Amelia takes him hesitantly.

"Do you want me to tell you a story?" Rachel asks.

"OK, I guess."

"Do you like milk and cookies?"

"Yes."

"Wait here and I'll see what I can do."

She goes back upstairs. Pete is on the porch trying to convince American Express to put his charge through. If he doesn't convince them, a crazy woman will murder her daughter in two hours.

She taps the kitchen door and Pete turns to look at her. "What do they say?" she asks.

"I'm still talking to them."

Rachel reads the label on Lorna Doone cookies and Googles the ingredients just to be on the safe side. They are nut-free. She goes back downstairs with the milk and Lorna Doones.

She tells Amelia the story of Goldilocks and the Three Bears and Amelia is happy because she knows that one.

She does "Hansel and Gretel" next and Amelia knows that one too.

Stories of kids surviving peril in the woods.

Poor little Amelia, vanished like that other Amelia all those years ago.

She's a good kid. A smart kid. Rachel likes her. How could she not? And how could she possibly harm this child?

Half an hour later Pete appears at the top of the stairs. He gives Rachel the thumbs-up.

"The charge went through?"

"Yes."

"Thank God for that."

"How's Amelia?"

"Come down and see."

"She's sleeping. How did you do that?" Pete whispers at the bottom of the basement steps.

"Milk, cookies, and Marshmallow, apparently."

"What kind of cookies?"

"Lorna Doone. They're OK. I checked them."

"The EpiPen is on the way. I ordered it from eBay."

"You're not getting it sent here?"

"No. It'll go to an eBay drop box in Newbury."

"Good."

"I'll stay here tonight," Pete says. "You go on home, you look beat."

"I should stay."

"No, go home, please."

She doesn't want to fight him. She *is* beat. Utterly defeated. She takes a picture of Amelia with one of the burner phones. "I'll send this to them."

"Get some sleep, Rachel."

"I'm not tired," she insists.

Pete is scratching his arm and sweating. He looks vacant, unwell.

"Are you sure you're all right?" she asks.

"Me? Great. You go home, I'll be fine here."

She nods and goes up the basement steps. Down the porch. Along the beach. Home.

She's glad for the freezing rain. She deserves discomfort and misery and pain. She stands in front of her house and calls the Dunleavys on a new burner phone.

"Yes?" Helen says between breathy gasps of panic.

"You better be working on the money and the target. I'm sending you a picture of Amelia. She's sleeping, she's OK."

"Let me talk to her!"

"She's sleeping. I'm sending you a picture."

When the picture goes through, Rachel destroys the phone and walks into her house.

She makes a cup of coffee and begins monitoring the

Dunleavys' activities through their mirrored home PC. No e-mails or texts to the cops.

At midnight, Rachel's iPhone rings. "Hello?"

"Rachel?" a voice whispers.

"Yes."

"I'm not supposed to call you, but I want you to know that my boy was released an hour ago. He's with us now!"

"You got your boy back?"

"Yes. I can't believe it! I'm so happy! He's safe and he's back with us in the house. I was afraid to hope but . . . he came back."

"But . . . so . . . is there any way you can release Kylie now?"

"I can't. You know I can't. The Chain has to continue. You have to trust the process. If I break The Chain, the blowback will begin. I'll be in danger, my boy will be in danger, and you and Kylie will be in danger."

"Unless they're bluffing about that."

"They're not the kind of people who bluff. I think they would enjoy it if it all went wrong and we started killing one another. You saw what happened to that family."

"Yes."

"They told me about one time years ago when someone defected, and the punishments went seven levels back along The Chain before it sorted itself out."

"Shit!"

"But I want to let you know that you're one step closer to getting Kylie back. It'll be over soon, Rachel, it really will."

"Oh God, I hope so."

"It will."

"How did you do it? How did you get through it all? How did you find the strength?"

"I don't know, Rachel. I suppose you just have to imagine

that moment when you're together again with Kylie. Everything you do, every choice you make, is a means to that end, you know?"

"Yes."

"There was an incident when we took Kylie, something terrible. Nothing happened to her, she's fine. But I had to do something awful, and the old me would be in agony about what I did back there. But you know what I feel? I feel nothing. Nothing but relief. I did what I had to do and I got my son back. And that's all there is to it."

"I think I understand."

"You just have to hold on a little bit longer."

"I will."

28

Mike Dunleavy looks at his wife sobbing and curled up in a fetal position on the bathroom floor. He lies down beside her and he begins to cry too.

He puts the gun on the floor. There's no reason now to be walking around the house with a loaded gun.

The gun is useless. There's nobody to kill.

"How's Toby?" Helen asks him, tears flowing down her face.

"He's asleep. I told him Amelia was going to stay at a friend's house for a few days."

"Did he believe that?"

"He didn't care. He just wanted to know where his archery stuff was. I told him it was safe."

"Do you think it's OK to pray for God's help?" Helen wonders.

"Are we going to do this?"

"We have to."

"We don't have to. We could go to the police."

"They'll kill her if we go to the police. The woman who has her is a monster. I heard it in her voice. We're the worst parents in America. You know those people who overdose

148

in the front seats of their cars? We're dumber than that."

Helen begins weeping again. Great, big breathy sobs, like she's dying. He looks at her face in the dim light coming through the bathroom window.

She seems frail and broken, utterly lost. He has no words.

"How can Amelia sleep without Mr. Boo?" she asks.

"I don't know."

"We'll get her back, won't we? Tell me we'll get her back," Helen says.

"We'll get her back. We'll do everything we can. If I have to kill every one of those scumbags, we'll get her back."

29

It's still dark out but perhaps it's a little lighter in the east. Kylie can't sleep. She hasn't slept at all since she managed to get the wrench.

The adrenaline has been pumping all night and sleep was impossible. She's going to get one shot at this and she's going to have to take it.

The plan is simple. All the best plans are simple. Aren't they?

Get in the boat, find the whale, kill it.

Get in the boat, find the shark, kill it.

The man or woman is going to come down the steps with a tray holding a bowl of cereal and a glass of orange juice. He or she is going to bend over to set down the tray. Then he or she is going to take the cereal bowl and orange juice off the tray.

That's when Kylie is going to hit him or her with the wrench.

A blow as hard as she can on the top of the head. A two-handed blow that will render him or her unconscious.

That person will then be on the ground and down for the count. If she gets lucky, he or she will have the handcuff key. Kylie will uncuff herself, run up the steps, and head for the nearest road. If, however, there is no handcuff key, the gun will come into play. The gun is the crucial part of it. Without fail, every time they have come down here, they have been armed.

If there's no key, Kylie will take the gun and wait until the man or woman wakes up and then she'll point the gun at that person's head and call for the other one and tell them both to give her the handcuff key or she'll shoot.

If they don't believe she'll shoot, she'll plug whoever she's got in the kneecap. She's gone shooting in the woods with her uncle Pete a couple of times. She knows how to fire a revolver. Safety off, check the chamber, pull the trigger. The partner will get the key and give it to her, but if either of them balks, she'll make a deal with them: after she gets home to her mom, she'll claim she can't remember where she was held. She won't remember for a full day. That will give them twenty-four hours to get out of the country.

Kylie is pleased with the plan. It's logical and rational and she can't see any reason why it won't work. The hardest part will be the first step, and that will be over in a second. *You can do it, Kyles, you really can do it,* she tells herself. But she's shaking with fear in the sleeping bag.

Shaking isn't the right word. *Convulsing* might be closer to what's going on. But courage runs in the family. She thinks about her mom going through all those chemo treatments. She thinks about her grandmother fighting NYU for all those years to stay in faculty housing after Grandpa ran off with one of his students. And she thinks about her great-grandmother Irina, the determined little girl who browbeat and bullied her family onto a donkey cart and drove them east with the retreating Red Army to a train that transported them to a strange domed city called Tashkent. Four years they'd spent there as penniless outcasts, and when they got back to the shtetl in Belarus in the fall of 1945, they discovered, of course, that every single person who had stayed there had been murdered by the Germans. But for her great-grandmother's courage, Kylie wouldn't be here today.

That's what she needs now, the courage and determination of little Irina and her mom and her grandma. All the women, all the way back. She examines the wrench again. Heavy. Seven inches long. Someone probably left it there after fixing the boiler. More likely a workman than one of the house's owners. They don't seem like the boiler-fixing types. It isn't the sort of wrench that will help break a chain, but it's maybe big enough to break someone's head.

She'll soon find out.

30

Rachel checks for Amber Alerts and police reports and breaking news about a missing child, and she keeps one eye always on the mirror of the Dunleavys' home PC.

Wee hours. Robert Lowell's Skunk Hour. So late. So tired.

Don't fall asleep, don't fall asleep, don't fall asleep . . .

She closes her eyes for the briefest of moments.

Void.

Sunlight.

Birdsong.

Shit.

What day is it?

The hours are like years and the days are decades. How many millennia into this goddamn nightmare is she?

Another morning. That feeling in her stomach, those butterflies of terror, of gut-churning horror. You've never experienced fear until something or someone puts your child in danger. Dying is not the worst thing that can happen to you. The worst thing that can happen to you is for something to happen to your kid. Having a child instantly turns you into a grown-up. Absurdity is the ontological mismatch between the desire for meaning and the inability to find meaning in this world. Absurdity is a luxury parents of missing children can't afford.

She sits at the living-room table. Eli the cat meows next to her. He hasn't been fed in almost two days.

She fills his bowl, drinks a mug of cold coffee, and steps out onto the deck. Then she puts on a coat and walks along the basin trail to the Appenzellers' house.

The sun comes up over the Atlantic and the big houses on the eastern side of the island. Her iPhone rings. *Unknown Caller.* Her stomach lurches. What now? "Hello?"

"I need you! Get over here!" Pete yells.

"I'm two minutes away."

"Run! I need help."

She sprints along the basin trail and onto Northern Boulevard. Heart pounding, she runs down the path onto the beach and up the back steps of the Appenzellers'.

Worryingly, the door is open.

She goes inside.

On the kitchen table there's Pete's .45 and a bag of what looks like drugs. What the hell? Is Pete a user? Her mind races.

Can he be trusted? Jesus, is he part of all this?

Rachel thinks she knows Pete, but can you ever really know anybody? He's crazy about Kylie but there were those arrests a while back, and what has he been doing all these years since getting out of the Corps?

She shakes her head. No, it's Pete, for heaven's sake. This is the paranoia talking. The Chain has nothing to do with Tammy and it has nothing to do with Pete.

But drugs? This is serious. She'll have to—

"Rachel! Down here! Put your mask on."

She puts on her ski mask and runs down the basement stairs.

Pete is holding Amelia, who is wrapped in a towel, writhing and shaking. Cereal is spilled all over the floor.

"What happened?"

"Gave her the Rice Krispies. I thought it would be fine! I didn't see the small print. It says that it might contain trace nuts."

"My God!"

"The EpiPen won't be here until later this morning," Pete says in a complete panic.

Amelia's lips have swollen and she's deathly white. There are specks of foam at the corners of her mouth and her breaths are shallow and raspy.

Rachel puts the back of her hand on Amelia's forehead.

Fever.

She lifts Amelia's shirt.

Hives.

Rachel opens Amelia's mouth and looks inside. No obstruction. Her tongue isn't swollen. Yet.

"Are you having trouble breathing, Amelia?" Rachel asks. "Can you breathe? Answer me."

Amelia nods.

"What does your mom do when you're like this?"

"Doctor."

She's covered with sweat and her breathing is getting more labored.

"We need to take her to a hospital," Pete says.

Rachel turns to face him. What the hell is he thinking? Hospital? There's no way they can take her to the hospital. If they take her to the hospital the jig is up and Kylie's dead.

"No," she says.

"She's having an allergic reaction," Pete says.

"I can see that."

"She has to see a doctor. We don't have the EpiPen."

"No doctor," Rachel insists. "I'll hold her."

She takes the girl and Pete finally understands. "Are you sure?"

"Yes. I've made the decision."

A terrible decision, but one The Chain has forced on her. Either the little girl is going to die in her arms here and now or she's somehow going to get better.

"I'll stay here with her. You get an EpiPen any way you can!"

"How?"

"Rob a goddamn pharmacy! I don't know. Go!"

Pete runs upstairs. "I'll leave you the gun," he says from the kitchen.

"Fine. Just go!"

She hears the back door slam.

She holds Amelia.

"Doctor," Amelia says.

"Yes, honey," Rachel replies.

There will be no doctors and no hospitals.

If she dies, she and Pete will abandon the house and try again. The cops will find a dead little girl chained to a pillar, covered in spit and vomit, surrounded by dolls and toys and games. They will think it's one of the most evil crime scenes they've ever laid eyes on.

Amelia's face is pale. Her eyes are glassy. She begins coughing.

The hospital could save her.

A paramedic unit from the Newburyport Fire Department could save her.

But Rachel isn't going to call the paramedics or a doctor or a hospital. That path will kill Kylie. If she has to choose between Amelia and Kylie, it's going to be Kylie.

Rachel starts to cry. "Try to breathe more slowly," she says to Amelia. "Slow, easy, big breaths."

She feels Amelia's pulse. It's getting weaker. Amelia looks green. Her skin is soaking, as if she's just had a bath. "Want Daddy," Amelia moans.

"Help's coming, I promise."

Rachel rocks the little girl in her arms. She's dying. Amelia is dying and there's nothing Rachel can do.

Maybe antihistamines would help? There might be some upstairs in the medicine cabinet.

She picks up her phone and Googles *peanut allergy and antihistamines*. The very first article that comes up tells her not to give antihistamines to a child having a severe allergic reaction because antihistamines don't treat anaphylaxis and might make things worse.

"Come on, Pete," Rachel says out loud. "Come on."

Amelia's limp and hot and bubbles are frothing on her lips.

"Mom," she says and moans again.

"It's OK," Rachel lies. "It's OK."

She holds the little girl tightly against her.

The minutes tick past. Amelia gets no better but no worse.

The house is quiet.

She can hear gulls, the sea, a *rat-a-tat* . . .

Huh?

She sits up on the mattress and listens.

She hears the *rat-a-tat* again.

What is that?

"Elaine?" someone says.

Someone is knocking at the front door.

Someone is upstairs right now.

A woman.

She lays Amelia down on the mattress, quietly runs up the basement steps, and crawls into the corridor.

Rat-a-tat again and then another "Elaine? Are you home?"

Rachel flattens herself on the corridor floor.

"Elaine? Is there anybody home?"

Amelia's little voice drifts up through the open basement door. "Mommy . . ."

"Elaine? Are you guys there?"

Rachel crawls along the hall and into the kitchen.

The bag of drugs is gone but Pete left the .45.

Rachel takes it off the kitchen table and slips back out into the hall. This is one stupid woman out there. Even if Elaine were home, she wouldn't want someone knocking on her door at six thirty in the morning.

"Uhh," Amelia moans.

Heart in mouth, Rachel slithers down the basement stairs, almost slipping and breaking her goddamn neck. She runs to Amelia and puts her finger to her lips.

"Shhh," she hisses.

"Elaine, are you in there or not?" the voice at the front door demands. "I thought I saw you moving around!"

Amelia moans louder and Rachel has no choice but to put her hand over the little girl's mouth. Amelia can't breathe properly through her nose. She begins thrashing against Rachel's grip but she's far too weak to put up any kind of resistance.

"Shhh," Rachel whispers. "Take it easy. It's OK, it's OK."

She holds her tight.

No more noise from upstairs.

Ten seconds go by.

Fifteen.

Twenty.

Thirty.

"I guess nobody's home," the voice outside says.

Rachel hears the woman walk down the porch steps, and a moment later she hears the heavy front gate swing closed. Rachel takes her hand away from Amelia's mouth and the little girl gasps for air.

Rachel runs upstairs to the first-floor window. The busybody is an elderly lady in galoshes and a purple raincoat. "Wow," Rachel says to herself.

Utterly exhausted, she sits on the floor and waits for the cops to show up.

When they don't come, she goes back downstairs to Amelia.

She seems to be doing a little better. Or is that just wishful thinking?

She phones Pete but he doesn't answer.

She waits two minutes and calls again. No answer.

Where is he? What the hell is he doing?

Were those drugs? Was he high? She knows he's been in and out of the VA clinic in Worcester for the past year but she hasn't asked what the problem is. Pete's never been one to share and she didn't want to push it.

Where is he?

Has he run out on them?

Amelia is lying on her side now, coughing.

Rachel tucks her in the sleeping bag and puts her arms around her the way a mother would. She strokes her forehead and rocks her.

"It's going to be OK, baby," she says gently. "Sweetie, I promise, in a couple of hours, you'll feel fine."

Rachel holds her and talks to her and she feels like the biggest dirtbag fraud in the world. Five minutes crawl by in slow motion. She'd been willing to let her die. Would have let her die. Still will let her die if—

KNOCK.

KNOCK.

KNOCK.

Rachel creeps back up the basement steps again.

KNOCK.

KNOCK.

KNOCK.

She tiptoes up the stairs to the second-floor bedroom and looks out the window.

It's a Newburyport Police officer.

The old lady looking for Elaine *had* called the frickin' cops.

"Hello?" the policeman says, knocking again.

Rachel holds her breath. If Amelia somehow manages to scream, the cop will certainly hear.

"Anybody home?" the cop says.

He looks through the mail slot and examines the windows. Rachel flinches back behind the curtain. If he's suspicious, he'll break the door down. Then what?

If Rachel shoots him, it won't solve the problem. More cops will come to investigate. And more. And the kidnapping will be compromised, and Kylie will be killed. But if he discovers Amelia, Rachel will be arrested and Kylie will die.

The cop takes a few steps back and looks at the side of the house. If he spots where the window has been recently boarded up—

Rachel flies down the stairs.

Amelia is gurgling in the basement. A terrible choking noise.

She is maybe actually going into cardiac arrest now. Rachel runs through the kitchen, tucking the .45 into the back of her jeans. She has to stop the policeman. If the game is up, Kylie is dead. Simple as that.

Rachel sprints down the back porch and along the sandy path to the front of the house.

"Hello there!" she says from the street.

The cop turns to look at her. She recognizes him. She's seen him at the ice-cream place in Ipswich a couple of times, and he'd given Marty a ticket once when they parked too close to the hydrant at the farm stand. He's in his midtwenties. Kenny something.

"Hi," he says.

"Are you out here 'cause I called you?" she asks.

"Did you call the police?"

"Elaine Appenzeller asked me to keep an eye on the house while she's in Florida. I saw some kids playing around in here. I told them to scram or I would call the cops. And, well . . ."

"They didn't scram?"

"No. They have now, obviously, now that you're here. I'm sorry, did I do the wrong thing? I mean, they were trespassing. That's against the law, right?"

"What did these kids look like?"

"Oh, no, we don't have to make a federal case out of it. They were only about ten. Look, I'm sorry. I was just bluffing when I told them I would call the cops and then they were looking at me the way boys that age do, and I said, 'I'm pressing the number,' and I sort of pressed it."

Kenny smiles. "You did the right thing, ma'am. I don't know if we could prove aggravated criminal trespass on ten-year-olds, but if you don't stop them young, the next step is breaking and entering. You'd be surprised how many of these big old empty summer houses get broken into in the off-season."

"Really?"

"Oh yes. Kids usually, of course, very few actual burglaries, but quite often for recreational drug use or immoral purposes."

"Immoral purposes?"

Kenny's cheeks flush red. "Sex," he says.

"Oh."

They stare at each other.

"Well, I'll just check that the front and back doors are locked and then I'll get going," Kenny says.

Rachel can't allow that to happen. The back door will give the game away.

She wonders if Amelia is still alive down in the basement. She wonders how the Rachel of today can think such a thing in so offhand and chilly a manner. The Rachel of yesterday would have been heartbroken. The Rachel of yesterday is dead and gone.

She plucks at the loose red thread on her sweater and feels the .45 behind her back. His gun is holstered. She could march him into the house at gunpoint and execute him, take Amelia out of there, and move her to a different safe house.

"Did I see you at the White Farms ice-cream stand in Ipswich a few times?" Rachel says.

"Yeah, I've been there," he replies.

"I'm a butter-crunch girl. What's your favorite flavor?"

"Raspberry."

"I've never tried that one."

"It's good."

"You know what flavor I've never tried but want to? The Outrageous. The one that has a bit of everything."

"Yeah, I know. Sounds weird."

"Perhaps if you're not doing anything, I don't know . . ." she says and smiles.

Kenny is a bit slow on the uptake and Rachel guesses that it isn't every day that a somewhat attractive older woman comes on to him, but eventually he begins to see that she's making a pass at him. In fact, he probably thinks she made up the whole story about the kids in the yard just to manufacture this little encounter.

"If you could give me your number, I—"

"Yes," Rachel says. "This week isn't good, but next week if you're not too busy . . . or we could go for a drink or something. You know, if it's too cold for ice cream," she adds, giving her winningest smile.

Kenny smiles back.

"Have you got a pen and paper?" she asks, noting that he doesn't have them on him. "Back at your car?"

She walks him back to the cop car, touching his arm a couple of times accidentally on purpose. She gives him her number and thanks him for coming out. "I'll check the locks. I'm supposed to go in and feed the fish anyway," Rachel says.

"I can go with you," Kenny offers.

She shakes her head. "Nah, I'll be OK, I have the heart of a lion . . . and a lifetime ban from the Boston zoo."

Kenny hasn't heard that one before and he laughs. He gets in the police car and she smiles again and waves as he drives off.

When he's out of sight, she rushes to the back door, enters through the kitchen, and runs down the basement steps, putting on her ski mask as she goes. "Hang on, honey! Hang on!"

Amelia is covered in hives and sweat but, incredibly, is still alive.

Barely.

"Oh my God, sweetie, hold on, just hold on."

Amelia is drooling and her breathing is getting shallower.

Rachel pulls her out of the sleeping bag.

She's on fire. Her eyes flutter.

Her breathing slows, slows, slows, and then stops completely.

"Amelia?"

She isn't breathing. Oh my God! CPR! How do you—

Rachel remembers what to do and begins giving her mouth-to-mouth.

She inhales deeply and then breathes life back into Amelia. Once, twice.

She changes position and pumps Amelia's chest hard and fast, thirty times.

The little girl is breathing again but she needs help, now. Rachel taps 911 into her phone but doesn't press send.

One call and the paramedics will come and save Amelia's life.

They'll save Amelia and condemn her own daughter to death.

She squeezes the iPhone so hard she thinks the glass is going to crack.

Amelia's face.

Kylie's face.

No. She can't do it. Sobbing on the concrete floor, she puts the phone down.

31

The door at the top of the basement steps opens.

"Breakfast on time this morning," the man says, coming down the stairs with a jug of orange juice, toast, and a bowl of cereal. Kylie looks for the gun and there it is, tucked in the front of his pants, something her uncle Pete says nobody should ever do with firearms.

"Are you awake?" he asks.

"Yeah," Kylie says, sitting up in the sleeping bag.

"That's good. Do you like marmalade? I love it. I never had it before I went to London a few years ago. Had it on my toast at breakfast."

"Yes, I do like it. My mom gets it sometimes."

"Toast cut into triangles, Maine butter—from grass-fed cows, of course—Coco Pops, and OJ. That should keep you going for a while."

He sets the tray down on the ground.

She has deliberately placed *Moby-Dick* on the floor, opened, facedown, two-fifths from the end. She knows he'll pick it up, impressed.

"My goodness, you're doing well with this. You're over halfway—"

While he is bending over, Kylie clubs him on the head with the wrench. The fact that he's wearing the ski mask makes it easier to do because she can pretend she's not hitting a human at all. The man groans and she hits him again.

He falls forward and lands with a sort of pathetic clump on the edge of the mattress.

She has no idea where on the head she's hit him but it has done the trick, all right. He's out.

Now she knows she's in a race against time.

She has to flip him over, get the handcuff key out of his pocket, uncuff herself, and run up the steps.

Out in the yard, there could be a dog or the woman or anything. She'll have the gun. She'll have to shoot. If there's no one there, she'll have to run straight for the fence as fast as she can. If she's in the part of New Hampshire she thinks she is, it'll be marshy and boggy, but if she keeps going east, she'll hit I-95 or Route 1 or the ocean. She'll keep going even if they yell at her to stop.

He's a heavy man but she manages to roll him over onto his back, pushing on his sweaty chest and his armpits that smell like onions.

She takes the gun out of his waistband and searches in all his pockets for the key to the handcuffs.

No wallet, no ID, no nothing, but especially no key.

She searches again just to be sure. He's wearing old-fashioned brown slacks with deep pockets, but they're totally empty. There are no rear pockets in the pants, but his shirt has a pocket at the front. It would be the perfect place to hide a handcuff key.

Yes! she thinks, but there's no key there either. *Damn it.*

On to plan B. Kylie examines the gun. There are six bullets in the cylinder. *OK,* she thinks, *all he has to do is wake up.*

166

A minute goes by.

Two.

Oh my God, has she killed him? All she did was hit him with a wrench. That didn't kill people in the movies. She didn't mean to kill—

The man begins to stir.

"Oh, my head," he says, smiling weakly. "Right in the noggin. You got me good."

He groans, and after a few seconds he sits up and looks at her. She has the gun in her hand. The loaded gun.

"What did you hit me with?" he asks. He puts his hands under the ski mask and rubs his eyes, moaning.

"I found a wrench on the floor," Kylie says.

"What wrench?"

Kylie holds up the wrench in her left hand.

"Oh, wow. How did we miss that?"

"It was under the boiler."

"Impossible! I checked this room."

"You had to be in a certain spot at a certain time. I remembered what Howard Carter said when he found King Tut's tomb. You have to be looking, not just seeing."

The man nods. "I like that. You're very smart, Kylie. All right, so what is supposed to happen next in your plan?"

"I've searched you. You don't have the key to the handcuffs, but *she* must. I want you to yell for her and tell her to bring the handcuff key."

"Or what?"

"Or I'll shoot you."

"Do you think you're capable of doing that?"

"Yes. I think so. My uncle Pete took me target shooting a few times. I know what to do."

"It's a different thing, though, isn't it, shooting a target, a piece of paper, and shooting a person?"

"I'm going to shoot you in the leg first to show you that I'm serious."

"And then what?"

"She'll give me the handcuff key and I'll go."

"Why would she let you go?"

"Because otherwise I'll kill you," Kylie says. "But I know you didn't mean to do all this and I'll make you both a promise. After I get out of here, I'll say to my mom that I can't remember anything. I'll wait twenty-four hours until I tell the cops where this place is. That will give you both a day to fly anywhere you want. Anywhere there isn't a, um, one of those—"

"Extradition treaties?"

"Yeah."

The man shakes his head sadly. "I'm sorry, Kylie. It was a good effort, but you've miscalculated. Heather doesn't really care about me. She'd let you shoot me. She'd let you plug as many bullets as you'd like into me."

"Of course she'll care! Call her. Tell her to bring the key!"

"No." He sighs. "She hasn't cared for years, if she ever really did. Jared's her son from her first marriage. I was kind of a stopgap measure, I guess. A stopgap she got stuck with. I love her but I think the feeling's never really been mutual."

Kylie makes a mental note of the two names he let slip in his dazed state, Heather and Jared. That information might be useful later but for now she has to get out.

"I don't care about any of that stuff, mister. I want to get out of here! I'm not bluffing."

"I don't think you're bluffing. You seem like a very determined young lady. You should pull the trigger."

"I will."

"Do it, then."

She stands up, aims the revolver at the man's kneecap,

and squeezes the trigger the way her uncle Pete taught her.

The hammer falls down on the percussion cap. There's a click, and then silence. She squeezes the trigger again. The chamber revolves; the hammer goes back and comes down on another percussion cap. Another click, then more silence. She pulls the trigger four more times until she has gone through the entire six bullets in the gun.

"I don't understand," she says.

The man reaches out and takes the gun from her. He clicks open the revolver and shows her the six gleaming *empty* brass cartridges that he put in the weapon.

32

There's a noise upstairs in the kitchen.

Has the cop come back?

Rachel picks up the gun and points it at the top of the basement steps. "Who is it?" she asks.

She sights the gun. Holds her breath.

Pete comes running down the steps.

"I got the EpiPen. It arrived at the drop box!" he says.

"Thank God!"

Rachel backs away as Pete injects Amelia in the leg. It works almost immediately. Like a goddamn miracle. Amelia gasps and begins to cough.

She coughs and sucks air and coughs again.

Pete gives her water and she drinks it and wheezes.

He takes her wrist. "Pulse coming down to normal. And she's breathing better."

Rachel nods, walks upstairs, finds the Appenzellers' liquor cabinet, and pours herself a large tumbler of Scotch.

She drinks it and refills the glass.

Forty-five minutes later, Pete comes up to join her. "How is she?" Rachel asks.

"Doing much better," Pete says. "Fever's way down."

"She was in a very bad way. I think her breathing stopped."

"It was my fault. I didn't check the cereal."

"I would have let her die, Pete."

Pete shakes his head but he knows she would have and that he probably would have too.

"I've become them," Rachel whispers.

They stare at each other for a beat or two. Their eyes tell the same story: shame, exhaustion, fear.

"When you were out, some woman came to the door looking for Elaine Appenzeller. She went away but she called the cops," Rachel says.

"Did the cops come here?"

"Yeah."

"Are we compromised?"

"I don't think so. I flirted with the cop and I think he thinks I'm some horny old lady who nuisance-calls the police just to get dates with them."

"You're not old," Pete says with a smile, trying to lighten the mood.

I'm probably dying, Pete, Rachel thinks, *how much older can you get?* "So Amelia's OK?"

"She's on the mend, yeah."

"I'll go down and see her."

Amelia's breathing and complexion don't fully return to normal for another half an hour. If only a trace amount of nuts has done this to her, then a full-blown exposure would certainly have killed her.

"Why do you always wear those masks on your face?" Amelia asks her.

"It's because when we give you back to your mommy, we don't want you to be able to tell her what we look like," Rachel says.

"Doesn't Mommy know what you look like?"

"No."

"You should Friend her on Facebook and then she'll know," Amelia says definitively.

"Maybe I'll do that. Do you want a juice box?"

"Is it apple juice?"

"Yes," Rachel says as she hands it to her.

"I hate apple juice. Everybody knows I hate apple juice." Amelia groans and throws away the apple juice and then she throws the Lego horse she's playing with. It smashes into half a dozen pieces. "I hate it here and I hate you!" she yells.

"You have to keep your voice down, sweetie," Rachel says. They had done a good job with the soundproofing but still . . .

"Why?"

"Because if you don't, I guess we'll have to put tape over your mouth to keep you quiet."

Amelia looks at her in amazement. "How would I breathe?"

"You'd breathe through your nose."

"Would you really do that?"

"Yes."

"You're mean."

Rachel nods. The little girl is right. She is mean. She's so mean that she'd been willing to let her die down here.

Rachel takes a burner phone out of her bag. "Would you like to speak to your mom?" she asks.

"Yes!" Amelia says.

Rachel dials Helen Dunleavy's number.

"Hello?" Helen says. She sounds frazzled, exhausted, afraid.

"Would you like to speak to Amelia?"

"Yes, please."

She puts the phone on speaker and hands it to the little girl.

"Sweetie, are you there?" Helen asks.

"Mommy, when can I come home?"

"Soon, sweetie, real soon."

"I don't like it here. It's dark and scary. When is Daddy coming for me? I don't feel well. I'm really bored."

"Soon, sweetie. He'll come soon."

"Am I going to have to miss much school?"

"I think so. I don't know."

"I hate this chain on my hand. I hate it!"

"I know."

"Say goodbye to your mommy," Rachel says, reaching for the phone.

"I have to go now," Amelia says.

"'Bye, honey! I love you!"

Rachel takes the phone and begins walking up the stairs. "As you can see, she's safe and well. For now. You need to get moving with parts one and two."

Rachel closes the basement door behind her and walks into the kitchen.

"I think we can transfer the money tonight," Helen says.

"Do it now! And then get scouting for a target. We'll kill Amelia if we have to. I want my daughter back and you are in my goddamn way," Rachel says and then she breaks the phone in half. She takes the back off it, removes the SIM card, and stamps on it repeatedly until it's broken in two. She puts the remains in the garbage bag Pete keeps in the kitchen.

She stands there, shaking with anger and frustration.

Horizontal lines of dust levitate in the beams of sunlight coming through the shuttered windows. She can hear the sea breaking on the beach a hundred yards in front of her, and downstairs the little girl is humming to herself.

She breathes in and out, in and out. Life is a cascade of nows falling on top of one another without meaning or purpose. Of all the philosophers, only Schopenhauer ever got that right.

"I'm going back home," she shouts to Pete and when the coast is clear, she slips out the back and walks over the dunes. She feels like crying, but she's all cried out. She is stone. The Rock of Gibraltar. And again that thought—the Rachel of yesterday is gone. She Lady Macbethed the tears out eons ago, and she is a different person now.

33

The man is taking a few minutes to pull himself together.
Kylie stares at him in disbelief.

Her plan A is gone; her plan B is gone.

There is no plan C.

"I don't understand—why didn't you load the gun?"
Kylie asks at last.

"You think I would ever point a loaded gun at a child?
Me? When all my professional life has been about . . . ooh,
my head. And not after that incident with the ... . after what
happened when we got you. Wow. It's still throbbing. You
hit me twice? That was really something. Now, be a good
girl and give me the wrench."

Kylie hands him the wrench and he puts it on the breakfast tray.

"I must say, Kylie, I really admire you. You're resourceful
and you're determined and brave. If this were any other
situation, I would be rooting for you to succeed."

"Then please let me—"

"But I don't want you to think I'm a pushover or that I'm
not serious. I'm deadly serious. We're so close to the end
now. And we've been through so much. So I'm afraid that

I'm going to have to punish you so you don't do anything like this again."

"I won't. I can't."

"It's a little too late for you to give your word on that."

He leans forward and slaps her so hard that the chain jerks taut and she twists and falls to the concrete floor.

A ringing in her head.

White spots before her eyes.

Darkness.

An ellipsis of time.

White spots again.

Pain.

Blood pouring from her nostrils and her mouth.

Where is she?

Somewhere musty.

An attic?

A basement?

A—

Oh yeah.

She's been unconscious for how long? A minute? Two? A day?

When she opens her eyes, the man is gone. He's taken the wrench and the gun with him. The breakfast tray is still there.

Her face is stinging. Her head is light.

She sits up. If she tries to stand, she knows she'll fall down again.

Her eyes aren't focusing too well either. The far wall of the basement is blurring into one long smear of color.

Blood drips from her nose onto the sleeping bag.

Drip. Drip. Drip.

Crimson blood pooling on the shiny nylon surface, making a shape like South America.

She dips her finger in the milk of the cereal bowl. Still cold. She's been unconscious for only a few minutes, then.

She begins to cry. She's so lonely and so afraid. Abandoned by the whole world with no ideas and no hope and no plan at all.

34

Rachel drives to the mall in New Hampshire and brings back a first-aid kit, dolls, DVDs, a princess dome tent, and games. Pure guilt. Pure guilt after the fact. Amelia is doing better now. She played Snakes and Ladders with Pete and ate a ham sandwich.

They put up the dome tent and stick *Frozen* in the portable DVD player. They watch Amelia watch the movie for an hour until the Wickr app chimes on Rachel's phone. She goes upstairs to read it.

A message from 2348383hudykdy2.

The Dunleavy ransom has been paid, the message says simply.

Rachel takes one of the powered-up burner phones and dials the Dunleavys.

"Hello?" Helen says.

"The ransom has been paid. You know what to do now."

"How can we do that? It's madness. It's impossible," Helen says.

There's a brief scuffle and then someone says, "No."

Mike Dunleavy comes on the line. "Now, look here—" he begins but Rachel cuts him off immediately.

"Put your wife back on the phone now or your daughter's

dead," Rachel says.

"I want to know who—"

"Put your wife on the phone now, asshole! I've got a gun pointed at Amelia's head!" she yells.

A second later Helen comes back on. "I'm sorry—"

"You will be sorry, you stupid bitch. Do what you're supposed to or you'll never see Amelia again. Once you have a list of targets, send it to the contact on Wickr for final approval," Rachel snarls, and she hangs up.

She removes the SIM card and smashes it and the phone on the kitchen floor. She puts the broken phone in the garbage bag.

A few minutes later, she mirrors the Dunleavys' home computer on Pete's laptop and sees, sure enough, that they are trawling through Facebook feeds and Instagram accounts. Yup, that's how you do it in this day and age.

Pete comes upstairs. "News?"

"They paid the ransom."

"They could afford it. It's the second part . . ."

"Yeah. How's our girl?"

"She's OK. Still watching Disney movies. I promised to play Operation with her later."

Rachel nods absently.

"Look, Rach, you can go home, I'll be OK here," Pete says.

"No, I'm staying the night with Amelia," Rachel insists.

"She asked me to stay tonight, not you," he says gently.

"Why's that?"

"She's scared of you."

"Oh."

"It's better if I stay. I'm used to roughing it. Sleeping bag on the floor is no problem."

Rachel nods. "I guess that's the way it is, then."

"I guess."

They stare at each other and say nothing. Rachel observes him. She knows that something is amiss but cannot put her finger on it. Something to do with that bag of what might have been drugs?

"You're OK, aren't you, Pete?" Rachel asks.

"I'm fine," he says.

"I'm really relying on you," she says.

"I'm fine. Trust me," he says.

Pete knows that she knows. It's time for him to cook up again. He needs it. His body craves it. He had thought he might use this experience as a way to force himself to quit, but it isn't that simple. There's a reason it's called a fix.

Finally Rachel stands. "Call me," she says.

"I will."

She gives him a sad little wave goodbye and goes out.

The sea lashes the dunes, and a freezing, bitter wind is coming at Rachel from the north. A slantwise rain is falling, and lightning stabs at the Dry Salvages off Cape Ann.

Rachel goes home and takes a Sam Adams out of the fridge. The beer isn't cutting it. She pours herself half a glass of vodka and tops it up with tonic. She thinks about the first unknown caller. That voice on the phone. That thing they said about the living being only a species of the dead. It was the kind of thing she'd said to her friends when she was a freshman. A young person's idea of depth. As if whoever was behind The Chain was pretending to be a wise fifty-year-old but was really about her own age or younger.

Rachel would have thought it would take someone a lifetime to get this evil, but no. *And what about you yourself, Rachel? A kidnapper, a torturer of children, an incompetent mom. All of the above. And you know in your heart that you would have let Amelia die. The intent was there and that's what counts in moral philosophy, in law, and in life.*

Your fall has been vertiginous and swift. You're in the cage plummeting to hell. And it's going to get worse. It always gets worse. First comes the cancer, then the divorce, then your daughter gets kidnapped, then you become the monster.

35

Mike and Helen Dunleavy were everything Rachel hoped they would be. For all their procrastination and panic on Saturday morning, by Saturday afternoon they had really gotten their shit together.

They chose a kid from East Providence named Henry Hogg, a boy in a wheelchair whose father was a junior vice president of an oil company, so he could pay $150,000 without sneezing. On Saturday night, Henry's father attended a Rotary Club dinner in Boston, and at nine o'clock, Henry's stepmother picked Henry up from his friend's house, three blocks away from theirs. She started wheeling him home alone through the streets of Providence.

The Dunleavys made sure he never got home.

Kylie doesn't know about any of this, but a few hours after midnight on Sunday, the basement door opens and the woman—Heather—tells Kylie to get up.

Rachel doesn't know about this until her phone rings at 2:17 on Sunday morning.

She's at home, curled up on the couch, drifting in and out of sleep. She's a mess. She's stopped eating, stopped showering. She can't sleep for more than a few minutes.

Her head throbs constantly. Her left breast hurts.

The *I Ching* is open next to her at the hexagram *hsieh*—deliverance. Her fingers linger by the line *You kill three foxes in the field and receive a yellow arrow*. Will the yellow arrow be a sign that her daughter is safe?

The phone call startles her out of her torpor and she grabs the phone like it's a life vest.

Unknown Caller.

"Hello?" Rachel says.

"Rachel, I've got some very good news for you," the woman holding Kylie says.

"Yes?"

"Kylie will be released within the hour. She will be given a burner phone and she'll call you."

Rachel bursts into tears. "Oh God! Are you serious?"

"Yes. And she's fine. She's completely unharmed. But you have to remember that you and she are both still in grave danger. You have to keep your victim until you get the OK from The Chain. If you attempt to defect, they will kill you. Remember the Williams family. They might order me to kill you and Kylie, and I'll do it to protect my boy. If I don't do it, they'll get the people above me on The Chain to kill me and you and our kids. They mean it. They're truly evil."

"I know," Rachel replies.

"It was so tempting for me to let Kylie go when I got my boy home safe. I just wanted to be done with the whole business, but I knew if I did that, she and you and me and my son would all be in jeopardy."

"I promise you, I won't endanger us. Where's my Kylie?"

"We're going to blindfold her and drive her around for forty-five minutes and then drop her off near a rest stop. We'll give her a phone and she'll tell you where she is."

"Thank you."

"Thank you, Rachel, for not screwing up. We were very unlucky, but it's all over now. Please let it be over, please let the people you're managing not screw up. Goodbye, Rachel."

She hangs up.

Rachel calls Pete at the Appenzellers' and tells him the news. Pete is ecstatic. "I can't believe it. I hope it's true."

"I hope so too," Rachel says. "I'm praying."

"Me too."

"How's Amelia?"

"She's sleeping in the princess tent."

"I better get off the line."

"Let me know what's happening."

An hour goes by.

An hour and fifteen minutes.

An hour and twenty.

One hour and twenty-five minutes.

"I wonder if something has—"

Rachel's iPhone begins ringing. *Unknown Caller.*

"Hello?"

"Mommy!" Kylie says.

"Kylie, where are you?"

"I don't know. They told me to wait one minute to take the blindfold off. They're gone now and I'm just on a road in the middle of nowhere. It's dark."

"Can you see anything?"

"There seems to be a bigger road down the way."

"Walk toward it. Oh, Kylie, are you really out?"

"Mommy, I'm out. Come and get me!"

"Where are you, darling? As soon as I know where you are, I will come for you."

"I think I can see a Dunkin' Donuts sign. Yeah, there's

a Dunkin' Donuts. It's a gas station rest stop. I can see it!"

"Is it open?"

"Yes, I think so."

"Go there and ask them where you are. Don't hang up, be careful crossing the road, and just stay on the line."

"No, I gotta hang up, they didn't charge this phone all the way, there's only one rectangle left in the battery. I'll call you from the garage."

"No! Kylie! Don't hang up! Please!"

The line goes dead.

"No!"

A tense five minutes of silence before it rings again.

"OK, Mom, I'm on Route 101 in the Dunkin' Donuts bit of a Sunoco station."

"What town?"

"I don't know, Mom, I don't want to ask again. It seems weird showing up at this time of the night and not knowing where you are."

"Jesus, Kylie, just ask them."

"Mom, listen, Google it, I'm in New Hampshire on 101 just off I-95."

Rachel Googles it. "Is it the Sunoco near Exeter?"

"Yes. There's a sign that says Exeter."

"I'll be there in twenty minutes! Can you wait twenty minutes?"

"OK, Mom."

"Get a drink of water if you don't have money to buy food."

"No, they gave me money. I'll get a doughnut and a Coke. I asked them for my phone and they said they didn't have it."

"We found your phone," Rachel says, running out to the car.

"Can you bring it?"

"Later. I'm in the car now."

"What did you tell Stuart?" Kylie asks.

"I told Stuart you were sick and I told your father you had gone to New York. Oh my God, Kylie, is it really you? Did you really come back to me?"

"It's really me, Mom. I'm hungry. I'm going to get a doughnut. Maybe a couple of them. I'm hanging up to get a doughnut, Mom," Kylie says.

"Don't hang up! I'll be there in a minute," Rachel says but Kylie is gone again.

I-95 is only a few minutes away and Rachel tears up it at eighty miles an hour, pretty much the Volvo's maximum velocity.

Google Maps takes her to the 101 turnoff and there right in front of her is the Sunoco station.

Kylie is sitting in the window seat of the Dunkin' Donuts by herself. Her brown hair, her freckly face, the little silver headband. It's really her!

She looks so small and frail under the harsh lights.

"Kylie!" Rachel screams. She slides the Volvo into a parking spot, opens the door, and runs in.

They hug each other and burst into tears.

Kylie is crying. Rachel is crying.

It's real.

It's actually real.

Her little girl back again. The *I Ching* promised a yellow arrow when it would all be over.

There's no yellow arrow anywhere, but Kylie is back with her in the world.

Thank you, God. Thank you, God. Thank you.

"Oh, Mommy, I thought I was never going to see you again," Kylie says.

Rachel can't believe it. She isn't sure the world is big enough to contain the relief and gladness she feels. "I knew I'd see you again! I knew I'd get you back," Rachel replies and holds her close. So close. Her little girl smells like her little girl. She's trembling and cold. She must be hungry and so, so scared.

The tears flow.

Rivers of relief and happiness.

A weird, unbalanced, off-kilter kind of joy.

"Are you hungry?" Rachel asks.

"No. I ate a doughnut and the people fed me while I was there."

"What did they feed you?"

"Normal stuff. Cereal. Graham crackers."

"Come on, let's get out of here. I'll take you home. Uncle Pete's here."

"Uncle Pete?"

"Yeah, he's been helping me out."

"You didn't tell Dad?"

"No."

"'Cause of Tammy?"

Rachel nods.

"They told me that if I said anything, we could all be in danger," Kylie says.

"That's what they told me. Come on, let me take you home."

"I need to go to the bathroom," Kylie says.

"I'll go with you."

"No, Mom, no. I'll be OK."

"I'm not going to let you out of my sight."

"Mom, I'm not having you go into the bathroom with me. I'll be one minute."

Rachel walks her to the Dunkin' Donuts bathroom and

stands outside the door. It's one of those unisex, single-person toilets so there's no way there's someone in there who's going to drag Kylie out a window or anything, but still, Rachel hates to lose visual contact with her for even a few seconds.

The middle-aged cashier catches her eye.

"Is she yours?" the woman asks.

"Yes."

"I was just gonna call the cops. I thought she was a runaway."

Rachel smiles and texts Pete that Kylie is safe.

"You gotta keep an eye on them when they start hitting their teens," the cashier says. "It's a difficult age. I should know. Four daughters."

"This one is my whole world," Rachel replies.

The woman nods. "You can't let them out of your sight."

"You can say that again."

Kylie comes out of the bathroom and Rachel hugs her. They leave the gas station hand in hand.

"I want to have a long, hot shower when I get home," Kylie says as they get in the car.

"Of course. Anything you want."

"I feel dirty."

"Are you OK? Did they touch you? Hurt you?"

"No . . . yes. The man yesterday. What day is it?"

"Sunday morning, I think."

"I tried to escape and he slapped me," Kylie says matter-of-factly.

"Oh my God. He hit you?" Rachel asks.

"Yes. And the funny thing was, he wasn't the bad one. She was the bad one. She was so scary," Kylie says and starts crying again.

Rachel hugs her tightly.

"Come on, let's go, I want to go home. I want to see my cat and Uncle Pete," Kylie says.

Rachel starts the car and turns on the lights and drives south.

"There's something else, Mom," Kylie says.

"What?" Rachel asks, expecting the worst.

"I'm not really sure but I think maybe they shot a cop. We were pulled over by a state trooper and I think they shot him."

Rachel nods. "I think there were reports of a New Hampshire state trooper being shot on Thursday morning."

Kylie gasps. "Did he die?"

"I'm not sure," Rachel lies.

"We have to go to the police," Kylie says.

"No! It's too dangerous. They'll kill us all. They'll hunt us down and get us. You, me, Pete, your father, all of us. We can't say or do anything, Kylie."

"So what do we do?"

"We don't do anything. We keep quiet and try to put this behind us."

"No!"

"We have to, Kylie. I'm sorry, but it's the only way."

When they arrive back on Plum Island ten minutes later, Pete is waiting for them. He hugs Kylie when she gets out of the car and then lifts her up and spins her around.

"Honey, you're safe!" he says and helps her inside.

Eli jumps up onto the sofa next to Kylie and she picks him up and kisses him.

"How's . . ." Rachel whispers to Pete.

"Sleeping. I'll go back there in five. I just wanted to see you guys," Pete replies.

"Uncle Pete," Kylie says and puts her arms out for another hug.

Rachel sits on one side of her and Pete sits on the other. Eli nestles in her lap. *It's a miracle, that's what it is,* Rachel thinks. Sometimes kids do come back, but often they do not, especially girls.

"Do you know everything that's happened?" Kylie asks Pete.

"Yeah, I've been helping your mom."

"Group hug," Kylie says, crying again.

Pete puts his arms around both of them.

"I can't believe it," Kylie says. "I thought I was going to be down there for a million years."

They all sit there for a few minutes before Kylie looks up and grins at the two of them. "I'm hungry," she says.

"Anything you like," Rachel tells her.

"Pizza."

"I'll microwave one right now."

She tries to get up and go to the kitchen, but Kylie won't release her.

"Are you OK, Kylie?" Pete asks. "Did they hurt you?"

"The man hit me after I hit him and tried to escape. It really hurt," Kylie says.

"Shit," Pete says, his fists clenching by his sides.

"You must have been terrified," Rachel says.

Kylie speaks and Pete and Rachel listen.

She tells them everything.

They let her words spill out. If she wants to talk about it, they'll let her talk. Kylie isn't one who clams up, and for this Rachel is grateful. She strokes her daughter's hair and smiles at her bravery.

She heats the pizza while Pete goes back to the Appenzellers' to check on Amelia.

Kylie goes up to her bedroom to see all her stuff.

"Mom, can I text with Stuart and all my friends now? Would that be OK?" Kylie asks.

"Yes, but you have to tell him that you had a stomach bug, OK?"

"OK, I guess. And what do I tell Dad?"

"Oh, crap, that's a whole thing. You have to tell your father that you went to New York," Rachel says, and she explains the situation with her father and Tammy and her grandmother.

"I need my phone!"

Rachel gets the phone. "I couldn't fake-text for you because I didn't know your passcode."

"It's so obvious: two-one-nine-four."

"What's that?"

"Harry Styles's birthday! Oh my God, I have a million messages."

"You have to tell people you were sick."

"I will. But I want to go to school Monday. What day is it tomorrow?"

"Monday."

"I wanna go to school."

"I don't think that's a good idea. I want you to get checked out by a doctor."

"I'm fine. I want to go to school! I want to see everybody."

"Are you sure?"

"I don't want to be cooped up in a house again."

"Well, no school bus, not anymore. I don't know what I was thinking."

"Hey, where's my stuffed bunny? Where's Marshmallow?" Kylie asks.

"I'll get Marshmallow back for you tonight."

"He's not lost?"

"No."

Kylie sends texts to her friends, who are probably all sleeping. She and Rachel lie in bed and watch her favorite YouTube clips: A-Ha's "Take On Me" video, the Monty Python fish–slapping dance, half a dozen videos from the rap group Brockhampton, the bit in *Duck Soup* where Groucho is suspicious of his own reflection.

Kylie showers and asks for some alone time, and when Rachel goes to check on her half an hour later, she is fast asleep. Rachel collapses on the couch and weeps.

Pete comes back at six in the morning and puts a couple of logs on the fire. "Everything OK over there?" Rachel asks.

"Amelia is still asleep."

Pete makes a pot of coffee and they sit by the fire.

Everything seems back to the way it was before. Fishing boats heading out into the Merrimack. Bernstein on WCRB. The *Globe* arriving in its plastic wrap in front of the house.

"I can't believe she's home," Rachel says. "There were times when I thought I'd lost her forever."

They watch the logs whiten and slowly turn to ash. Rachel's phone rings. *Unknown Caller*. She answers it on speaker.

It's the distorted voice. It is The Chain speaking directly to her: "I know what you're thinking. It's what everyone thinks when they get their loved ones back. You think you can release your hostage and end this. But the thing is, you can't fight tradition. Do you know what a tradition is, Rachel?"

"What do you mean?"

"A tradition is a living argument. A living argument for a practice that began a long time ago. And it works for our particular tradition. If you mess with The Chain, it will be sure to get you and your family. Leave the country, go to

Saudi Arabia or Japan or wherever. Change your name, change your identity. We'll always find you."

"I get it."

"Do you get it? I hope so. Because it's not over. It won't be over until the people you've recruited do what they're supposed to do without screwing up and the ones they've recruited do their job without screwing up. We haven't had a defection in The Chain for a few years now, but they happen. People think they can beat the system. They can't. No one can, and you're not going to."

"The Williams family."

"There are others who have tried. No one has ever succeeded."

"I'm going to keep my word."

"Be sure that you do. We put ten thousand dollars in your bank account this morning—that's ten percent of the money the Dunleavys paid. We took it out of the same Bitcoin account they put their money into. I don't know how you would ever explain that to the federal authorities. Even if you somehow escaped our assassins, which no one ever has, we'd release all this information and you'd go to prison. The evidence is all there to reveal you as the genius behind a sophisticated kidnapping ring. You're smart. You can see the big picture, can't you?"

"Yes, I can."

"Good," the voice says. "We probably won't speak again. Goodbye, Rachel, it's been a pleasure doing business with you."

"I can't say the same."

"It could have been worse. It could have been a lot worse."

When the call ends, Rachel shudders and Pete puts his arms around her. She's so pale and thin and fragile, and her heart is beating so fast. Like a wounded bird that you put in a shoe box and nurse back to life, hoping that one day it will be able to fly again.

36

Kylie finally comes down the stairs. She's got her iPad in one hand, her phone in the other, and Eli over her shoulder.

"I had over a hundred and fifty Facebook, Instagram, and Twitter notifications," Kylie says, trying to sound upbeat.

Rachel smiles. So much for her idea of going full tinfoil hat and killing social media. Kylie returns her mother's smile. *Both of us faking it for each other,* Rachel thinks. "You're a popular girl," she says.

"I talked to Stuart. Everybody seems to have bought the whole sickness story. And I texted Grandma too. She's fine. I even e-mailed Dad."

"I'm sorry I made you do that."

Kylie nods and doesn't say *It's OK* because it's not OK to make your daughter lie to her friends and family.

"You were careful what you said?"

"I was."

"If you say one thing on social media, the whole world sees."

"I know, Mom. I can't ever tell anyone, can I?"

"No . . . are you OK, my darling?" Rachel asks, stroking Kylie's face.

"Not really," Kylie says. "I was so scared down there. There were times when I thought I was going to—I don't know—*disappear?* You know that thing where some people think that if other people leave the room, they just don't exist anymore."

"Solipsism?"

"That's what I thought was happening to me down there in the basement. I thought that I was starting not to exist because no one was thinking about me."

Rachel hugs her tight. "All I did was think about you! Every minute of every second of every day."

"And then there were times when I thought that maybe those two would just leave me there. Maybe if they thought they'd been discovered, they'd go, and the food would run out and the water would run out and I would just die."

"I wouldn't have let that happen," Rachel says. "I wouldn't. I would have found you no matter what."

Kylie nods but Rachel sees that she doesn't believe it. How would she have found her? She wouldn't have found her. Her daughter would have been trapped down there forever.

Kylie walks to the screen door and looks out at the basin.

"Your flip-flops are onomatopoeia-ing," Rachel says, trying to shift the mood.

Kylie turns to face her. "Mom?"

"Yeah?"

"They explained to me that they couldn't release me until you continued The Chain."

Rachel looks at the floor.

"Mom?"

Rachel swallows hard. She can't lie about this—it would

make everything worse. "That's right," she says.

"So, wait, did you . . . have you . . ." Kylie asks, horrified.

"I'm sorry. I, I, I had to."

"You kidnapped someone?"

"I had to."

"You still have them?"

"Yes. I can't release them until The Chain continues."

"Oh my God!" Kylie says, her eyes wide. "Where?"

"We found a . . . I found an empty house on the other side of the basin. A house with a basement."

"They're over there right now? Alone?"

"That's where Pete is."

"Is it a boy or a girl?"

"The less you know, the better."

"I want to know!"

"A girl," Rachel says, feeling great waves of shame course through her.

A great river of shame as brown as shit.

"Can't you just let her go?"

Rachel fights her gag reflex and the flight response and forces herself to confront the present reality. She looks Kylie in the eye and shakes her head.

"C—can't we go to the FBI and have them hide us and give us new identities or something like that?" Kylie asks.

"It's not so simple. We've—I've—actually kidnapped someone. They'll send me to jail. And you won't be safe. I believe them when they say that The Chain has never been successfully broken. I think they'll find us wherever we go. I can't take that risk."

"Can I see the girl? Can I talk to her?"

Rachel shudders at the thought of dragging Kylie deeper into this. "No, you go back to school. We'll handle this. Me and Pete."

"What's her name?"

"It's best that you don't know."

"Does she have Marshmallow?"

"Yes." Rachel tries to hug her, but Kylie pushes her away.

"Don't touch me!" Kylie says.

"I can get Marshmallow back. I—"

"That's not the point! It's not about Marshmallow. It's about what you've done. How could you kidnap someone, Mom? How could you do that?"

"I don't know. I had to."

"Did you hurt her?"

"No. Not really," Rachel says, again swimming in that river of lies and shame.

"How could you do that, Mom?"

"I don't know."

Kylie takes a step back and then another until she bumps into the screen door.

Rachel looks at her grubby fingernails and catches a glimpse of herself in the glass. She's like some skinny, deranged prophet trying to bring a suddenly clear-minded former follower back into the fold. No, she's not. It's worse than that. She's a demon, dragging her daughter down with her into the pit. She's the opposite of good and kind Demeter. She has made Kylie lie. She's made her a party to a crime. This fissure between them will widen into a gulf. Nothing will ever be the same again.

She looks into Kylie's betrayed, teary eyes.

Rachel imagines a sulfurous reek to the air. No, they are not yet escaped from hell. The escape will take months, perhaps years.

Kylie begins to sob. "You had to do it to get me back?"

"Yes."

"You and Uncle Pete?"

"Yes."

Kylie slides open the door, and a cold wind blows in from the basin.

"Can we go outside?" Kylie asks.

"It's freezing."

"We can wrap ourselves in the comforter. I don't want to be inside."

They go onto the deck.

"Can I hold you?" Rachel asks tentatively.

"Yes," a meek Kylie responds.

Kylie sits on her mother's lap in the Adirondack chair, wrapped in a blanket, the long tie of Rachel's robe threaded around them like an umbilical. They don't talk. They just sit there.

The day dwindles to an end in a line of reds and yellows along the Merrimack Valley. It grows dark, and when the stars come out, mother and daughter are swallowed up by the night. What is going to be a long, terrible night indeed.

37

Her instinct's right. The Chain is screwing up. Well, her instinct is *partially* right. The problem, however, is not Rachel Klein. And the problem is not Helen Dunleavy. The problem is Seamus Hogg. Using standard spyware tech, she has mirrored the Hoggs' phones and read Seamus's e-mails. Seamus e-mailed his uncle, a guy named Thomas Anderson Hogg, who lives in Stamford, Connecticut, and asked him if they could meet at a Starbucks in Stamford tomorrow morning at ten.

This is a big problem because Thomas Anderson Hogg is a retired U.S. marshal.

Seamus is going to rat.

And not even to the cops but to the goddamn U.S. Marshals Service.

She looks at the data on Rachel again. An uninteresting but surprisingly competent link so far. She has done everything right. Paid the ransom fast, paid the increased ransom fast, carried out a successful kidnap.

She is capable and good. Her ex-brother-in-law is helping her. Another interesting dude. Honorably discharged from the Marines but he had taken some heat for the September

2012 Camp Bastion incident. No pension. Only the minimum VA benefits. Arrested in Worcester, Massachusetts, in 2017 for possession of one gram of brown-tar heroin. Charges subsequently dropped. The mug shot is of a haunted, dour, prematurely middle-aged-looking man.

Is the ex-husband helping too?

She Googles Rachel's ex-husband, Marty O'Neill.

Now, that's a good-looking guy. A very good-looking guy indeed. She's surprised she hasn't come across him before. The pool of eligible bachelors in Boston is remarkably shallow. Harvard grad, lawyer, dating some drippy blonde. Born in Worcester, lives in Boston, is a partner at the white-shoe law firm of Banner and Witcoff. Yeah, he's the brains of the family.

Well, let's see how they collectively handle a little curveball.

She logs into the Wickr app and messages Rachel:

Seamus Hogg is defecting. He is going to rat. He e-mailed his uncle, a retired U.S. marshal, and he's meeting him tomorrow at ten a.m. in Stamford, Connecticut. Obviously, this meeting cannot be allowed to take place. The Dunleavys have screwed up. They have picked an unreliable target. And their screwup is your screwup, Rachel. Kill your hostage and pick another target or stop this meeting and remind the Dunleavys and the Hoggs that they are part of The Chain. If you do neither of these things, the blowback will come for you and your family. We know where you live. There is nowhere you can go where we will not find you.

38

Black Atlantic. Black sky. A dusting of drab stars. Rachel is sitting on the deck smoking a cigarette when the Wickr app on her phone sounds an alert. A message for her.

She reads it, digests it, goes into panic mode, calms herself, gets a burner phone, calls Pete at the Appenzellers', and reads him the message.

"Aren't the Dunleavys supposed to take care of this?" he asks.

"The Chain bastards contacted *me*. This is the blowback they were talking about, Pete. If the Hoggs screw it all up, that means the Dunleavys have screwed up, and I'm supposed to kill Amelia and pick a new target or they'll come for me."

"Wait there. I'll be right over," Pete says. "Amelia's asleep."

Rachel dials Helen Dunleavy's number but the phone rings and rings and eventually goes to voice mail. She dials again, but no one answers. She waits a minute and dials a third time, but still nothing—either the stupid bitch is dead or she's turned her phone off.

Their PC is off too. There are no traces from any of their

electronic devices. What's happened to them? What the hell?

She signs into Wickr and sends a message to 2348383hudyk-dy2: Dunleavys not answering phone.

There's an immediate response: That's not our problem, Rachel. That's your problem.

A minute later Pete arrives. "What did the Dunleavys say?" he asks.

"No answer. The stupid bastards have their phone turned off."

"So what are we going to do?"

"I'm not going to kill Amelia and start again."

"Of course not."

Pete hopes that Rachel doesn't notice his glazed eyes. He shot up about fifteen minutes earlier. He'd thought they were done for the night, and his body was craving opiates. He had to give in and shoot up in the Appenzellers' kitchen.

"Pete?" Rachel says.

"I'm out of ideas," he replies dully.

"We go down to the Dunleavys' now, tonight, and we tell them they have to get their boy in line."

"Call them up."

"I've called them! They're not answering. Aren't you listening?"

"Who doesn't leave the phone on when their daughter's been kidnapped?" Pete wonders.

"Maybe they're already dead. Maybe the blowback has killed them and we're going to be next," Rachel says.

"They might be coming for us right now."

"We'll bring Kylie to the Appenzellers' house. Nobody knows about that place except us," Rachel says.

"I'll get things ready."

Rachel goes to Kylie's room. She's still awake and on her

iPad. "I'm sorry, honey, but it's not safe for you to be here tonight. Something's happening with The Chain."

Kylie is terrified. "What? Are they coming for us?"

"No. Not yet. I have to sort something out. I'm going to take you over to the Appenzellers'. You'll be safe there."

"They're coming back for me, aren't they?"

"No. It's not that. You're safe. It's fine. It's just a precaution. Your uncle Pete and I are going to take care of everything. Come on, pack a bag."

Rachel and Kylie drive over to the Appenzellers' and slip in the back. Pete is waiting in the kitchen with his .45 and Rachel's shotgun.

Kylie looks at the weapons, swallows, then gives Pete a hug.

"Is the little girl here?" Kylie asks.

Rachel nods.

"Where is she?"

"Basement. Asleep," Pete says.

"Pete and I have to go out. Amelia probably won't wake up, but if you need to go down there, put this on," Rachel says, giving her a black ski mask.

"So she can't identify me," Kylie says, fascinated and appalled.

"I was praying you wouldn't get further involved, but if Amelia starts to cry, I guess you'll have to go down there and comfort her," Rachel says. "We can't have her making too much noise."

"I think she'll sleep until morning, though. I had her skipping rope for an hour," Pete says.

"Where are you guys going to be?" Kylie asks her mom.

"Pete and I have to go deal with an emergency."

"What sort of emergency?"

"It's OK, honey, it's not bad, but both of us have to go

and you'll have to stay here with Amelia."

"You need to tell me what's happening!"

Rachel nods. She deserved that. "One of the families far-ther down The Chain is thinking about going to the police. We have to stop them. If they go to the police, we could all be in danger."

"So where are you going?"

"Providence."

"You're going down there to tell them to pay the ransom and do everything you did?"

"Yes."

"What if you . . . what if you don't come back?"

"If we're not back by morning, call your father to come and get you. Stay in this house. Don't go home. When he gets here, tell him everything. Keep your phone turned off until then."

Kylie nods solemnly. "What time in the morning?"

"If you haven't heard from either of us by, say, eleven, it probably means we've been compromised," Pete says.

"Dead?" Kylie asks, her lip trembling.

"Not necessarily. Just that something's going wrong," Rachel says, although she thinks *dead* is the most likely scenario.

Kylie hugs her mom and Pete. "I'll be OK," she says. "And I'll keep an eye on her."

Her daughter is now co-opted into a kidnapping scheme. Rachel feels mortified and angry. But she can't indulge these feelings for very long. The clock is ticking. She wipes the tears from her cheeks. "Let's get this show on the road, then," she says to Pete. "I'll drive."

39

Sunday, 11:27 p.m.

Swamp to the left, marsh to the right. High beam on the headlights. Smell of gun oil, sweat, fear. Nobody talking. Rachel driving. Pete literally riding shotgun.

Beverly, Mass.

Old wooden houses. Oak trees. The occasional apartment building. Quiet. Blue light from TVs and burglar alarms.

Suburban-nighttime ennui. Which is good. Fewer busy-bodies on the sidewalks.

Poseidon Street.

The lights are off in the Dunleavy house.

"Drive around the block," Pete says. "Don't stop."

Rachel does and then parks one street over.

Quiet town. No one around. Only one question: Why won't Helen Dunleavy answer her goddamn phone?

Rachel has an image of the entire family tied to chairs in the kitchen with their throats cut.

"We can go in through those little scrubby woods next door to their house," Pete says. "And then in through the back door."

"How?" Rachel asks.

Pete holds up a wrench and a lock-pick kit. "If we're

definitely going to do this," he says.

"Yeah. We're pot committed," she replies.

Pot committed is the polite way of putting it. She's going to have to go full-on Lady Macbeth now. Act it. Believe it. Be it. For Pete, for herself, for Kylie—the lives of her family are at stake.

"I've got an EM-pulse kit to baffle the alarm system if there is an alarm system. Once we're in, we use handguns," he says, handing her his glove-compartment .38 revolver. He's also got a .45 and a nine-millimeter.

The guns. The scrubby wood.

Pete struggles to get over the Dunleavys' north fence. Rachel stares at him. What is the matter with him? She wonders again if he's on something or if he's had an injury he hasn't told her about. She needs him to be 100 percent.

"Are you OK, Pete?" she says severely.

"Yeah! I'm fine. Are you OK?"

She glares at him in the darkness.

"We should probably get moving, right?" he says.

"Sure."

The Dunleavys' backyard. Toys, lawn furniture, a swing. The back door, which leads to the kitchen.

"Come on," Rachel says.

Flashlights on. EM-pulse kit on.

Pete fiddles with the lock. There's a little tremor in his right hand.

"Can you get it?"

"Yeah. Done this before. It will not resist my attentions for long, trust me," he says.

Three minutes. Four minutes.

"Are you sure?"

The door finally unlocks. Pete turns the handle. There is no safety chain. No burglar alarm goes off.

"Are we OK?" Rachel asks.

"Yeah."

They put on their ski masks and enter the kitchen. Rachel darts her flashlight around the room.

No dead bodies. No assassins.

"Do we know where we're going?" Rachel whispers.

"Yes," Pete says. "Follow me."

She follows Pete upstairs.

Carpet on floor. Pictures on wall. A big clock at the top of the steps. A mirror that scares her for a sec when she sees a person with a gun in it.

"First bedroom on the left," Pete hisses.

Through the bedroom door. Body odor. Smell of booze. A woman snoring on the bed. Flashlight into the corners. No one else there. Pete tiptoes to the bed, kneels beside the woman, and puts his hand over her mouth. She yelps under Pete's hand and he holds her down.

Rachel checks the en suite bathroom while Pete smothers her cries with his big paw.

"It's clear," Rachel says.

"Are you Helen Dunleavy?" Pete asks. "Just nod your response."

She nods.

"Where's your husband?" Pete asks. "One-word answer. The name of a room. Whisper it. If you're loud, you're dead."

"Basement," Helen croaks.

"I tried to phone you. Do you recognize my voice?" Rachel asks.

"You've got Amelia," Helen says and begins to cry.

"Where's the kid? Henry Hogg?" Rachel asks.

"Basement."

"With your husband?"

"We take turns to—"

Rachel glances at Pete. "Bring the husband up here. I'll stay with this one."

She switches on the bedroom light and points the .38 at Helen while Pete goes downstairs.

"What happened to your phone?" Rachel asks, seething. "Why isn't it on? Why aren't you sleeping with it under your pillow like a normal person would in this situation?"

"I, I, I don't know. Isn't it over there on the dresser?" Helen asks. Her face looks haggard, frightened. Her eyes are red and hollow. At least that's something.

Rachel looks at the dresser. The phone's dead. "You forgot to charge it," she says.

"I—I didn't know."

"Sleeping while your daughter's a hostage? What is your goddamned problem?"

"I, I was just taking a—" she begins when the bedroom door opens.

Mike Dunleavy walks in with his hands up. He doesn't resemble his photos online or on Facebook. He looks much older, grayer, fatter, stupider. Isn't he supposed to be some kind of smart guy with money? He looks like every dumb dad picking his kids up late from school because he forgot it was his day to get them. No wonder these clowns screwed it up. How did they ever kidnap anybody? Maybe they even lied about that.

"Is the kid in the basement?" Rachel asks Pete.

"Oh yes," Pete says and he lets out a kind of half whistle as if to say it isn't a pretty sight down there.

"You're the ones that took Amelia?" Mike asks with just a trace of an English accent.

"We have her."

"Is she OK?" Helen asks desperately.

"She's fine. We're looking after her."

"Why are you here?" Mike says. "We've done everything you've asked."

"No. You screwed up. We tried to call you, but your phone was dead and your computer was turned off," Rachel says.

Helen is looking at her strangely now. *If she says something like "I think I know who you are," then, Jesus Christ, I'm going to have to shoot her on the spot,* Rachel thinks.

"This is about the Hoggs, isn't it?" Helen says. "They've done something."

"It's what they're about to do," Pete says.

"Oh God! What are they about to do?" Helen asks.

"Seamus has an uncle in the U.S. Marshals Service. And he's going to go see him tomorrow in Stamford," Rachel informs her.

"Wh—what does that mean?" Helen asks, appalled.

"In theory, it means you have to kill little Henry and start again or else we have to kill Amelia and start again. Simple as that. I'm not having The Chain come near me or my family. Is that understood?" Rachel snarls.

"There must be some other—" Mike begins.

"There is. The three of us drive down to Providence and explain things to Mr. Hogg in person," Rachel says.

"The three of us?" Pete inquires.

"The three of us," Rachel insists. "Can't trust these clowns."

She turns to Helen. "You'll stay and watch the kid. Your husband will come with us. We'll take your car. It's a BMW, isn't it?"

"Yeah," Mike says.

"Should be fast enough. Put some goddamn shoes on. Oh, and go find Mr. Boo. We need Mr. Boo," Rachel says.

"Mr. Boo?" Mike wonders.

"Amelia's bear. She wants it."

Helen gets Mr. Boo.

"If you call the cops or warn the Hoggs or do anything stupid while we're out, Amelia's dead. They'll kill her and then they'll come for you and Toby. Do you understand?" Rachel says.

Helen nods.

They go outside to Mike's BMW, a large, black top-of-the-line job. The kind they give to big earners at Standard. Plush. Comfortable. Fast.

Mike hands Rachel the keys. She gets in the driver's seat.

Pete gets in the back with Mike.

She turns the key in the ignition and the car growls to life.

She looks in the rearview. Pete's still a bit dazed. Mike's shitting himself. She can handle both of them. She will handle both of them.

"Buckle up," she says.

40

She merges with the traffic.
  The highway hums. The highway sings. The highway luminesces.

It is an adder moving south.

Diesel and gasoline.

Water and light.

Sodium filament and neon.

Interstate 95 at midnight. America's spinal cord, splicing lifelines and destinies and unrelated narratives.

The highway drifts. The highway dreams. The highway examines itself.

All those threads of fate weaving together on this cold midnight.

Towns and exits gliding south, shutting down other possibilities, other paths. Peabody. Newton. Norwood.

The Google map making its own zodiac.

Pawtucket.

Providence.

The Brown University exit. Lovecraft country. An old coach road to East Providence. Big houses. Even bigger houses.

212

Maple Avenue. Bluff Street. Narragansett Avenue.

"Here," Mike says.

"Is this it?"

"Yeah."

The house is a large, ugly, mock-Tudor job, an early 2000s McMansion on a street filled with similar properties.

They drive past it and park a little way up the road.

"Front or back entrance?" Rachel asks Pete.

"Hard to say," Pete mutters. "We don't know about dogs, alarms, that kind of thing."

"Back, then," Rachel decides.

The three of them exit the BMW, walk around the block to the Hoggs' backyard, and climb a metal fence at the rear of the property. No dog comes tearing toward them. No floodlights come on. No shotgun blast comes roaring out of the night.

The back door is a solid-looking thing but there's another door attached to a kind of mudroom on the side of the house. It has only a latch lock on the other side of a piece of glass. Pete turns on his EM-pulse kit and breaks the glass.

They wait for a response. A yell. A light coming on.

There's no reaction.

Pete puts his hand through the broken window and undoes the latch on the external door.

They go inside the mudroom, which is a small, narrow wooden chamber filled with coats and boots.

Flashlights on.

Mudroom to kitchen to dining room.

A dining room with pictures on the wall.

Rachel's flashlight catches a family portrait. Two boys, a man, and his wife. Tall man with jet-black hair. Small, doughy, attractive wife who looks like she's nice. The kids are about the same age, early teens. One of the boys is in a wheelchair. Why did the Dunleavys kidnap the one in the wheelchair? Why make it so difficult?

What kind of a person kidnaps a disabled child?

Then again, what kind of person kidnaps a kid who might die of an anaphylactic reaction to nuts?

What kind of person kidnaps a child?

They walk into a games room that has a full-length pool table, a dartboard, and a Nintendo Wii console. At least the Hoggs appear to have money.

"I guess you better take this," Pete says absently, giving Mike a nine-millimeter pistol.

Rachel looks at him, amazed. Why would he give—

Mike turns and points the nine-millimeter at Rachel's head.

"Now, you bloody bitch, you're going to get yours. You're going to release Amelia tonight or I'm going to—"

"You're going to do what?" Rachel snaps. "You think we're dumb enough to give you a loaded gun?"

Mike stares at the weapon. "I—"

Rachel snatches the pistol out of his hands and gives it back to Pete, who finally seems to realize his mistake.

Rachel shoves the barrel of the .38 into Mike's cheek.

"You still don't get how it works, do you? Even if we gave you Amelia back, that won't be the end of it. The Chain has to continue. That's the way it's set up. They'll kill you and Amelia and your wife and Toby. They'll kill all of you and start again. They'll kill me and my family too."

Mike shakes his head. "But I—" he begins.

Rachel pistol-whips the .38 across his face. He winces and staggers back toward a fish tank. She grabs the lapel of his jacket and stops him from falling.

She pulls him close. "Do you get it now?"

"I think so," Mike whimpers.

She puts the gun under his chin. "Do you get it?" she insists.

"I get it," he bleats and then he actually starts to cry.

She takes off his ski mask and lets the gun fall to her side. She looks at him and holds the moment for a beat, two, three.

"Close your eyes," she says.

He closes them, and she takes off her ski mask, pulls his head down, and leans her forehead against his.

"Don't you see? I'm saving you, Michael," she says very softly. "I'm saving you and your family."

He nods.

He understands now. Forehead against forehead. Victim and accomplice. Accomplice and victim.

"It's going to be OK," she whispers.

"Are you sure?" he asks.

"Yes," she says. "I promise."

She puts her ski mask back on and hands Mike his mask.

She glares at Pete. "What the hell's the matter with you? Get it together," she hisses.

A dog appears from a side door, a big tawny-brown Alsatian. It freezes when it sees them. "Hey, boy," Pete says. The dog comes over and sniffs Pete's hand and likes what it smells there.

He pats it on the head. It sniffs Rachel and Mike and, satisfied, heads for the kitchen.

A TV is blaring from a room at the front of the house.

They follow the sound down a corridor hung with more family portraits.

In the living room, they find a large man snoozing on a recliner in front of Fox News. A jowly, powerful, fallen man taken down by events, like Gulliver.

He was reading the Bible. It has slipped to the floor next to him. There's a gun in his lap.

Rachel nods at Pete.

Pete carefully lifts the gun and puts it in his own jacket pocket. "Is that Seamus Hogg?" Rachel whispers.

Mike nods.

Rachel picks up the Bible.

He was reading Deuteronomy.

Now, she thinks, *it is time to teach him a new religion.*

41

Empty beach. Indifferent sky. Waves iterating on the cold black ocean.

Rachel walks up the back steps of the Appenzellers' home.

From the outside, the house looks deserted.

In through the kitchen.

To the top of the basement steps.

"Kylie?"

Voices down below.

Dutch angle. Tight on Rachel's face. Jesus. What now?

She takes out the .38, levels it in front of her, and walks downstairs.

Kylie and Amelia are in the dome tent.

They are playing Operation. Kylie isn't wearing her ski mask. They are eating potato chips and Amelia is laughing her head off.

This is the first time Rachel has heard her laugh.

She sits down on the basement steps and puts away the gun.

She wants to be angry at Kylie for not following the protocol. But she can't be. Kylie is looking after the little girl the way a human being should care for another human being.

Kylie has more empathy than she does. Kylie is braver than her.

Rachel goes back upstairs.

She puts the gun on the kitchen table and sits.

She is filled with self-hatred and revulsion. None of this would have happened if she had been a better mom.

For a moment she wonders what it would feel like to put the barrel of the nine-millimeter in her own mouth. That cool carbon steel resting on her tongue as if it belonged there. The thought scares her, and she pushes the weapon away.

"When is this going to end?" she whispers to the darkness.

The darkness keeps its own counsel.

42

Seamus Hogg has been thoroughly educated. He gets it now. He makes a plan and executes it rapidly. Apparently, he's a quick study in the child-abduction business. He drives to Enfield, Connecticut, and waits outside a football field for a fourteen-year-old boy named Gary Bishop who plays defensive tackle.

Rachel doesn't know much about football, but she knows that defensive tackles are big. That worries her, but the target has been approved by the Wickr contact. How carefully do they vet these things? Do they even care if it all goes wrong? Do they occasionally long for it all to go wrong? What is the psychology of a monster?

She looks at the clock above the tide marker.

It says 6:01 p.m.

She goes outside to wait on the deck.

Kylie's in the living room doing her homework. Pretending everything is normal, sitting there doing her math but letting out little whimpers. Rachel wants to sit with her, but Kylie says no. Rachel watches her through the glass. An OK day at school, she said. She looked terrible and had no trouble convincing anyone that she had been ill.

Pete is over at the Appenzellers' house with Amelia. Amelia is in her princess tent playing Operation by herself now. Amelia hates Rachel. She told Pete that. "Don't want the lady. I hate her."

Rachel doesn't blame her in the slightest.

Rachel looks at her phone and the burner phone next to it on the deck: 7:15.

If it all gets screwed up again, could the Dunleavys be trusted to kill Henry Hogg and wipe the slate clean?

If they can't, will she have to kill little Amelia over there at the Appenzellers'? Kill that terrified, sad, lovely little girl in the tent? The .38 revolver is in the pocket of her robe. It'll have to be her. Letting Pete do it would be a cop-out. Pete had, she knew, actually shot people. Possibly killed people. In Afghanistan he had been in several firefights, and in Iraq he'd been in too many to count.

But she had brought him in. So it had to be her. No choice.

She'd ask Pete to wait in the kitchen and she'd go down the basement steps in her socks. Amelia wouldn't hear her approach across the concrete floor. She'd shoot Amelia in the back of the head while she played. Amelia would never know what happened. Existence to nonexistence just like that.

Killing a child—the worst thing anyone could ever do.

But better that than have Kylie sucked back into the void.

Rachel begins to cry. Great waves of anguish and anger. Did this make them smile? Forcing virtuous people to do terrible things? Every human being walking this earth can be forced to violate his or her deepest beliefs and principles. Isn't that hilarious?

She waits until 7:25 before phoning the Dunleavys. "Well?"

"We've just called Seamus Hogg. The kidnap was successful. The kid was almost no trouble at all. He got him."

"That's great."

"How's Amelia?"

"Amelia's fine. Playing Operation again. Safe." Rachel hangs up.

She walks to her bedroom and sits on the edge of the bed.

She puts the .38 on the dresser, lets the hammer down gently, puts the safety back on, unclicks the cylinder, removes the bullets, puts them in the dresser drawer, and breathes.

An hour later the Wickr app on Rachel's phone chimes. Her contact informs her that she can release Amelia Dunleavy.

With only a slight hiccup, The Chain is marching on its merry way.

Rachel calls Helen Dunleavy on a burner phone.

"Hello?"

"We're going to release Amelia in the next thirty minutes. Will call with instructions," Rachel says and hangs up.

She goes to the Appenzellers' house and puts on her ski mask, and she and Pete unchain little Amelia and get her out of the basement. They put on gloves and Rachel dresses her in a brand-new fingerprint-free pair of jeans and a sweater. When the coast is clear, they drape a towel over her head and move her to the back seat of Pete's pickup.

They drive her to the playground at Rowley Common and get her out of the car. They tell her to keep the towel on for a count of sixty and then play on the swings until her mom comes to pick her up. They leave her with a wiped-down Mr. Boo and a toy octopus she has become particularly fond of.

They park the Dodge across the street from the common

and Pete watches Amelia through binoculars while Rachel calls the Dunleavys. She reminds them about The Chain and the blowback and the terrible consequences of releasing their victim early or of anybody talking. They have already been given this speech by the voice of The Chain, and they assure her that they will do the right thing.

Rachel tells them where their daughter is and hangs up.

She and Pete wait in the Dodge Ram.

A little girl left by herself on the swings in the gathering dark in early twenty-first-century America. How scary is that?

Five minutes go by.

Amelia gets bored.

She gets off the swings and walks to the edge of Route 1A. Cars are roaring by at fifty miles an hour.

"Damn it!" Pete says.

Rachel's heart is in her mouth.

There are other people in the park now, a couple of teenage boys in hoodies. "She's going to get herself killed," Pete says.

"I'll handle it," Rachel replies. She puts her ski mask back on. She gets out of the car and runs over the road to Amelia. "Amelia, this road is dangerous. I told you to wait by the swings! Your mommy and daddy will be here in five minutes."

"I don't want to play on the swings," Amelia says.

"If you don't go over to the swings, Amelia, I'm going to tell your mommy and daddy you don't want them to come for you, and they won't come!"

"Would you really do that?" Amelia asks, suddenly frightened.

"Yes! I would," Rachel says. "Now go play on the swings."

"You are such a meanie! I hate you!"

Amelia turns and begins walking back to the playground.

Rachel sprints over the road before the teenagers register the ski mask and maybe begin wondering if something is wrong. When she's sure they aren't looking in her direction, she gets in the Dodge.

Amelia sits glumly on the swings by herself as the two teenagers go into the playhouse, apparently to light up a joint.

Time crawls by.

Finally the Dunleavys pull up in their car and run to their daughter and hug her and cry.

And it's done.

The spotlight is off them and they can only hope that the people farther along The Chain don't screw everything up and send it spiraling back toward them again.

They drive home to check on Kylie and then go straight to the Appenzellers' to remove all traces of their presence there. They clean out the basement and take down the board over the basement window, return the mattress to the upstairs bedroom, scrub away the prints. They put the mechanism into the back door and lock it as best as they can. The Appenzellers will definitely notice that something is wrong with it when they return in the spring, but spring is a long way away.

They drive the garbage to a dump in Lowell. When they get back, it's late, but Kylie is still awake.

"It's over," Rachel says. "The little girl is back with her parents."

"Is it really over?" Kylie asks.

Rachel banishes all uncertainty from her voice and looks Kylie straight in her big brown eyes.

"Yes," she says.

Kylie bursts into tears and Rachel hugs her.

They order pizza and Rachel lies next to Kylie until she falls asleep. When Kylie is finally down for the count, Rachel texts her oncologist that she'll call her in the morning. She hopes she isn't dying. That would be the kicker to all of this.

She goes downstairs. Pete's outside in his sweats chopping firewood. There are now half a dozen stacks of wood, each about six feet high. Definitely enough firewood to get through the winter and a zombie apocalypse or two. He comes in with a bundle of wood and lights a fire in the grate.

Rachel gets him a Sam Adams and he pops it and sits with her on the sofa. Something stirred in her when she saw Pete chopping that wood. Something ridiculously silly and primal.

She's never known Pete well enough to have a crush on him. He's always been away somewhere. Iraq, Camp Lejeune, Okinawa, Afghanistan, or just traveling. He's very different from Marty. Taller, leaner, darker, moodier, quieter. Marty is handsome from fifty paces; Pete is more of an acquired taste. They don't look alike or act alike. Pete is introspective; Marty's an extrovert. Marty is the life and soul of the party; Pete is the guy in the corner browsing the bookshelf, checking his watch to see if he can quietly slip away.

Pete finishes the beer in one gulp and gets another. She lights him a Marlboro from Marty's emergency bar-exam carton. "And we have this," she says, producing a bottle of twelve-year-old Bowmore. She pours them two fingers each.

"This is good," Pete says. He likes this feeling. This little booze buzz. He'd forgotten what that felt like. It's a completely different type of high than you get with the opiates. Heroin is a protective blanket you throw over yourself. The most beautiful blanket in the world, a blanket that eases the pain and lets you sink into an autumnal universe of bliss.

Booze brings you out of yourself. Or it brings him out, anyway. And yet he doesn't quite trust these emotions.

"I'll just check the doors," he says, clearing his throat. He gets up abruptly, takes the nine-millimeter from his bag, patrols the perimeter, and locks the doors.

Task completed, he has no choice but to sit back down on the sofa. He makes a decision. Time for him to tell Rachel the truth about himself. Both big secrets. "There's something you should know about me," he starts hesitantly.

"Oh?"

"It's about the Marines. I was . . . I was honorably discharged, but it was a close-run thing. I avoided a court-martial by a whisker for what happened at Bastion."

"What are you talking about?"

"September fourteenth, 2012," he says in a monotone.

"In Iraq?"

"Afghanistan. Camp Bastion. The Taliban dressed in U.S. Army uniforms and infiltrated the perimeter fencing and got onto the base and started shooting up planes and tents. I was the duty officer of the engineering unit at hangar twenty-two. Except, well, except I wasn't on duty. I was high in my tent. Just pot. But still. I'd left a senior sergeant in charge."

Rachel nods.

"When I got over there, all hell had broken loose. Tracers and RPGs and total confusion. RAF guards shooting at Marines shooting at army. There were these private security contractors who just happened to be there, and they prevented a massacre. Never in a million years would I have thought that a Taliban team could penetrate that deep into the base. Prince Harry from England was there that night. The VIP area was two hundred meters from the firefight. It was a complete disaster, as you can imagine, and I owned a big chunk of it."

"Pete, come on, that was six years ago," Rachel protests.

"You don't understand, Rach. Marines died, and I played a part in that. They punished me under Article Fifteen, but it would have been a GCM if they hadn't been worried about the publicity. I quit anyway a couple of years later. Six years before my twenty. No real pension or benefits. What a complete asshole."

She leans forward and kisses him gently on the lips.

"It's OK," she says.

The kiss takes his breath away.

You're very beautiful, he wants to say but can't. She's exhausted, thin, and frail but still gorgeous. That isn't the problem. The problem is articulating the feeling. He feels his cheeks redden and he looks away.

She pushes back a strand of dark hair from his furrowed brow.

She kisses him again, this time more seriously. It's something she has been wanting to do. She's worried it will be anticlimactic.

It isn't.

His lips are soft but his kiss is strong and powerful. He tastes of coffee, cigarettes, Scotch, and other good things.

Pete kisses her back hungrily, but then after a minute, he hesitates.

"What?"

"I don't know if I can," he says softly.

"What do you mean? Don't you find me—"

"It's not that. That's not it at all. You're incredibly hot."

"I'm skin and bones, I—"

"No, you look amazing. It's not that."

"What is it, then?"

"I haven't . . . for a long time . . ." he says. It isn't really a lie. He's thinking about the second big secret—the heroin—and wondering whether he will be able to perform.

"I'm sure it will all come roaring back," Rachel says as she leads him to the bedroom.

She takes off her clothes and lies on the bed.

She doesn't know it but she's wildly sexy, Pete thinks. Brown hair, long, long legs.

"Come on," she says teasingly. "Is that a pistol in your pocket or are you just . . . oh, it is a pistol."

Pete puts the nine-millimeter on the bedside table and takes off his T-shirt.

When he drops his sweats, he's somewhat surprised to see that everything is in full working order.

"Well, well, well," Rachel says.

Pete grins. *That's a relief,* he thinks, and climbs into bed next to her.

It's pure we-survived-the-plane-crash sex.

Frantic, fraught, desperate, hungry.

Twenty minutes later, she climaxes and he climaxes.

A spectacular oasis after months of drought.

"So that was . . ." Pete says.

"Yeah," Rachel agrees.

She goes to get the cigarettes and Scotch. "And also, you know, weird," she says. "Even perverted. I mean, Christ, two brothers, who does that?"

"Just stay away from my father. I don't think his heart could take it."

"That is so gross."

Pete gets up, walks to the living room, and thumbs through her vinyl collection, which is mostly Motown and jazz. Her CDs are all Max Richter and Jóhann Jóhannsson and Philip Glass.

"My God, Rachel, ever hear of a thing called rock and roll?"

He puts on Sam Cooke's *Night Beat*.

When he comes back to the bed, she clearly sees the track marks on his arms.

It isn't a surprise. She suspected something like this. She touches the track lines and then, gently, kisses him.

"If you're going to stay here, you'll need to be clean," she says.

"Yeah," he agrees.

"No, Pete, I'm serious. You gave Amelia the wrong food. You gave the gun to Mike Dunleavy. You need to be off that shit."

Pete can feel the force of her gaze.

He's ashamed of himself.

"I'm sorry. I'm so, so sorry. You're right. You deserve it and Kylie deserves it. This isn't just about me anymore. I'll get clean."

"You need to promise me, Pete."

"I promise."

"Chemo isn't the same thing, but I got through some hard times. I'll be there to help."

"Thank you, Rach."

"What happened last night in East Providence? In Seamus Hogg's house? You were high?"

"No. Not high, but . . ."

"What?"

"On the tail end. I just wasn't thinking when I gave Mike Dunleavy that gun. I'm sorry. He could have killed us."

"But he didn't."

"No."

She climbs onto his chest and looks him in the eye.

"I couldn't have done this without you, Pete. I mean

228

that." She kisses him on the lips.

"It was you, honey, it was you who saved your family," Pete insists. "You did it. You can do anything."

"Ha! I've felt like such a failure these past few years. Waitressing and all those menial jobs so Marty could study for the bar. Even earlier. You know that when I was coaching Marty for the LSAT, I got one seventy on the practice test. He got one fifty-nine. I had all this potential, Pete. I blew it."

"You've turned everything around, Rach. It's amazing what you did, getting Kylie back," Pete tells her.

She shakes her head. It's a miracle that Kylie is back with them, and you don't congratulate yourself for a miracle.

Rachel puts her hand on his chest and feels his heart beating. Calm, slow, deliberate. He has three tattoos: an ouroboros serpent, the Marine Corps logo, and the Roman numeral V.

"What's the V stand for?" she asks.

"Five combat tours."

"The ouroboros?"

"To remind myself that there ain't nothing new under the sun. People have survived worse."

She sighs and kisses him again and feels him stirring underneath her. "It would be nice if this moment could last forever," Rachel says.

"It will," Pete replies happily.

No, Rachel thinks, *it won't*.

PART TWO

THE MONSTER IN THE LABYRINTH

43

A muddy hippie commune in Crete, New York, sometime in the late 1980s. It's a morning in early fall, gray and drizzling. The community is built around a series of decrepit farm buildings. It's been a going concern since the summer of 1974, but no one recruited since then has evidently had much competence in animal husbandry, agriculture, or even basic maintenance.

The name of the commune has changed several times over the previous decade and a half. It's been called the Children of Asterion, the Children of Europa, the Children of Love, and so on. But the name isn't important. When what takes place that particular fall morning makes it into the *New York Daily News* the attention-grabbing headline will simply read "Upstate Drug-Sex-Cult Massacre."

But for the moment all is peaceful.

A toddler maybe around two, a little boy named Moonbeam, is outside with his twin sister, Mushroom, and an assorted bunch of other toddlers, older kids, chickens, and dogs. They are playing in a muddy field behind the barnyard without adult supervision. The kids seem happy enough although they are all damp and dirty.

Inside the barn, a dozen or so young adults are sitting in a circle tripping on Orange Barrel and Clear Light LSD. At the end of the seventies, there would have been thirty or forty people in here, but that was the heyday for this kind of experiment in alternative living, and it was a long time ago. The eighties have a very different vibe and the commune is slowly dying.

The events of today will be its grisly final chapter.

A station wagon pulls up at the edge of the farmyard. An old man and a young man get out. The two men look at each other and put on ski masks. Both men are armed with ugly snub-nosed .38 Saturday-night-special revolvers.

The men walk into the barn and start asking the tripping young adults where Alicia is.

Nobody seems to know where Alicia is or even, indeed, *who* Alicia is.

"Let's try the house," the old man says.

They leave the barn, walk by a rusting tractor, and enter the massive old farmhouse.

The place is a maze, an obstacle course. Mattresses, furniture, clothes, toys, and games are strewn everywhere. The men draw their weapons and clear the rooms on the first and second floors.

The men look up the stairs to the third floor. Somewhere up there, music is playing.

The young man recognizes the album as *Sticky Fingers* by the Rolling Stones, which was one of Alicia's favorites.

As they climb the stairs, the music gets louder. They enter a large master bedroom at the bit where "Sister Morphine" transitions into "Dead Flowers."

They find Alicia, a young blond woman, naked with another young woman and a red-haired man with a ginger beard. They are in a large, old-fashioned four-poster bed.

Alicia and the bearded man are tripping. The other woman appears to be deeply asleep.

The old man kneels down next to Alicia, slaps her on the cheek, and tries to get her to respond. "Where are the kids, Alicia?" he asks, but she doesn't answer.

The young man shakes her and asks her the same thing, but she doesn't respond to him either.

Eventually he gives up asking.

The old man grabs a pillow and gives it to the young man.

The young man looks at the pillow and shakes his head.

"Only way to be safe," the old man says. "Lawyers will give them back to her."

The young man thinks about it for a while, nods, and then, reluctantly at first, but then with growing anger, starts smothering Alicia with the pillow. Alicia struggles, scratching at the young man's hands, thrashing her legs.

The bearded man comes to and sees what's happening.

"Hey, man!" he says.

The old man takes out the revolver and shoots the bearded man in the head, killing him instantly.

The young man drops the pillow and takes out his .38.

"Tom?" Alicia gasps.

The old man shoots her in the head too.

Despite all the commotion, the other young woman hasn't woken up, or perhaps she is pretending to be asleep. The old man shoots her anyway.

Feathers are flying and the sheets are drenched with blood.

The bathroom door opens and a naked young man enters the room holding a roll of toilet paper.

"What's going on?" he demands.

The old man takes careful aim and shoots the perplexed young man in the chest. It's a heart shot and it probably kills him, but the old man crosses the room and double taps him in the head anyway.

"Jesus, what a mess," Tom says.

"I'll take care of this while you look for the kids," the old man tells him.

Ten minutes later Tom finds Moonbeam and Mushroom playing in the dirt behind the barn. He takes them to the station wagon.

With a bowie knife, the old man has cut off four fingers on Alicia's left hand—the four fingers that scratched the young man and got his DNA on them.

He finds a jerrican of gasoline and trails gas all through the farmhouse. He wipes the jerrican with a handkerchief, goes to the kitchen sink, and pours himself a glass of water. He drinks the water and wipes the glass clean of prints.

He steps through the screen door, holds the door open with his foot, lights a book of matches, and throws it onto the kitchen floor.

A line of scarlet flame races across the linoleum.

The old man joins Tom back at the station wagon.

They drive away from the commune, the old man at the wheel, Tom in the back with the kids.

They don't meet any other cars on the narrow road that leads away from the farm—which is fortunate for everyone.

Tom looks through the rear window to see the farmhouse erupting in flames.

They drive for forty minutes, until they encounter a reservoir. The old man stops the station wagon, gets out, cleans both pistols and the bowie knife with a handkerchief.

He adds the bowie knife to the paper bag containing Alicia's fingers. He pokes a hole in the bag and throws the bag and both pistols into the glassy water.

They sink immediately.

Three sets of ripples in the pond intersect briefly like the triple spiral one finds at the entrance to passage graves in Neolithic Europe.

The spirals fade and the black water is still again.

"Come on," the old man says. "Let's go."

44

A blizzard. Cold. The bundles at her feet are birds who have frozen and fallen from the trees. Snow stings her face but she can barely feel it. She is here and not here. She is watching herself in a cinema of confession.

All she's trying to do is get back to the house from the mailbox. But she can't see through the white translucent depths of Old Point Road.

She doesn't want to take a wrong turn and wander into the marsh. She walks gingerly in her bedroom slippers and her robe.

Why is she so underdressed? Underprepared? Unready?

The marsh waits for her to fill an absence. *You owe the void a life because you got your daughter back.*

On the water ducks raise an alarm. Something is lurking out there on the edge of the tidal basin.

The wind swirls the snow in front of her. What possessed her to come out in weather like this?

The whiteness darkens into the shape of a creature. A man. The curve in the hood of his coat makes it seem like he has horns.

Maybe he does have horns. Maybe he has the body

of a man and the face of a bull.

He comes closer.

No, it is a man. He is wearing a long black coat and he is carrying a gun. The gun is pointed at her chest. "I'm looking for Kylie O'Neill," he says.

"She's not home—she, she, she went to New York," Rachel stutters.

The man raises the gun . . .

She wakes with a start.

The bed's empty. Pete is gone. The house is quiet. She's had this dream before. Variations on a theme. You don't need to be a genius to interpret this nightmare: You are in debt. You will always be in debt. You owe. Once you are on The Chain, you are on forever. And if you even think about trying to emancipate yourself, the blowback will come for you.

It's like her cancer.

It will always be there, lurking in the background, for the rest of her life. For the rest of all their lives.

Cancer.

Yeah.

She looks at the pillow, and sure enough, there are a few dozen brown and black hairs and—oh, how charming—quite a few gray ones now too.

When she'd gone to see her oncologist on that fateful Tuesday morning, Dr. Reed had immediately sent her for an MRI. The results were sufficiently concerning for Dr. Reed to recommend a surgical intervention that afternoon.

It was the same cream-colored room at Mass. General.

The same kind Texan anesthetist.

The same no-nonsense Hungarian surgeon.

Even the same Shostakovich symphony playing in the background.

"Honey, everything's going to be just dandy. I'm going to count down from ten," the anesthetist said.

Come on, who says "just dandy" anymore, Rachel thought.

"Ten, nine, eight . . ."

The surgery was declared a success. She would "require only one cycle of adjuvant chemotherapy," which was easy for Dr. Reed to say because she didn't have to go through it. She didn't have to have the poison dripped into her veins.

Still, once every two weeks for four months is something Rachel can handle. Nothing is all that terrible now that her little girl is back again.

She brushes the hairs off the pillow and the bad dream from her mind. She can hear Kylie upstairs above her in the shower. Kylie used to sing in the shower. She doesn't do that anymore.

Rachel pulls back the blinds and picks up the mug of coffee Pete left for her by the bed. It looks like a nice morning. She's surprised to see that there's no snow. The dream felt so real. The bedroom faces east toward the tidal basin. She takes a sip of coffee, slides the glass doors open, and goes out onto the deck. It's crisp and cool, and the mudflats are full of wading birds.

She sees Dr. Havercamp walking through the dunes in front of the house. He waves and she waves back. He disappears behind a large beach plum bush from which this island and the one in New York got its name. The beach plums are ripe now. They'd made jars of preserved plums last fall, selling them at the farmers' market. She and Kylie split the proceeds. *Vineland Jam Corporation,* Kylie had called it, writing that on the homemade labels. Kylie had loved the fact that dangerous piratical Vikings had maybe made it as far south as Plum Island. Those were days when you could long for danger from a place of safety.

Rachel tightens the belt on the robe and goes into the living room. "Honey, do you want me to make you breakfast?" she calls to her daughter.

"Toast, please," Kylie says from somewhere upstairs.

Rachel pads into the kitchen and puts two slices of bread in the toaster.

"Happy Thanksgiving," someone says behind her.

"Shit!" she says, spinning around and holding up the bread knife.

Stuart comically puts his hands in the air.

"Stuart, I'm so sorry, I didn't know you were over," Rachel says.

"You can put the knife down now, Mrs. O'Neill," Stuart replies, faking terror.

"Sorry about the S-word too. Don't tell your mother."

"It's fine. I might have heard that word once or twice before in various, um, contexts."

"Would you like some toast?"

"No, thanks. I just came by to say hi to Kylie before you guys leave."

Rachel nods and makes some toast for Stuart anyway. She and Kylie and Pete are going to Boston for Thanksgiving. Thanksgiving was only two days after a chemo Tuesday, so Marty had stepped into the breach and invited them all to his place for the holiday.

It's OK. Everything is OK.

Rachel makes two more slices of toast, puts them on a plate.

Pete comes in from his run, looking breathless but happy. He's been running a lot the past two weeks and getting stronger. The VA in Worcester got him into a methadone program, which allows him to ease the opiates out of his system gradually. It's working so far. And it would have to

241

keep working. Her family is the priority. Pete knows that.

Pete kisses her on the lips.

"Good run?" she asks.

He looks at her. He can tell. "Bad dream?" he whispers.

She nods. "The same," she says.

"You should talk to someone."

"You know I can't."

They can tell no one that they have gone through the looking glass and into the world where nightmares are real.

Pete gets himself coffee and sits next to Rachel at the living-room table.

He had never formally asked to move in. He had driven to Worcester and brought the stuff he'd wanted—which wasn't a whole lot—and then just sort of stayed.

Out of the three of them, Pete perhaps is doing best.

If he has bad dreams he doesn't mention them, and the methadone keeps away the worst of his cravings.

Out of the three of them, Kylie is definitely doing the worst.

That night at the Appenzellers', Kylie went down to little Amelia. The girl had woken up and Kylie had comforted her and told her that everything was going to be all right. But that isn't the point. The point is that she went down there. She was part of the apparatus keeping Amelia prisoner. Thus Kylie had been both victim and abuser. Like all of them. Victims and accomplices. That's what The Chain does to you. It tortures you and then makes you complicit in the torture of others.

Kylie hasn't wet the bed since she was four years old. Now nearly every single morning, the sheets are soaked.

When she dreams, the dreams are always the same—she's thrown in a dungeon and left to die alone.

Everything is changed on Plum Island. Kylie doesn't walk

to school or to the store or anywhere by herself.

Before, they seldom locked the doors; now they always do. Pete has reinforced and changed all the locks. He cleared Rachel's devices of spyware and his friend Stan came in and professionally debugged the house and put coin-size GPS trackers in Kylie's shoes. They monitor Kylie constantly when she goes anywhere, especially when she stays with her dad in the city.

Kylie knows she can't tell her father about what happened. Not her father, not Stuart, not the school counselor, not her grandmother. Nobody. But Marty is no fool and he sees that something is wrong. Maybe something to do with a boy? He isn't going to press it. He's having his own problems. Tammy had suddenly moved back to California to take care of her mother who had recently been in an accident. Tammy wasn't interested in a bicoastal relationship. A few curt e-mails, and just like that, so long, Marty.

Pete wasn't too surprised. Marty had bailed Tammy out of bankruptcy, restored her credit, sorted out all her legal woes, and then she'd said, *Thank you very much, I'm off to the coast.* She socially engineered them, Pete thinks. He's seen Tammy's type before; in fact, he married a girl almost exactly like Tammy. And he knows plenty of male Tammys.

Kylie finally comes downstairs. She's changed out of her pajamas into sweats and a T-shirt.

Rachel knows what that means. Her pajamas are in the laundry basket.

"Oh, hi, Stuart," Kylie says.

She looks so very sad. Thanksgiving will hopefully give her something else to think about. Rachel watches her while pretending to look through her philosophy books. Stuart is talking and Kylie is giving him vague, halfhearted answers.

Finally Stuart says goodbye; they all have breakfast and then get dressed.

At one o'clock, Pete drives them down to Marty's new place in Longwood, which is almost within home-run range of Fenway Park. Good neighborhood. Lawyers, doctors, accountants. White picket fences, well-kept lawns. "Whatever Marty's giving you in child support, ask for more," Pete says, parking the Dodge.

Marty hasn't even tried to cook. He ordered in everything from a gourmet-delivery app, which is fine. The house is barely furnished and he does not have a new girlfriend in tow, which surprises Rachel a little. Marty always seemed to be a plan A and plan B kind of guy.

They get the lowdown on Tammy's sudden departure and Marty's career. He's upset about Tammy breaking up with him via text message and then ghosting him from California, but Marty's not one to let something like that get him down. He riffs about clients, tells a hilarious story about a will reading, and then does some of his better lawyer jokes.

He doesn't ask about Kylie's school. He already knows about the collapse in grades and he thinks it's best not to bring it up.

Kylie is distant, and Rachel is too exhausted to say anything, but for once Pete keeps up his end of the conversation. He says he's thinking of kayaking up the Intracoastal Waterway and he talks about the intricacies of the Cape Cod canal and the Chesapeake.

Rachel's mom calls from Florida, and Marty insists on speaking to her. There's a heart-in-mouth moment when Marty asks her about *Hamilton,* but Judith remembers to lie about that.

Judith tells Rachel privately that she needs to make a clean break from that awful O'Neill family, and Rachel listens, agrees, wishes her a happy Thanksgiving, and hangs up.

"What did you do for Thanksgiving last year, Uncle Pete?" Kylie asks.

"I was in Singapore traveling. Didn't do much. Couldn't get turkey."

"What was your last proper Thanksgiving at home? With family?" Rachel wonders.

Pete thinks about it. "It's been a few years. The last Thanksgiving I remember was in Okinawa at Camp Butler. Mess hall had turkey and mashed potatoes. It was pretty good."

Rachel listens and smiles. She holds Kylie's hand under the table and moves the food around on her plate and pretends to eat. She looks at Kylie—now laughing at her dad's jokes but almost always on the verge of tears. She looks at Pete—broody and quiet but trying his damnedest to keep the convo going. She looks at Marty—handsome and ebullient and funny. Tammy is an idiot. Marty's a keeper.

She excuses herself to go to the restroom.

She catches her reflection in the hallway mirror.

She's fading away again. Dissolving into the background. She goes into the bathroom and plucks at that annoying red thread on her favorite red sweater.

She sits there on the toilet with her head in her hands, thinking.

The bell sounds on her phone. A new message on the encrypted Wickr app. She had only gotten messages from one person on Wickr: the Unknown Caller. The Chain.

She opens the message.

You have a lot to be thankful for this year, Rachel. We have given you back your daughter. We have given you back your life. Be thankful for our mercy and remember that once you are on The Chain, you are on it forever. You are not the first and you will not be the last. We are watching, we are listening; we can come for you at any time.

Rachel drops the phone and stifles a scream.

She bursts into tears. It will never be over. Never.

She sinks to the floor and after a few seconds remembers to breathe.

She weeps and washes her face and flushes the toilet and takes a deep breath and rejoins her family.

Everyone looks at her. Everyone knows that she has been crying. Two of them guess the reason why.

45

Fifty-Five Fruit Street, Boston, Mass.

She tells them not to come. She wants them to come, but she always tells them not to. Pete has to drive her, of course, but there's no reason Kylie and Marty have to be there.

As ex-husbands go, Marty is pretty high up there.

They wait outside in the family room.

The family room is fine. There's a TV tuned to CNN and a stack of *National Geographic*s going back to the 1960s. There's a view of Boston Harbor. You can just see the USS *Constitution*.

She's glad they aren't in here to watch her gasp in pain when the nurse accesses the port or to see her when the poisons flow and the shivering begins and the nausea makes the room spin.

Chemo is a little death that you invite in in order to keep the big death waiting outside on the porch.

When the humiliation and the agony are done, they wheel her into the recovery room and they smile at her. Hugs from Kylie and Pete. Marty talking a mile a minute.

That's what you need. Family. Friends. Support.

Dr. Reed is happy with her treatment. And her prognosis is good. And the trajectory is pointing to the upper right of the chart.

But the terrible secret truth is that she isn't doing well.

Her body is failing.

She's getting weaker.

And she knows it isn't the cancer that's consuming her. That isn't the big C.

Not the cancer.

It.

The Chain.

46

A family has just finished moving into a house in Bethesda, Maryland. It's been a long day but now the delivery guys are gone and all the boxes are inside.

The family are posing for a photo outside their new home. A happy family in sunlit suburbs. Imagine an early-1990s version of Robert Bechtle's painting *'61 Pontiac,* except the kids are the same age. Twins. The husband, Tom Fitzpatrick, is a small, trim, dark-haired man in a white shirt and thin black tie. He looks rather like the first Darrin on *Bewitched.* He seems harmless enough. His new wife, Cheryl, is pregnant. She has long, straight golden hair and bangs that hover a couple of inches above her pretty brown eyes. Without straining the analogy, you could say that she has a bit of a Samantha Stephens vibe.

The little boy, Moonbeam, is now called Oliver. A chubby, harmless-looking kid with maybe a slightly eerie unblinking intensity about him. The girl, Mushroom, is called Margaret. She too does the eerie unblinking thing, but you don't notice as much with her curly red hair and perpetual-motion antics. If Tom were one for taking his kids to head doctors, Margaret would probably be on Ritalin, but Tom is not one for doctors. He's old-fashioned like that. "You don't need a pill for every ill," his father says.

Two days after they move in, they hold a housewarming party and invite all the neighbors. There are congressional aides living on this street, employees of the State Department, the Treasury Department.

There are three parties taking place in the house at the same time that night. There is the party where the men are getting to know one another. Tom comes off OK. He seems like a square, boring kind of a guy with his GI Joe hair and pocket protector and fridge full of Coors Light.

There's the women's party. Cheryl seems pretty and dull and maybe a bit simple. Cheryl is a typical suburban mom who had her own dreams but who has given them up to be a supportive wife. Cheryl wanted to be a baker like her grandfather.

And then there's the kids' party taking place in the TV room. The kids' party is the most interesting. The boys are dissecting the record collection and declaring it lame: John Denver, Linda Ronstadt, Juice Newton, the Carpenters. The girls are spilling the family secrets. Ted's dad is a drunk who is having an affair with his secretary. Mary's mom crashed her car two years ago and killed a woman on a bicycle. Janine's mom thinks the neighborhood has gone straight to hell now that an Indian family has moved in.

As the party continues well past the kids' bedtimes, Oliver is informed that the Jets and the Giants both suck but the Giants suck more because they're in the same division as the Redskins.

Oliver says that he doesn't even really like football. A ten-year-old boy named Zachary tells Oliver that he is a little queer who smells. Zachary also informs him that his mom looks like a whore.

Oliver calmly tells the boy that his mom is dead. His mom was murdered and her body was mutilated and then burned in a fire.

Zach looks pale. He looks even paler a minute after Margaret dares him to drink half a can of beer she found. Zachary chugs the can and says he has drunk beer before. That might be the case, but not beer laced with a teaspoon of ipecac syrup.

Zach begins projectile vomiting, and this effectively puts an end to the party.

47

She stares at the computer screen. A blank page, a winking cursor.

It's a frosty December morning, an hour from high tide. The tidal basin is filled with wintering geese and eider.

She takes a deep breath and types: *Lecture 2: Introduction to Existentialism. The existentialists believed that our lives are an attempt to impose meaning on an existence where there is no meaning. For them this world is an ouroboros—a serpent that eats itself. Patterns repeat. There is no progress. Civilization is a rope bridge dangling over an abyss.*

She shakes her head. Wrong tone. She clicks Delete and watches her hard work vanish in an instant.

Kylie comes downstairs in her new red coat. She looks happy today. She, like her mother, is getting good at faking happy. A little turned-up-corner-of-the-mouth smile and a phony lilt to the voice. But the eyes tell a different story.

She'd been having a lot of stomach cramps lately. The doctors haven't found anything. They say it's probably stress. Stress that doubles her up in pain and gives her nightmares and causes her to wet the bed.

She puts a brave face on it, but Rachel knows.

"Can we go?" Kylie asks.

"Sure. This isn't working anyway," Rachel says and shuts the laptop.

"Just give me five minutes to shower and we can head out," Pete says.

"We probably shouldn't be late," Kylie replies.

"If he says five minutes, he means five minutes," Rachel says. On a planet filled with unreliable men—fathers who desert their families, husbands who run off with younger women—Pete is someone who won't let you down. Still, she isn't going to allow an addict to share a house with her daughter, so she makes sure that Pete is religiously following his methadone program. He is, and shoring up his responsible-provider street cred, he has taken a security-guard gig to pay off his sudden massive credit-card debt.

Exactly five minutes later they are in the Volvo traveling into town. They park at the Starbucks, and Rachel hugs a hot tea in a window seat while Kylie and Pete go off to get a few things.

It's a busy Saturday morning, and Newburyport is full of locals and tourists. Marty is picking them up soon with his new girlfriend. Of course he has a new girlfriend. The plan B at last. But rather than rendezvousing on Plum Island, they are meeting in the safer, more neutral Starbucks in Newburyport.

As soon as Kylie is out of sight, Rachel takes her phone and checks the app for the GPS tracker in Kylie's shoes. Yup, there she is, walking up High Street and turning left to go into the Tannery. Every child of every parent is a hostage to fortune, but not every parent has been reminded of this so vividly.

She sees Pete across the street carrying a whole bunch of

shopping bags. She waves to him and he enters the Starbucks and kisses her on the cheek.

"What did you get?" she asks.

"A few things for Kyles."

"I hope you didn't spend too much money, you've already done more than—"

"Shhh," Pete says. "One of my great frickin' joys in this life is getting presents for my niece."

They sit there and talk and wait for Marty. He's late, as usual.

"Finally, here's the man himself," Pete says, tapping his watch and getting to his feet. "Of course this new girl is a beauty. And, oh my God, even younger than the last one, by the looks of it."

Marty comes in all smiles. He's wearing faded jeans, a V-necked gray T-shirt, and an Armani leather jacket. His hair is cut short and he's acquired a tan somewhere.

The girl is a spiky-blond-haired little thing. Shorter than Marty, unlike Tammy, but still gorgeous. Adorable upturned nose, dark blue eyes, dimples. She looks as if she's barely out of high school.

Introductions are made. Hands are shaken. Rachel deliberately doesn't bother to catch the name because she knows that this one is probably going to be succeeded by another one just like her a few weeks from now.

Kylie comes in and hugs her dad and shakes the new girlfriend's hand.

The new girlfriend says that Kylie looks very snuggly and hip in her red wool coat, which pleases Kylie.

They talk briefly and Rachel smiles and fades slowly into the background. How easy it is to fade when you are so light. When the only thing giving you substance is the poison in your veins.

"It's time to go," Marty says, and it's all hugs and kisses again and then they're off in Marty's white Mercedes.

"Kylie will be fine," Pete says over dinner that night. "She likes the new girlfriend."

"She shouldn't get too used to that one; there will probably be another even younger one next week," Rachel replies with a touch of bitterness, surprising herself a little.

After dinner, they check Kylie's location on the GPS (she's at Marty's house) and they FaceTime her.

Later, Pete goes to the bathroom to take his methadone. He has started mixing a little Mexican brown-tar heroin back into the methadone program, just to help get through the night.

Rachel doesn't know that but she has to take two Ambien and two fingers of Scotch to get any sleep these days. She sits down at the computer and tries to get back to the lecture she's writing but it isn't going anywhere. She watches YouTube, but even Ella Fitzgerald singing Cole Porter can't lift her spirits.

Blank page on the screen. Flashing cursor.

Rachel feeds the cat and decides to straighten up the house. Who can work in a dirty house?

She goes upstairs to Kylie's room and lifts the duvet from the bed. The sheets are soaking and the mattress is damp. She should have changed the bed this morning. This is now a nightly occurrence. No one sleeps. Everyone has bad dreams. Kylie goes to bed on two beach towels at her father's house so he won't find out.

Rachel sits on the edge of Kylie's mattress and puts her head in her hands. On the floor next to her feet, she sees Kylie's Moleskine notebook. She picks it up and fights the urge to look inside. This is Kylie's sacred, private space.

Don't open it, don't open it, don't—

She opens it and begins flipping the pages. There are drawings, journal entries, lists of favorite songs and movies, names for potential dogs, and so on, starting at the beginning of the year. All that stopped the day she was kidnapped. After that, the notebook has increasingly random violent scrawls, pages colored all black, a drawing of the basement where Kylie was held, and information on her kidnappers: *Man was possibly a teacher. Woman named Heather. Boy named Jared.* A reference to the Ultimate Houdini Magic Kit she had gotten as an early Christmas present and its tips on escaping from handcuffs. More black pages and spirals so heavily drawn that the page is torn. One of the last diary entries, from just two days ago, is an address for a website that discusses painless ways to kill yourself. *Pills? Drowning?* Kylie scrawled in the margin.

Rachel gasps.

"This is never going to end," she says to herself.

She goes downstairs to her computer and texts Kylie to ask how she's doing. Half an hour later, Kylie texts back that she's fine. They are all watching *The Maze Runner*.

Rachel closes her laptop and stares out at the dark.

"I'm going to do this," she whispers to the night.

Even though it had been thoroughly scrubbed clean of worms and spyware, she decides to get Pete's computer instead. She checks that the antivirus and antimalware programs are all running smoothly. They are. She runs a program that hides her IP address. She logs in to Tor. From Tor, she goes to Google and creates a fake identity—TheGirlCalledAriadne@gmail.com, because all the other versions of the name Ariadne are already taken.

She finds Google's blogger platform and logs in with her new fake e-mail address. She creates a blog with a minimalist template. She calls the blog *Information on The Chain*.

Its web address is simple: TheChainInformation.blogspot.com.

For the blog description, she writes: *This is a blog for anyone to leave anonymous tips or information on the entity known as The Chain. The comments section is open below. Please be careful. Anonymous comments only.*

Is there a way The Chain can track her down? She doesn't think so. They'll only uncover a fake person she has just made up. Even Google doesn't know who she is. *Create blog now?* Google asks her.

She clicks *Yes.*

48

It's moving day again. The year is 1997. The twins have a little brother now, Anthony. This time they're moving to a place called Anaheim. Tom has gotten a promotion. He's in charge of something. Something to do with drugs. It's going to be a high-stress job, he says, but he doesn't appear to be worried about it.

Oliver and Margaret have grown up to be normal-looking kids. Margaret has freckles and striking orangey-red hair like her grandfather but also like the man her mother was sleeping with at the commune. Oliver is plump with very pale skin and darker red hair. He still has the same unblinking intensity of eye that has unnerved people since he was a baby.

Their new street in Anaheim is almost a carbon copy of their street in Bethesda.

Little Anthony plays on the sidewalk with a whole bunch of new friends.

Oliver and Margaret watch from the upstairs window. They don't spend a lot of time with kids their age. Margaret is the more social of the two, but she doesn't want to abandon her twin brother.

Cheryl finds them in their bedroom.

"Come on, now, go outside like your little brother," she says.

The twins don't move.

Cheryl wants the house to herself so she can take a couple of diazepam and have a vodka tonic.

"Don't want to go outside," Oliver says.

"Do you want to go to Disneyland or not?" she asks.

"Yes," Oliver says.

"Then get the hell outside now and play like normal kids!" she says.

Their first day playing on the new street does not go well.

A little girl from across the road, the alpha girl, Jennifer Grant, bullies Margaret and makes her cry. She calls Margaret ugly and laughs at her because she doesn't know any of the skipping rhymes.

Oliver knows that he can't hit a girl, but he hits her anyway. Jennifer runs inside, and her older brother comes out of the house. He grabs Oliver by the throat and lifts him off the ground, shaking him and choking him at the same time. Oliver can't breathe, can't cry out. The older boy throws him to the asphalt, and Jennifer comes out of the house and crosses her arms and laughs, and so do some of the other kids. Even little Anthony, but you can't blame him for siding with the majority.

It's the kind of scene you'd see in an after-school special. It doesn't feel real. But it is real. And it's only a moment. Bored, the kids drift off to other diversions.

The twins slip back inside the house, hide in the garage, and wait for their father to get home.

He gets home late. He works in the FBI field office on Wilshire Boulevard, which is a hell of a commute.

At dinner that night, the twins don't mention the incident,

and Anthony has actually forgotten about it. Tom is full of chat. He talks about his new job and new opportunities. Cheryl reminds him that he wanted to tell the kids something. Tom grins and asks the kids if they want to go to Disneyland this very Saturday. They all say yes.

When Saturday comes, however, Tom has to work, but he tells them they'll do it the following weekend.

"I bet we never end up going," Margaret says prophetically to Oliver that night in their bedroom.

"I bet we don't," Oliver agrees.

"Does your neck still hurt?" Margaret asks.

"No," Oliver says, but she can tell that he's lying.

Margaret sits in bed reading one of the Baby-Sitters Club books. It's the one where Mary Anne gets one of those chain letters, and it really upsets her. Her friends tell her to rip up the chain letter and nothing bad will happen.

Mary Anne rips up the letter. Nothing bad happens. That's the problem with chain letters.

An idea occurs to Margaret.

The bad thing has to happen first.

The following Tuesday, Jennifer Grant's rabbit escapes from its hutch and runs away.

The next day at school, Jennifer finds a note in her lunch box: *Spill grape juice on yourself at lunchtime or your rabbit will die.*

In the cafeteria, in front of everyone, Jennifer spills grape juice on herself.

The notes continue.

The demands escalate.

Jennifer stands up and says "Shit" in class. She asks to go to the bathroom five times in one lesson.

The most disturbing one orders Jennifer to go outside naked at six in the morning and stand in front of her house for ten seconds. If she does that, her rabbit will be returned.

Jennifer stands outside the house naked for ten seconds, and a note in her cubby that day tells her where to find her dead rabbit.

Margaret and Oliver put the Polaroid they took of Jennifer naked under the chest of drawers in their room. No doubt it will come in useful later.

Life rolls on as normal. Little Anthony is adjusting well to his new school and his new friends. The twins finally seem to be settling in.

Cheryl is lonely and bored. She calls her mother, and her mother tells her to suck it up. Plenty of people have it worse. Cheryl continues to self-medicate with diazepam, vodka tonics, and Cuba libres.

Two months into the LA gig, Tom comes home drunk. He has dinged the car and is furious about it. Cheryl and he get into a big argument. Tom smacks her and she goes down like a ton of bricks.

Little Anthony starts to wail but Oliver and Margaret watch with cool indifference.

49

The therapist is in Brookline in a new office building over a store that sells bespoke umbrellas. *Très* hipster.

Rachel waits in a plush reception area and skims nervously through copies of British *Vogue*.

Rain lashes the windows, and the minute hand on the refurbished antique clock moves slowly. She stares at a reproduction of Manet's *Devant la glace*. A woman is looking in a mirror but you can't see her face, which Rachel thinks is somehow appropriate considering her own looking-glass phobia. The music being piped in is from one of the later Miles Davis albums. *You're Under Arrest,* she thinks, which is also some kind of ironic commentary on her situation.

Rachel wonders what Kylie is talking about. She's told Kylie that she can't mention The Chain or what happened to her, but she hopes that the therapist will give her strategies to cope with her suicidal thoughts, bed-wetting, and anxiety.

She and Kylie both know that it won't work but they still have to try. What else can they do?

Fifty minutes later, the therapist comes out and gives Rachel a little encouraging nod. The therapist seems to be in her midtwenties. *What does someone in her twenties know about the human heart or, indeed, anything?* Rachel thinks and smiles back.

During the car ride home, Kylie doesn't speak.

They drive over the PI bridge and along the turnpike and up the lane to the house. Rachel doesn't want to press her daughter, but Kylie has given her nothing.

"Well?" Rachel says at last.

"She asked if I was being sexually abused. I said no. She asked if I was being bullied at school. I said no. She asked if I was having boyfriend trouble. I said no. She says that I'm exhibiting the signs of someone who has gone through a physical trauma."

"Well, that's true. They did actually hit you."

"Yes. But I can't tell her that, can I? I can't tell anyone about that. I just had to sit there and lie about teenage problems and stress and worries about starting high school. I can't tell her that a policeman got murdered in front of me or that people put a gun in my face and threatened to kill me and my mom. I can't tell her that I had to lie on the floor with a little girl who had been kidnapped by my mom. And I can't tell her that they still might come back for us if we ever breathe a word of this," Kylie says and begins to cry.

Rachel reaches out to her as the rain hammers on the roof and pours down the windshield of the Volvo.

"We're trapped, aren't we, Mom? If we go to the police, you and Pete will go to prison for kidnapping. And they'll still try to kill us, won't they?"

There's nothing Rachel can say.

When they go inside, the house is cold and Pete is trying to fix the woodstove. "How did it go?" he asks.

She shakes her head. *Don't bring it up,* she mouths.

A silent dinner. Kylie moves the food around her plate.

Rachel's unable to eat. Pete's worried sick about both of them.

When Pete and Kylie go to bed, Rachel logs on to her blog. There is a new notification in the comments section. From Anonymous. She scrolls down the screen and reads the comment.

It says, *Delete blog* now *before they see it. Keep eye on personal column of* Boston Globe.

She doesn't need to be told twice. She logs in to Blogger and clicks *Delete blog.*

Are you sure you wish to erase this blog and all of its contents? Blogger asks her.

She clicks *Yes* and logs out.

50

Wednesday, 5:00 a.m. Rachel can't sleep.

She gets up, puts on her comfy red sweater and her robe, and makes some coffee. She sits in the dark living room for a while looking at the lights of the houses on the far side of the tidal basin.

Then she goes outside and waits. She plucks at that loose thread on her sweater. Eli the cat comes to investigate, and after accepting a few strokes, he slips off into the sand and reeds to war with the possums.

A bristle of alertness lights the nerve endings on the nape of her neck. This is an eons-deep response. Humans are both predators and prey.

The insistent pounding of her heart. The talismanic trembling of her limbs.

Today is going to be important.

The curtains are opening on the third act.

The morning sun is low and dim, and the air is cold but not bitingly so.

The smell of the marsh.

The sound of birds.

The yellow of a bicycle headlight on Old Point Road.

Little Paul Weston makes more or less directly for her house. Almost no one now gets home delivery of the *Globe*. Paul cycles down the lane. She waves from the stoop so as not to freak him out, but he's spooked anyway.

"Jesus, Mrs. O'Neill! You scared the life out of me," he says.

"Sorry, Paul. I couldn't sleep. Thought I'd wait for the paper."

Instead of throwing the *Globe* vaguely in the direction of the house he cycles up to her and puts it in her hand.

"Have a nice day," he says and bikes off.

She goes in, unfolds the paper on the living-room table, and turns on the main light.

She ignores the headlines and goes straight to the personal columns and the small ads. Despite Craigslist and eBay, the *Boston Globe* still has dozens of small ads every day.

She skims through the obits and love connections and car ads and finally finds what she's looking for under the heading Miscellaneous:

Chains bought and sold: 1-202-965-9970.

She wakes Pete and shows him the ad.

He shakes his head. "I don't know."

"We are going to do this," Rachel insists.

"Why?"

"Because it's never going to end unless we do something. It's killing Kylie and it's out there right now, stalking us, remembering us, and drawing in other families, other moms, other kids."

"You're talking like The Chain has a life of its own."

"That's exactly what it has. It's a monster demanding a human sacrifice every few days."

"I don't know, Rachel. Sleeping dogs."

"They're *not* sleeping. That's the issue. I'll call this number on a burner phone."

"Maybe I should call. I don't think anyone at The Chain knows my voice. If it's a trap, I mean."

"I'll disguise my voice. I'll do my grandmother's accent."

Pete gets the bag of burner phones from the closet and they select one at random and go onto the deck so as not to wake Kylie. Pete looks at the clock. It's only six thirty in the morning. "Too early to call someone?"

"I want to call before Kylie gets up."

Pete nods. He doesn't like any of this but it's Rachel's show and he just has to go along with it. She dials the number.

A male voice answers immediately: "Hello?"

"I'm callink about ze ad in ze paper," Rachel replies in an approximation of her grandmother's Polish accent.

"What about it?" the man asks.

"I've been having trouble with a chain and I vas vondering if you vere having ze same trouble and vhether ve could help each other," Rachel says.

There is a significant pause on the phone.

"Are you the one who wrote the blog?" he asks in a deep baritone that also has a tinge of a foreign accent to it.

"Yes."

Another long pause.

"I don't know if I can trust you. And you should be wary about trusting me. Don't give out any personal information at all, OK?" he says.

"OK."

"They could be listening. In fact, they could be you. Or me. Do you understand?"

"Yes."

"Do you really understand? The danger is real."

"I know. I've seen it up close," Rachel says, kind of abandoning the accent now.

A few seconds pass. Then: "Since you're calling yourself Ariadne, you can call me Theseus. Perhaps we shall go into the labyrinth together."

"Yes."

"I hope you are not a fool, Ariadne. Your blog was foolish. This call was foolish."

"I don't think I'm a fool. I'm just someone who wants to put a stop to this."

"That is ambitious. What makes you think you can stop this entity?"

She looks at Pete. "I've figured out a few things."

"Have you indeed? All right, Ariadne, this is what I want you to do. Go to Logan Airport today at noon. Buy a domestic ticket going anywhere that departs from terminal A. Go through security and wait in the departures lounge. I have the number of this phone. Bring it with you. I may call you; I may not. Trust no one, least of all me. Recall that one builds a labyrinth not to hide but to lie in wait."

The line goes dead.

"Well?" Pete asks.

"I'm going."

"Trust no one. Not even him."

"This needs to end. I'm going," she insists.

"No. You're not going. This is crazy."

Pete is genuinely concerned, but his misgivings are also partly due to his own difficulties. Rachel doesn't know that the methadone isn't fixing him as well as it should. When you're coming off pure golden-brown, high-altitude Mexican heroin, Bayer methadone is not the solution that the VA addiction-and-recovery counselors think it is.

He's jittery, buzzing, not thinking clearly. To take on

51

Rachel has never liked Logan. People are always on edge; 9/11 began here. The long lines. The bad vibes. The Red Sox merch.

She and Pete go to the Delta counter and buy tickets to Cleveland.

They go through security and wait. She has her sunglasses on and her Yankees cap pulled down low, as if that will help.

Noon comes and goes.

"What now?" Pete asks.

"I don't know," Rachel replies.

"Why don't you call the number from the paper?"

She waits five minutes and calls.

"I'm sorry but this number has been disconnected," an automated voice says.

Twelve thirty arrives, and finally her burner phone rings.

"Go to Legal's Test Kitchen near the Delta shuttle gates and order a Cthulhu black ale and a chowder. Come alone," the voice says.

"I'm with someone. He helped. We're in this together," she says.

"Hmmm. OK, order two Cthulhu ales and two chowders. Table number seventy-three seems to be available. It's a booth on the left-hand side."

"Then what?"

"Then we'll see, won't we?"

They go to Legal's, sit at table 73, and order the beers and two cups of clam chowder. They have the feeling that they are being watched, which, of course, they are.

"Who do you think it is?" Rachel asks, looking around at the customers and the staff. The place is packed. There are a lot of people glancing in her direction. It's impossible to tell which one is the one.

She pulls her cap lower.

"This is a bad idea. Now they know who we are but we don't know who they are," Pete mutters.

Rachel nods. Her instincts have been to trust this person, although why should she? Pete's paranoia would have been the safer default position.

But she is so desperately worried about Kylie. Every choice she has is a bad one. Action is bad. Inaction is bad. It is a classic zugzwang situation. You have parachuted into the minefield and there is no safe way out. Maybe this is how The Chain tests people, by sending someone out as bait for potential defectors? Any person in here could be The Chain's agent. And now she and Pete are going to have to—

A large man wearing glasses shuffles over and sits down in the booth with them. "You took a hell of a risk coming here," he says with a hint of an Eastern European accent. He holds out a large hairy paw. "I suppose I am the bold Theseus. You must be the brilliant Ariadne."

"Yes," Rachel says, shaking his hand.

He's very tall, six five or six six, and he's big too, somewhere between 275 and 300 pounds. He's maybe in his early fifties. He still has most of his hair, which is long and straggly. His scruffy beard is turning gray. He's wearing faded brown jeans, Converse sneakers, and a trench coat over a corduroy jacket and a T-shirt with an image of the cover of *Zen and the Art of Motorcycle Maintenance*. He doesn't seem like the diabolical mastermind behind The Chain. But you never can tell, can you? He's holding what looks like a double Scotch or bourbon.

Pete offers his hand. "You come with her?" the man asks, shaking it.

Pete nods.

The man gives them a vulnerable, weak, rueful, scared kind of smile and swigs the remainder of his drink. "Well, you can't have gotten guns or knives or nerve poison through security, but that's only delaying the inevitable, isn't it? If you're from The Chain, you know who I am now, and I'm dead," he says. "However, if *I'm* from The Chain, I know who you are and *you're* dead."

"Would you really know us? How many people do you think have been through The Chain? It must be hundreds," Pete says.

"You're right. Hundreds. Maybe thousands; who knows? My point is that you'll have a photograph of me by now and you can match it up against the database and have me killed as soon as I leave this airport. Just add me to the to-do list of whoever is currently on The Chain and they'll kill me and my daughter. Anyone can be gotten to. You can kill presidents and kings and heirs apparent and pretty much anybody if you're motivated enough."

He takes off his glasses and sets them on the table. His hazel eyes are keen and intelligent and sad, Rachel thinks. And there's a professorial or clerical air about them. They are, perhaps, a pair of hazel eyes to believe in.

"We'll have to trust each other," Rachel says.

"Why?" the man asks.

"Because you've got the look of someone who has gone through what I've gone through."

The man examines her carefully and nods. "And you?" he asks Pete.

"I helped. At the end. I'm her ex-brother-in-law."

"A military man, by the looks of it. I'm surprised they allowed that—or did you try to sneak that past them?"

"He's retired, and they said that he was OK. I really had nobody else," Rachel explains.

"The Chain is a cage always in search of the most vulnerable birds," the man mutters, and he stops a passing waiter and orders another double bourbon.

"Either of you ever done any kriging or matrix programming or regression analysis?" he asks.

"Kriging?" Rachel asks, wondering what the hell he's talking about.

"It's a Gaussian-process regression. A tool for statistical analysis. No?"

Pete and Rachel shake their heads.

He taps the table number. "The number seventy-three means what to you?"

"John Hannah, offensive lineman for the Pats," Pete says quickly.

"Gary Sanchez briefly wore number seventy-three when he first came up with the Yanks," Rachel says.

The man shakes his head.

"What does it mean to you?" Rachel asks.

"It is the twenty-first prime number. The number twenty-one has prime factors seven and three. A pleasing coincidence. Table seventy-seven is also free over there. It's not prime, of course, but it is the sum of the first eight prime numbers and the atomic number of iridium. Iridium is how they finally proved what killed the dinosaurs, which was the big mystery when I was a kid. The iridium–marker layer in the K-T boundary. Atomic number seventy-seven was the harbinger of death for the dinosaurs. It's an ending number. All books should end on the seventy-seventh chapter. They never do, though. But we're beginning something here, aren't we? Hence table seventy-three, which is a little more appropriate than seventy-seven, yes?"

Rachel and Pete look at him in utter bafflement.

He sighs. "All right. Mathematics is not your forte, I see. Well, that's not important. The story's more important than the technique. How long?" he asks.

"How long what?"

"How long have you been out?"

"About a month."

A hungry look plays across his face. A grisly smile. "That's good," he says. "That's what I was hoping for. I've been out three and a half years. The trail has gone cold. I need someone with the scent still on them."

"For what?" Rachel asks.

His bourbon comes and he drinks it in one. He stands and leaves a fifty-dollar bill on the table. "I guess you're right, I guess we are going to have to trust each other," he says to Rachel. "Him, I don't like. I can't read him. But you—you're no liar. Let's go."

Pete shakes his head. "I don't think so. I think we're fine here."

The man runs his hands through his stringy hair and ties it back in a ponytail. "Well, I'll tell you what: I'll be at the Four Provinces pub on Massachusetts Avenue in Cambridge in about forty-five minutes. I'll get one of the private rooms at the back of the pub. They'll let me have it. I'm a regular.

Maybe I'll see you there. Maybe I won't. It's up to you."

"What's wrong with this place?" Rachel asks.

"I want a bit of privacy to tell my story. And for us to make our plan."

"A plan for what?"

"The reason you've come here," he replies.

"And what's that?" Pete asks.

"To break The Chain, of course."

52

They are moving again. This time it's back east. This time it's closer to home: Boston. They pack boxes. Decide what to keep, what to donate, what to throw away. Little Anthony and Tom will miss LA, but the twins and Cheryl have never really fit in here.

Maybe Boston will be easier. Tom's dad lives nearby and dotes on the grandkids.

Anyway, it's another moving weekend.

Cheryl shifts the dresser in the twins' room.

She finds the Polaroid Oliver took of Jennifer with no clothes on. The girl is in front of her house, and the photograph was probably taken from Oliver's bunk in his bedroom.

She shows him the photograph and demands an explanation. Oliver can't think of one. He doesn't deny he took the Polaroid, though. Cheryl calls him a little pervert and slaps his face. "Wait till your father gets home," she says. Tom returns with boxes from the supermarket. He's been away a long time. He stopped at a bar on the way back.

Oliver and Margaret are waiting upstairs. They hear Cheryl talk to Tom. They hear Tom say, "Jesus H. Christ!"

Tom comes upstairs. He grabs Oliver by the collar of his T-shirt, drags him down from the top bunk, and throws him against the wall.

"You little sicko! You know what I think? I think they put LSD in your baby food. Who knows? I mean, Jesus, you might not even be my goddamn kids!" he yells.

Anthony has come upstairs to watch the fun. Margaret sees him standing in the doorway grinning. It's a grin that is going to cost Anthony his life.

"It was just a joke," Oliver says.

"I'll show you a joke," Tom says. He picks Oliver up off the floor, drags him to the bathroom, throws him into the shower, and turns the cold water on.

Oliver yelps as the water hits him.

"This is funny, isn't it?" Tom says.

Tom keeps the shower on for two minutes and then finally turns it off.

Oliver is bawling his guts out. Tom shakes his head, puts his arm around Anthony, and leads him downstairs.

Oliver is sprawled in a corner of the shower, still sobbing. Margaret climbs into the shower next to him and takes his hand. Oliver is ashamed of his tears and everything that's happened.

"Go away," he says.

But he doesn't mean it and Margaret knows he doesn't mean it.

His sobs turn to whimpers. The day lengthens. The sun sets right down Orange Avenue, silhouetting the planes landing at Long Beach Airport.

"It's OK," Margaret says, holding her twin brother's trembling hand. "We'll get them."

53

The three of them are in a private room at the back of the Four Provinces pub in Cambridge.

Rachel and Pete are sitting opposite the big man. There's a festive air in the pub but not in here. Three pints of Guinness and three double Scotches in front of them, which should keep them from being bothered by waitresses for a while. Rachel takes her baseball cap off and sets it next to her pint. She looks at Pete, but he merely shrugs. He isn't sure how this is supposed to commence either.

Rachel checks her watch. It's 2:15 now. Kylie is going over to Stuart's after school, and Stuart's mom will be picking them up. Stuart's mom is a tough-as-nails attorney and completely dependable. Stuart's father is ex-army; he works from home and is still in the Massachusetts National Guard. Outside of Marty, Stuart's mom and dad are just about the only people Rachel trusts to keep Kylie safe. But still, time is marching on. Rachel wants to get back before dark. "One of us is going to have to go first," she says.

The big, shambling, sad-eyed man nods. "You're right. I contacted you," he says. "First things first. Security. No blogs, no e-mails, no paper trail, and when we meet, you make damn sure you're not being followed. Get off the T at random stops, *French Connection*–style. Do it again and again and again until you *know* you're not being tailed."

"Sure," Rachel says absently.

The man's expression darkens. "No, no *sure*. *Sure* is not good enough. You need to be certain. Your life depends on this. You took a hell of a risk meeting me at the airport. And coming here? How do you know I didn't lure you here so I could kill you both and slip out the back?"

"I wasn't armed at the airport, but I am now," Pete says, patting his jacket pocket.

"No, no, no! You're missing the point!"

"What is the point?" Rachel asks gently.

"The point is you have to be vigilant. The last few weeks . . . well, I don't know. There was a break-in in the math department. They ransacked half a dozen offices, not just mine. But that could have been cover. Even though I've been discreet, I've been making waves. Ripples in the pond. Maybe I've stirred things up. Maybe I'm being researched. Targeted. I don't know. And more important, you don't know. You don't know me from Adam."

Rachel nods. A few weeks ago she would have thought this kind of talk was crazy paranoia. Not now.

The man sighs deeply and takes a battered notebook out of his raincoat pocket.

"This is my third journal on The Chain," he says. "My real name is Erik Lonnrott. I work there," he says, pointing behind himself with his thumb.

"The kitchen?" Pete asks.

"MIT. I'm a mathematician. Coming to Cambridge was the worst thing that ever happened to me and my family."

"What did happen?" Rachel asks.

Erik takes a large swig from the Guinness. "I'll begin

279

at the beginning. I was born in Moscow, but my parents moved to America when I was thirteen. I grew up mostly in Texas. I went to Texas A and M. I got my PhD in mathematics there and I met my wife, Carolyn, there. She was a painter. Huge, beautiful canvases, mostly with religious subjects. We had a daughter, Anna, when I was doing my postdoc in topology at Stanford. Those were the good days."

"And then you came here," Rachel says.

"We moved to Cambridge in 2004. I was offered an associate professorship with tenure. Who turns down something like that at MIT? All was good until 2010, when . . ." He chokes up and his voice dies away. He takes another drink and pulls himself together. "My wife was bicycling home from her studio in Newton and was hit by an SUV. She was killed immediately."

"I'm sorry," Rachel says.

He smiles weakly at her and nods. "It was terrible. I wanted to die, but I had a daughter. We got through it. A thing like that. You think you won't, but you do. It took us five years. Five long years. Things were finally starting to turn around, and then . . ."

"The Chain," Pete says.

"March fourth, 2015. They took Anna when she was walking home from school. In Cambridge, in broad daylight. It was only four blocks."

"They took my daughter at the school-bus stop."

Erik takes out his wallet and shows them a picture of a bright-looking curly-haired girl in jeans and a T-shirt.

"Anna was thirteen years old, but very shy, young for her age. Vulnerable. When they told me what I had to do to free her, I could not believe it. How can anyone contemplate such things? Nevertheless, I did what I had to do. Anna was kept underground in the darkness for four days before she was released."

"Oh my God."

"She never recovered from the ordeal. She began having seizures, hearing voices. A year later, she tried to kill herself by cutting her wrists in the bathtub and she's now in a psychiatric hospital in Vermont. When I go to see her, sometimes she doesn't even know me. My own daughter. She has good days and bad days. Very bad days. My beautiful, intelligent Anna, in a bib, being fed baby food with a plastic spoon. The Chain has ruined my life and my daughter's life and ever since then, I have been looking for a way to kill it."

"Is there a way to kill it?" Rachel asks.

"Perhaps," Erik replies. "Now it is your turn to speak. What's your story?"

Pete shakes his head. "No, this isn't a quid pro quo. Like you say, we don't know you from Adam—"

"They took my daughter," Rachel says. "I had to take someone else's little girl. I've been having nightmares ever since. My daughter's in a very, very bad place."

"And you have cancer," Erik comments.

Rachel smiles and unconsciously touches her thinning hair. "You don't miss much, do you?"

"And you are from New York," Erik says.

"Maybe I'm just a Yankees fan," Rachel replies.

"You are both. And you are a brave Yankees fan. One who does not mind getting dirty looks from every single person in this town."

"I'd be happy if it was only looks," Rachel says and manages another smile.

"I have been researching the entity known as The Chain for over a year now," he says and passes his notebook to Rachel and Pete. They undo the elastic strap and open it.

It is filled with dates, names, charts, observations, data points, extrapolations, diary entries, essays. All written in black in a spidery, tiny script. Written, they note, in a cipher.

"At first there was nothing; fear kept people quiet. But then I dug deeper and I found references to The Chain in anonymous personal ads in newspapers. I noticed one or two obscure hints here and there. An odd crime report that did not add up. I did a sieve-map analysis, statistical-regression analysis, Markov chain modeling, a temporal-event analysis. I collated the results and regressed them, and I have come to a few conclusions. Not many, but a few."

"What conclusions?" Rachel asks.

"I believe The Chain began sometime between 2012 and 2014. The regression analysis leads back to a median date of 2013. The ones who run it, of course, want us to believe that it is an ancient entity that has not been bested in scores, even hundreds, of years, but I think this is a lie."

"An ancient provenance makes it seem even more un-beatable," Rachel agrees.

"Exactly. But I do not think it is ancient," Erik says and he takes another sip from his glass.

"I don't think so either," Rachel says.

"What other conclusions have you reached?" Pete asks.

"Obviously, the builder of The Chain is very intelligent. College-educated. Genius-level IQ. Very well read. Proba-bly around my age. Probably a white male."

Rachel shakes her head slowly. "I don't think so," she says.

"I have done the research. Predators like this generally operate within their ethnic group. Even allowing for the pseudorandom element in victim selection. He's around my age or perhaps a little older."

Rachel frowns but says nothing.

"The Chain is a self-perpetuating mechanism whose purpose is to protect itself and make money for its founder," Erik goes on. "I believe The Chain was designed by a white male in his late forties early in this decade, perhaps as a response to the recession and banking crisis. Possibly adapted from Latin American replacement-victim kidnapping models."

Rachel takes a sip of her Guinness. "You might be right about the inception date but you're wrong about the age and the gender."

Erik and Pete both look at her with surprise.

"She's not as old as she pretends to be and she's not as smart as she thinks she is. She was bluffing with me when she was talking about philosophy," Rachel continues. "That's not her area of expertise."

"What makes you think it is a woman?"

"I can't put my finger on that. But I know I'm right. I was talking to a woman who was using a voice-distortion machine."

Erik nods and writes something in his notebook.

"Were you contacted by burner phone and the Wickr app?" he asks.

"Yes."

He smiles. "The Chain has protected its security very cleverly. The anonymous phone calls using burner phones, the anonymous Bitcoin accounts that last a few weeks and disappear, the anonymous encrypted Wickr app whose ID gets changed periodically. The hiring of proxies to do the dirty work. Very clever. Almost foolproof."

"Almost?"

"Some of it is unassailable. In my opinion, it would be impossible to backtrack through all the links of The Chain to find its origins. This is, of course, because of the pseudorandom element in the selection of the victims. You had a free choice of target, as did I, and so on and so on all the way back. Attempting to trace that trail to its origin will not work. I know. I have tried."

"So how do we find the people who run The Chain?" Pete asks.

Erik picks up his notebook and flips through it. "For all my research, actually, I have come up with very little in the way of solutions. I—"

"You're not telling me this whole meeting was a waste of time?" Pete interrupts.

"No. Their methods are good but when you are dealing with human agents, mistakes can be made. No agent is perfect in his or her tradecraft. Or so I suspect."

"What mistake has The Chain made?"

"Perhaps they have become a little complacent, a little lazy. We shall see. Tell me about your last interaction with them."

Rachel opens her mouth to speak, but Pete puts a hand on her arm. "Don't tell him anything else."

"We have to trust one another," Rachel says.

"No, Rach, we don't," Pete says.

He doesn't catch his own mistake but Rachel does and Erik does. Erik takes the notebook and presumably writes down *Rachel*.

We've come this far, she thinks. "It was a month ago. The first week of November," Rachel says.

"They called you?"

"Yes."

"And used the Wickr app?"

"Yes. Why is that so important?"

"The Wickr and Bitcoin accounts are protected by the highest levels of encryption commercially available, which would take tens of thousands of hours of supercomputing time to break. And I am certain that, at least in the beginning, they changed their Wickr app ID periodically for extra security. And, of course, there may be various layers of redundancy and dummy accounts. But even so, I believe I have found a flaw in their method of communication."

"What flaw?"

The waitress opens the door and pokes her head in. "Will you be wanting to order food?" she asks in a Scottish accent.

"No," Erik says coldly.

When she's closed the door, he begins putting on his coat. "She's new," he says. "I don't like new. Come on."

54

A bench on Boston Common. A cold wind whistling in from the harbor. They're opposite the memorial to Robert Gould Shaw and the men of the Fifty-Fourth Regiment. Not many people around. Just a few joggers, college students, people pushing strollers.

Rachel watches him and waits. When Erik finally feels safe he continues: "The standard construction of pseudorandom encrypted functions is generally believed to be leakage-resistant, but I don't think it is. And when you have sloppy tradecraft, you make it slightly easier for people like me."

"I don't understand," Rachel says. She looks at Pete. He's in the dark too and he has a software background.

"They reach out to us in two ways, and both ways, I believe, can be decrypted," Erik goes on.

"How?"

"The burner phones aren't as safe as everyone thinks they are, even if all the calls are made from brand-new burner phones housed inside a Faraday cage. The consensus is that calls made by such a method would be completely untraceable," Erik says with a grin.

"But you've thought of a way to crack it, haven't you?" Pete says.

Erik's grin broadens.

"This has been my primary area of research for the past year."

"What's the trick?"

"It is theoretically possible to measure power levels and antenna patterns through software that can be installed on a smartphone. The phone can then analyze the incoming call in real time."

"You've done this?" Pete asks, impressed.

"I have been tinkering with such a concept."

"You can trace a call made on a burner phone?"

"No, but the cell phone's base station—the closest wireless tower—could possibly be found," Erik says cagily.

"You've done it! Haven't you?" Pete insists.

"Tell us," Rachel pleads.

Erik waits until a jogger passes before continuing. "I am in the process of finishing up my design of a hunter-killer application that can seek out the base station closest to where a cell-phone call has been made, even a burner-phone call made from inside a Faraday cage. Once the base station has been pinpointed, it might be possible to narrow the frequency of the phone's signal, giving you a rough vector from the phone tower to the phone itself within, say, two or three hundred meters."

Rachel isn't sure she understands all this. "So what does that mean?" she asks.

"There may be a way of following the thread into the heart of the labyrinth," Erik replies.

"And the Wickr app?" Rachel asks. "That's their primary method of communication."

"A not-too-dissimilar technique. My hunter-killer

algorithm can't break the message's encryption or find the sender, but it can find the cell-phone base station that's closest to where the message was sent from. Obviously, if they're communicating from Times Square in New York City, we're screwed, but if they're calling from a private residence, we might be able to trace them."

"Why haven't you done it?" Pete asks.

"Because I was last in contact with them two and a half years ago and the burner phone they used to talk to me has been destroyed and the Wickr ID they used to communicate with me has been changed. The trail has gone cold. Whereas you . . ." he says, looking at Rachel.

"Me what?"

"If I'm right about their tradecraft, they still might be using the same app ID to speak to you."

"They are. They sent me a message at Thanksgiving."

"Perfect!" Erik exclaims.

"How would it work?" Rachel asks.

"You would have to provoke them or threaten them or worry them sufficiently so that they want to communicate with you. They may message you or, better yet, call you on a burner phone. If they talk long enough, we run the software, and we can possibly triangulate the base cell tower their phone is in contact with."

"And if they're in Times Square or driving or otherwise on the move? We'll have pissed them off with no hope of finding them. And we'll have painted a target on our backs and they can come after us!" Pete protests.

"The plan is not without risk," Erik says.

"For *us*. It's all risk for us. It's zero risk for you," Pete says.

"What would I have to do, exactly?" Rachel asks.

"No! Rachel, don't agree to—" Pete begins.

"What would I have to do?" Rachel repeats.

"You must get in a dialogue with our Unknown Caller on Wickr or, better, on the phone and let me run a live trace when they contact you."

"What do you mean, a dialogue?"

"You draw out the conversation as long as you can. The Wickr trace isn't very accurate, I'm still working on the software, but a phone trace? A phone trace from a conversation that could last two or three minutes? That would be great."

"What would happen?"

"I trace them through the hunter-killer algorithm and eventually with a little luck I find the base cell tower that the call is coming from."

"Does it work with landlines?" Pete asks.

"If they're dumb enough to call us on a landline, I'll have them in two seconds."

"I think that will make them think I'm some kind of a problem," Rachel says. "A long conversation like that. I'll be drawing their attention to me and my family."

"Yes," Erik agrees. "And I must confess that the app is not fully functional. I am very much in the beta stage. Tracing a phone call that could be anywhere in the whole of the United States requires a lot of computing power."

"What if you could ignore most of the United States and just focus on one area?" Rachel asks.

"That would make things a lot easier," Erik says. "But I can't do that. They could be calling from anywhere. Even abroad. I—"

"She's from Boston. And The Chain seems to operate mainly in New England. Close to home. They're keeping it nearby. That's what I would do in case of trouble."

"How do you know 'she' is from Boston?" Erik asks. "I didn't notice a Boston accent."

"She's gotten rid of it. She talks very deliberately when

289

she's using the voice-distortion machine. But you can't quite get rid of all the intonation, can you? I started to suspect it, and I tried something with her in one of our conversations. We were talking about the Boston police and I said that they would arrest you for *banging a uey*. She laughed at that because she understood it. I'd never heard that expression before I moved here. There's probably a lot of people outside of Boston who would also understand it, but my hunch is that she's a Bostonian."

Erik nods. "This is helpful. If the app doesn't have to search anywhere but New England, it would be a lot more efficient. Orders of magnitude more efficient. North America has five hundred million people and billions of phone lines. New England has perhaps ten million people."

"Your app might work fifty times faster," Rachel says.

Erik nods. "Perhaps."

"But there must be some other way of doing this, one that doesn't involve drawing attention to ourselves," Pete says.

"None that I've been able to come up with. You still have a direct contact with them. It will be risky but not recklessly so. We run the app, and when we find out where they are, we leave an anonymous tip with the police. Maybe even wait a month or so, so they don't make the connection between our call and their arrest."

"I don't like the sound of this at all," Pete says.

"Time is of the essence. Soon they will change their Wickr ID and we will have no way of directly communicating with them. And that recent break-in has given me pause," Erik says. He writes something down on a piece of paper. "This is my new burner-phone number. I will need you to make a decision soon."

Rachel takes the number and looks at him and then at the

war memorial behind him. A line of verse goes through her head, that one about Colonel Shaw riding on his bubble, "waiting for the blessèd break."

We're all riding on our bubbles, she thinks, *we're all waiting for the blessèd break.*

She offers Erik her hand. He shakes it.

She gets up from the bench. "We'll have to think it over," she says.

55

Erik goes back to his office at MIT feeling good.

He has some hope at last after the long information drought that has hollowed him to the bone. This is a chance. The game is well and truly afoot now and those bastards are going to get theirs.

He had thought that he was going to have to take out a newspaper ad in the *New York Times* challenging The Chain to call him or he would reveal their existence. But they would not have responded to the ad, and, worse, sooner or later they would have found out who placed it, and thus his life and his daughter's life would have been in grave jeopardy.

Rachel is right to be nervous about antagonizing The Chain, but better her than him, he thinks, and then he immediately feels guilty about this thought.

It's us against them. All of us. Rachel. A godsend, meeting her. She's smart too. Such superb insights. Of course he should have focused on Boston. Most of the data points he has are in New England. Those potential hits he discovered in Colorado and New Mexico are outliers.

Yes. This is real progress.

Almost with a lightness in his step, he gets into his battered Chevy Malibu and drives out of the MIT staff parking lot.

He doesn't notice the stressed-looking woman watching him through her windshield. He doesn't notice her follow him home to Newton.

Perhaps he shouldn't be unduly alarmed. He's not the only person being followed.

He hasn't quite moved to the top of the to-do list just yet. If he were to take a few days off or go on vacation or something like that he might be safe.

But unfortunately for Erik the fire is in his belly now and he has no idea that his movements and, more important, his Google searches are being monitored, recorded, and sent for processing to The Chain.

56

Tom, Cheryl, Oliver, Margaret, and little Anthony are on a Caribbean cruise to celebrate Tom's promotion to senior special agent.

Tom and the whole organized-crime division of the Boston field office have been getting a lot of positive attention in the press. The Patriarca crime family, originally from Providence and once so powerful in Boston, has been crippled by rats, wiretaps, and sting operations. The Winter Hill Gang has been broken up, and Whitey Bulger himself is on the run. Tom is quite the golden boy at the Bureau. Sure, he has his temper issues, but who doesn't? He works hard, and this vacation is well earned.

Tom booked the family a junior suite near the promenade deck. For some reason little Anthony has his own bunk, while the older children, Margaret and Oliver, are forced to share a bunk.

Margaret and Oliver actually don't mind that much, and Anthony's attempts to lord it over them are quietly ignored.

The ship visits Nassau and leaves at dusk with a fireworks display. The cruise is nearly over and they are steaming toward Miami. It's really been a great trip.

Anthony feels a hand on his arm in the middle of the night. It's Margaret.

"Shhh," she whispers. "There's something really cool I have to show you on the deck."

"What?" Anthony replies sleepily.

"It's a surprise. A secret. It's really cool, though."

"What is it?"

"Maybe you should go back to sleep. It's only for big boys. Oliver is up there now."

"Is it a whale?"

"Come with me and I'll show you."

Margaret leads Anthony to the ship's stern. Oliver is indeed waiting for them.

"What is it?"

"Over there," Oliver says, pointing into the darkness. "Here, let me lift you up and show you."

"No, I—" Anthony says, but it's too late for that now.

Margaret and Oliver have been planning this for months. They made sure the vessel they ended up on was an older one without CCTV cameras. They laid the groundwork with a couple of false reports about Anthony's humorous sleepwalking adventures.

They hoist Anthony onto the guardrail and push him over into the foaming wake behind the ship.

57

Another handover of Kylie in Newburyport. The girlfriend is the same one. The little blonde. Rachel is determined to pay attention this time and at least get her name while Kylie retrieves her complicated Starbucks order.

"Rachel's teaching college now," Marty is saying to the girl.

"Wow, that's great," the little blonde says.

"I'm so embarrassed, I really am, but what's your name again? I'm sure you've told me a couple of times, but I've been a bit out of it, as you can imagine," Rachel says.

Marty looks really concerned by this. Not angry, but actually concerned for Rachel's mental health. Chemo can mess you up in many different ways. "It's Ginger," Marty says gently.

"And what is it that you do?" Rachel asks.

"Ginger, believe it or not, works for the feds," Marty says, speaking for her again.

Pete and Rachel look at each other, eyes wide. This information has clearly never come up before because Rachel can see Pete is as stunned as she is. Kylie has never mentioned it, which is less surprising. It's been drilled into her that they can't have anything to do with law enforcement.

"The FBI?" Rachel asks.

"The FBI," Ginger says, doing a sonorous, deep movie-trailer voice.

"She's not just an agent, though, she's also getting her PhD in criminal psychology at BU. Busy gal," Marty adds.

"That wasn't my idea. The Bureau sort of forced me into that," Ginger says modestly in a charming Boston accent.

"PhD? You can't be old enough—" Rachel begins, wondering if the woman is some kind of freaky Doogie Howser type.

"She's thirty," Marty says.

Rachel can't figure out if he's saying that apologetically or boastfully. A woman nearly his own age? Who's a grown-up with a grown-up job? Boastfully, she decides. "You barely look eighteen," Rachel blurts out. "You must be . . ." She trails off, not sure how to complete the sentence.

"Bathing in the blood of virgins every night?" Marty finishes for her.

"I wasn't going to say that," Rachel says, but her little protest is lost in Ginger's gales of laughter. She thinks Marty is hilarious.

"Just a healthy skin-care regimen," Ginger says.

"Where exactly did you two lovebirds meet?" Pete asks, taking more of an interest in Ginger himself now.

"We almost literally bumped into each other jogging on the common," Marty says.

"He's done that before," Pete says. "That's assault, buddy. One day it's not going to work and you'll be headed for the Big House."

Ginger laughs at that too. She thinks both brothers are a riot.

She's pretty, she's young, she has a great sense of humor, and she's smart; if she comes from money too, that'll just about seal it for Marty, Rachel thinks. "So you're a local, Ginger?" she asks.

"Oh my God, is my accent that outrageous?"

"No, that's not what I was getting at. I just wondered what high school you went to. Maybe you guys went to the same one. I'm not from around these parts."

Marty shakes his head. "Nah, she went to Innsmouth High," he says. Rachel hasn't heard of it. "Redneckville," Marty explains.

"I guess I was a real boonie kid," Ginger says. "Lucky to get out."

Yeah, yeah, Rachel thinks. *Real* boonie kids don't get PhDs at BU. Although, Jesus, she shouldn't talk. Harvard. I mean, come on. Partial scholarship, yes, but even so.

"So what do you do in the FBI?" Rachel asks with another quick look at Pete.

"Profiling, right?" Pete suggests.

Ginger laughs. "You'd think, huh? I've been angling for the BAU for years, but the Bureau in its ineffable wisdom has stuck me in its white-collar-crime division."

"Fun work?" Rachel asks.

They talk about evil bankers for a bit and in a lull, Marty asks how Kylie is doing in school. Rachel shakes her head. "She's been under a lot of stress."

"Have you read those e-mails her teachers have been sending?"

"Yeah," Rachel replies. "I don't think we should talk about this, er, you know, here."

"No, sure, of course," Marty says. "Only, um, if Kylie is going through something, Ginger works with psychologists and psychotherapists."

"We already tried a psychotherapist. It's complicated," Rachel replies.

"I do know some really good people," Ginger says helpfully. "Both inside the Bureau and out."

"Drop it. Here she comes," Pete says.

Despite her family's concern, Kylie is all smiles. She's got some crazy Starbucks concoction with a bunch of whipped cream and chocolate on top.

"We should go," Marty says.

"Really? Can't we all just sit together for a minute?" Kylie begs.

They sit at the window table and talk as the sky threatens snow. Marty observes that New England does Christmas better than anywhere else.

Rachel smiles and tries to contribute but Pete sees that she's getting tired. They all say their goodbyes, and he takes her home.

She can't hold down food that night.

She can't sleep.

She sits in bed with a cold cup of tea.

Again that thought to punish herself: If she had succumbed to the cancer a year ago, none of this would have happened.

58

And still they don't stop. The dreams. The man in the snow. The fear. The bed-wetting. The stomach cramps. Every day, Kylie is getting weaker. She puts a brave face on it but Rachel sees. Rachel knows. And she is getting weaker too. Fading away. The longer the cancer treatment goes on, the longer the process of recovery.

They have to strike now.

Pete counsels against the plan. He has his own demons. The pain is coming back. The hunger. He is failing too.

Kylie's nightmares. Rachel's nightmares. Kylie crying behind the bathroom door. Pete sneaking off in the Dodge Ram to be by himself. Rachel's hair coming out in clumps. Kylie refusing sleepovers because she doesn't want anyone to find out. They have all sipped from the Drink Me bottle. They have all unwound the clew of red thread. They have all fallen through the looking glass.

Rachel and Pete sit on the cold deck behind the house.

Atlantic breakers. A sickle moon. The chilly, indifferent winter constellations.

Pete is waiting for her decision.

She finishes her Scotch and hugs herself.

"We have to do it," she says.

Pete shakes his head. "We don't have to do a goddamn thing."

"Erik is—"

"He can do it. He can take the risk."

"He can't do it without us, without me—you know that."

"We're out. We escaped by the skin of our teeth. We were lucky. This thing nearly got all of us," Pete says.

She looks at him. This doesn't sound like the Marine Corps officer who's done five combat tours. Doubt is crippling him. Or maybe now that he has something to lose—a family—he has become more cautious. He doesn't realize that the family will be lost if they do nothing.

"It's not a *thing,* Pete. The Chain isn't mythology. It isn't self-perpetuating. It's human. It's made up of humans. It's fallible, vulnerable, just like we all are. What we do is find the human heart at the center of it and break it."

Pete thinks for a long time and then nods. "OK," he says quietly.

"Good."

Rachel calls Erik's number. "We're in," she says.

"When?"

"I want my daughter away. Safe."

"So when? It must be soon, before they change the protocols."

Marty and his girlfriend can probably take Kylie on the weekend, Rachel thinks. "Saturday," she says.

"I'll call you at ten in the morning. You're going to have to provoke them. You've got to make them call you back."

"I know."
"It's going to be dangerous."
"I know."
"Until Saturday comes."

59

Marty laughs with pleasure. "I would love to have Kylie. Actually, it's perfect. Ginger suggested we go meet her grandfather this weekend. I'll take the Kylester."

Rachel's heart skips a beat or two. "Wow, you're at that stage already? Meeting the parents?" she says, trying to be jocular and lighthearted, but she doesn't feel *that* jocular. Marty would never have married someone like Tammy. But a whip-smart FBI agent who is still young enough to give him the couple of boys he's always wanted?

"It's nothing like that. I'm not going to ask for her hand in marriage. And it's her grandfather, not her dad. Nothing serious. Just a meet-and-greet. Her twin brother's going to be there too. But I'd like Kylie to come. And you're welcome too. And Pete. They've got a big old tumbledown house by a river, apparently, lots of swings and woods to play in if the weather stays mild."

"That sounds lovely but I'm just going to take it easy this weekend."

"Why don't you do something fun, if you're feeling up to it? A spa day. Send me the bill."

"Maybe I will. You know, as ex-husbands go, you're not too bad."

"Damning with faint praise."

Rachel says goodbye and goes upstairs to tell Kylie the plans.

"You goofed, Mom. Stuart's supposed to stay here this weekend. His parents are going to his stepsister's graduation in Arizona," Kylie says.

"Oh, crap, yeah."

She calls Marty again. "We can't do it. I'm an idiot. Sorry. Stuart's staying with us this weekend. His mom is going to Phoenix."

"Stuart? That weird freckly kid? He can come too. Ginger won't mind."

"You'll have to ask Stuart's mom. I doubt she'll say yes. She doesn't completely trust me, and therefore, by association, she won't trust you."

"No, it'll work the opposite way. She'll see that I am the dependable one. Text me her number and I'll call her."

Rachel texts him the number and of course Marty works his charms with Stuart's mom. The weekend is Rachel's.

Any other chemo patient would spend that time taking it easy and recovering.

Rachel is going to hunt for the monster's lair.

She goes downstairs to Pete.

"I mean, it's sensible, right? If we find them with Erik's app, they won't be able to track us or anything, will they?" she asks, looking for reassurance.

"I guess as long as you don't piss them off too much, we should be fine. We're just doing the equivalent of a phone trace. They won't even know we're looking for them. I doubt we'll find them, but if we do we'll let the authorities take care of it. An anonymous call to the FBI should do the trick."

"So we'll be safe?" Rachel asks again, thinking more about Kylie than herself.

Pete nods.

"OK," Rachel says and she knocks the wooden tabletop as a charm against the possibility of something going wrong.

60

A house in Watertown, Massachusetts, in the late 1990s. It's another one of those Spielbergian suburbs filled with kids shooting hoops, riding bikes, playing street hockey. There's the sound of trash talk, skipping rhymes, laughter . . .

But 17 Summer Street is a house of mourning, not a house of mirth.

It's been six months since the Princess Cruise from Nassau. Cheryl isn't over it. How do you get over something like that?

She's been going to therapy and she's on several different antianxiety medications. None of that helps.

What helps is being numb.

Every morning, as soon as Tom and the twins are gone, she makes herself a vodka tonic that is mostly vodka. Then she puts on the TV and swallows a Klonopin and a Xanax and zones out.

The morning creeps by.

At eleven thirty, the mail will come. When she was a little girl, there were two deliveries a day. Now there's only the one, at eleven thirty.

She knows what the postman will bring.

A few bills, some flyers, and another one of those letters.

She closes her eyes, and when she opens them, the sun has moved across the sky and it's time to check the mail.

She ignores the junk and the bills and opens the letter that is addressed to her. *Dear Whore,* it begins.

The rest of it accuses her of being a slut and a terrible mother who is responsible for her son's death.

This is the thirteenth letter she's gotten like this. All of them written in block capitals with a black ballpoint pen.

She puts it with the others in a shoe box in the linen closet.

She makes herself another vodka tonic. She finds a cocktail umbrella and floats it in the glass. She watches a bit of *Days of Our Lives* and goes upstairs.

She sits on the bathroom floor and opens up a bottle of Nembutal. She pops one in her mouth and takes a drink. She pops another in her mouth and takes another drink.

She swallows the entire bottle and lies down on the bathroom floor.

At four o'clock, Margaret and Oliver come home.

They've gotten used to walking home from school by themselves.

Oliver turns on the TV. Margaret goes upstairs to read. She's a good reader. Two years above her grade level. She's reading *The Tombs of Atuan* by Ursula Le Guin. It's very gripping but eventually she needs to go to the bathroom. She finds Cheryl lying on the floor in there.

There's foam around her mouth, her pupils are fixed and dilated, but she's still breathing. Margaret brings Oliver upstairs and both children stare at Cheryl.

"The letters," Margaret says.

"The letters," Oliver agrees.

They look at her for a while. Her face is the color of the

wallpaper in Tom's study, a kind of pale yellow.

Tom doesn't get home until seven thirty. The kids are in front of the TV eating microwaved pizza.

"Where's your mother?" he asks.

"She must have gone out," Margaret says. "She wasn't here when we got home."

"But her car is parked across the street," he says.

"Oh, really?" Margaret says and goes back to the TV.

"Cheryl!" Tom shouts upstairs but there is no answer. He storms into the kitchen and grabs a Sam Adams from the fridge. He takes a bite of pizza.

When he does finally go upstairs, it's too late. The Nembutal has induced respiratory failure leading to cardiac arrest.

He sinks to his knees and takes his wife's cold hand.

He begins to cry.

"What have I done to deserve this?" he wonders out loud. And then he remembers.

61

Erik's been at it all night. He is five cups of coffee in. He is six layers down in the Russian doll of anonymity and fake identities. He has scrubbed the traces and is using a brand-new MacBook with a bogus IP address that locates it in far-off Melbourne, Australia. He is deep in the maze, but he is safe. Or thinks he is.

He's pleased with his research. All the building blocks are in place.

Always were in place.

The Karush-Kuhn-Tucker conditions are optimal. The information is there if you know where and how to look. All those hints, all those personal ads, all those confessions. Every new person introduced to The Chain adds a geometric level of instability. The thing has been teetering on the verge of collapse for a long time. It's just figuring out a way to harness the data points into a shape.

He sips coffee and reads an interesting paper by Maria Schuld, Ilya Sinayskiy, and Francesco Petruccione on prediction by linear regression on a quantum computer. Their algorithm is fascinating.

But it is, he knows, a distraction, something for future analysis.

Amazon's Alexa is playing *Physical Graffiti* for the third time tonight. He stops to listen to the opening riff of "Trampled Under Foot."

He looks at the photograph of himself, his wife, and his daughter in front of MoMA, in New York. His wife's favorite place in all the world. His wife and daughter are grinning while he looks pained.

He shakes his head and fights the tears and looks at the bullet points on the screen that he will have to condense for his Chain notebook.

Things are OK. While he hasn't completely tested the app, he thinks it *should* work. And it should work only for Rachel.

He reorders the list on his screen. These are the things he is fairly certain of now:

1. At least two individuals. Two different signatures and modes of operation. Family members. Siblings?
2. Boston-based
3. Not organized crime
4. Some kind of law enforcement background

"Trampled Under Foot" ends and "Kashmir" begins.

The woman has been watching him for ninety seconds now. Her heart rate is through the roof.

Her instructions are clear: kill Erik, retrieve his notebook. She knows why The Chain picked her—because of her two previous breaking-and-entering convictions. They think she's some kind of expert. She's not. Those were teenage indiscretions. She's a respectable fifth-grade teacher now. She got lucky that Erik's back door was such an old

310

lock. There was barely any skill required.

She got lucky.

Erik got unlucky.

She has in fact killed before. A dog on the road out on Cape Cod. She'd hit it, and she had to put it out of its misery with a snow shovel.

Maybe that's what she's doing to Erik.

His wife is dead. His daughter is in an asylum.

Yes, she thinks and aims the gun at his back.

this new project now in his condition? With Rachel in chemotherapy?

It's insane. They're out of it. Better to let it go.

"You can't tell me what to do, Pete. I'm sick of people telling me what to do!" Rachel says.

"Your life is at stake here. Kylie's life."

"I know that! Don't you think I know that? I'm trying to save our lives!" Rachel takes his hands. "We have to do this, Pete," she whispers.

Pete looks at her.

Rachel is being literally poisoned every other week at 55 Fruit Street.

She's surviving. She's coping. She's still alive.

"OK," he says. "But I'm going too."

62

Pete's alarm goes off at five o'clock. He kills it before it wakes Rachel and quickly rolls out of bed.

His skin and eyes and internal organs are craving the fix. It has been a full day now. One of his longest fasts yet. He is trying a technique called stretching that some guys in the program have recommended. You stretch out the time between hits as long as you can—you go a full day, then a day and a half, and then two days. He looks at the clock. Twenty-five hours and five minutes. Getting up there. Getting close to his record. He feels OK. So far.

He makes coffee, does a few pushups, and goes into the bathroom and locks the door. What would happen if he boils half as much as normal? Can he wean himself off that way? Could that work? Half is crazy. Two-thirds, maybe.

He measures out two-thirds of his normal dose, boils it up on a spoon, sucks it into the syringe, injects himself with the good stuff.

He lies down on the sofa and the beautiful dreams take hold of him for an hour.

He wakes up again.

He could have gone longer. He's feeling fine.

He makes more coffee, showers, and preps the pancake batter. He thinks about the guns and for the third time goes to check that they're still locked in his truck. They are. He examines the hunting rifle, the .45, Rachel's shotgun, and the nine-millimeter.

He took all four to the range yesterday and he'd gotten some good practice in. He'd been an engineering officer in the Corps, but no matter the job, every Marine is an infantryman first.

Rachel wakes up next.

She hasn't really slept.

She'd vomited in the middle of the night.

Eleven days since her last chemo treatment, but it happened like that sometimes. Or it could just be the fear.

The Boy Called Theseus will be phoning the Girl Called Ariadne at ten o'clock sharp.

She comes out of the bedroom and sits at the living-room table.

Pete kisses her on the top of the head. "You didn't sleep?"

"I did. A little. I had another dream."

Pete doesn't need to ask what about.

Another nightmare.

Another glimpse into the future.

Kylie finally wakes at eight and Stuart comes over promptly at eight thirty.

"Pancakes, anyone?" Pete asks.

He has just poured the batter into the frying pan when Marty and Ginger arrive in Marty's big white boat of a Mercedes.

Pete turns down the gas on the stove and he, Rachel, and Kylie go out to greet them.

"Well, if it isn't Lily, Rosemary, and the Jack of Hearts,"

Marty says, slapping Pete on the back and kissing Rachel and Kylie.

"And if it isn't . . ." Pete says, but he can't think of a good response.

Marty's definitely the one who got the family's gift of the gab.

They're an attractive couple, Rachel thinks. Ginger's hair has grown some and she has washed out all the dye, so that now it's a pretty copper color, which suits her much better. Marty's eyes are somehow greener.

"Pete's made pancakes and I'll fry up some bacon," Rachel says.

They sit at the living-room table and eat breakfast.

"These are good, big brother—did you make them from a mix?" Marty asks.

Pete shakes his head. "I'm with Mark Bittman. Pancake mixes are the sign of a decadent civilization."

"My childhood was exactly like that," Marty tells Ginger and Kylie. "You ask an innocent question and you get some lecture about everything that's wrong with the world."

"He's lying. He was the spoiled one in the family," Pete says.

"What was your childhood like, Ginger?" Rachel wonders.

"Wow. Crazy. Don't get me started. I don't even remember the commune years. We lived all over before coming back to Boston," Ginger says.

"Is that why you were attracted to the FBI? For stability?" Rachel asks.

"Not really. My dad was an agent, my grandfather was Boston PD, so I guess it's the family business," Ginger says.

"Are you sure it's OK that we dump two kids on you?" Rachel asks Marty in private when breakfast is over.

"I talked it over with Ginger. She'd love to have Kylie and her little pal down to her grandfather's house. It's a big old fun-packed place on the Inn River. Kids will go nuts down there. Love it."

"A lot of those old houses in that part of Massachusetts, on the floodplain, are dangerous. Just be careful, OK?"

"Don't worry, the house is gorgeous—they've spent a lot of dough doing it up."

"Ginger does come from money, then? Lucky you," Rachel says.

"Yeah, it must be family money, because you don't make that much as an FBI agent," Marty replies.

"Unless she's one of them corrupt cops," Rachel jokes.

"Come on, Rach, look at her—she's from law-and-order central casting."

Stuart and Kylie are finally ready, and Pete and Rachel walk everyone to the car. "Look after the kids," Rachel says.

Ginger hugs her. "Don't worry, they'll be safe with us," she promises.

Yeah, family money, Rachel decides, looking at Ginger's bag, a small but gorgeous Hermès Birkin.

Hugs and kisses all around, and the four of them are off.

Back in the house, Pete places a map of New England on the table.

"Somewhere in here," he says.

"Now we just have to wait for Erik's call. I'll check that the GPS tabs we put in her shoes are working."

She turns on her phone, and, yup, there is Kylie heading south.

They check the weather. Drizzle, maybe some snow flurries.

Could be worse.

They wait for Erik's call.

Ten o'clock comes and goes.

Ten fifteen.

Ten thirty.

Eleven o'clock.

Something is wrong.

"What do we do?" Pete asks.

"We just wait, I guess," Rachel replies. But something terrible has happened, she knows it.

Pete knows it too. It's that feeling you get a minute before the alarms go off and the ordnance comes raining down.

Eleven fifteen.

Eleven thirty.

A thick sea fog is rolling in from the Atlantic. Ominous pathetic-fallacy weather.

At eleven forty-five, a text comes through to Rachel's burner phone.

If you are receiving this text, it means I have been compromised or incapacitated. Most likely I am dead. I am sending you a link to a place where you can anonymously download the hunter-killer app for phone communications and text messages. A reminder: The longer you are in direct communication, the closer you will get to finding who you are talking to, so if you choose to use it, keep them talking as long as you can. I was not able to get the app to work properly with Wickr or Kik or other encrypted apps. If they communicate with you that way, it will not work properly. Maybe version 2.0 if I'm still alive. Good luck.

The next text is a link to a site where they can download Erik's application.

She shows the message to Pete and turns on the TV news.

It takes another forty-five minutes for the news to hit WBZ Boston.

"An MIT professor was murdered this morning. Erik Lonnrott was shot three times at his home . . ."

The report goes on to say that there were no witnesses to the incident. The police's working theory is that this was a robbery gone wrong, as the house appeared to have been ransacked and various items were apparently stolen.

"He wrote my name in his notebook," Rachel says.

63

A few weeks after Cheryl's death, Tom promises the kids a new start. He's a changed man and a better man, he says. He's going to book that trip to Disneyland. He's going to work less. He's going to make them the focus of his life.

The better-man shtick is convincing for about ten days. Then something at work annoys him and he stops at a bar on the way home.

The bar becomes a regular watering hole on his drive back from the FBI.

One night he meets someone at the bar and doesn't come home at all.

Oliver and Margaret don't mind.

They're self-reliant. Oliver spends much of his time on his home computer. Margaret is still reading a lot. Detective novels and romances are her favorites. She's writing too. Anonymous letters.

A boy she liked asked another girl to the school disco.

The girl got a letter that convinced her not to go to the disco.

The teacher who gave her an F got a letter threatening to expose his secret. It was an old trick she'd read in a Mark

Twain book, but the teacher came in the next day as pale as a ghost.

Margaret has another project she's working on. She spends a lot of time copying and perfecting her father's handwriting.

On the one-year anniversary of Cheryl's death, Tom comes home drunk.

The kids can hear him downstairs in a royal rage about something.

They wait trembling in their bedroom for Tom to come crashing up the stairs.

They don't have to wait long.

Stomp, stomp, stomp, stomp.

The bedroom door is kicked open.

"Where's the meat loaf?" he says, which is such a silly line that Margaret almost giggles.

He turns the light on and the laughs evaporate. Tom has taken off his belt.

Tom had asked Margaret to save him some of the meat loaf, but she and Oliver finished it. There was nothing else in the refrigerator.

"Do you ever listen, you stupid little shit?" Tom says and he pulls her from the bed so hard that he dislocates her shoulder.

He slaps her twice with the double-folded belt and then he tells her to stop crying because he barely touched her.

He storms back downstairs.

Margaret is in agony all night and it's the school nurse who finally sends her to the hospital the following day. Tom is guilty and remorseful. He stops drinking. He starts going to church and to Promise Keepers.

Margaret and Oliver bide their time.

Church doesn't last.

A couple of months later, the drinking begins again in earnest.

One night when Tom is blind-drunk on the sofa, Margaret removes the revolver from his shoulder holster. She and Oliver gently open Tom's mouth and put the barrel of the revolver between his lips, and together they pull the trigger. Then they wipe their fingerprints off the gun and place it in Tom's right hand.

They put the suicide note they've written on the coffee table.

They work themselves up into fake tears and dial 911.

After being taken into foster care, the kids are dumped with their grandfather Daniel at his fly-ridden tumbledown house by the Inn River in a swampy part of Massachusetts.

Grandfather Daniel is retired Boston PD.

They haven't seen a lot of him but he sure as hell remembers them. He remembers them when they were only so high and living on a commune in upstate New York.

Daniel doesn't go into the city much anymore. He lives by fishing, hunting, and trapping, and his house is decorated with the skulls of many different animals.

Daniel meets the woman from social services with a broken-open shotgun over his shoulder. Margaret and Oliver give their grandfather a hug.

The woman from social services is relieved that the kids seem to know and like the old man.

"Their stepmom wasn't too fond of me or this place, but I seen the kids a couple of times," Daniel explains.

When the social services woman has gone, Daniel takes them into the kitchen and gives them each a can of Budweiser, which they accept nervously. A butchered hog is hanging upside down over the large kitchen sink. Its white skin is black with flies.

Daniel shows the kids how to open the beer cans. It's just like with a Coke. He tells them they can call him Red or Grandpa. He asks them what they want to do with their lives. Oliver says he wants to make a lot of money, maybe in computers, and Margaret says she wants to be an FBI agent like her dad.

Daniel considers that. "We'll see," he says. "First thing we have to do is fix them names." He looks at the boy. "We'll call you Olly. You like that?"

"Yes, sir," Olly says.

He examines the girl. "And with you, it's obvious. That mop of yours. We're going to call you Ginger."

64

The monster is out there, right out there through the glass in the fog.

It killed Erik and when it finds the name Rachel in the notebook, it will kill her too. Her and Kylie and Pete and Marty and Ginger and everybody connected with her.

There's no choice now. Choice was always an illusion.

There's only one thing to do.

Her hand is trembling.

Pete is looking at her expectantly.

She knows what she is going to do next.

First of all, she calls Marty to check that Kylie is safe and sound. Kylie isn't answering her phone, as usual, but the GPS locator has them at the mall at Copley Place.

Marty answers immediately. "Yeah, she's fine, we're just finishing up at the mall," he says.

"You have her in your line of sight?"

"Yeah, of course. She's at the Adidas store with Stuart."

"And then you're going to Ginger's dad's house?"

"Grandfather's house. What's the matter, Rach? I can tell something's up."

"I just want to know that Kylie's safe."

"She's safe. Ginger's twin brother will be there, and Ginger is an actual card-carrying FBI agent, and her grandfather is ex–Boston PD. I can't think of much safer than that."

"That's good, Marty. Keep her safe, OK?"

"I will, sweetie. You take care now. Take it easy this weekend, for God's sake. You need your strength, okay?"

"I will."

They say goodbye and hang up.

"What now?" Pete asks. "The cops?"

Rachel ties her hair back in a ponytail. "Kylie's safe but they are going to be coming for us. We need to get out of this house."

"What's the plan?" Pete asks.

"We download the app, see if it works. If we can find them, we'll locate their residence and call the police."

"And if we can't?"

"We call Ginger and tell her everything and ask her to take Kylie into protective custody. Then I guess we turn ourselves in."

Pete looks at her. "How long do you think we have?"

"I don't know. Hours? Let's get started," Rachel says.

She turns on Erik's app. It has downloaded successfully but when she tries to open it, a message flashes on the phone's home screen: For this app to work you need to enter the next number in this sequence: 8, 9, 10, 15, 16, 20 . . . If you enter the wrong number your phone will be locked and all devices associated with your account will be disabled for twenty-four hours.

Rachel shows the message to Pete.

"That is a powerful bit of tech. We need the exact digits or we're screwed," Pete mutters.

"What about the number pattern? Recognize it?"

He shakes his head. "It's not prime numbers. It's not the

sum of the numbers before. It's not any series that I know of offhand."

"We get only one shot at this. If we mess this up, we won't be able to get back in until tomorrow."

"And tomorrow will be too damn late."

"Eight, nine, ten, fifteen, sixteen, twenty," Rachel says aloud.

"I'll Google it," Pete says, but all he gets are links to YouTube videos teaching kids how to count.

Rachel closes her eyes and tries to think. What sequence is this? It's something she has seen before somewhere.

"An additional security protocol makes no sense at this stage, does it, Pete?" she says, thinking out loud. "I mean, Erik knows that the only person who is going to download this app is me. Right?"

"That's right," Pete agrees.

"And possibly The Chain, if The Chain has gotten his notebook and begun deciphering it. So what code would he have introduced here that would slow them down but allow me to pass through freely?"

"I don't know," Pete says.

Rachel puts the phone down on the table and paces the living room. Rain pounds on the skylight. A foghorn sounds from the Coast Guard ship.

"Something from your philosophy background?" Pete suggests.

"All he knows about me is that I have cancer, I'm a mom, and my team is the New York—shit, I have it!"

She picks up the phone and types in *23*.

A message flashes on the screen: That is the correct number. You may start the application after entering your username.

"Twenty-three?" Pete says. "I don't get it. It's prime, but twenty isn't prime."

324

"They're retired Yankees' numbers. A Bostonian's not going to know that, but a Yankees fan will," Rachel says.

The app opens up on a map of the Eastern Seaboard of the United States. The app is simple and user-friendly. There's a green Begin Trace button and a red End Trace button. The simplicity, however, conceals some pretty clever mathematics and statistical analysis.

"What's the username?" Pete asks.

Rachel types Rachel.

Username not recognized. Two more login attempts, a message on the screen says.

She types Erik.

Username not recognized. One more login attempt.

She types Ariadne.

A screen full of text appears.

Welcome, Ariadne. This app should work with text messages and with phone communications. The beta version will also work, to some extent, with encrypted communication apps. Version 2 will work with most encrypted message apps. Simply click the red button when you are on the phone and this app will attempt to locate the cell phone tower nearest to the call's point of origin. The longer you are in communication with your interlocutor, the closer and more accurate the app will be.

She shows the text to Pete.

He reads it, nods. "So if they respond to your Wickr text with Wickr only, it might not work."

"I guess not."

"If we weren't under time pressure, I'd say wait until tomorrow morning. Sunday morning, early, most people are generally at home. Saturday afternoon . . ."

"It's now or never. We have to take the gamble."

"OK, then."

"Here goes," Rachel says.

She clicks the Wickr button on her phone and begins typing.

I was thinking about what you said on Thanksgiving. I want to know if there's a way of getting off The Chain forever. I'm having nightmares. My daughter gets terrible stomach cramps. Can we somehow buy ourselves off The Chain permanently? Thank you.

She shows the message to Pete and sends it to Wickr 2348383hudykdy2.

Ten minutes later, she gets a notification that her interlocutor is sending her a response. She clicks Begin Trace, and Erik's hunter-killer algorithm powers up immediately.

It is a pleasant surprise to hear from you. It is a little early for Christmas presents, don't you think? It is with regret that I must inform you that we do not offer the service you require, the message says.

The GPS map on Rachel's phone lights up, but then nothing happens. The map freezes and the app crashes. She stabs at the screen, but it's dead.

"It didn't work," she says.

"He didn't think it was going to work with the encrypted apps. He said the phone trace works better."

"If I say 'Please call me,' it will definitely make them suspicious," Rachel says.

"I don't know."

A thought occurs to Rachel. "You know, Erik might be a crazy person. This might have no hope whatsoever of working."

"MIT doesn't employ dummies."

"But he still might be crazy. Maybe the grief has driven

him mad?"

"Do you think you can risk another communication without pissing them off?"

"What does it matter? As soon as they find my name in the notebook, they'll come for us."

"We don't know that they've got the notebook. He might have hidden it in a safe or something."

Rachel looks through the windows. "They have it," she says. "They're reading it right now. Sooner or later, they'll put two and two together."

"My fault. I'm really sorry about that," Pete says.

"I couldn't have gotten Kylie back without you, Pete."

Rachel opens the Wickr app again.

There must be some way of getting off The Chain forever. Something I can do for you or some amount of money I can pay. A way to close things off permanently, so we know that we are safe. Please, for the sake of my little girl, tell me what it is, she types and sends the message.

They have to wait only two minutes for a response. Again it comes through Wickr, not the phone. She fires up the hunter-killer application.

You must be pretty stupid. What was the first thing we told you? It's not about the money. It's about The Chain itself. It's got to keep going forever. Lose one link in The Chain and the whole thing collapses. OK, dummy? Wickr 2348383hudykdy2 replies.

The hunter-killer algorithm searches and recalibrates, and Erik's GPS locator lights up but once more crashes with no result. Rachel's phone freezes and she has to turn it off and on again.

"Nothing," Rachel says.

"Shit!"

"I'll try one more," Rachel says.

Please. I'm begging you. For the sake of my family, is there

327

anything I can do to get off The Chain? she types.

She shows it to Pete. "Send it," he says.

She sends the message. This time there is no quick response.

Five minutes go by.

Ten.

"That's it, then," Rachel says.

Her iPhone rings.

She fumbles for it and drops it onto the floor.

It bounces on its edge and the screen cracks.

"Shit!" Rachel screams and grabs the phone and turns on Erik's app. "Hello?" she says.

It's the Unknown Caller. The voice, as usual, is disguised.

"There is one thing you can do for us, Rachel. Why don't you kill yourself, you stupid bitch!" the voice says.

The hunter–killer algorithm flares to life and begins zooming in on an area of Massachusetts north of Boston.

"Please, I—"

"Goodbye, Rachel," the Unknown Caller says.

Keep her talking, Pete mouths.

"Wait. Don't go. I know things about you. I've found out stuff," Rachel says.

There's a pause before the voice asks, "What things?"

Rachel's mind races. She doesn't want to be associated with Erik in case they haven't got the notebook after all. What things about The Chain could she have found out on her own?

"The woman who took my daughter was named Heather. Her husband accidentally told Kylie that her son is named Jared. It shouldn't be difficult to find a woman named Heather with a son named Jared."

"What would you do with that information?" the voice

asks.

"We could start tracing our way backward to the very beginning of The Chain."

"That would be signing your own death warrant, Rachel. You're a very stupid woman, gambling with your life and your daughter's life like this," the voice says.

All the while they talk, the app zeros in on a smaller and smaller area of Massachusetts. A diminishing circle whose focus is now somewhere south of Ipswich and north of Boston.

"I don't want to cause any trouble. I—I just want to feel safe," Rachel says.

"If you ever contact us again, you'll be dead by the end of the day," the voice says. The call is disconnected.

But the app worked. The phone call was made in the Choate Island area in the marshes of Essex County. The cell tower nearest the caller is on Choate Island itself.

Rachel takes a screenshot of the map and shows it to Pete.

"This is it!" he cries.

"Let's go!" Rachel agrees.

They run outside to the truck.

They speed south along Route 1A through Rowley and Ipswich. In Ipswich they get onto 133, a narrow road through Ipswich's Great Marsh.

They drive as close as they can to Choate Island but there are no roads onto the boggy island itself, so they'll have to walk if they're going to find the cell tower. The fog isn't so bad down here, but the rain is chilly and coming at them slantwise from the ocean.

They park the pickup and get out. They put on coats and hiking boots. Pete's armed himself with the rifle, the Glock, the .45, and two flash-bang stun grenades that he thinks might come in handy. Rachel takes her shotgun. She's shaking. She's so afraid, she's finding it hard to breathe.

"Don't worry, Rach. There's not going to be any trouble today. This is a scouting mission. We'll get the info and call the feds."

They walk along a trail into the swampy terrain near Choate. Despite the rain and the cold, it's surprisingly insect-ridden. The land on either side of the path is choked and overgrown, dense and claustrophobic. Here and there they get glimpses of the Inn River, thick and sludgy under a layer of brown algae. The Inn is a tributary of the Miskatonic River, which curves through the mire somewhere to the north. The whole marsh seems to be caving inward, leaning toward some hidden center of mass. Something like Spanish moss is hanging from the trees; birds screech in the upper branches, and winter hasn't had its usual culling effect on the biting flies.

Rachel's spooked. They're getting close. She can feel it.

The dreams and song lines and nightmares are leading here.

They have been warned off probing into The Chain, and here she is following The Chain backward along Ariadne's thread.

But the labyrinth is not going to give up its secrets so easily.

They search the swamps and bogs on Choate for the next three freezing, filthy hours and come up with nothing.

No cell-phone tower.

No cell-phone relay station.

Barely any sign of civilization at all.

They stop at a little clearing and drink from their water bottles and then they start out again. More frustrating hours of this. By dusk, they are utterly soaked and exhausted and bitten raw by bugs. Rachel isn't sure if they are on Choate

330

Island or back on the mainland or on a different island in a different river system completely. They have crossed a hundred little streams and trails. She's beat. Chemotherapy patients do not go trekking through bogs in December.

She gasps for air.

She's dying right here, right now, out in the swamp. Pete can't know this.

She looks at the threatening sky overhead. Towering gray-black clouds looming over the marshes to the west. "Didn't the weather forecast say snow?" she says.

"Possibly, yeah. And we definitely do not want to be out here in the snow."

"If you were going to build a cell-phone tower, where would you put it?" Rachel asks him. "You're the engineer."

"On the high ground," Pete says.

"Is there any high ground?"

"What about that hill over there?" Pete says.

It's a very little hill, maybe thirty feet above sea level. It's five hundred yards away through the thicket.

"Why not?"

They are two-thirds of the way up it when they begin to see the outline of the cell-phone tower. It has fallen over, or perhaps it partially sank and tipped into the ground.

They reach the top of the hill, their breathing ragged.

From up here, you can see the whole Inn River system stretching to the west. The sickly green alluvial plain is vast, fetid, and unholy, as if it's covering up a lost corsair city waiting to be exhumed from its own sewers.

Rachel's heart sinks.

Erik's plan had been what, exactly? What did he expect them to do after they found the cell-phone tower closest to where The Chain's calls had come from?

"Now what?" she asks Pete.

Pete looks at the clouds and checks his watch. It's five. They've been hiking all day. They're cold and very wet and he doesn't want Rachel to be in the swamps at night. Not without proper equipment and with a snowstorm coming.

And he has other issues. He messed up this morning with that two-thirds-dose bullshit. His skin is starting to crawl. His eyes are dry. He's getting the sweats real bad. It hasn't fully hit yet, but it will.

He needs the fix.

Soon.

"Do you think we should call it a day?" he asks.

Rachel shakes her head. They're so close. She has to find them before they come back for her. They won't get another chance at this. It has to be now.

"Call it a day?" Pete asks again.

"And then what?" Rachel asks.

"Go to the feds? Tell them everything. Let them search for the house."

"We'll go to jail."

"The Dunleavys might not cooperate with the cops," Pete says.

Rachel shakes her head again. "They'll help us only if they know The Chain is finished."

Pete nods.

"What's that over there by the river to the north?" Rachel asks, taking Pete's binoculars. "Is that a cabin?"

She scans the structure.

It's about three-quarters of a mile ahead. A big old house with a deck that goes all the way around the outside. And it's on a direct vector with the cell-phone tower.

"It's definitely worth a closer look," Pete says. "But we're going to have to wade another stream or two. It's actually over on the mainland, I think."

They hike through an icy stream that comes up to their thighs and then up through a sparse little wood to within a few hundred yards of the cabin.

It's a large dwelling built partially on stilts near a river. It's next to a couple of derelict farm buildings sinking back into the marsh to the east. Several vehicles are parked under the veranda on the north side of the structure.

The hairs on the back of Rachel's neck are standing up.

Something about this place screams *denouement*.

"What do you want to do, Rach?" Pete asks.

"Let's try to go a little closer. If we can get a look at those license plates . . ."

"We'll have to crawl. Nice and low to the ground. The cover's not so dense here; we could be seen," Pete says.

Rachel shoulders her shotgun on its strap, drinks the last of her water, and follows Pete as they crawl toward the cabin.

The terrain is boggy and damp with brambles, thistles, and beach-plum bushes.

Within thirty seconds they are scratched, cut, bleeding.

Snow begins to fall.

They're a hundred yards away now.

It's an ugly property, all angles and ungainly additions from different eras with different timbers. It has been expanded very recently to accommodate what appear to be a couple of extra bedrooms on the upper story.

Pete takes out the binoculars and tries to read the plates on the vehicles under the house, but he can't quite make them out. "Rachel, you've got good eyes, do you want to try?"

She scans the cars. A Mercedes, a couple of pickup trucks, a Toyota.

She sees someone stepping onto the wraparound balcony.

"Kylie! Oh my God!" she screams. She scrambles to her

feet and begins running toward the house.

"What the hell?" Pete yells, momentarily stunned.

She has twenty yards on him, but Pete catches her in seven seconds. He tackles her and she goes down just in front of an old tree stump.

"What the hell are you doing?" Pete says, turning her to face him.

She struggles violently to break free of his grip. "They've got Kylie! They've got her! I saw her on the balcony," Rachel says breathlessly.

Pete looks up over the tree stump toward the balcony. There's no one there. "You're mistaken."

"It was her! I saw her!"

Pete shakes his head. There's no way they've gotten Kylie. She's with Marty and they've been careful.

Rachel is hyperventilating.

"It's not Kylie," Pete whispers. "And I can prove it. We put the GPS tracker in her shoes, remember? I can show you exactly where she is, and I promise you it's not here."

"Show me on the GPS," Rachel demands. "I know what I saw."

Pete opens the GPS app and shows Rachel that Kylie is nowhere near them. "She's in Boston."

Rachel looks at the phone. Sure enough, Kylie's GPS is beeping from downtown Boston, not here. "I was sure that was her," she says, confused.

"Come on, let's get back to the cover of those bushes before we're seen," Pete says.

65

Innsmouth High. Ginger at her tenth-grade career day.

"So what do you want to do with your life, Margaret?"

"I want to be an FBI agent like my father."

"This is very laudable, sweetie, but you'll need to improve some of your grades."

"Which ones?"

"Your English is great, but your math and science need a little work. Your brother can help you, I'm sure."

"Yeah, he loves that stuff."

Oliver helping Ginger with her homework in their grandfather's big ramshackle house by the Inn River. Screens and ant traps and bugs in the summer. Woodstoves and cold and kerosene heaters in the winter.

Daniel teaching the twins how to hunt in the dark places of the Miskatonic Valley. Daniel teaching the twins how to skin and smoke and preserve the meat.

Daniel telling the kids old cop stories. Old war stories.

Ginger and Oliver work hard and they both get into BU, which makes Daniel proud. Olly studies software engineering. Ginger studies psychology.

Both of them do very well indeed. The only fly in the

ointment is the amount of money they have to borrow for student loans. Daniel is not a wealthy man and they have grown up poor.

But after graduation, Oliver is headhunted by half a dozen Silicon Valley start-ups and Ginger is headhunted by the FBI, the CIA, and the ATF.

Ginger joins the Bureau.

There's a lot of affection in the FBI for Ginger and her father. *Shame what happened to your pop, real shame . . .*

Ginger works hard and gets fast-tracked. She makes connections. *I knew your old man. He was a hell of an agent. He and me, we used to—*

Ginger burning the midnight oil.

Ginger slowly rising up the chain of command.

Sometimes she wonders if she's doing this for herself or to please her grandfather or maybe to one-up her father. Is Ginger's life a result of or a reaction to her relationship with her dad?

She takes classes at the Behavioral Analysis Unit in Quantico, where they have all sorts of shrinks and investigators who can help her explore these questions if she wants. One of her instructors quotes the German poet Novalis: "Inward goes the way full of mystery." She likes that and she'd like to someday go on that inward journey to get at the root of why she's the way she is, but it's a journey she'll make by herself. She'll never trust any shrink with her past history and the thoughts in her head.

Oliver moves to California to work, first for Apple and then for Uber and then for a few riskier start-ups of which he has a piece. "When one of these hits, we'll be millionaires."

When one of these hits . . . he's worked for two companies in a row that have gone bankrupt.

That doesn't matter.

Ginger has come up with an alternative way to make money.

Serious money. Serious power.

Ginger hears about the Jalisco boys in the early 2010s.

The Jalisco boys brought north from Mexico an entirely new model of heroin distribution. The cartels and the gangs were too violent and too scary for Middle America. The Jalisco boys saw that and realized that there was a vast untapped market for their product if they approached the customers just right.

They gave out free heroin outside VA clinics, methadone clinics, and pharmacies to build up their clientele. Clinicians' overprescribing of OxyContin had created a vast user base of opiate and painkiller addicts who were all slipping into panic mode now that the DEA was finally beginning to crack down on narcotics.

Brown-tar heroin filled the gap nicely. It worked better than OxyContin or methadone and it was free, at least at first. And the guys giving it away weren't scary. The dealers didn't carry guns and they smiled a lot.

The Jalisco cartel had a million users within two years.

They diversified into other criminal enterprises.

Ginger ends up on a Jalisco task force. She is looking into links between the Jalisco cartel and the Boston mob. Thanks to rats and FBI penetration, the Patriarca crime family is on the decline, but the Jalisco cartel is on the upswing.

Ginger comes across a Jalisco hostage scheme in which people who owe money are kidnapped until their families pay their debts, but there's an element of humanity to it: a different member of the family can take the place of the kidnap victim.

The Jalisco boys' hostage model works largely through minimal violence, but seeing its underutilized potential,

Ginger wonders if it can be modified for her own ends.

She remembers how effective the chain letters were in her childhood.

She discusses it with Olly.

With the help of her programming-genius brother, The Chain is born in Boston in 2013.

It isn't an immediate success. There are teething troubles. A little too much blood.

Needing to distance themselves from the wet work, they use Jalisco and Tijuana enforcers who are desperate for money. They don't know who their employer is. The mysterious woman behind it all is known as the Mujer Roja or the Muerte Roja. They say she's the wife of a cartel over-lord. They say she is a Yankee follower of Nuestra Señora de la Santa Muerte.

The Jalisco and Tijuana assassins are somewhat trigger-happy. They don't really understand that operations in the United States require finesse. There's a little too much killing in the early days. The whole thing is on the verge of collapse.

Ginger gets rid of the Mexican assassins and uses her contacts in the dying New England Patriarca crime family instead. They understand the American way of death. They've been doing this kind of thing for decades.

Eventually The Chain begins to run like a well-oiled machine.

Things start to settle.

The Patriarca goons are disposed of, and The Chain begins to self-regulate.

Ginger sending out the letters.

Ginger making the phone calls.

Ginger calling in the hits.

It grows to become a million-dollar blackmail, kidnapping,

and terrorism scheme run as a family business by Oliver and Ginger.

"It is," says Olly, "the goddamn Uber of kidnapping with the clients doing most of the work themselves."

If they could launch it as an IPO, he says, it could be worth tens of millions.

But as it is, they're comfortable enough.

They pay off their college loans. They get rich.

They open bank accounts in Switzerland and the Cayman Islands.

The Chain works beautifully now and it's foolproof.

Oliver has done several red-team failure analyses of The Chain and he sees only three areas of concern that might conceivably lead to trouble.

First, there's Ginger's often lazy tradecraft. He's told her to use a new Wickr address, a new burner phone, and a new Bitcoin account at every new stage of The Chain. But she doesn't always do that. It's a big hassle and usually she changes the addresses and accounts only about once a month. He's also told her never to make one of the anonymous Chain phone calls when she's at work or when she's at her house in the Back Bay or at Daniel's house on the Inn River.

She promises to work on the tradecraft, although it's hard to hold down her job in the Bureau, study for a PhD, and run a very sophisticated criminal enterprise all at the same time. Still, there are many layers of encryption between them and The Chain. Encryption, Faraday cages, redundancies . . .

The second major area of concern is Ginger's use of The Chain to settle personal scores. Three times (that Olly knows of) she's done this. Ideally, the business and the personal should never mix, but with human beings there's always going to be some blurring of the lines. And improvising a set of rules to delineate the system was always going to seem contingent on and provisional to that system's inventor.

Some of this score-settling ties into the third area of concern—Ginger's sex life.

Olly realizes that he's a bit of an odd duck, relationship-wise. He's never had a serious girlfriend or a real romantic interest of any kind. He's an introvert and he doesn't like parties or physical contact. Maybe the hippies really did mess with his brain chemistry early?

Ginger, however, is thoroughly engaged with the world. They would be a neat example in any psychological study of twins. She had boyfriends throughout high school and college, and she has dated a dozen different men since joining the Bureau, two of whom were married.

Sex is important; Olly appreciates that intellectually. Sex is the joker that keeps mammalian DNA forever changing and one step ahead of all the viruses and pathogens that are trying to wipe the species out. Olly understands this on a scientific and mathematical level. But sex is still a wild card, and love—God forbid—is an even wilder card.

Power corrupts and absolute power corrupts absolutely. And when you mix power with sex, well, you get what Ginger has occasionally done with The Chain. Several times he's caught her using information from the FBI databases for purposes unrelated to Chain business. He suspects there are other incidents he doesn't even know about.

It isn't good.

He has to get her to put a stop to it.

Oliver sits in his grandfather's study with Erik Lonnrott's notebook in his hand. There's a fire burning in the grate. He can see snow flurries through the window.

Olly examines the notebook carefully. It's mostly a fair copy of a previous notebook. Or even notebooks. Erik has been working on this for some time. Olly was aware that someone was looking into The Chain and he had suspected that Erik might be the one. Erik had shaken off too many tails for him to be entirely innocent, and a lot of search histories and analyses led straight back to the computers at MIT.

They hadn't been able to find Erik's laptop or phone, but the notebook was on his person.

Erik took the trouble to write most of his text in cipher. Olly isn't too bothered about that. There is no cipher devised by man that is unbreakable. Additionally, poor old Erik had gotten quite excited in the last few weeks of his life, and instead of carefully coding all of his entries, he had simply written them down in Russian or Hebrew. As if that would conceal anything. The poor deluded fool.

Olly looks at these final entries and is not impressed. Erik hadn't gotten very far with his work. He had no suspects, he hadn't made the connection to the Jalisco boys, his reasoning was all over the place.

Some of the last few entries are just random words and names.

There are hints about an app he was designing but no indication of what said app was supposed to do.

The very last entry in the book was clearly written very recently—perhaps a few days ago.

It says simply: דתל

It's a word that means "ewe" in Hebrew.

It's a word that's pronounced "Rachel" in English.

Olly sighs and looks out the window.

Marty, Ginger's new boyfriend, has an ex-wife named Rachel, doesn't he?

This little family get-together is going to be a lot more

interesting than he initially expected. He picks up his phone and texts his sister: Ginger, can you do me a favor and come talk to me when you get a chance?

66

Rachel tries to call Kylie but she can't get through.

"No signal," she says. "Thank God she's safe, though."

Pete, however, is looking worried. "Shit. Maybe not," he says.

"What is it?"

"Look at the time stamp on the GPS trace in her sneakers."

"Oh my God. She's been at the Adidas store in Boston for nine hours!" Rachel says. "I know what happened. She bought new shoes, threw the old ones out, and forgot about the GPS."

"How could they have taken her in broad daylight from the mall? It doesn't make sense," Pete says.

Rachel is poleaxed.

Her world has been pulled out from under her.

Again.

And this time it's 100 percent her fault. They had warned her. They told her to leave well enough alone, and she had blundered ahead with this idiotic plan.

She feels sick.

Dizzy.

Nauseous.

She dry-heaves.

The old thoughts: *You stupid cow. You stupid bitch. Why didn't you just die when you had the chance? Everyone would have been better off.*

They have taken her beautiful, innocent, wonderful girl. Her fault.

Stupid, stupid, stupid, stupid!

Stupid no more.

She unslings her shotgun. She'll go in the back door under the balcony. She'll shoot the lock off if she has to and she'll kill everyone inside and get her daughter out of there.

She brushes snowflakes off her face and heads for the house.

"Where are you going?" Pete asks.

"To get Kylie."

"You don't know what or who is in there," he says.

"I don't care. You can stay here, I'm going in," Rachel says.

Pete grabs her arm. "No. We'll both go. Wait here for two minutes and I'll scout ahead."

"I'm going with you."

Pete shakes his head. "I'm the expert, Rachel. I did the Marine Corps recon course. I've done this kind of thing many, many times."

"I'm going with you."

"Just hold on here for two minutes, OK? Let me check it out first."

"Two minutes?"

"Two minutes. I'll signal you from under the deck. Wait here."

Pete knows he should have done this whole thing by himself today. What was he thinking, bringing a cancer patient?

He slithers across the open ground toward the carport

under the house. There are five vehicles parked here: a white Mercedes, a red Mustang, two pickup trucks, and a Corolla. That could translate to a lot of people. He goes low past the cars. A security light comes on and he freezes, but no one comes out to investigate and he slowly moves on again. Next to the carport is a drive-in garage and next to that appears to be the front door and the large windows of a lower living room. Pete can't risk going past those, so he goes back the way he came. He tries the door next to the garage. Locked. The garage door itself, however, is not closed properly. There's about half an inch of clearance between the bottom of the door and the ground. He lies down on his belly and slides his fingers underneath. If it's just a buckle in the aluminum, it wouldn't do them any good, but if it's a damaged torsion spring . . .

He puts two hands under the door and tries to lift, and the door gradually begins to rise.

This is how they'll get in, Marine Corps urban warfare–style. You gain entry, you clear the room, you move to the next room, you work level after level until the house is secured. Unknown number of unfriendlies, but he and Rachel have surprise on their side. He gets to his feet and staggers a little.

Oh no.

He feels dizzy.

His skin's on fire.

It's the hunger.

He's screwed himself this morning. *Can't suddenly start messing around with your fix, you know better than that, Pete.*

Soon there will be a million ants crawling up his legs and arms, into his mouth, down his throat . . .

Stop it! he tells himself. *Stop it now!*

Hubris to play the hero card. Rachel would be the better

345

scout in these circumstances. *Gotta get back,* he thinks, and he turns and runs straight into a man holding a shotgun.

"Yeah, I thought I heard something," the man says.

Pete thinks about a move, but instead of thinking about a move he should have actually *moved.* Flashlight into the man's skull. Boot into his knee. Gun butt to face. One guard taken out. But he's done nothing. Too slow. Too slow not because he's too old or because he doesn't have the muscle memory; too slow because he has damaged himself with heroin and oxycodone and every other opiate he has been able to get his hands on.

And now Pete has Rachel's exact thought: *Stupid, stupid, stupid, stupid.* Stupid and weak. The man takes a step back and points the shotgun at Pete's face.

"Drop the flashlight and the gun," the man says.

Pete drops the flashlight and the nine-millimeter.

"Now, with two fingers, take that forty-five out of your belt and drop it on the ground too."

Pete takes out his precious .45 ACP and lets it fall into the gathering snowflakes at his feet. Now he feels naked. The ACP had belonged to his grandfather in the U.S. Navy. The old man had fired it in anger once—at a kamikaze ramming his ship at the Battle of Okinawa. It had been Pete's good-luck charm in Iraq and Afghanistan.

"Shit," Pete says.

"Yeah, pal, you're in the shit. Daniel don't tolerate nobody on his property. And by 'don't tolerate,' I don't mean he's gonna turn you over to the local cops. Put your hands on your head."

Pete puts his hands on his head. "This is all a misunderstanding. I got lost," he begins, but the man shushes him.

"We'll see what Daniel has to say about that. He's got his grandkids with him today. I don't believe he'll be right

346

pleased. Kneel on the ground, and keep your hands behind your head."

The guard kicks him in the back and Pete goes down.

Dirt. Gravel. Snow.

Pete's mind is racing. He's trying to think. Nothing comes.

"Now, you just lay down there, boy, you just lay there while I ring the doorbell and bring everybody running."

67

Ginger walks into the big remodeled master bedroom feeling pretty pleased with herself. The Chain has neutralized the Erik Lonnrott threat, and her new boyfriend is getting along like a house on fire with Daniel. They are both big Red Sox fans and Marty can throw out names like Ted Williams, Carl Yastrzemski, and Roger Clemens and know what he is talking about. Daniel told Marty he could call him Red if he wanted. A rare honor.

A big decision, bringing him here. It's not every partner she brings to meet her grandfather and her brother. But Marty O'Neill is special. He's funny. He's smart—Harvard College and Harvard Law; I mean, come on. He's very good-looking if you like dark-haired, green-eyed, and Irish. And she does.

It's true that he has a daughter, a thirteen-year-old daughter, a slightly annoying thirteen-year-old daughter, but her recent tribulations have obviously taken the wind out of her sails, and the thirteen-year-old is very appreciative of both Marty and his new young girlfriend who has an awesome job and who taps into the coolest hipster frequencies.

Oliver would no doubt be furious if he found out that

she had met Marty by stalking him through The Chain, but Marty wasn't exactly a victim or anything. His ex-wife had kept him out of it. And she'd just chanced upon his Facebook page sort of accidentally while researching her.

Sort of.

True, she had The Chain get Marty's previous girlfriend, Tammy, out of the picture, but that's as far as it went.

This time.

If Olly knew how many times she has used inside knowledge from The Chain for her own little adventures, he would no doubt have a fit, but what's the point of having all this power and ignoring it? It's fine to dip your toe in from time to time. It would be perverse not to.

The Chain is her invention, after all. Her thing. All Olly's talk of IPOs and internet millions is just talk. The Chain got Olly his house in San Francisco, her house in Boston, and the apartment on Fifth Avenue. The Chain. Her idea.

So if she wants to play with Marty O'Neill, she can. Marty is handsome, witty, and fun. Olly need not worry. She's in control. She's the spider. The annoying fly, of course, is the ex-wife. The nerve of her on Wickr today. People *never* Wickr'd once they were off The Chain. They normally were so grateful. Grateful and scared. Maybe it would be better to have the ex-wife disappeared. All it would take was one little phone call or message: *We've added a new condition for your child's safe return. A woman named Rachel Klein O'Neill who lives on Plum Island, Massachusetts—get rid of her by the end of the week. The body must never be found.*

Rachel can be removed from the picture at any time.

"The children seem happy. I just saw Kylie on the deck," Marty says, coming up behind her and kissing her on the back of the neck.

Ginger turns to face him and Marty puts his arms around

her. "This is so good for Kyles. I'm not the world's best judge of teenagers, but she seems to have been going through a really hard time in the past few weeks."

"Yeah, I did give Rachel the name of one of our therapists."

"Well, Rachel's been out of it too, as you can imagine," Marty says.

Ginger's phone pings to let her know that she has a message.

"What's up?" Marty asks as she reads the message from her brother.

"Oh, it's only Olly. Something about dinner, I'll bet. No doubt Grandpa is going to try to burn the house down with his barbecue again. Hold that thought, I'll be right back."

Ginger walks along the second-floor landing to her grandfather's study, goes inside, closes the door, and sits down. Olly has that look of superiority he assumes sometimes, a look that would try the patience of a saint.

"Yes?" she says. "What is it?"

"You've been using The Chain for your own ends again, haven't you?"

"No."

"Yes, you have."

"It's all for *our* own ends."

"You know what I mean. You've been meddling. Like you did with Noah Lippman."

"No."

"Or that girl crush you had on Laura what's-her-name a few years ago. Poor Laura made the mistake of her life by rebuffing you, and then she vanished without a trace three months later. You waited a whole three months before unleashing The Chain on her. Very tactful."

"Noah's still alive."

"Just about. We don't use The Chain for our own personal vendettas, Ginger—we've discussed this."

"I didn't."

"Or to meet handsome young men."

Ginger groans. He's onto her. "Do you know how difficult it is to meet people in this city?" she protests.

"Not difficult at all. There are a million dating apps."

"I'm supposed to ignore any man who might have come in contact, even peripherally, with The Chain?"

"Yes! You know the protocols."

"Who set up the protocols? Who invented The Chain?"

"It's a security issue, sweetie."

"It's all my handiwork. It wasn't you. It was me. I can do what I like with it."

Olly closes his eyes and sighs. All good things have to come to an end eventually, he supposes. He is surprised that it has lasted this long, actually. The models all said that The Chain would probably last only about three years before it collapsed. You could intimidate so many folks for only so long. The number of people involved grows almost exponentially, and no conspiracy can survive exponential growth. It's a typical stochastic fast-slow system and when the breaking point comes, it will break spectacularly.

Olly strokes the little goatee he has been cultivating without much success for the past few months. "We should have retired The Chain years ago," he mutters. "I mean, why keep it going when we have enough money?"

"Why stop it? You're just jealous because it was my creation."

"Wasn't the purpose of The Chain to set us up for life? It's done that."

"Was that its purpose?" she asks with a sneer.

He frowns and shakes his head.

"You just don't get it, do you?" Ginger says. Not for Olly the peregrine-hovering-over-the-hay-field thing. Olly isn't a true predator like her. A true predator sometimes kills even when it isn't hungry. "Wasn't it us against the world? Remember?" she says.

Olly's frown deepens.

"All right, what's gone wrong?" Ginger asks.

"It has to do with that notebook," Olly says.

"You've decoded it, haven't you?"

"No, not yet."

"Then what?"

"Near the end, crazy Erik didn't write everything in code."

"And?"

"What did you say your new boyfriend's ex-wife's name was?"

"Oh, shit."

"Sometime in the last week or so, Erik apparently met with a woman named Rachel."

"Shit, shit, shit."

"Come on, spill."

Now it's Ginger's turn to sigh. "You know what your problem is, Olly? You're completely bloodless. You're like Spock or something. You should probably see someone about that. It's not normal."

"This is serious, Ginger. This is crash-bag, fake-IDs, flee-the-country stuff."

"How much do we have in Switzerland?"

"Enough." Olly goes to the gun cabinet, unlocks it, and opens it. "I always thought that if we were going to go down, it would be because of you tangling emotions with business."

She smiles. "Christ, Olly, that's how everybody goes

down in the end. Didn't you know that? You can't fight biology."

"You can try," he says.

68

Back in the master bedroom, Marty is looking through the plate-glass window at the oak-tree stump between the house and the swampy, scrubby woods beyond. Snow is falling in big powdery flakes on the river and the living trees and the dead oak. It's a frickin' Robert Frost poem.

Lovely down here. Ginger undersold it. This is no crazy old cabin in the middle of a swamp. This is some spread. A beautiful house. Art on the walls. Expensive shit. The old man, Daniel, must have a chunk of change. And as advertised, he's a character.

The kids are loving it and Ginger is loving showing it off. She's a good one, he thinks. Rachel was a mistake. They were both so young. He'd told everybody that he'd fallen in love with Rachel reading her brilliant book reviews in the *Crimson,* but that was crap. It was a physical thing. They really didn't have much in common.

When you got past thirty, you had better judgment. Tammy was merely a fling, but Ginger's different. Special. With her he could settle down. Live in the city. Have a couple more—

"I was just thinking about you," he says as Ginger comes

back into the room holding her handbag.

A strand of red hair is curling down between her breasts.

He has a sudden urge to throw her on the bed and ravish her.

"Ginger, do these doors lock? I know there's kids wandering around, so I—" he begins, but something in his peripheral vision catches his eye.

He turns to look at it.

"What is that?" he says to Ginger.

"What?"

"Is that someone coming toward the house from behind that tree?"

"Where?"

"I thought I saw someone coming through the snow. Yeah, look . . . oh my God! You're not going to believe this, but, um, I think that's my ex-wife," Marty says.

Ginger takes the Smith and Wesson .38 out of her handbag and points it at his head.

"I believe you," she says.

69

Rachel puts the shotgun against her shoulder and aims it at the guard.

"Hold it right there," she says.

The guard spins to face her. "Whoa! Take it easy, lady. I don't think you know what you're doing with that thing," he says.

"You'll be thinking something else when I blow you in half with it," Rachel replies.

Pete picks up his .45. "Drop the shotgun, pal," Pete says.

The guard places the gun on the ground and puts his hands up.

"Lie facedown on the ground," Pete orders and the man complies as Pete kicks the gun away.

"You don't have to hurt me. There's duct tape and rope in the garage. I got the garage-door opener in my jacket pocket," the guard says quickly.

"How many armed men inside the house?" Pete asks.

"I'm the only—" the man begins.

"Nobody move!" someone says, and there's the sound of a gunshot.

A spotlight comes on. Standing at the front door are

Ginger and a man about her age—her twin brother, Rachel assumes. Both of them have handguns.

"Rachel, is that you? What's going on?" Ginger asks innocently.

Ginger? What the hell? Doubt courses through Rachel. Did Erik's tracker somehow cross signals with the GPS tracker they put in Kylie's shoes? Did Kylie transfer the GPS tiles after all? Was this whole ridiculous hunt through the swamp an enormous mistake?

Oh my God, yes. If it's a mistake, Kylie is safe. Yes! Rachel has to explain before someone gets hurt.

"I'm so sorry, Ginger. This must look completely crazy. I was just telling this gentleman here—"

The garage door opens to reveal a skinny old geezer with white hair holding what looks like an assault rifle. "What are you doing here on my property?" the old man demands.

"Grandpa, we've got this!" Ginger's brother says.

"Olly's right, Red, we've got it under control," Ginger says. "Rachel, you and your friend should really drop your weapons."

"Everyone, please, I think we've made a huge mistake. I'm sorry. I put a GPS tracker in Kylie's sneakers. I thought she'd been kidnapped."

"Drop your gun, please, Rachel. Why on earth would you think she'd been kidnapped?" Ginger asks.

"It's complicated," Rachel replies.

Ginger is under the floodlight above the door, and Rachel can see her face.

She sees her clearly for the first time.

That copper hair. Those blue eyes. Those beautiful blue eyes. A cold blue. A chilly bottom-of-the-abyss blue. Blue eyes that are watching this whole scene with cool disdain.

Ginger seems to be enjoying it, even.

And then Ginger's eyes meet Rachel's and the two women look at each other for what seems like an age but is perhaps little more than a second.

That second is enough.

They recognize each other.

You.

You.

Rachel knows and Ginger knows, and Ginger knows that Rachel knows.

Erik's app hasn't made a mistake.

The Chain leads here and Ginger is not going to let any of them leave this place alive. They have uncovered the secret, and to protect it Ginger is going to have to kill all of them. Rachel, Pete, Marty, Stu, and Kylie.

Rachel had been about to tell Pete that they should drop their weapons and put their hands up. But if they do that, Ginger will murder them on the spot.

Rachel turns to Pete. She looks up at the floodlight above the porch. Pete follows her gaze.

"She's The Chain and she's going to kill us," Rachel says.

Pete nods.

The twins are behind a low wall. Hitting them will be difficult, so instead, he raises the .45 and shoots out the light.

70

Immediate darkness and confusion. Yelling and an arc of yellow flame from the garage as Daniel opens up with the automatic weapon.

"Hit the deck!" Pete shouts.

Rachel throws herself to the ground.

Tracer rounds fly from the barrel of the gun and hurl themselves into the space where Rachel had been seventenths of a second ago. The rounds miss and continue to spin on their long axes, traveling thousands of yards across the night.

Then all the guns open up at once. A .38, a nine-millimeter, and that big assault rifle again. Fire from several angles triangulates two yards above Rachel's head.

She buries her face in the snow and screams.

None of this matters. The guns, the gunfire, the sickly-sweet smell of gunpowder. What matters is Kylie. She's in the house somewhere and Rachel is going to get her. Pete is doing a ten-count in his head. Ten seconds on automatic will burn through the magazine on the assault rifle in the garage.

After ten seconds, he looks up. The shooters on the porch

have slipped back inside. The old man has gone through his mag and is reloading.

Pete shoots three rounds into the garage to give the man something to think about and then scrambles to a new firing position. Shoot and move. Shoot and move. That's what kept you alive in a limited-cover firefight, and the big ACP rounds would take you down with a shoulder shot at this range. Might even take you out.

He rolls into the snow to his right, crawls behind a bush, and shoots again. His whole body is aching with need for the fix, but he'll fight it and them. "Rachel? Are you OK?" Pete says.

No answer.

He has to think of a plan. Any plan. In infantry training, they tell you that a sloppy plan executed immediately is better than a great plan executed an hour later. They're right about that. Out here he's going to die. He has to go in.

Maybe fifteen seconds have passed since the shooting began.

Here goes, he thinks.

"Not so fast, smart guy," someone says, grabbing at him. He ducks a fist coming at his face and blocks a knife coming at his rib cage.

It's the guard who'd originally found him. He'd forgotten all about that asshole. The man has grabbed his gun hand and is trying to kill him with a large hunting knife. The knife slashes at his face; Pete flinches, and the knife nicks his left cheek. Pete kicks hard into the darkness and connects with soft tissue. He frees his gun hand and shoots once.

There's a hollow, sickening thump and then silence.

"Pete?" a voice says next to him.

"Rachel?"

"I'm going into the house," she whispers. "Through the garage, it's the only way."

"What's the plan?"

"We go inside the house, rescue the kids, and kill everybody who isn't Kylie, Marty, or Stuart," Rachel says.

"Sounds good to me."

71

They enter the garage. The shooter is gone but boxes holding something flammable have caught fire and are burning furiously next to a dozen cans of paint. They can't stay here.

"There's a door that leads to the main house," Rachel says.

She's up for this. It's the moment she's been subconsciously training for all her life. The radiation, the chemo, those hard days in Guatemala, those long shifts waitressing at the diner, the midnight Uber runs to Logan. All of it was preparation for this. She's ready. It's all for family, isn't it? Everything is for family. Even an imbecile knows you don't get between a grizzly-bear mama and her cub.

Pete fishes one of the two flash-bang grenades from his coat pocket. "I'm going to open the door and throw in a flash-bang. Close your eyes and cover your ears," Pete whispers to Rachel, then tosses the stick as he opens the door. A second later, the flash-bang goes off with a deafening roar and a white juddering light. It's an essentially harmless weapon meant to stun at close quarters. It won't hurt the kids, but it'll scare the shit out of people who don't know it's coming.

"Wait here," Pete says and goes through the door.

A dozen smoke alarms begin ringing. It's an old house but it's been remodeled, and in one of those remodelings a sprinkler system has been installed to protect the artwork the grandchildren have been collecting. Rachel has never been in a home that has its own sprinkler system and she's shocked when cold water starts pouring down on her. She has no idea what's happening.

Pete pops his head around the doorway. "No one there now. We should go. Those paint tins are going to start exploding in a minute."

"Which way?" Rachel asks, coughing.

Pete has no idea. "Room by room. Stay behind me. Check my blind spots," he says.

Pete forges ahead but he wonders if he can last much longer. He's having trouble breathing. Adrenaline is putting off the collapse, but that won't work forever. *Hang in there, Pete,* he tells himself, *until you get Kylie safe.*

The house has been haphazardly extended so that now it's a maze of rooms and corridors and alcoves.

A hallway.

A room.

A big TV, a sofa, hunting trophies.

Another door.

Dining table, chairs, artwork.

A distant scream.

"Kylie!" Rachel yells.

No answer.

Back to the hallway.

Pete kicks open another door and swings his weapon into the corners of a kitchen. "Kylie! Stuart!" he says.

Nothing.

The house lights flicker as smoke from the garage fire fills the entire ground floor. Water is still dripping from the sprinklers and pooling at their feet. The smell is pungent, sour, Neolithic.

In a downstairs bedroom, Rachel spies Kylie's coat but no Kylie.

The lights fail and come back on again, a dim, yellow goblin glow.

The bedroom connects to another room.

Pete eases the door open and looks inside.

Empty, but they can hear footsteps outside in the hallway. Rachel points to the door and puts her finger over her lips. Pete takes his remaining flash-bang from his pocket, violently tugs open the bedroom door, and throws the grenade into the corridor.

Another loud explosion and a burst of white light followed by machine-gun fire. Pete waits until the shooting stops and then in one clean, fast movement he goes out with Rachel, swinging right as Rachel swings left.

There, in front of her, at the end of the hallway, a man is reloading an assault rifle. The old man again. Not one of the twins. His hair is white; his stance is remote, tough, confident. He's the one that Olly calls Grandpa and Ginger calls Red.

Rachel raises her shotgun.

She remembers what she was told at the range: wait until your target is close or your target flees. But this man is not running toward her or running away from her. He's just standing there at the end of the long corridor.

He finishes reloading. He looks at Rachel and raises a long black gun.

Rachel pulls the trigger.

Her aim is off.

The wall to her right erupts in fire. The kick takes her in the shoulder. The man yells, drops his gun, and staggers into a room next to him. Pete turns, checks that Rachel's OK, and goes down the hallway after the man, but he's gone.

Pete picks up a dropped MP5. A perfect weapon for close work. He clears the mechanism and shoulders it.

"I think I'm out of ammunition," Rachel says. Pete hands her the nine-millimeter and she sets down the shotgun, which has served its Chekhovian purpose.

The house's lights finally go off and stay off.

The darkness is nearly complete.

Darkness. Smoke. Pools of dank water.

What can they do but forge on by iPhone light?

They come upon a big open-plan living room. Dozens of hunting trophies on the walls, and not just local animals—antelope, cheetahs, lions, a leopard. Predators and prey together.

Fear is coursing through her, but fear is a liberation too. Fear releases power and is the precursor to action.

Pete is drenched with sweat. "Are you OK?" she asks.

"Fine," he replies. He feels the opposite of fine but the MP5 is comforting against his shoulder, there's nine left in the magazine, and he still has his trusty .45. All good.

"Mommy!" a distant voice calls from somewhere outside.

They slide open a set of glass doors and find themselves in the snow. It's blowing hard from the north and swirling about them in an icy wind.

"Over there, I think," Rachel says, pointing to a series of disused farm buildings. There are footprints in the snow heading toward the closest structure.

They follow the prints toward the entrance to an old abattoir. This had presumably been a working slaughterhouse once but now there are gaping holes in the walls and roof, and ivy covers everything.

They kill the phone lights and go inside.

They're immediately hit by the stench of blood, putrefaction, and rot.

Broken glass litters the floor and crunches under their feet.

It's hard to see; the only illumination comes from the flickering lights of the house erupting in flames behind them.

Wind howls through the ruined walls and the roof.

Rachel jumps as she almost collides with a sow hanging from a ceiling beam. The pig's lifeless dead eyes are level with her own.

Adjusting to the dark, she sees other animals on hooks—pheasants, crows, a badger, a deer.

The abattoir is on two levels with a small set of steps between them.

"They must be on the upper level," Pete whispers. "Stairs are a classic place for an ambush. Watch out."

Rachel nods and tries not to make so much noise with her boots.

They move forward slowly.

Broken glass, wet snow, stale air. Rust, dried blood, death.

They get only halfway up the concrete steps before someone starts shooting.

"Handgun, three o'clock!" Pete screams and returns fire with the MP5 as he runs to the top of the steps. He shoots three more times as his target ducks behind a piece of machinery and vanishes.

He smiles grimly to himself. The bastards have wasted their chance.

He looks at his clip. The MP5 is empty now. He drops it and pulls out his trusty .45.

"Did you hit someone?" Rachel whispers.

"No."

"Be careful of the kids," Rachel says, following him up the steps.

Her hands are shaking and she forces herself to grip the pistol tighter. She can't lose it now, not when they are so—

An overhead arc light comes on.

Rachel spins the nine-millimeter in a 360 around her. The abattoir is a filthy concrete ruin with bits of old farm machinery and garbage everywhere. Near her, two more pigs are hanging from hooks in the ceiling. One of them has been freshly slaughtered and is dripping blood into a bucket.

But none of that is relevant.

What's relevant is what she sees thirty feet away at the end of the upper level of the abattoir: Ginger is standing there with her twin brother, Olly, both holding pistols aimed at Kylie and Stuart.

Kylie and Stuart are crying and terrified; their wrists are handcuffed in front of them. Marty is sprawled near them on the floor, apparently only semiconscious. His head is bleeding and he's breathing hard and moaning in agony. Ginger is holding Kylie by the collar of her T-shirt and pointing the gun straight down onto her skull. Olly has his arm around Stuart's neck and the barrel of his weapon is shoved into Stuart's ear.

Pete and Rachel both freeze.

"Mom!" Kylie cries.

"Let her go!" Rachel screams at Ginger.

"That doesn't seem likely, now, does it?" Ginger says.

Rachel aims the nine-millimeter at Ginger's face. "I'll kill you right here," she says.

"You're that confident about hitting me from this distance? How many times have you even fired a pistol, Rachel?" Ginger asks.

"I won't miss you, you bitch."

"Drop your gun or I drop the kids."

"We're not dropping our guns," Pete says. "That's not how this is going to work. You're going to let the children go and we'll leave, and you'll have plenty of time to get your crash bags and your dummy passports and everybody wins."

He sways a little before catching himself and getting his balance.

"Whoa, steady there, sailor boy. Why don't you sit down and take a load off?" Ginger says, looking significantly at Olly.

"You should listen to me," Pete mutters, inching his way closer. They are a confident pair. Overconfident. Another few feet and he'll have a clear shot at Olly. Stuart comes only halfway up his chest, so if he aims at the top of Olly's skull, the big powerful .45 round will kill Olly instantly. Has to be soon. The adrenaline in his system has definitely plateaued and he's on the downslope now.

"Clicking the hammer back is such a cliché," Ginger says. "Do you really need me to do that? Are you so dense that you need a visual aid? I will kill this little girl if you don't drop your goddamn gun."

"Then you'll die," Pete says. He's about twenty feet from them now. A fast shot might just do the trick.

"Put the gun down now, asshole!" Olly barks with a cool, imperious air.

Pete takes aim at the top of Olly's skull. He should act. He should act now. But everything hurts. Everything aches. His hand is shaking.

"You need to drop the gun now or—" Olly begins.

There's a loud bang, and a bullet from Ginger's .38 hits Pete in the torso and he's down.

Rachel dives behind a concrete blood-collecting trough as another bullet misses her by inches.

"You shot him," Olly says to Ginger.

"The theatrics were getting on my nerves," Ginger replies. "Now, Rachel, it's your turn. Drop the gun and put your hands up or we kill Kylie. Olly, keep your arm around that one's neck but put your gun in little Kylie's cheek."

Olly sticks the barrel of his pistol in Kylie's right cheek.

"Mommy!" Kylie wails.

Rachel's stomach lurches. Her eyes are streaming. Pete is shot; Marty is down. And she's so exhausted. Weeks of this. Years of this. Everything has gone wrong since that very first oncologist's report from Mass. General.

She's doomed and part of her wants to lie down on the filthy floor, close her eyes, and sleep.

But she can see Kylie's face, and Kylie is her world. She crouches behind the blood trough and points the nine-millimeter over its lip at Ginger.

"Drop your gun and put your hands up!" Ginger screams as the snow whirls around her.

"No! You drop your gun," Rachel replies, tears running down her cheeks.

"Put your hands up and we'll let you go. You and the kids. Like your friend said. We know the game's over," Olly says. "Ginger here has screwed it up for us. Not for the first time. We'll let you go and you'll let us go. We can make a deal. Give us twenty-four hours and we'll be in South America."

Rachel's heart leaps. Here's a new possibility. A slim lifeline of hope.

"Promise it! Promise me you'll let us walk out of here," Rachel says. "If—if you're fleeing the country, there's no need for any more killing."

"Put your hands up, drop your gun, and I give you my word that you and the kids will be unharmed," Olly says.

"You'll let me take the children and go?" Rachel asks.

Once she gets the children to safety, she can call the police and come back for Marty and Pete.

Olly nods. "I'm not a monster. You can leave with your family. And in return, you give us a day before you call the cops. All you have to do is drop your gun and put your hands up. Come on, Mrs. O'Neill, let's work together on this, for all our sakes!"

Her mind is in overload. A collage of competing images and instincts. *Don't trust them, get the kids, don't trust them, get the kids . . .*

She has to choose, so she decides to believe him.

Get the children back first, worry about his intentions later, she tells herself.

She stands, puts her hands up, and lets the nine-millimeter fall to the floor.

"Come out from behind that trough, put your hands on your head, and get down on your knees," Ginger says.

Rachel does as she's ordered and Ginger pushes Kylie toward her. Kylie falls into her mother's arms and Rachel hugs her.

"This time I'm never letting you go," Rachel whispers.

Olly shoves Stuart toward the little pietà. He turns to his sister. "That, Ginger, is how you do these things. That is how it's supposed to work. Not with this," he says, waving the gun at her. "With this," he says, touching the side of his own head. "You see what I did there? All I did was talk to her. No guns, no violence—a self-correcting mechanism. All you need is a phone and a voice. And a little bit of brains."

"So you're really going to let them go?" Ginger asks.

"Of course not! How can we possibly let them go? Jesus Christ, Ginger, I worry about you."

"We're going to kill them?"

"Yes!" Olly says with exasperation.

"Might as well do it now," Ginger says. "It feels like we've been here half the night playing reindeer games in the snow. Better close your eyes, folks. For you the war is over."

72

As early Christmas presents go, the Ultimate Houdini Magic Kit couldn't be more geeky, and Kylie is at the age where her friends will tease her about such things. *Magic? I mean, seriously, who does magic?*

So she didn't tell any of them. Except Stuart, of course. She told Stuart.

And she learned a few tricks. As she promised herself in that basement when she'd been chained to the oven, she did, in fact, learn how to escape from handcuffs. She watched those YouTube videos and she practiced. A lot. She got good at it. As good as one can get in a few weeks. She can escape from a standard handcuff in under thirty seconds. Now, zip ties are a different story, but all metal handcuffs can be opened with a universal key if you know what you are doing. As a good-luck totem, she always carries a handcuff escape key with her on her key chain.

Always.

Unseen by anyone, she unpicks the lock that is cuffing her hands in front of her.

Now what? Snow is pouring in through the holes in the roof. Her mother is holding her, Stuart is crying, and there on the floor right in front of her is the pistol that her mom dropped.

She reaches down and picks up the gun. It feels heavy. Impossibly heavy. The twins are talking. "Might as well do it now," Ginger says. "It feels like we've been here half the night playing reindeer games in the snow. Better close your eyes, folks. For you the war is over."

Kylie lifts the nine-millimeter, aims, and pulls the trigger.

73

Olly's face caves inward, rushes out the back of his skull, and sprays over the cinder-block wall behind him. Kylie has never seen anything like it. It's beyond horrific. But she has only a fraction of a second to be horrified. Ginger swings her gun around and points it at her.

"You little bitch!" Ginger screams and shoots blindly at Kylie.

Kylie fires again, but this time she's miles high and the bullet clangs into the ceiling.

A rusted piece of the roof thuds to the floor between Ginger and the body of her brother. Startled, she turns to see what it is. Kylie hustles her mom and Stuart behind the concrete blood-collecting trough.

Ginger recovers herself and fires four times in quick succession.

Four shots slam hard into the trough.

Ginger moves, closes one eye, and aims carefully at Kylie's shoulder peeking out from behind a crack in the concrete, but there isn't going to be another shot. The revolver is empty.

"Shit!" Ginger says.

She's out of ammo, Rachel thinks, and she takes the nine-millimeter from Kylie, stands, aims, and deliberately pulls the trigger. The trigger doesn't do anything. The nine-millimeter is empty or, more likely, jammed and she has no idea how to fix a jam.

The two women glare at each other.

Another look of recognition.

Mirror Rachel, Mirror Ginger, you could be me, I could be you.

Rachel shakes her head. She's not buying into that we're-not-so-different-you-and-I bullshit. *We all have choices.*

Ginger smiles and drops her gun.

"I'm coming for you," Rachel snarls and runs at her.

Ginger quickly assumes a self-defense stance, but Rachel's momentum knocks them both to the ground.

Ginger springs to her feet and Rachel finds something metal on the floor and tosses it at her; it misses and thuds into the cinder-block wall.

Rachel gets up and throws a fist at Ginger but she's far too slow and Ginger easily dodges it with a neat sidestep. Ginger's blue eyes glint with pleasure as she head-butts a stunned Rachel in the face.

Rachel has never had her nose broken before, and the pain is so shocking that she is momentarily blinded. Ginger punches her in the ribs, stomach, and the left breast.

Rachel winces, collapses onto one knee, and then somehow gets up again.

"You liked that, bitch? You'll love this," Ginger says and she punches her in the throat, the left breast again, and then square on her bloody nose.

Heavy, well-placed, well-aimed blows that hurt.

Rachel goes down hard.

Ginger leaps on top of her and flips Rachel onto her back. Ginger is so quick and efficient that Rachel has no chance.

"No, ugh." Rachel gasps as Ginger's hands wrap around her throat and squeeze.

"I knew you were trouble. Knew it right from the start," Ginger says, her wild, ecstatic, crazy face leering above Rachel. Spittle is flying from her mouth. She's grinning. She's enjoying this. "I knew it!" Ginger says and squeezes harder. In FBI self-defense class, she learned how to choke someone out in a few seconds.

Rachel's vision is tunneling.

Everything is becoming white.

"You're going to die, bitch!" Ginger yells.

Tunnel.

Whiteness.

Nothingness.

Rachel knows she is disappearing forever now.

She can feel her life dribbling away onto the grimy concrete floor.

How to tell Kylie she loves her but that she isn't going to make it?

Can't tell her. Can't talk. Can't breathe.

Nothing anyone can do.

Rachel understands everything now.

The Chain is a cruel method of exploiting the most important human emotion—the capacity for love—to make money. It wouldn't work in a world where there was no filial or sibling or romantic love, and only a sociopath who is without love or who doesn't understand love could use it for her ends.

Love is what undid Ariadne and Theseus.

The Minotaur too, in the Borges story.

Love, or a fumbling attempt at love, is what nearly undid Ginger.

Rachel sees all that.

She understands.

The Chain is a metaphor for the ties that bind all of us to friends and family. It is the umbilical link between mother and child, the way or path that the hero must travel in a quest, and it is the thin clew of crimson thread that is the solution Ariadne comes up with to the problem of the labyrinth.

Rachel understands it all.

Knowledge is sorrow.

She closes her eyes and feels the darkness wrap around her.

The world is diminishing, fading, falling far away . . .

Then she feels something else.

Something sharp. Something that cuts. Something that hurts. A long, thin shard of glass.

Her thumb drags it across the floor and her hand wraps around it.

Her hands are bloody but her grip is strong.

Rachel Klein, avoider of mirrors, has tumbled through the looking glass and taken a piece of that glass with her.

She will give it to Ginger as a gift.

Yes.

And with the last breath in her body, she arcs the splinter of glass hard into Ginger's throat.

Ginger screams and lets go of Rachel and claws at her neck.

She fumbles at the glass and tries to save herself but the carotid is severed and a fount of crimson arterial blood is already pouring from the wound.

Rachel rolls away from her and gulps air. Ginger's eyes widen. "I knew you were . . ." she says and collapses to the floor, dead.

Rachel breathes and closes her eyes and opens them again.

And now it is only Kylie hugging her.

Hugging her for twenty seconds and then getting up and pressing a rag against the wound in Pete's abdomen.

The bullet somehow missed the major blood vessels, but he needs medical attention. Quick.

Kylie finds her mom's phone and dials 911. She tells the dispatcher that she needs the police and an ambulance.

Kylie hands the phone to Stuart and goes to help her dad.

Stuart tells the dispatcher exactly how to get to them from Route 1A. When he sees the house behind them is burning, he tells them to send the fire department too. "Stay on the line, honey, help is on the way," the dispatcher says.

Kylie finds pieces of tarp and puts one over her uncle Pete and her dad and another around her mom and Stuart as protection against the wind and snow howling through the abattoir.

"Come here," Rachel says to Kylie and Stuart, and she pulls the two kids close.

She tells them it's going to be all right in the voice mothers have used to reassure their little ones for tens of thousands of years.

"How can I help?" Marty asks, crawling toward them.

"Help Uncle Pete. Keep pressure on his wound," Kylie says to her dad.

Marty nods and presses the rag hard against Pete's stomach. "Hang in there, big brother, I'm sure you've faced worse than this," Marty says.

Pete's wound looks terrible, but his dark eyes still have fire in them. Death is going to have to deal with a force that is shamanic, strong, inimical.

Embers are falling onto the remains of the abattoir's roof.

"Guys, we may have to get out of here," Marty says.

Rachel looks at the ferocious blaze taking hold of the entire west side of the house.

"Can we move Pete?" she asks.

"I think we need to," Marty replies.

Flames engulf the house's upper story and send the wooden deck crashing to the ground.

Snow and embers mingle in the slaughterhouse, drifting down from the black sky.

"I think I hear them coming," Rachel says as the sound of sirens comes out of the night.

Kylie smiles and Stuart nods and Rachel tightens the tarpaulin around them. It will be hard to ever let her daughter go again. Impossible. Rachel kisses Kylie on the top of her head.

Pete is glad to see it.

He blinks slowly.

He tries to say something but there are no words now.

He knows he's going into shock. He has seen it a million times. He'll need a medic soon if he's going to survive.

Marty is speaking to him, but he needs the—where is it?

His fingers search the ground until they touch his grandfather's Colt .45, supposedly fired in anger at a Zero heading for the USS *Missouri*.

Pete somehow manages to lift it.

His grandfather's .45 . . . the lucky charm that kept the old man safe through the Pacific and kept Pete himself safe through five combat tours.

Pete hopes there is just one ounce of luck left in it.

74

Ever since he was little, people have called him Red. They'd christened him Daniel, after his father, but the old man is a little too free with his fists to be popular with the boy.

In the service they call him Red. Or Sarge. Or Sergeant Fitzpatrick. Red he likes.

The army is good for him. The army teaches him his letters.

There's Red in the remedial reading class. Red skimming the funny papers. Red digging the comics. A swollen red Krypton sun. Superman walking the red road.

The army sends him overseas.

Red in the jungle.

Red in the delta.

Red in a whorehouse in Nha Trang.

Red in a whorehouse in Saigon.

He knows the whores are scared of him. The whores don't like his eyes or the fish-scale birthmark on his neck. The whores don't call him Red or Daniel or Sergeant. Behind his back they call him *ông ma quy,* which means "sea demon."

Red in a chopper.

Red in a firefight in the Ia Drang Valley. Red keeping cool as mortars come in. Red getting recommended for the Silver Star.

Red back in America being presented with a baby boy by his Southie girlfriend.

Red joining the Boston PD.

It's the mid-1960s and there are a lot of opportunities for a young man on the make. Sometimes you have to smack a few people around.

Sometimes you have to do a lot worse.

Red stains on the floor of a Dorchester shebeen.

Red all over the walls of a snitch's basement apartment.

Red the hands. Red the eyes. Rooms full of red.

Red's wife runs off with another man to Michigan. Red footprints in the snow outside a house in Ann Arbor.

Red's boy grows up and follows his old man into law enforcement.

Glory days.

Red-letter days.

Before the fall. Before that hippie bitch comes into his boy's life.

He is an old man now. His hair is white. But the old Red is still there.

They think they can kill me?

I'm hard to kill.

Red picks himself up off the linen-closet floor where he has been recovering. He limps to the room next to the library. Smoke is everywhere. The house is on fire. He finds the first-aid kit. He looks at the shotgun wound in his side. He's had worse. Worse in that gun battle with hoods in '77. Worse when a collection went wrong in Revere in '85.

A younger man then, though. A much younger man.

He's bleeding bad. Red the bandages. Red the lint. He limps to the gun rack. There's yelling and shooting coming from the old abattoir outside.

He gets himself an M16 with an underslung M203 grenade launcher.

The only weapon to choose when you need something more convincing.

He staggers to the kitchen, coughing in the thick black smoke.

The hurt is incredible. At least four broken ribs and probably a punctured lung. But he'll get through it. Red would get through it and he's still Red even if his hair is white.

He staggers out into the blizzard and shuffles toward the back of the old slaughterhouse.

One step at a time through searing pain.

He blinks the snow out of his eyes.

It's only fifty feet but it might as well be fifty yards.

He is reduced to crawling. His outbreaths are frothing blood. Definitely a punctured lung.

He reaches the rear door of the abattoir. The death entrance.

Red on the dirt. Red the handrail and the snow.

Breathing is hard. He has only one working lung and that is filling with blood too.

He climbs the last concrete step and peers over the lip of the back door.

The arc light is on and he can see everything.

There are his two beloved grandchildren dead on the floor. The kids he'd rescued all those years ago. The only ones who ever really loved him or understood him. Olly and Ginger in the world of red.

That woman is there, huddled with the two kids under a tarp. Marty and another man are lying on the floor next to them—both, apparently, still alive. Not for long.

Red raises the M16 and puts his finger on the trigger of the underslung grenade launcher. It is loaded with an armor-piercing high-explosive grenade that will kill everyone in the room. Probably including him.

That's good, he thinks, and he pulls the trigger.

75

People talking from a long way off. Something cold and wet falling on his face.

Where is he?

Oh yeah.

Blacked out for a second there. Marty is talking to him. Trying to lift him up. Rachel is holding Kylie and Stuart.

Pete's holding his .45. He looks along the line of the floor and sees Daniel at the back entrance of the abattoir at the same time that Daniel sees him. The old man has an M16 with a grenade-launcher attachment.

Rachel's wrong. It *is* deep stuff. It *is* mythology. Old versus young, army versus navy, catharsis versus chaos. Clearly the god of war is keeping one of them alive just for his own amusement.

Both of them pull their triggers. The old man pulls his first and he has only the briefest moment of confusion when the metal trigger stays in place. Confusion and then realization: He forgot to flick off the manual safety on the M203 grenade launcher. The M203 is dangerous. You can't have it going off willy-nilly. It needs to be armed and the safety switched off by hand.

Shit.

He fumbles for the clunky safety catch for a split second before Pete's gun barrel flares a brilliant white and Daniel's chest explodes in pain and fire and his soul is cleaved by a slug from a World War II .45.

76

S hapes. Sirens. Snow.
    A blanket.

"I'm sorry, Pete, but this place is going up in flames. We gotta get you outside."

Rachel, Kylie, and Stuart help Marty and Pete across the abattoir floor to the exit.

They stagger away from the burning building and collapse in the snow. Behind them, bottled gas tanks under the kitchen begin exploding.

"Come on!" Rachel says and carries and drags them farther away from the property.

Blue flames.

Snowflakes.

Flashing lights.

A Miskatonic River Valley fire engine is coming up the road. The word *Fire* is spelled out mirror-backward above a big yellow arrow.

Rachel nods.

Three dead foxes and the yellow arrow at last. Deliverance finally at hand.

Pete beckons Rachel close.

"Yes?"

"If I don't make it, don't let them cast some asshole to play me in the movie version of this," he croaks.

She grins and kisses him.

"One more thing," he says, but his voice dies in his throat.

"Me too," she agrees and kisses him again.

77

No one is going to play Pete in the movie version of this. Pete is far too controversial a figure for a movie. After their confessions, Pete and Rachel are charged with felony kidnapping, false imprisonment, and child endangerment. For that alone it's fifty years in prison.

And then there's the little expedition to Innsmouth. Was that a vigilante rescue attempt or a home invasion?

It has taken a long time to sort everything out.

It has taken a team of federal agents weeks to fully analyze The Chain documents they found on Ginger's hard drive.

It has taken the Dunleavy family to heroically step forward and tell the police that Rachel took Amelia with their consent because she told them that she was going to break The Chain. That explains the money too. The cops don't believe a word of it, but it's clear that the Dunleavys are going to be hostile witnesses for any prosecution.

By this time, the tide of compassion is fully with Rachel and Pete and all the victims of The Chain. The public is overwhelmingly behind them; Rachel and Pete are sympathetic defendants, and there's a high probability of jury nullification. The Massachusetts Attorney General's office can see which way the wind is blowing. Rachel and Pete are released from custody pending further inquiries. And without the Dunleavy family testifying against them, with the public on their side, and with Ginger's career of evil becoming more and more apparent, Rachel's lawyers tell her that an expensive, unpopular trial now looks very unlikely indeed. Rachel has killed the monster. The Chain has been stopped forever and everyone who was a link in that chain has been freed.

The history of The Chain itself is being investigated by dozens of reporters. A journalist from the *Boston Globe* discovers its roots in a substitute-kidnapping scheme that began in Mexico.

There are hundreds of victims of The Chain but the fear of retaliation and the occasional brutal, bloody reprisal were enough to keep almost all of them quiet over the years.

That, anyway, is what Rachel has read in the press. That's the *Globe* summary. There are more sensational accounts in the tabloids and on the internet. But for self-preservation, Rachel doesn't read the tabloids and she hasn't really gone on the internet since she's been released from custody.

Rachel doesn't give interviews; she avoids the limelight; she doesn't do anything much but pick up her daughter from school and write her community-college philosophy lectures, and eventually, through these prudent un-twenty-first-century measures, she becomes old news.

Gradually she's no longer a trending topic on Twitter or Instagram. Some other poor devil has come along to take her place. And then another one will come along after that. And then another. It's all very familiar . . .

In Newburyport she's still recognized—how could she not be?—but when she drives up to the malls in New Hampshire or into the Boston suburbs, she's anonymous again and that's the way she likes it.

A sunny morning in late March.

Rachel is in bed with her laptop. She deletes the twenty new requests from her e-mail inbox asking for interviews and closes the computer. Pete is next door in the shower. Singing. Badly.

She smiles. Pete is doing really great now on his methadone program and at his brand-new job as a security consultant for a high-tech firm in Cambridge. She walks barefoot into the kitchen, lights the stove, fills the kettle, and puts the water on to boil.

Upstairs, she can hear the occasional ping of Kylie's iPad. Kylie's awake and hunkered under the sheets, chatting with her friends. Kylie is also doing amazingly well. They always say that kids are resilient and can bounce back from trauma, but it's still incredible to see how high she is bouncing back.

At eight o'clock, Stuart comes by and she gives him a hug and he sits there petting the cat, waiting patiently for Kylie to be ready. Stuart also is doing great, and out of all of them he seems to be the one digging the fame the most. Although Marty also appears to be enjoying all the attention. He has popped up on the TV several times to talk about his experiences. And with each telling, his own role in the rescue has become a little bit more extravagant. Marty is all right and his new, *very* young girlfriend, Julie, seems to believe that they are all in some kind of romcom together in which Rachel, the gloomy first wife, will eventually be won over by her effervescent charms.

Rachel sits down at the dining-room table and opens her laptop again. Her thoughts drift. She thumbs through Sarah Bakewell's *At the Existentialist Café* and is momentarily taken aback by a striking picture of Simone de Beauvoir wearing a brooch in the shape of a labyrinth.

She shuts the book and waves at Dr. Havercamp as he walks through the reeds to pump the bilge from his boat.

"Trying to start this lecture with a joke, Stuart. How does this sound? 'My friend is opening a bookstore to sell German philosophy texts. I told him it wouldn't work—it's too much of a Nietzsche market,'" Rachel says with a look of triumph.

Stuart grimaces.

"Not good?" Rachel asks.

"I'm not really qualified to judge the, uh . . ."

"What he's trying to say, Mother, is that your comedy stylings skew to an older demographic," Kylie says, leaning over the balcony rail.

Pete comes out of the shower and shakes his head. "I hope your plan B isn't a career in stand-up," he says.

"To hell with all of you!" Rachel says and shuts the laptop.

When everyone's ready they go out to the car, and since they're early for school, they swing by Dunkin' Donuts on Route 1.

Rachel looks at her daughter as she takes a bite of a bear claw. Kylie and Stuart are arguing about spoilers for season three of *Stranger Things*. This is nearly the old, carefree, bullshitty Kylie again. The splinter will always be there, of course. The darkness. They'll never quite be able to get that out. It's part of her now, part of all of them. But the bed-wetting has stopped and the bad dreams are fewer. And that's something.

"OK, here's one that's a winner. How many hipsters does it take to change a light bulb?" she asks.

"Mom, don't! Please. Don't even!" Kylie pleads.

"How many?" Stuart asks.

"It's a pretty obscure number, you've probably never heard of it," Rachel says, and at least Pete grins.

She leaves the kids at school and she drops Pete at the commuter-rail stop in Newburyport. His new job requires him to wear a suit and he hates that. He is continually fussing with his tie.

"Leave it alone! You look fabulous," she says and means it.

When his train comes, she walks back to the Volvo, drives into town, and goes straight to the Walgreens. She checks that Mary Anne, the cashier she knows, isn't working, and she slinks down the aisles to the pregnancy-test-kit section.

There's a baffling number of choices. She grabs a kit more or less at random and takes it to the counter.

The cashier is a high-school-age girl whose name tag claims that she's Ripley. She's reading *Moby-Dick*.

She doesn't appear to be at the "devious-cruising *Rachel*" bit. Their eyes meet.

"What chapter are you on?" Rachel asks.

"Seventy-six."

"A man once told me that all books should end at chapter seventy-seven."

"God, I wish this one did. I have loads to go. Hey, um, you should probably get the Clearblue kit," the girl says.

"The Clearblue?"

"You think you're saving money by getting the Fast-Response. But the FastResponse has a higher rate of false positives." She lowers her voice. "I speak from experience."

"I'll get the Clearblue," Rachel says.

She pays for the kit, gets another coffee from the Starbucks on State Street, and drives back to the island.

She goes to the bathroom, takes the kit out of the box, reads the instructions, urinates on the stick over the toilet bowl, and puts the stick back in the box.

It's surprisingly warm for March, so she takes the box and

goes outside and sits on the edge of the deck with her feet dangling above the sand.

The tide's in. The smell of the sea is strong. Wisps of heat are rising above the big houses on the Atlantic side. A gawking white heron wades among the weeds as a hawk flies westward toward the mainland.

Fishing boats. Crabbers. The lazy bark of a dog down near the convenience store.

She feels the force of the metaphors—comfort, stability, safety.

Thoreau called Plum Island the "bleak Sahara of New England," but it isn't that today.

She looks at the box in her hand. The box that contains two possible futures. Two futures that are tumbling toward her at sixty seconds in every minute, sixty minutes in every hour.

One heartbeat at a time.

She smiles.

Either future will be OK.

All futures will be OK.

She has rescued her daughter from the dark.

She has slain the monster.

There are challenges ahead.

A million challenges.

But she has Kylie back.

She has Pete.

She has survived.

Life is fragile, fleeting, and precious.

And to live at all is miracle enough.

AFTERWORD AND ACKNOWLEDGMENTS

It only takes two facing mirrors to construct a labyrinth.

Jorge Luis Borges, *Seven Nights*

I wrote the first draft of *The Chain* in Mexico City in 2012 after learning about the Mexican concept of exchange kidnappings, whereby a family member offers himself or herself as a replacement hostage for a more vulnerable kidnap victim. I tied that idea to an event from the late 1970s—the era of poisonous chain letters. The part of Ireland I grew up in was very superstitious, and we completely believed in the power of written enchantments. My fifth-grade teacher told the class to bring in any of these letters that were upsetting us, and I gave her a chain letter that was worrying me. She destroyed it along with the others, defying the author's promises of jinxes, disasters, and bad luck and effectively breaking the chain. This incident deeply impressed me as a kid, and it stayed with me. Periodically over the next three decades, I'd ask my mother how Mrs. Carlisle was doing, and I was always relieved to hear that she was getting through life relatively unscathed.

Back in 2012 I wrote *The Chain* as a short story, but I thought it had the makings of a novel, so I basically left it unfinished in a drawer for five years. In 2017 I finally got myself a full-time literary agent, Shane Salerno, founder of the Story Factory. I had been writing the Sean Duffy series of detective novels set in the Belfast of my youth, and although these books were getting well reviewed and winning a few awards, they weren't quite breaking through in the way I wanted. Shane phoned and asked if I had an American book in me, and I pitched him the short-story version of *The Chain*. I heard something drop and smash in his kitchen, and he urged me to stop whatever I was doing and immediately begin writing *The Chain* as a novel, which is what I did.

All books are something of a collaborative process, and I'd like to thank Don Winslow, Steve Hamilton, Steve Cavanagh, John McFetridge, and Shane Salerno for looking at early drafts of *The Chain* and lobbing intelligent suggestions my way.

My actual brilliant editor at Mulholland, Josh Kendall, pored over the manuscript with the keen eyes of a forensic diagnostician. He continually forced me to consider whether an idea or concept was as tight or compelling as it could be. At Mulholland and Little, Brown I would also like to thank the tireless and brilliant Tracy Roe, Pamela Marshall, Katharine Myers, Pamela Brown, Craig Young, Reagan Arthur and Michael Pietsch, and the entire sales team. At Orion I am indebted to Emad Akhtar, Leanne Oliver, Tom Noble, Jen Wilson, Sarah Benton, and Katie Espiner for their blood, sweat, and tears. And at Hachette Australia, special thanks to Vanessa Radnidge, Justin Ratcliffe, and Daniel Pilkington.

I want to thank the staff of the Newburyport Public Library, where I did much of the research for *The Chain,* and the staff of the George Bruce branch of the New York Public Library in Harlem, who provided me with a quiet space to write. Riding either coincidence or sympathetic magic, while on assignment in Prague for a magazine article on writer's block, I wrote the final chapters of *The Chain* in Franz Kafka's old office (now a hotel) at Na Poříčí 7.

To conclude these acknowledgments I'd like to express my gratitude to Seamus Heaney, Ruth Rendell, Don Winslow, Ian Rankin, Brian Evenson, Val McDermid, and Diana Gabaldon, who have given me encouragement and advice over the years and who told me to just hang in there when I often wondered if I was really cut out for this writing malarkey.

And finally, to my wife, Leah Garrett, always my first and most perceptive reader, and to my daughters, Arwynn and Sophie, for not only providing me with advice on teen mores and vernacular but for teaching me what you are capable of when your kids' health or happiness is threatened.

Sláinte.